DAWN OF AFFLICTION

Other Books by D.I. Telbat

The COIL Series: Christian Suspense

The COIL Legacy Series: Christian Suspense

COIL Legacy Collection: 3 Books in 1 Volume

The Resolution Series: America's Last Days

The STEADFAST Series: America's Last Days

STEADFAST Collection: 6 Novellas in 1 Volume

Last Dawn Series: America's Last Days

Leeward Set: Where Christians Dare

Never Lost Series: Trafficking Rescue Novels

Arabian Variable

Called To Gobi

God's Colonel

Soldier of Hope

Short Story Collections

DAWN OF AFFLICTION
America's Last Days

BOOK ONE OF THE LAST DAWN SERIES

D.I. TELBAT

IN SEASON PUBLICATIONS
USA

Printed in the United States of America

DAWN OF AFFLICTION: America's Last Days
/ D.I. Telbat -- 1st ed.
Categories: Futuristic Christian Fiction;
Christian Suspense

D.I. Telbat / In Season Publications
https://ditelbat.com
https://books2read.com/DITelbat

ISBN 978-1-7371777-6-0

Cover Design by Streetlight Graphics

This book is for
those who know their need and look to the Cross,
and for those who see the needs of others
and respond without delay.

Acknowledgements

Every book requires a team,
and every series requires commitment.
Thanks to the individuals who bless me
by striving alongside me in
correcting, editing, proofing, and advising—
Dee, Jamie, Sharon, and Ed.
And special thanks to my Beta Reader friends,
for blessing me with their kind service.
Most of all, I acknowledge
the finished work of Jesus Christ for us,
and the saving work of God in us.
May our work bring Him glory and honor.

Character Sketch

Alice Prine – long-limbed black woman who's lived in Eagle Mountain for almost twenty years. Her faith is rivaled only by her loyalty to Levi.

Annette Sheffield-Caspertein – Levi's stepmother, now in her sixties, but she still carries herself with the grace of her days as a model. Now as a Christian woman, she takes the role of matriarch, skilled and protective—and able to shoot a rifle with the most elite soldiers.

Galt Brogdon – General of the Pacific States' most elite soldiers, run out of San Diego's Coronado Island, the new capital. His zeal for control and domination tends to crowd his sense of right and wrong, which he isn't afraid to express through the troops he commands.

Jenna Dowler – old friend of Levi's and blind daughter of the legendary Corban Dowler, COIL's founder. It is her communication to Levi for help that prompts him to leave California and head toward New York where she is.

Kendrick Obrador – Chancellor of the Appalachian Federation on the East Coast.

Kip Brogdon – son of the mighty General, a curly-haired, spoiled young man who is used to taking what he wants and not looking back.

Levi Caspertein – son of COIL's top operative, Titus. This broad-shouldered man in his late thirties has been trained as a soldier, but now he must learn to lead his family across a dangerous wasteland.

Lyla Suzanne Grady – a dark-haired native of Nebraska. She's outspoken and fierce, independent yet devoted.

Mia Trimble – Levi's cousin by Wynter & Wes Trimble. This nineteen-year-old young woman is thrust into the brutal land of violence where she must learn to trust in God's healing hand more than that of her cousin.

President Criswell – the head of the Pacific States

Vorca – a young, plump Native American woman who speaks no known language, though she finds her place quite naturally within the family who accepts her.

Glossary

Appalachian Federation – the government that rules the East Coast of the American mainland, run by Chancellor Obrador.

C.E.E. – Citizenship Entrance Exam, enforced by the Appalachian Federation.

COIL – Commission of International Laborers, a Christian Special Forces relief organization.

Pacific States – the government that rules the West Coast of the American mainland, from Mexico to Canada, run by President Criswell

Plains Zone – the No-Man's-Land which spans the lawless territory between the Pacific States and the Appalachian Federation.

Map 1 – San Diego

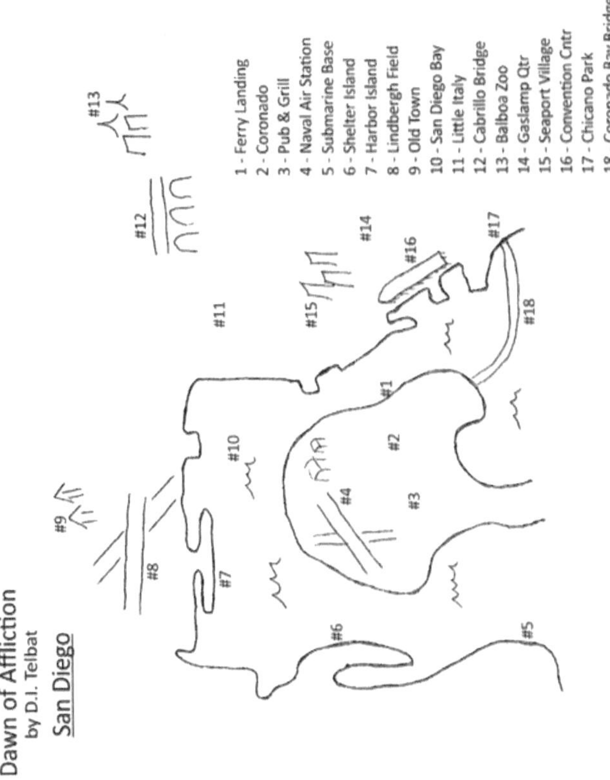

Map 2 – SW US & City Route

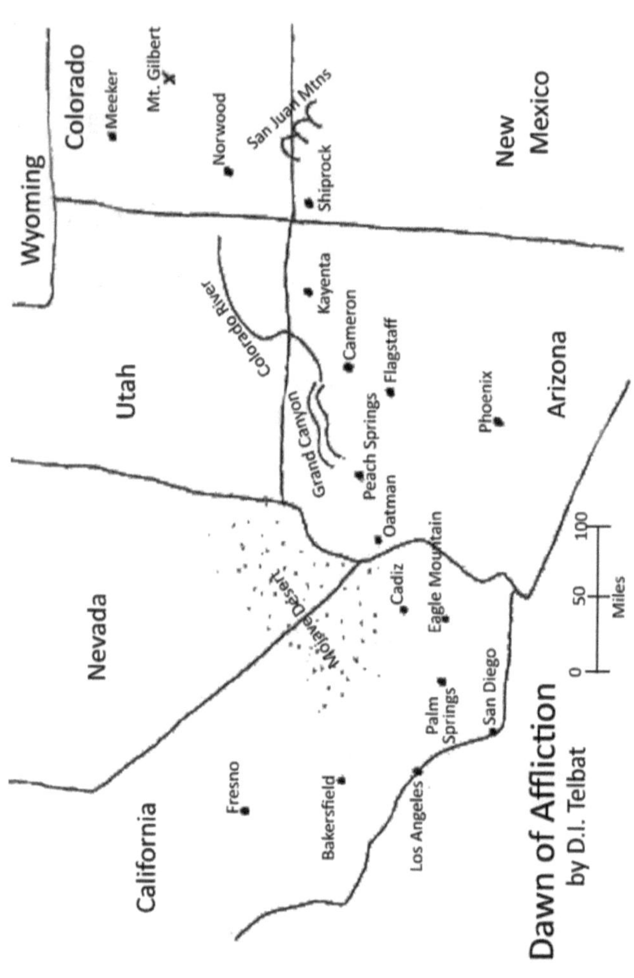

Map 3 – City of Aporax

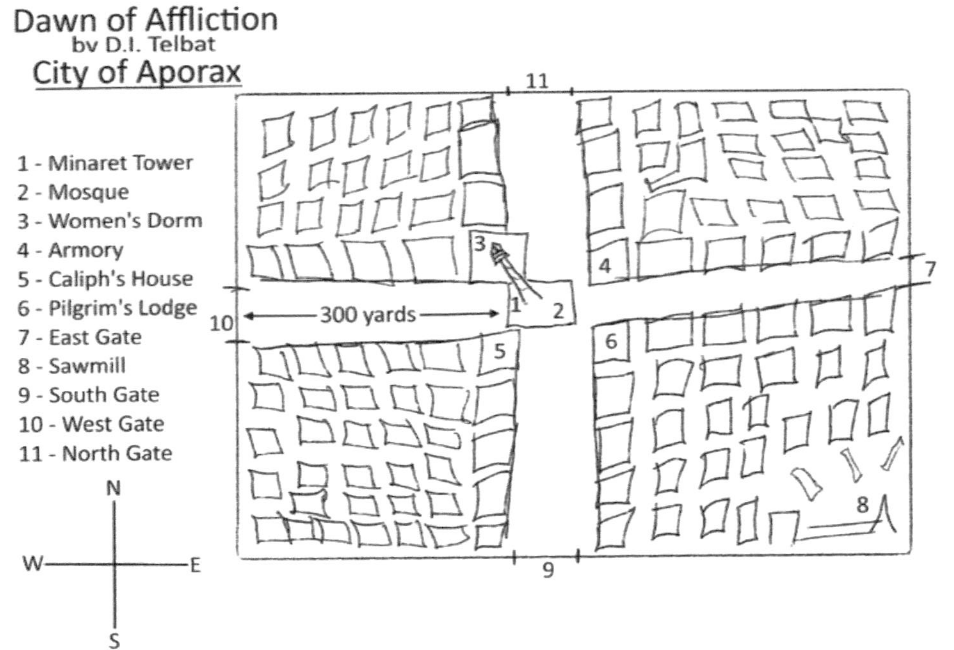

A Note from the Author

Dear Reading Friend,

The start of this new series warrants a few comments about the story you're about to read.

I have written this series for the current state of mind in America, all while remaining true to the *COIL* and *STEADFAST* tradition many are familiar with. This world is certainly unraveling, but God's people need not unravel with it.

Levi Caspertein is meant to inspire genuine believers as to how to behave and react in the most dire of circumstances. True, we will not relate to all of Levi's situations in his post-apocalyptic era, but we can glimpse his Christ-likeness and attitude of bold compassion in the midst of upheaval.

As for the apocalyptic timeline I've chosen, I've theorized a "what if" scenario. What if Christ's prophetic return to reign on earth didn't happen as soon as believers thought? What if America is brought low through disaster before the Tribulation era of Revelation happens? At this time, I only feel called to write about the era leading up to what many Bible students call Daniel's 70th Week.

The geographical locations and facts in this book are accurate, from San Diego's Coronado Island, to Oatman, Arizona, where wild burros roam the town. Eagle Mountain, California, which plays a big role in this story, is a real ghost town today. The aquifer under Cadiz, CA, is owned today by a Los Angeles-based company, but it seemed a legitimate desert location in the story for a water dispute where lines are drawn between races. The bridge outside Cameron, AZ, which is destroyed in this book, really spans the canyon today, across US Route 99.

From San Diego, California, to Meeker, Colorado, Levi travels eastward through a nation that has sinfully devoured itself, one town after another. This is futuristic fiction, of course, and I don't intend to vilify the pleasant and decent folks who live in these fine towns today, even though my fictional character, Levi, is met in the future by many evils in various communities.

Finally, after years of contemplating the telling of this story, I have chosen to write the entire novel in first person. Levi's internal struggles as a family man, his growth as a Christian, and his character as a soldier and survivalist seemed best told through his own eyes. He embodies an imperfect man, but a man I hope we would desire to emulate, or perhaps stand beside.

In these challenging times in America and beyond, may we focus intently on God's promises of security, preservation, and loving care. In this way, and in no other way, will we best care for others as the world is shaken. Jesus Christ is the only answer to all of man's problems. He died for us, that we might live again!

Thank you for your faithful example, my brothers and sisters, wherever God has placed you.

Sincerely in Christ,
David Telbat

Prologue

"Levi, are you there? I couldn't raise you on the radio for our scheduled relay to tell you of the emergency we're facing here in the Appalachian Federation. Our radios are about to be confiscated, and I have no doubt that mine will be among those taken. Over the years, I've used this radio to inform others in New York about events across the nation. And now, I'll be required to surrender my only method with which you and I can communicate.

"It's been twenty years since you and I were with our parents in San Diego, anticipating the collapse of America. During these years, we've grown from immature children to mature adults—even becoming leaders in our own communities. God has used each of us in different ways, and I couldn't be happier than to be serving Him now.

"Our radios aren't the only things that the government will be restricting in the weeks and months to come. Since the Bible claims exclusivity over all other religions and gods, as well as condemns immorality and violence, the Bible will also become an item of abolishment within a few weeks. Many of us Christians already in the underground church have been preparing for this day, but we know it still won't be easy. Persecution will certainly increase, since numerous believers will refuse to give up their Bibles, and others will be outspoken about their faith in Jesus Christ. The new government's laws are strict for these types of insurrections. Imprisonment and even death by execution will become commonplace, I fear, throughout the Christian church. Yes, even here in America where some still claim that we live in the land of the free and the home of the brave.

"I can't give you all the details, Levi, since I don't know all of what will happen tomorrow and in the weeks to come, but I will say this: I need the help of someone I can trust. I'm willing to stand for God against the dangers that are confronting us, but I'm just one blind woman. The last I heard, you said your father had caught the virus. That grieves me, since many around the world have known Titus Caspertein as a strong and vibrant man of God. However, I plead with you and ask what seems even to me to be an unreasonable request—if your father has gone to be with the Lord, and you are able to come east, please come to us here.

"In my selfishness, Levi, I want you here. As you know, you and I are the son and daughter of what remains of COIL. The Commission of International Laborers once spanned the globe, rescuing the persecuted from affliction, but now COIL is needed in America. Here, on the East Coast, Christians are under fire, and I need your help to help others. Please, Levi, come to me. I know this is asking a lot. You would need to cover hundreds of dangerous miles to reach me, but I can think of no one else to ask, nor do I doubt that you can survive the journey.

"How I wish we could've spoken one last time! But it wasn't meant to be. I'll leave you with this final message, and pray you receive it. I, and those with me, will wait for you. We need all that COIL once was, and we need that mighty hand of God to extend itself through you to us, to save us, to lift us up, to glorify our Lord and Savior. Every day, I will pray for your safe travels, and for comfort in your grief at the passing of your father. At least he is with the Lord now, where we will all be soon.

"Until you arrive, Levi, God will preserve us. But please hurry. There are many unknowns, and I fear the worst from our government. As your sister in the Lord, I love you and Annette and Mia. May God be with us all. This is Jenna Dowler signing off permanently. I hope and pray you receive this. Goodbye, Levi."

Chapter One

I hadn't expected to wake up from such an attack, but when I did, my first thoughts were of my cousin, Mia Trimble. They had taken her, and I had to get her back. Though fists had pounded my skull, and boots had kicked at my ribs, we Casperteins are hard-headed—and harder yet to kill.

Just the day before, I had buried my father, Titus Caspertein, after he'd fought for days against the virus. He'd been a rogue and an arms smuggler in his youth. Then, when he'd become a believer, he'd given his life to the work of Christ, and that was the only side of my father I ever witnessed. But still, his reputation as a criminal had daunted many in power after the collapse of the United States. I understood why Kip Brogdon hadn't stolen Mia before this dark night—it was because my father had still been alive. However, Kip Brogdon was underestimating my father's son. Since I'd found my father twenty years earlier, he'd taught me how to survive in the world of evil people, and even how to thrive and remain victorious as a man of God. This meant Kip Brogdon was in trouble!

On the bank of Seaport Village in San Diego, I rolled to my knees. My head was spinning and I could tell I had a few loosened teeth. There was dried blood in my nose, and one ear felt like it was hanging on by mere flesh. Feeling my torso, I winced at painful ribs. At least Kip Brogdon and his cohorts hadn't shot me dead, though I guessed they would wish they had killed me once I came for Mia. How could they leave me alive and expect me to do nothing?

Rising slowly to my feet, I steadied myself against the burnt remnants of a wall, once belonging to the convention center on Harbor Drive. All of America seemed to have burned in the early days of the Meridia Pandemic—or known as the Meridia Panic in other parts of the country. Thus, it had become known as Pan-Day. I remembered watching the flames consume the building and the Hilton Bayfront from my father's high-rise condo overlooking Santa Fe Depot. The charred ruins of the structure now gave me cover as I walked toward the water and gazed toward Coronado Island.

Coronado Island was the fortress-capital of the Pacific States, the government established in the years after Pan-Day, headed by President Criswell and the military's awe-inspiring might. Unfortunately, the Brogdon family was under the rule of the president, and that meant I had to go to Coronado Island to rescue my nineteen-year-old cousin. What Kip Brogdon and his father, Galt, didn't know was that for days, I'd been planning to leave the city. I was leaving San Diego and the Pacific States, leaving her corrupt empire to the dark hearts that ruled her.

As complete as my plans were for crossing the Rockies to the east, walking into the jaws of Coronado Island hadn't been part of those plans. But my father was gone, and my mother, Annette, was waiting across the city for me. She was expecting Mia and me before dawn. I couldn't go to my mother without my cousin.

Straining, I lifted and set aside a heavy steel beam from the floor of the convention center. It weighed over three hundred pounds. A weaker man would've passed it by, but I knew that underneath it was a trapdoor in the floor. With a glance over my shoulder to check for onlookers, I thrust my hand into a jagged hole and pulled the door open. It revealed a second door, this one vaulted with an electronic keypad. I typed in my birthdate, and the vault clicked loudly. After throwing open the door, I climbed down a short flight of steep stairs, allowing the door to close above me.

A flashlight lay where I'd left it. I set it on a shelf from where the beam lit the bunker—once a storage room for convention equipment. Now, the shelves held rows of NL-X2 battle rifles and other equipment designed or stockpiled by COIL operators. Long ago, COIL's technology and non-lethal weapons had been used to protect persecuted Christians in far-away lands. Now, we were the persecuted Christians, and it was in this land that we needed protection.

"Never give these weapons to the military, Levi," my father had told me often, warning me of the danger of the battle rifle falling into the hands of the Pacific States military forces. The Brogdon family wanted to utilize the compact rifle's versatility for lethal means, but COIL had designed the rifle strictly for non-lethal purposes. Thus, my father and I had kept the stash of NL-X2 rifles a secret, both of us praying for a day when responsible men once again reigned the mainland, and peaceful means could be used to enforce a moral civilization.

As I selected ammunition and donned a vest to carry magazines, I prayed for Mia. She was as thin as a pole, but willing to work as hard as a man, which was often required in the life we now lived. For years, she'd been sheltered by my father and mother, and even myself, from suitors. Many times, we'd sent young and old men alike away from our house in Little Italy—men who had eyes for Mia. Healthy women of children-bearing age were rare in the Pacific States. Most families who had means had fled inland, but the Casperteins had remained on the coast, caring for those who couldn't travel. It put us all at risk, since the Pacific States were concentrated along the West Coast. But we Casperteins aren't afraid of facing threats or danger, if the cause is just and requires a Christ-like presence.

Thus, my father had instructed Mia, when she was a young teen, never to leave the house alone or unarmed. Usually, this was no problem, since I often took her with me to scavenge the city for parts, food, and equipment to use or sell. Earlier that night, we'd been paying the bunker one last visit to arm ourselves for our trip east. Jenna Dowler had broadcasted a message for me, and I needed to go to her. Although she was in faraway New York, I couldn't dwell on the obstacles between us. The Pacific States under President Criswell was a mess of corruption and violence, but Jenna had communicated that the Appalachian Federation along the East Coast was actually persecuting Christians. The Federation spanned from Florida to Vermont, and thousands of Christians were in potential danger, as well as Jenna, who was a close friend from before Pan-Day. It ain't easy being a Caspertein sometimes, but there is a certain honor that comes with persevering through hardship for the sake of another. I couldn't let Jenna down, but since I was leaving, Annette and Mia had to leave as well. They both seemed to be ready for a change from the city, like me.

With two NL-X2 rifles in my arms, and enough non-lethal ammunition to tranquilize a family of rhinos, I emerged from the bunker and set the beam back across the trapdoor. If I were ever to return to San Diego, I prayed the weapons would remain safe. I left the convention center and jogged up the shoreline to a rubber raft I often used for fishing. San Diego Bay provided a staple for civilians who still lived in the city, and a couple of households had depended on my netting skills to provide them with fresh fish.

I found the raft where I'd left it—in the bushes next to what was once the USS Midway Museum. The raft had had a leak for a month and I hadn't patched it, figuring I was leaving the city soon. Now, I spent ten minutes blowing on the valve, filling the compartment with air. Paddling across the channel was no small feat; I would need a raft worthy of the task.

Shoving off the bank, I didn't dip my paddles right away. Instead, I studied Coronado Island with more than a little dread. No one visited the island like the old days. Surfing its western shores or touring the military installation was strictly prohibited now. No ferries churned the waters around the island, and the only vehicles allowed across the Coronado Bay Bridge belonged to President Criswell's army. It was run by General Galt Brogdon—the cunning father of the spoiled son, Kip Brogdon, with whom I had an appointment, of sorts.

Paddling straight across the bay would land me at Coronado Island's Ferry Landing, which was lit up as much as the naval air station on the north end of the island. Instead, I aimed my raft toward a darker section of the shoreline where I knew a few palm trees still stood. In the past, I'd viewed the island from elevated perches through a high-powered telescope, but I'd never imagined assaulting the heavily-guarded facility at night, or alone.

I prayed as I rowed the wobbly boat into the current. Going after Mia like this was instinctively rash. My ribs were sore, and my scalp needed stitches. A couple fingers felt broken, and my stomach ached from the last few punches I'd received before blacking out. Eight men had tangled with me while Kip Brogdon had held Mia back. If he'd not held on to her, she would've attacked the men with teeth and nails to protect her older cousin.

The eight men had attacked and beaten me senseless. But I'd been unarmed and unprepared. Now, I was armed and ready, and I was facing a lot more than eight men. But the terrifying odds couldn't stop me. The Casperteins believe in a mighty God, a God who had empowered weaker men than me against stronger forces. Besides, I had the NL-X2 rifles, which may have kept Kip Brogdon from killing me altogether, since he and his father had assumed for years that we had a stash of the battle rifles hidden somewhere in the city.

I checked my analog watch. Annette was waiting for me at Balboa Zoo, northeast of downtown. If I didn't make it back to her by dawn with Mia, she would come looking for us, and that would put her in harm's way. The three of us would need a miracle to make it out of the rotting city alive.

The NL-X2 was a standard .308 caliber rifle, but it was called a bullpup, on account of the action of the rifle resting behind the trigger guard. Its squat appearance made it look like a little bull. The barrel was a lengthy eighteen inches, nearly the entire length of the weapon, making it the coveted weapon of the century. Overall, it was short and had a reach of six hundred yards in the hands of a skilled operator. Thanks to my father and other COIL operatives who'd taught me to shoot before Pan-Day, I was one of those skilled operators.

The wind worked against me as I paddled. By the time I reached Coronado Island, my raft was nearly flat and my adrenalin had worn off. I was thinking clearer and feeling all of my injuries. On the island before me were thousands of men who would kill me on sight since I didn't wear their uniform of denim pants and a crimson-colored jacket. But to leave San Diego without Mia was to abandon her to the likes of Kip Brogdon. The cruelties of his fists and forced childbearing were surely just the beginning of what he had in mind for his captured bride. Since Pan-Day, such abductions were commonplace. Men had a mind to leave sons behind, and Christian women many times made submissive wives.

The only problem with Kip's plan was that Mia had a cousin who was too stubborn to give up. It was true that my father had taught me to submit to the government over us—President Criswell in this case—even as unreasonable as he was. But I had also been taught to pursue justice, and any normal man's conscience would've told him a crime had been committed. If my intentions were evil against the Brogdons, I would've loaded the bullpup with lethal rounds instead of the gel-tranquilizers. For over a decade, the Casperteins had submitted to the martial authority reigning from Coronado Island, but now that authority had crossed the line.

Scrambling up the beach, I reached the first palm tree and lay on my belly. I carried one bullpup in my hands, with the second on a sling on my back. Coronado Ferry Landing was to my left, three hundred yards. First Street lay perpendicular to my position. It was the first of ten residential streets on the island. The naval air station property lay to my right, through a barricade two hundred yards away. The residential barracks weren't well-lit, and I hoped to exploit that error.

For twenty years, I'd lived across the bay. As any young man with a good scope might, I had watched the island soldiers and their maneuvers. Through my father, I'd learned that President Criswell lived at Hotel Del Coronado, and his chief administrators lived in the residences nearest the hotel.

Instead of running or prowling along the houses with their untrimmed hedges, I walked calmly up one avenue to Second Street. A Humvee's headlights and engine caught my eye and ear one street east, but I didn't panic. I was one of the last visitors the Brogdons or anyone on the island might expect, especially after the beating they'd given me. Obviously, they needed to realize that courage among us Casperteins hadn't died with my renowned father, in whose shadow I had lived since a teen.

His last days had been agonizing to witness—and lonely. The Meridia Virus—thought to be eradicated after so many years—had been the culprit that finally killed Titus Caspertein. From the early years, we all knew the symptoms and its origins in Meridia, Oregon. My father had been exposed to the contagion from somewhere, but since he'd often mingled with refugees out on the highways, we hadn't been able to trace where he'd contracted the terrible disease. The country had lost one hundred million people, the estimate was, and a resurgence of the virus had been unlikely since people had been living more isolated and traveling less. Human contact, some said, was more limited in the east, so many had left California. Annette had guarded my father's passing with caution, ensuring that the mighty man of valor and faith was the last Caspertein to die of the virus. My father had passed without being touched or embraced by any of his family. That was the way he wanted it.

I reached Tenth Street without opposition, then knelt against the wall of what I knew had been a pub, but was now the mess hall for the army. It was two o'clock in the morning. Arriving may have been without notice, but my departure was certain to be a combination of noise and commotion.

A line of Humvees were parked on the nearby curb. I jogged to one and checked for keys. The third in line had keys. President Criswell had never been challenged by an opposing force on his home turf. Surely, in their eyes, there was no reason for them to be on guard. The only skirmishes his military had experienced were against certain mountain populations who occasionally ventured to the coast in search of supplies or women. Brogdon's forces, equipped from Coronado's Navy SEAL armory, always overwhelmed any other force. Criswell had become comfortable—a glutton for resources and expansion, some said—and the once hardy men of Coronado Beach, the US Navy SEALs, had been replaced by undisciplined yet savage predators. They knew no honor, and showing Mia any dignity wouldn't be part of their military motto.

From the Humvee's bumper, I studied the residences nearest the Hotel Del Coronado. Two hours had passed since my beating. I guessed that the only house with most of its lights still on was bound to be the Brogdon residence, early morning or not. Kip would be celebrating the spoils of his deeds. The immediate problem for me was that three men in Pacific States uniforms were lingering outside. My father had been enough of a leader with local civilians that the Brogdons, both father and son, had visited our house several times over the years. President Criswell had often sought resourceful men like my father to become part of his government, and General Galt Brogdon had many times questioned my father about the stash of bullpups. But my father had declined to join Criswell's administration, and he'd not disclosed anything about the COIL equipment in the bunker. Now, that secret was my own.

Thus, from seeing the military around the city, and from visits by the Brogdons, I had become acquainted with several of the soldiers who were especially close to Kip. Of course, I'd gotten an up-close view of their faces and fists that very evening. So, I recognized the three on the lawn outside the residence, and I knelt for a careful shot.

My father had taught me to hunt and shoot deer, not men. But we had, once or twice a year, been called to the edges of the city where small communities were barely surviving. There, my father and I had organized the people to withstand minor attacks from mountain raiders, who were hardly more than thieves preying on the civilians. So I knew well the feel of firing a non-lethal gel-tranq at a man, incapacitating a target to wake up later. Annette had said that sometimes taking the hard line with a man was better than taking a passive line to make that man question the direction of his life. I believed she was right.

I gazed through the scope mounted on top of my battle rifle and pulled the trigger. The .308 has a bucking recoil, but I was a healthy two hundred pounds, with broad shoulders and a frame a little over six feet tall. The recoil from the first shot didn't faze me as I lined up for the second and third shots.

The non-lethal rounds I used were gel-based, a capsule shaped like a bullet, but pliable like putty on impact. The butt of each round contained an internal needle, which was water soluble, meant to pierce the skin and distribute the tranquilizer toxin into the bloodstream. On average, the toxin lasted for one hour on a grown man, longer for smaller body masses. The aftereffects were short-term: a nasty bruise.

Unfortunately, my father and the COIL engineers had never fine-tuned subsonic rounds for the gel-tranq cartridge. They'd come to a point when they had to make a choice between the stopping power and accuracy of the large caliber, or silencing it. The .308 round couldn't be silent and powerful at the same time. They chose power over the silencing feature. Hence, my three gunshots on that dangerous night announced the presence of an adversary to everyone on the island—about five thousand men and a few women.

Before the last of the three men had settled on the lawn, I ran past them and kicked in the front door. Two uniformed men rose from their easy chairs and scratched for their sidearms. Neither one of them was Kip Brogdon. I shot both men in their thigh muscles, the gun blast deafening indoors, and moved to my left toward a lit hallway. Another man emerged from a bathroom—this one wasn't Kip Brogdon, either. I silenced him and barged through two doors before I found Kip, half-dressed, standing over the bed where Mia lay, tears on her face. She clutched the sheets to her neck as Kip aimed a pistol at her head.

"You messed up, Kip," I said. "God's people aren't fair game. There are consequences for evil—eternal consequences. This might sting a bit."

Mia understood my intentions and rolled off the bed. Kip's weapon was no longer aimed at her. I shot him in the bare shoulder of the arm that held the weapon. His pistol fired harmlessly into the headboard as his arm jerked upward. A breath later, he collapsed onto the floor, unconscious.

"I was beginning to wonder if you were still alive." She wiped her face and blew her nose on the sheet.

"We have to leave in thirty seconds, Mia," I said as she gathered her clothes.

I returned to the front room. Outside, a siren was blaring from somewhere on the island. I'd heard it tested in previous years, but this was probably Coronado's first real emergency. I didn't anticipate a speedy response, but once they rubbed the sleep from their eyes and found their rifles, I expected heavy resistance.

Mia emerged from the room. I gave her a quick hug and handed her my primary bullpup along with one extra magazine of thirty rounds. She had hunted with me and my father, but only with regular rifles.

"You good?" I nodded at her. "It ain't gonna be easy pulling out of here."

Her blond hair was tangled and she was developing two black eyes from scrapping with Kip, but she cradled the rifle against her shoulder like she was a battle-hardened soldier. After all, she was a Caspertein.

"Lead the way, Cuz," she said with a sniff and a determined nod.

Chapter Two

When we exited through the front door of Kip Brogdon's house, I covered left as Mia went right. Soldiers, only a few with rifles, were running up the street, and two Humvees rushed toward us, their headlights in our eyes. Mia, not waiting for me to fire first, pulled the trigger time and again. Her small frame bucked against the recoil.

I saw four men fall before we reached the Humvee with the keys in it, and I took that moment to change rifle magazines to a cartridge my father had designed. When I fired with the second bullpup, it was with a phosphorus-hybrid round into the grill of the Humvees. The acidic round, designed specifically to disable vehicles, crashed into the engine and immediately went to work eating through every component it splashed on. Metal, plastic hoses, even the engine block itself was fair game to the acid that ate everything with which it came into contact. One round into each of the approaching Humvees was enough to disable them within a minute or two, but we weren't waiting to see the effects of the phosphorus. We needed to leave, and fast!

"Do you still remember how to drive?" Mia asked as we climbed into the front seats. She reloaded her bullpup and leaned outside the window as I studied the controls of the Humvee.

"Of course I remember!" I gulped. "It's just been twenty years . . ."

Vehicles weren't popular now since fuel required a nearby refinery, of which I only knew of one, and it was in President Criswell's control. Thousands of abandoned cars sat all over the city, most of them stripped of anything of possible value. I'd sat behind the wheel of a dozen vehicles over the years, imagining driving again, as I had as a youth.

Our Humvee lurched forward while bullets pinged off the armored body. We zoomed down a street before I realized we were headed west instead of east! I made two right turns, leaving our enemy behind, and flew up Orange Avenue.

"You ready?" I asked. "We have to cross the bridge."

Coronado Bay Bridge was about a mile long from the island to the mainland, and completely exposed, making a long arc to the east. Not only was it heavily guarded on the mainland end, the bridge was high above the water, so jumping off was out of the question. I'd seen the barricade on the far end, so I knew what we were up against.

I drove onto the bridge going eighty-miles-an-hour, starting the long curve to the east.

"There they are!" Mia readied her rifle. "You have a plan?"

After all she'd been through that night, she seemed a little too anxious for action, but it was understandable, I guessed. My father had told me stories of Christians overseas who'd been assaulted. With Christ's help, they were able to recover over time. I prayed that Mia would as well. Since I was still young, I really didn't know how to comfort her. Nor did our urgent escape give us any time to talk about what she'd survived.

"The barricade is meant to keep people out, not in." I sped the Humvee faster. "Hang on!"

The barricade was well-armed with .40 caliber mounted guns behind sandbags on both sides of the lane, but the lane itself had only a wooden crossing arm. As we drove near, I saw the mounted guns weren't manned, probably because they couldn't swivel to fire backward, only forward, toward the mainland.

Two men, their arms waving, tried to flag us down, but we didn't stop. The wooden arm splintered across our bulletproof windshield and we sped into Barrio Logan Chicano Park, a trash dumpsite for Coronado Island. I hit the brakes. A few civilians scattered in our headlights, the pre-dawn scavengers picking at Coronado's refuse.

"You have to drive to the zoo and get Mom." My heart was pounding fast. "Look, Mia—gas and brake. It's easy once you get going."

"What? Where are you going? You can't leave me now!"

"I've got to slow them down, and you and Mom have to get on the road. Drive as far as you can, until you run out of gas. Then follow my map in my pack. Mom has everything. I'll catch up in a few days."

"Levi, you . . ." She wrapped her arms around my neck. "Please don't tell Aunt Annette how you found me. Just . . . forget about it."

"I will. You sure you're okay?"

She sat back and touched my hairline. Her fingers came away bloody. My injuries from the beating had opened up from all the movement.

"I'll deal with it," she answered. "But look at you, you're bleeding! I thought they'd killed you!"

"We can talk later." I climbed out of the Humvee as she took the driver's seat. "Take care of Mom, and keep her moving east."

I started away on foot.

"Hey, Levi." She waited until I looked back then blew me a kiss. "Thanks for coming back for me."

"It's what family does for one another, even when it ain't easy. Get moving."

I jogged back to the bridge before her taillights were out of sight.

At the on-ramp to the bridge, I leaped down to the Hilton Bayfront where collapsed warehouses were still in the process of being rebuilt by the Pacific States government. I scaled the scaffolding to reach the roof and lay prone on top of it, aiming at the bridge. As I prayed for Mia and Mom's safety, I steadied my breathing.

Headlights approached, crossing the bridge in pursuit of us. In the darkness, I counted the concrete piles of the bridge and visually marked how far I guessed it was to six hundred yards—over a quarter-mile away. The rifle wasn't accurate any farther than that. I could see the approaching headlights at almost the highest point of the bridge. They started down toward me, coming into range.

My first round was high and broke phosphorus acid across the windshield of the first vehicle. They stopped suddenly and the second Humvee rear-ended the first one. I fired at both vehicles more accurately, destroying their engines. Other vehicles approached, their drivers curious rather than cautious about the incoming fire, and I disabled seven vehicles before someone radioed back to warn the others to stay back.

Just then, my location was discovered—I was certain it was from my muzzle flash—and I took fire from the checkpoint, from both guns at the same time. Forty-millimeter rounds tore into the roof around me, but both guns were meant for near-target devastation and their barrels were short. However, rather than risk one of their rounds catching my backside during my retreat, I switched from phosphorus rounds to non-lethal gel-tranqs. At two hundred paces, I put both men to sleep.

A few of the men on the bridge fired at me, but their smaller arms were inadequate. I climbed off the roof and ran on foot toward Petco Park and beyond.

Blocks later, I slowed to a jog and tried to focus on the journey before the three of us, but my nerves were on edge. A coyote yipped and I jumped. A feral cat hissed and I nearly tranquilized the little critter before moving on. San Diego, even after twenty years of trying to rebuild the city, was still a wild and untamed warzone. President Criswell had been more concerned about acquiring wealth and comfort for himself than putting priority in the safety and contentment of his constituents. My father had helped thousands, but civil disorder had crippled the city over time.

This wasn't the way I'd planned to leave for New York. Instead of leaving quietly by disappearing into the night with my mother and Mia, Mia's capture and rescue had awoken a force from Coronado that was already hungry for an excuse to shed blood. The Brogdons wouldn't know we'd made preparations to leave—until they visited our home. Once the damaged vehicles were towed away, others would resume the chase. How far would they chase me? How badly did Kip want Mia? Or how far was General Galt Brogdon willing to pursue me to find out if the stash of bullpups was really in the city?

Coronado Island didn't have another bridge, but there were navy vessels that could come to shore on the mainland. In case solders already on the mainland had been ordered by radio to capture me, I couldn't return home. But since Annette and Mia were moving ahead without me, I would need meager provisions to sustain me for a couple days.

I chose to call upon an elderly Mexican Christian named Gustavo, who lived across the street from the Air and Space Museum.

The house Gustavo occupied was two stories tall, which was common quarters for citizens in that area. Many lived on the second floor, since the first floor was sometimes flooded that close to the ocean.

Below the window of Gustavo's dining room, I pulled a cord that rang a small bell above. A moment passed, then I heard a window slide open in the darkness.

"Who's there?"

"Gustavo, it's me, Levi Caspertein. Keep your light off."

He'd attended my father's funeral the day before, since they'd been close, so I knew he still favored our family. I heard Gustavo set aside what was probably his .22 rifle he used to shoot stray dogs.

"It's early, Levi. What's happened?"

"I tangled with the Brogdons."

"Of course you did. You're a Caspertein. Casperteins always do what no one else will do." He chuckled at his own joke, definitely more amusing to him than to me that night, although what he had said seemed to be true. "What do you need?"

"I'm leaving the city. Can you spare some water and food?"

He was a known baker, so I hoped for something fresh to fill my empty stomach.

"You're leaving the city? Permanently?"

I could hear the disappointment in his voice.

"I have to. I'll die, otherwise. Mom and Mia are already on their way."

"What about us? Your father led half this city to Christ, including me."

"Dad's gone now, Gustavo. We all must find our own way—to walk and to stand. Because of Christ, none of us are alone. I'm confident you'll finish the race well, bringing glory to our Lord and Savior. Gustavo? Are you still there?"

"I'm here. I think if you're leaving the city, you should take my grandson. I'm getting too old, Levi, and the city is becoming more unruly. There are rumors that President Criswell will begin to transcript the youth for war training. Jose cannot fall into their hands to become a killer!"

I clenched my teeth. The journey hadn't even begun, and already I was picking up a seven-year-old boy?

"I'll be traveling too fast, Gustavo. Twenty miles a day is too much for a child."

"What would your father do?"

I smiled in the darkness, already conceding in my heart to the old man's request. My father was a sensitive subject for me since I'd just buried him, and everyone in the city knew how close we'd been. If it were Dad, he would definitely find a way to take Jose and keep him safe.

"It ain't easy arguing with you, Gustavo. How quickly can you have him ready? Every minute counts."

"Five minutes. Let me wake him."

I placed my back against the outside wall and prayed for guidance. Every hour, my departure from San Diego became more complicated, more burdensome. Our resources were few, and we were already carrying one hundred and forty pounds between Annette, Mia, and myself. Maybe a young boy wouldn't matter greatly to our resources. He probably wouldn't eat much.

A few minutes later, Gustavo walked out the front door, helping his grandson into a small backpack. The boy held a thick blanket in his arms, which would do for a sleeping bag for a few months, since the spring weather was still dry and warm. Gustavo knelt in front of Jose.

"You know Levi from your Sunday school classes, Jose. You do what he says, you hear?"

"Yes, Grandpa."

"I'll pray for you every night, and you pray for me. Understand?"

"Yes, Grandpa."

Gustavo embraced the boy and I sneaked a peek at my watch. Dawn was one hour away.

The boy had a thermos and Gustavo handed me a medium-sized water bottle and a sack of fresh bread.

"I'll see you in eternity, Levi Caspertein."

We shook hands like brothers.

"See you, Gustavo."

Jose and I cut through the trees near the museum and paused at the edge of Laurel Street before crossing Cabrillo Bridge over the gorge. The acoustics were tricky there, sounds in the night farther away than they seemed. I thought I heard a vehicle, but I doubted Galt Brogdon had cleared the bridge and mustered a search party so quickly.

"You warm enough?" I asked Jose. He struggled with the blanket, so I swapped the bread bag for his blanket. "You remember the story of the Israelites I taught last month?"

Jose was silent for a moment, then turned his face up to me. Every other Sunday, I taught the youth a Bible lesson down at the old cruise ship terminal.

"The exodus?"

"Exactly. That's us now, trusting God as we leave Egypt. The bondage of Pharaoh is behind us. We're gonna cross this bridge at a run. You ready?"

"Yep."

I jogged slowly for the boy, his backpack jostling. Already, I saw a determined boy who would do just fine during a lengthy trek. In a few days when we caught up to Annette and Mia, I'd see what he had in his pack, but for now, we needed to get beyond Highway 805.

Cabrillo Bridge was long and exposed, but it was our fastest route toward Balboa Zoo. I kept my eyes on El Prado's Archway, and tried to block out the sure sound of a vehicle approaching us from behind. When I chanced a glance back, I saw four pairs of headlights. We'd never make it to the archway! If Jose knew the danger we were in, he didn't show it by crying or slowing down.

When we were twenty feet from the archway, another vehicle emerged and blocked our way. I considered grabbing Jose and leaping off the bridge. Somewhere down there in the blackness was a steep slope and shrubs. But if we landed on rocks, we would die instantly. We stopped running. In the headlights from both directions, I leveled my rifle and waited for someone to show themselves.

"Look over the edge, Jose," I said softly. "You see anything down there?"

The boy leaned over the guardrail.

"No, it's too dark."

"Can you hang and drop?"

Men exited the vehicles and I searched through the bright lights for a familiar authority figure.

"Drop it, Caspertein!" a deep voice boomed from behind me. I turned and aimed at General Galt Brogdon, a bulky man known for his physical strength. Rumor had it, he'd been an actual officer in the military before Pan-Day, though he'd been dishonorably discharged. He was shorter than me, but his shoulders were just as broad. "It's over. Drop the rifle."

The rifle! Even one bullpup was too many to fall into the hands of someone like Galt Brogdon. I would throw it over the bridge into the gorge before I turned it over to him.

"We're walking away, Galt. San Diego is no longer my home. You don't want me here, and I don't want to be here."

"Walking away?" He chuckled and stood unconcerned ten feet from me, even though my rifle was aimed at his chest. Eight of his men surrounded us, some inching closer. "You dare assault the capital, and think there won't be consequences? The Caspertein pup is as bold as the jackal father. Come on, now. You've done enough damage tonight. Put the weapon down. We both know you only have non-lethal rounds."

"Unless I still have a phosphorus round loaded." That made him hesitate, perhaps recalling the image of phosphorus eating through his engines on the bridge. "Imagine what that could do to your ribcage, General."

I reacted too slowly to one of his men who lunged forward and grabbed Jose. I turned my head to see Jose squirming in a laughing man's arms, but I kept my gun aimed at Galt. He didn't know I wouldn't kill him, not for sure. Without my father, he might've thought I was willing to blaze my own path. Very few knew me as anyone but a boy who shadowed his resourceful, witty father.

"Where's my son's fiancee?" Galt drew his sidearm from a shoulder holster and aimed it at Jose. "You have ten seconds, then I kill this little monkey."

"You kill him, and you'll never know where the rest of the bullpups are."

"Yes, the rest of the bullpups. That would be a nice prize to torture out of you. I guess I don't need the boy."

His gun barked fire, a bright flash so close in the darkness that I thought maybe it had been a warning shot. But Jose's lifeless body fell to the pavement. All hopes I had to bargain for our lives disappeared. General Galt Brogdon had murdered the boy!

I turned and dove off the bridge. Since Galt wanted from me the whereabouts of the rifles, and his son Kip surely wanted to find Mia, killing me was probably not in their plan book, but I wasn't standing around to be tortured.

Tree leaves smacked my face as I fell, then I folded in half over a thick branch. The branch broke and I continued to fall and twist, until I suddenly hit the grassy slope. Rolling, I let go of my rifle, but on its sling around my shoulder, it battered me about the face and neck until I came to a stop on level ground.

Out of breath, I gathered my senses for a few seconds and rose to my feet. Exhausted and covered with bruises, my ribs tender and my scalp bleeding again, I staggered to the north. Somewhere above me, men were running down the bridge, and a search light was shining at the trees where I'd fallen. But I was already far from that place, limping away, now on the other side of the bridge, moving in the night shadows of other foliage. The cracked pavement of Highway 163 was under my feet. Moving was easier on the pavement, but I couldn't remain where Galt Brogdon's forces could travel with ease. I'd need to travel cross-country to throw them off my trail.

Somewhere to the northwest of San Diego Zoo, I walked into the oak trees, leaving the bridge and tower behind. I sat down against one tree and touched my jeans, which were soaked with blood. Frightened at what injury I might find, I searched for a wound, but found none. When I smelled my wet fingers, I sensed water rather than blood. Then I found the water bottle had broken that had been clipped to my belt. My stop at Gustavo's house had been fruitless, leading only to Jose's death and almost my capture.

I struggled with hatred as I gazed back toward the road. With a dozen clips of various .308 rounds in my vest pouches, I could return to the bridge and take my revenge then and there. A well-placed phosphorus round on Galt Brogdon's hip or shoulder would lead to an agonizing and slow death as the acidic substance gradually ate away his skin and bones.

But then I looked away and regretted such thinking. Galt Brogdon deserved to be dealt with justly, but revenge wasn't mine to give. He'd opposed my father while my father tolerated him for years, and Kip had assaulted Mia with what I assumed was his father's blessing. Now, Galt had killed a young boy—all to try to force my hand!

Tears filled my eyes. To hate was to be in bondage. Thankfully, Jose had been a Christian. As young as he was, he'd been among the few my father had baptized in the bay that early spring when the water was coldest. A child had gone to his Heavenly Father, where my own father had recently gone. By God's grace, Mia would recover from the assault, and we would all leave the Pacific States far behind. God would deal with those in our wake, and on that point I would pray most fervently.

Holding my head up with new resolve, I walked toward Highway 805. Annette and Mia were certainly hours ahead of me, since they'd driven the Humvee as far as they could. Having no provisions of my own, catching up to them would be arduous.

Leaving San Diego hadn't been easy.

Chapter Three

Six days passed before I found the Humvee on Highway 15 northeast of San Diego. They'd been hard days for me, traveling night and day, then sleeping in holes for a couple hours when I was too tired to continue. Once, I chanced a shot at a coyote, which turned out to be a feral German shepherd. Tearing down a metal mile-marker sign, I used it as a frying pan and cooked dog meat over a small fire the second night out.

But now I was farther east from San Diego than I'd been since I was a teenager, when Pan-Day had struck. Even on hunting excursions with Dad, we hadn't strayed this far into the hills, and I was now witnessing devastation we in San Diego had only heard rumors about. Whole communities had burned. Drivers had fled the city or their neighborhoods. Abandoned cars lined the roads, some caught in traffic jams as if they'd happened just the day before.

On the sides of chipped buildings, faded spray paint marked the territory of gangs, now long-decimated by the pandemic, or by their own brutality. Occasionally, I came upon human skeletons on the road, picked clean by wild animals. Each one had been a person, a victim, a soul. The fear in those first months had been so irrational. Families had abandoned their own loved ones who'd merely coughed or sneezed. Not many had known how to diagnose the virus in the beginning. Millions had died, cut off from food and water, and others were shot outright for fear they were infected.

Sometime before the radio stations had lost power, someone had blamed the Christians for spreading the

Ebola Virus. The accusation was aimed at missionaries who had traveled to infected countries in West Africa, even in past years, then returned and spread the virus. But I'd been there at the beginning, twenty years earlier, when a seemingly harmless missile fired from North Korea had detonated in the sky over Meridia, Oregon. It hadn't been Ebola from Africa, but a new virus, this time from Meridia. The spores of some wickedly-engineered weapon had spread in the weeks following, contaminating the water and food and air. There'd indeed been a pandemic, but it was made worse by the panic that had ignited man's irrationality, suspicion, and fear. Without God in their lives for stability, the whole country had sunk into sand.

Far up on a hill overlooking the highway, I had a fair view of the Humvee below. Placing my fingers to my lips, I blew a shrill whistle. There was no movement. Its doors were closed, and it sat at the back of a line of vehicles parked on the highway in front of a collapsed overpass. I'd seen other signs of earthquake damage through the past day, but this was the worst. The quake had apparently occurred during the flight of thousands out of the city. Unable to drive, the motorists had been forced to flee on foot, but without provisions or the prospect of shelter, or any experience in survival, travelers would've been easy targets for human predators and looters who were armed and thriving in the chaos.

A jackrabbit hopped curiously through the skeletons of rusting cars, under which brown grass sprouted through cracks in the pavement. I was hungry and thirsty, but a .308 was too large a caliber to shoot such a small creature. Even if I used a gel-tranq round, the little animal would've been one big bruise to eat, blood saturating its meat.

Sliding down the hill on my heels, I hopped the highway barricade and approached the Humvee. It was empty. Annette and Mia had packs of their own, besides mine, which weighed as much as both of theirs combined.

But they'd taken everything, moving on rather than waiting for me, which was wisest. It was a lot for the two women to carry, but it was exactly what I'd told Mia to do—not to wait for me. That had been almost six days earlier. If I traveled quickly, I would catch them in one day since they were so laden with packs.

I walked down the east side of the road until I found fresh boot tracks—the small boots of Mia, alongside the larger tracks of Annette. For most of her adult life, Annette had been a clothing model and humanitarian. She'd met Dad in Gaza, Israel, and both had received Christ during a brutal operation between Israel and Hamas. Dad had been an international smuggler, but after that, he and Annette had gotten married and started serving God alongside other COIL Christians, assisting the persecuted worldwide. Though Annette had been a nurse and homemaker while I worked with Dad the past twenty years, I wasn't ignorant of her wisdom and life experience that would help us make the trek now in one piece. After all, she'd been Dad's right hand for years.

Discovering their tracks gave me their approximate heading. Annette was in the lead and her prints were deepest in the sandy ground there. She was probably wearing my heavier pack and Mia was wearing Annette's. Mia's pack was much lighter, and the two, I guessed, were trading off the weight between them. Temporarily, they could travel like that, but long-term, both would be too weary to walk after a couple days. I had planned this trip carefully, and what I'd packed had been weighed and distributed amongst our packs for maximum travel speed. Those had been the saddest days. While Dad was barely lucid, he'd given us instructions from the nearby room of our house—then certain he wouldn't live, yet wanting to know for sure that we would be leaving the city safely.

Jenna Dowler was the reason I was leaving the city now. Her distress call over the radio had alerted me to the grave situation she faced in New York. She needed me, and I had begun to make plans immediately. Around that time, Galt Brogdon and Kip, with some of their troops, had come to the house and demanded that we give up our radio for Pacific States security. That day, Dad hadn't protested when the general declared the radio was a security risk for civilians to have, as if we were conspiring with the Appalachian Federation on the East Coast. But I'd already received Jenna's final radio message, so there'd been no reason to cling needlessly to the radio. Now, I needed to get to New York.

The Dowler family had been responsible for Dad and Annette's conversion to Christianity, and their subsequent discipling in their walk of faith. Jenna was about my age, and though I'd had a youthful crush on her twenty years earlier, she'd become a sister in the faith since then. Communicating weekly with vague reports that could be intercepted had been our only form of contact, but it had been enough to create a strong bond of love for this courageous woman who was Corban Dowler's adopted daughter. On top of all of Jenna's challenges with the persecution in the east, she'd been blind since a young girl, and because of her blindness, I felt a distinct need to protect her. Her parents, Corban and Janice, had long since died, I'd heard. Dad's death had simply urged me to leave more quickly to go to Jenna.

I crested a hill and gazed into the distance. Annette and Mia's footprints continued across the dry ground, interspersed with ugly shrubs. Nothing moved in that desert—within my sight, anyway. For a moment, I felt the desperation and weariness of the journey. Like the Israelites, I pondered the simplicity of returning to the familiar—my Egypt. Regardless of the dangerous oppression and crumbling infrastructure in San Diego, I had found some comfort in knowing every street, hiding place, and torched building in the city.

The whole world seemed dead, and that wild thought, upon reflection, was a sign of my own desperation and hunger. The whole world wasn't dead; I was just isolated and feeling self-pity from my exhaustion. God wasn't done with humanity, for Christ had promised to return again and reign on the earth. And in eternity, sin and death would be removed as God alone showed Himself worthy to be glorified.

But for a little while longer, before that great and awful day of reckoning, I had to endure suffering and shame, loss and pain. Christ was worth it all, and I had to live as He would live on this journey to help one of His own, Jenna Dowler. The past comforts of San Diego had to be thrown off and forgotten. The future hardships needed to be embraced, since there was rest on the other side of those difficulties.

Hungry, thirsty, and tired, I followed the tracks of Annette and Mia. The hills rolled up and down, and I marched forward. At the top on one rise, where once again I gazed upon the changeless terrain and endless trail, I considered setting up camp for the night. My previous camps had been very meager, consisting of coyote meat or a few roots cooked over a small fire, and a hole to hide myself from the night's chill. A skinning knife, my Bible, and a lighter were all I had in my pockets. If the bullpup rifle hadn't been on a sling, I would've abandoned even its weight miles back.

Suddenly, I stood in the descending sun's rays near a cluster of three palm trees. Was I imagining the sight before me? A backpack lay at the base of each tree! I recognized my pack, as well as Annette and Mia's.

I crouched on the desert floor and brought my rifle quickly to my shoulder. My heart pounded. The boot prints veered southward, their strides lengthening as if running. *They were being chased!* Studying the hills, I checked for an ambush, but saw no one. By the tracks and plants Annette had trampled, I guessed I was still a day behind her and Mia. Whatever had transpired had occurred the day or night before. If more recent, I would've found the plants in their tracks more trampled rather than now standing almost upright.

Before tracking the women southward, I prowled closer to the palm trees to check for booby-traps. A few years earlier, Galt Brogdon's forces had faced a string of IEDs during their patrols near the Mexican border. It wasn't out of the ordinary for ex-military survivors of Pan-Day to set traps for potential threats. A community nearby couldn't know that casual travelers moving through their territory weren't a threat.

The packs seemed safe, and by their placement, they appeared to have been hidden from view from the opposite direction. It was like Annette to understand they were about to be captured, I guessed, and rather than be taken with their packs, they'd left them behind. This was as clear to me as if she'd written it in a message on paper. My mother was no fool in the face of adversity.

Sure enough, in moving my heavy pack with its external frame, the bullpup Mia had carried was hidden there as well. Under Annette's pack was a twelve-gauge shotgun to use for shooting fowl, and a .22 rifle, which could fire a standard or gel-tranq cartridge.

I unzipped a pouch and tore open a package of dried banana chips as I prayed for God's direction. Next came dried granola, then I guzzled twenty ounces of water from a water bottle. Ten hours of sleep would have revived me the rest of the way, but Annette and Mia had already been in foul company long enough.

After fastening the water bottle to my belt, I loaded the .22 rifle with non-lethal ammunition to use for defense against people. I also selected a wind-direction indicator, binoculars, and jerked deer meat to eat on the way. Choosing a battery-powered headlamp, I strapped it to my head in case I needed to track in the dark.

In planning this journey, we'd considered the probability of coming across other people, hostile or otherwise. The question wasn't what kind of people we would meet as much as it was—how would we deal with them? The strength of their forces and the type of their weaponry mattered most.

I jogged alongside Annette's deeper and more visible tracks, hoping to find their destination in the daylight. Though weariness and the cares of our journey ahead weighed heavily on my mind, I postponed those necessities and focused on this recovery. It had been only a few days since my father's funeral, and already I was forced to respond to the family's most dire needs. This was simply the man God had made me to be, by my father's sound counsel and Annette's hearty cooking. A Caspertein doesn't shrink from danger!

Two hundred yards away from the three palm trees where I'd left the packs, I found where Annette and Mia's tracks were intercepted by eight pairs of boots. No tire tracks, which probably meant these men had no gas for trucks or dirt bikes. Annette had chosen to run rather than have a gun battle with them, which may have meant the strangers had been carrying rifles. Both women were fair rifle shots, and the bullpup, in Annette's hands, had an exceptional reach over the standard hunting rifle.

Now all ten pairs of boot tracks turned northeast. Like the responsible tracker I'd been taught to be, I kept my binoculars handy and checked the landscape every thirty or forty yards as I pursued them.

I found their hidden mountain oasis three miles later. The sun set behind me as I lay on my belly, spying on the village of forty shoddy houses below, probably founded since Pan-Day around a natural spring. Thousands of these towns existed, a trader had told Dad, who'd traveled along the Mexican border to the Gulf and back each year. People wanted to escape the cities and live independently. Maybe they'd been law-abiding citizens, but once again, fear of the unknown caused honest people to commit unspeakable atrocities. The latest gourmet food, the most fashionable clothing, and the hottest new technology—the world's interest in trends had shifted to basic survival. Society's desire to be cool had been replaced by the need to use a crossbow for that night's dinner. The problem had been, however, that most Americans didn't know how to even build a fire. Pan-Day had come in December to most states, and all households had lost basic utilities by February of that first year.

The village below me had no electricity, but they did have a sentry in an elevated crow's nest at the far side of the small valley. The sentry would've needed a powerful scope and a very good eye to spot me against the sunset, especially since I was clothed in earth tones.

To recover the women, I had before me two choices— a sophisticated assault, or a head-on civilized introduction—and pray they were hospitable. The man who stood in the crow's nest held a rifle, but that could've been a peaceful community's show of force to keep bandits at bay. However, peaceful communities didn't abduct travelers.

I withdrew from my position and out of sight to ready my rifles. The .22 was a Savage bolt action with one modified magazine that held thirty rounds. Those rounds were subsonic, which allowed for the silenced firing of the gel-tranqs. If I fired the .308, everyone within five miles would hear that canon.

Circling the ridge, I approached the crow's nest position in darkness. Nothing on me rattled or rustled as I stepped closer to the watchman. The .22 rifle was aimed at the thirty-foot platform, and my bullpup was slung on my back. Leaving family behind wasn't an option. This village had abducted the wrong women!

The creaking of boards above told me the sentry was moving around. The night was quiet. I didn't hear any coyotes, which probably meant the village had overhunted the game nearest their shelter, which was potentially a fatal mistake for their years ahead.

The sentry moved into sight, gazing far off and over my head. If he would've looked straight down, he would've seen me as a shadow. Maybe. Darkness plays tricks on even the keenest eyes.

I shot him in the thigh, causing him to flinch backwards rather than tumbling out and getting hurt. He dropped to the floor unconscious an instant later, and I chambered another round. The first village residence was thirty yards away. There was no wall, only a garden that circled the houses.

No longer feeling the previous week's wounds, I approached the village with anticipation, my mouth open for maximum oxygen intake for my reflexive muscles, and my eyes wide. I'd lived my whole life for this journey. Fear wasn't allowed to paralyze me, even though I was afraid. A whole day was a long time for my family to remain in the hands of wicked strangers.

By rounding the first dwelling, I found only one window to avoid. A pair of young women passed me in the darkness—so close, I could hear them giggling about boyfriends. Through the window of the dwelling, I saw an elderly man bent over an LED lamp, reading a book. Though I hoped it was a Bible, when he turned a page, I saw it was a novel. His clothing was army surplus, like most civilians wore now in San Diego.

Caspertein men pride ourselves on our wit, and though I'd been proactive with a rifle the last week, I was willing to take on the old man with mere conversation, if he would allow it.

In case the front door was locked, I put my shoulder to it as I turned the doorknob, but it easily swung open. The man looked up, surely expecting someone he knew. Instead, I barreled into his one-room hut and closed the door behind me. Rather than aim the rifle at him, I cradled it lightly in my right arm, pointing at the floor, which was canvas-covered over a warped cement foundation.

"Good evening," I said. "Hope you don't mind. I was walking past the window and saw you alone in here. Figured you could use some company."

His sad eyes strayed to the corner nearest me where a bird gun was leaning against the wall alongside a broom.

"Yeah, nice night." He closed his book, a bookmark in place, and sat back, hands in his lap. "You're new around here."

"Yep. Looking for a summer cottage. Something with a view." I nodded at a framed photograph on a crooked bookshelf where more novels sat. "Nice-looking family."

"Pan-Day took 'em."

"I don't know which was worse: losing some of them quickly that year, or the rest of them slowly in the years since, one at a time."

"You must've been just a boy back then." He seemed to relax his shoulders. "Now all I got are these reading books."

"I don't know of any other kind of book." Smiling, I gestured to a chair with dirty laundry in it. "You mind?"

"Go ahead."

I used my left hand to sweep the clothes onto the floor, keeping my right hand ready for action, and sat down.

"Loss and strife make us think desperate thoughts, even hopeless thoughts." I spoke softly as I had seen Dad speak to people whom he met for the first time. "As vile as people may be around us, near or far, we can't forget the priorities of life."

"Priorities?" He frowned, and I waited as his curiosity worked for me. Maybe he expected a young man in his late thirties to speak of silly ideas, but I'd been raised by mature men and women of God who had spoken with purpose. "What priorities?"

"We're meant for more than sheltered lives and self-pitying memories. We've all suffered loss. I buried my father a few days ago." I sighed, intent to use my words rather than my rifle to stir this man's soul. "We're a broken people, but I've learned that keeping our priorities straight gives life some meaning, both for now and for the hereafter."

He looked again at his gun and bit his lip, maybe remorsefully. I guessed the hunting gun wasn't even loaded.

"So, what priorities are those?"

"People who seek their Creator don't seek to harm their neighbors."

"You some sort of philosopher, or just a religious nut?"

"You decide. I believe in a God who came to earth and paid a debt He didn't owe, because we owed a sin debt we couldn't pay. I'm talking about the justice of three crosses. Christ was in the middle. On one side, a man mocked the Savior, the One who'd paid for the sins of the world. On the other side was the same sort of condemned man, but he humbled himself and believed in that perfect payment. Even in death, one man found peace, but the other died with a burdened conscience and faced the separation of hell for eternity. That was two thousand years ago, and the thief is still there awaiting judgement. Sometimes, it ain't easy hearing the truth. How long have you been this . . . miserable?"

His nostrils flared, but maybe he realized he wasn't facing a movable object. I stood securely on Christ, the Rock, and only when men hear the hard truth do they truly grasp their need for their Savior. There was no other safety for eternity.

"It's been too long, I guess." His eyes avoided mine. "Seems I've heard those words a thousand times in years past, being my age and all, but today they might mean something, coming from you."

"You have all these books, but do you have a Bible?"

He rose from his chair and moved several stacks of books. He selected one with a brown cover that was at the bottom of one stack on the cement, protecting other books from water damage. When he set it on the table before me, the musty smell confirmed it had been damaged by water, but when I opened the cover, the words were still clear on the yellowed, wrinkled pages.

"Where would I start?" he asked, leaning forward. "I mean, if I read it."

"You have to read it," I said, turning to the Gospel of John. "There's no point dying without knowing the truth of what awaits you. The Book of John is where I'd start. Then go to the front and read the whole Bible. You'll find that God shows Himself as a Person of justice in the first section, and then as a Person of peace and grace in the second section, when God came in the flesh as a Man. He'll change your life, if you're ready to believe."

He started to respond when a shrill cry came from somewhere in the village. It was a woman's cry, and I recognized her voice—it was my stepmother, Annette!

I was out the door before the old man found his feet. Down a dark alley between dwellings, I ran at full speed. She screamed again, and others shrieked. Darting to my left, I searched desperately for a doorway to a sizeable structure with plywood walls.

When I found the door, I kicked it inward. Leveling the .22 rifle, I entered a well-lit room. I moved to my right. The bullpup found its way into my left hand, so that I was holding two rifles at once. A dozen men and three women surrounded Annette and Mia. Annette's hands were bound behind her back, as were Mia's, but it was Annette who was wrestling against two grown men as they clutched her arms. One woman with a pair of hair shears looked up at me, and everyone froze.

The next thing I noticed was that no one was armed. One rifle leaned against the wall next to me, but none of this lot had expected me. I was deep inside their community where no lone traveler would've normally dared to confront them.

The men were all bald, or wore short-cropped hair. They'd already buzzed a part of Annette's head above her ear. She wasn't a vain woman, but since she'd been a model during her youth, her long hair identified her, even though it now showed streaks of gray. Mia was held by two sturdy men as well. She didn't appear to be harmed, except for the fading yellow bruising around her eyes from Kip Brogdon's abuse.

"I knew you'd come for us." Mia grinned and the men nearest her backed away. "Tell them, Cuz, how much trouble they're in."

"This is a .308 battle rifle," I said, gesturing to the bullpup. "I have eight thirty-round magazines, and I'm an expert marksman up to a quarter-mile. You'd better back off my family or you'll feel what it means to meet Caspertein justice."

I made a small gesture with the rifle barrels, and those nearest Annette stepped away from her as well. Both women came over to me, and I drew my skinning knife from my hip sheath to quickly cut their binds. Annette took the .22 rifle from me, and we moved out the door together.

"Not a minute too soon, Levi," Annette said, with laughter in her voice. I took her to mean I wouldn't believe the story she had to tell.

But outside the building, we ran into a crowd of armed citizens, all of them with very short hair and none too pleased, it seemed, that they'd been invaded.

"Move aside!" I demanded, wishing for once the bullpup looked as menacing as it really was, instead of like a compact assault rifle shorter than my arm. "Move back!"

Our situation worsened when the men from inside the building found their courage and pressed us from behind. Annette backed up against me and held her ground as I did the same, while Mia clung to my side, wielding the skinning blade like a sword.

A shotgun blast spat fire into the night sky. People made way for someone who pushed through the crowd. Suddenly, I was face-to-face with the old man with whom I'd shared the gospel message. His bird gun rested over his shoulder. The people were hushed.

"When we took these women in the desert," he yelled for all to hear, "we thought we were saving them from falling into the hands of those to the east of us. We didn't know they really belonged to a good man, a friend of mine named—"

"The Serval," I mumbled, claiming an old handle of my father's.

"The Serval." He looked at me and gave me a little nod of recognition. "When I founded this town, none of you had anywhere to go. It's your turn to welcome them on their own terms, or let them leave."

"They could be spies!" someone in the back blurted. "They could be from Aporax!"

"They aren't spies!" the old man defended. "If you want them gone, I'm sure they're willing to leave. None of us wants bloodshed. This man is obviously a veteran of conflict, more than any of us. Serval?"

"With your permission, we would like to continue our journey. Tonight. Can you walk us out?"

"Go home, everyone." The old man gestured for us to join him as he started to the north, giving no one time to protest further. I lowered my rifle, but Annette and Mia were still skittish. "You don't want to go directly east from here. We've been having skirmishes with another squatter town called Aporax."

"And what's your town called?" I asked, walking at his side along the dirt pathways between buildings.

"This is Hawkridge. Most of us are refugees from Chula Vista. I was mayor there, and a lot of the people followed me after Pan-Day. We stayed together, but many have come and gone. Nothing is the same anymore."

"And the head shaving?"

"Lice. We've been infested for months. If your women would've stayed, they needed to be shaved. Their husbands would've insisted."

"I see."

At the top of the hill, we stopped and looked back at Hawkridge. I had more questions, but I didn't want to push the narrow welcome we had by explaining their unconscious sentry. Without learning his name, I shook the hand of the founder of Hawkridge, and we walked into the night.

Chapter Four

Thunder rolled the next morning as I stood in the rain. It was a gray day and I wore a gray rain slicker, my bullpup in my arms. Between the thunder, I heard the sharp crack of gunfire somewhere out there, a mile or two away, I guessed.

I looked back at a lone birch tree where I'd hung a tarp. Annette and Mia were still asleep. They'd marched hard through the night and stinging rain. According to the founder of Hawkridge, a dangerous town called Aporax was out there, so we hadn't spoken aloud during our trek. We didn't want to take a chance that our voices would carry in the darkness. When we'd heard the gunfire, we'd stopped to rest while I stood watch. Something terrible had happened somewhere out there in the night.

Originally, when Jenna Dowler had sent word for me to come to New York, I'd been the only one planning to make the trek. Dad had catalogued some intel on the conditions of the Plains Zone, but no traders ever returned from beyond the Rockies. The best he'd done was provide me with rumors and a few maps from the days of electricity, cars, and thriving tourism.

When Dad had been diagnosed with the virus, he was the first one to insist I take Annette and Mia with me. Mia was a wanted commodity, as a fertile female, and Mom couldn't protect her alone. Even as terrible as conditions sounded in the east, particularly against Christians, we all agreed the family should remain together.

This created some problems I was just beginning to realize. My optimism regarding Mom's physical strength and Mia's stamina seemed to have been unfounded.

Through the night, they'd stumbled and fallen, trudging slowly along ridges where I was able to move twice as fast. Jenna needed my help. She was the reason I was going to New York. If the journey took me twice as long to get there, Jenna could be dead by then, by way of the Christian persecution now occurring.

The gunfire in the distance ceased. Visibility was only about fifty yards through the torrential rain. My father had been a Special Forces operative for COIL, and though he'd taught me his skills and said I was a better shot with a rifle than he, I wasn't about to walk through the rain into an unknown conflict. Dad had taught me to utilize the superiority of the bullpup, its range and versatility, to overwhelm an enemy with greater numbers. But that required intel, and I knew nothing about what lay ahead. We would probably have to backtrack once the rain stopped, maybe even pass the area in the dark. Aporax was out there.

"The shooting stopped." It was Mom, making me jump as she approached and spoke from behind me. Standing next to me in her waterproof parka, she was as tall as I was. "Mia hasn't said anything about her time with Kip Brogdon, just that he kidnapped her. I asked her, but she didn't tell me what happened. How'd you get her back? How'd you find her?"

"When it's time, she'll bring it up. When she's ready, Mom."

"You know, I wasn't sure you'd find us, but she never gave up." Annette hooked her arm around my elbow. "She kept saying, 'You don't know Levi like I do. He'll come for us.' But she was crying most of the time. I know she's been hurt."

"We can't make her talk, Mom." I'd called her Mom since I'd found her and Dad after my birth mother had died when I was a teenager. "I've been thinking. When we get to Colorado, I should probably leave you guys at Uncle Rudy and Rex's place."

"And you'll go the rest of the way to New York alone? What if Rudy and Rex aren't in Meeker, Colorado, anymore?"

"From Colorado, things could get tougher, especially when I get to New York. We've always had one another, but Jenna has no one now. How's a blind woman supposed to survive if it's as bad as we think? I have to get to New York as soon as possible. I can come back with her."

We stood like that for a moment, then she walked back to the tree. Had I been wrong to say I was leaving her with Dad's brother, Rudy Caspertein, and his son, Rex? Rudy had been a seismologist before Pan-Day—a scientist and an adventurer. If anyone had survived in Meeker, Rudy and his son had. But we hadn't had contact with them for years. Heading first northward to Meeker had been Dad's idea, to make contact with other Casperteins who might be able to help us, if nothing else.

A woman's shriek reached my ears, and I leveled my rifle toward the east. It had been a brief cry, as if someone had tripped or fallen.

"Come on!" the woman called to someone, then there was the sound of panting and the footfalls of more than one person, splashing through puddles and struggling forward.

I knelt for more stability, pulling the rifle firmly into my shoulder for maximum control in the wet environment. No one was taking my family!

A young woman with curly blond hair and no coat stumbled toward me. Seeing me, she stopped and raised her hands. A few steps behind her was a young man in his mid-twenties. Both were covered in mud. I didn't hear anyone pursuing them, so I waved them closer.

Rising to my feet, I approached them. Neither of the two were armed or had provisions. By the look on their faces, they were an instant from bolting away from me, so I lowered my rifle.

"I won't hurt you. You're safe now. Just tell me what's happened."

"Safe?" The woman wrapped her arms around her midsection. "No one's safe! They took Natasha!"

She turned and wept in the arms of the man who I quickly discovered was her husband. Annette took her to the tree and I kept the husband with me in the rain, though we gave him a spare rain poncho. He was tall with a strong frame and small eyes.

"They came at us from a place called Aporax." He had peach-fuzz for a beard and a bullet wound in his shoulder that needed to be treated, but it didn't seem too serious. "We were part of a caravan headed south from Idaho. The winter was bad. We couldn't survive another one like that."

"Tell me about Aporax. Tell me about your daughter."

His name was Forest Holter, and his wife's name was Sharly. Traveling south, they'd been welcomed into Aporax before realizing they were a fundamentalist Muslim colony. When they'd tried to escape with their whole caravan, Aporax extremists had followed and ambushed them outside the city walls.

"We were given a choice," Forest said. "We could return to Aporax, or die fighting. If we fought, they said they'd take our children after we died, to raise them for Allah."

"So you chose to fight?"

"We tried, but we were so outnumbered. We're loggers and farmers, some hunters like me. It was a massacre. Natasha's only four!"

"Can you draw me a map of this compound? Forest, listen to me! Tell me all about Aporax."

We'd had Muslims in San Diego. Most of the time, they were a peaceful lot, and my family had helped them along with others we cared for. Occasionally, Galt Brogdon had dealt quietly with an outspoken jihadist, but it seemed that during the Pan-Day riots, most Muslims had been run out of the city, pressured by many who remembered the atrocities in the Middle East and Europe, and even the attack on the Twin Towers in Manhattan. I had no personal feelings of aggression toward Muslims. But I was aware that their religious book identified me as their natural enemy since I rejected Muhammad as a prophet in any sense, and I believed Jesus Christ was God in the flesh, man's only answer to the sin curse.

The rain stopped as Forest completed his description of Aporax, along with a rough tracing of the compound in the mud. Forest guessed several thousand lived inside the walls, many of them women and children, which was rare in that day to have so many.

"I know what you're doing," Annette said as I gathered ammunition and extra magazines. Forest and his wife were with Mia as she treated them to hot tea over a small fire. "You can't do this, Levi. You said it yourself—Jenna needs you. We need you. There's a whole army inside Aporax. You heard what Forest said!"

I set my hand on her shoulder.

"For hours, we listened to them fighting this morning. I couldn't rush into a fight without knowing anything, but now we know something. Dad trained me for moments like this."

"You can't save everyone from here to New York, Levi. You need to understand something. You may not even be able to save Jenna."

"Mom, I know I can't save everyone, but the ones I can save, I should save. Dad would go right now himself. I can't save just those who are convenient for us. We're gonna get to Uncle Rudy's, but first, I'm going to get this Natasha kid back to her parents. From what I've learned, Aporax has enough people that I can probably get into their settlement without being noticed or causing a scene."

"I can back you up with the other bullpup. You know I can shoot it."

"You heard what Forest said about Aporax. Women have to have their heads covered. You don't know their traditions, their Sharia Law, or how to act like a docile, fearful woman. You can't be seen anywhere around that place, Mom. The most I want from you is to be ready to move out when I get back, and keep Mia and these other two safe."

"Listen to you." She smiled sadly. "Just like your father, always ready to sacrifice himself to keep others safe. We need you to stay alive, Mr. Caspertein. I won't stop praying while you're gone."

We embraced. It could've been the last time we'd be together on this earth, and as we parted, we wanted no regrets, even if we disagreed on how I should proceed. I hadn't hesitated to help Forest and Sharly because I knew myself. When I start considering all the angles that regarded my own skin, I stop trusting God. There's a time to look for smooth stones, and then there's a time to sling them at the giant. No more hesitation.

Since my boot prints left deep and obvious tracks in the wet earth, I traveled in an arc to the south, then approached Aporax from the west. If anything happened to me, or if I was delayed, at least a tracker wouldn't be able to travel directly to my family. But traveling fast, though still sluggish on account of my weariness, I was sure I was leaving enough sign that even a child could've followed my tracks in reverse.

By dusk, I came upon Aporax and spied on it through my binoculars from a wooded ridge that overlooked a trail leading into the city. It was too much to hope that from my vantage point I would spot a child who fit Natasha's description. Since she was indeed a kidnapped victim, she wouldn't be outside on the bustling streets. Instead, I focused on the features of the men in the compound and in the gates, of which there was one gate in each of the four walls. It was the largest walled city I'd seen since before Pan-Day—so many people in one place! Like Hawkridge, the cement foundations of the buildings in Aporax showed evidence of crumbling, but the wood structures were log and appeared to be sturdy. A sawmill in the southeast corner had surely contributed toward many furnishings in the city. As I studied the layout, a plan was formulated in my mind.

The men of Aporax all wore beards, and their clothing was loose rather than jeans and buttoned flannel shirts that most survivors of Pan-Day wore. The beard wasn't a problem for me since I hadn't shaved since I'd left San Diego, and we Casperteins grow them thick. But I had no loose pants, baggy shirt, or a skull cap, like the men also wore. I couldn't blend in with this crowd like I was.

My binoculars swung to the western trail that led to the city. A few travelers, maybe hunters, were moving toward Aporax. None of them were alone, which was what I needed for my plan to work. The fastest, most effective route into the city was to impersonate an Aporaxian, and if that meant I had to tranquilize more than one, so be it.

I left the ridge and approached the trail. At a blind spot, where the trail dipped through a seasonal stream bed, I laid my trap. By sitting high up on the bank of the bed, I could see both east and west, and shoot toward the south.

Darkness closed on the mountains, and I fought desperately for alertness through many yawns, but finally, a small group of people on horseback moved up the trail. By the light of the moon, I counted three, at least two of them men, I guessed by their posture and apparel.

Horses were rare in those days. I hadn't seen any others in Aporax, so perhaps these three were travelers like myself, though they wore the clothing of Aporaxians. The trail west behind the three was empty, so my only difficulty was the shadows.

Through the scope of the .22 rifle, the riders were exceptionally visible, and from my position north of them only seventy yards, my shot was as effortless as pulling the trigger. After the first shot, I worked the bolt quickly and fired twice more. Ready with a fourth shot, I watched all three people fall unconscious from their saddles. The horses didn't even spook. One stopped and looked back at its rider, and the other two moved off the trail to graze. I checked the trail again. It was still clear, so I approached the horses.

I stooped over the riders to see what I was working with. The lead rider was as broad in the shoulder as me, and almost as tall, but the second rider, another man, was under six feet. The third was a woman in a full-length black *burqa*, with only her eyes showing through a slit in the cloth. I hadn't been able to see that from a distance. When I shifted her to lay more comfortably, I found her wrists were bound by a leather strap!

A captive? This changed everything, but it didn't stop me from loading all three back onto their horses—draping the men roughly over their saddles, and the woman more gently—and lead them back up to the ridge. That took a half-hour, which left me another half-hour before they woke.

Both men had carried full saddle bags with rain gear that had been used earlier that morning. Since the clouds generally moved west to east in Southern California, I guessed they'd come from somewhere on the coast, maybe north of San Diego. In their rifle scabbards, one carried a hunting rifle, and the other had an assault rifle.

As I waited for them to wake, my plan continued to formulate. Rescuing young Natasha was still my priority, but I wasn't about to miss an opportunity to disrupt whatever I'd stumbled upon here, if it was nefarious. A bound criminal wouldn't have been too surprising, if Aporax was a city with some semblance of justice, but these men had no paperwork or peacekeeping paraphernalia. I sensed they might be kidnappers, or maybe bounty hunters.

The big man woke first. He had a gray patch on an otherwise black beard. Since we were out of sight of the city, I risked to light a small fire to assist my work. A strip of cotton cut from this man's shirt covered my face except for my eyes.

"What is this?" He strained against tight leather straps, which I'd found in his saddle bags, now around his wrists and ankles. They were the same type of leather I'd cut from the woman's wrists, and I growled at the thought of this man's many other captives, if he was what I thought he was. "You don't know what you've done!"

Instead of responding to him, I set a twig on the fire and waited. I'd seen Dad deal with troublemakers in such a way—patiently allowing them to show their true colors. Time and silence are voids that some men must fill with their true nature, and Patch wasted no time showing me his.

"You'll pay for this! Who are you? Let me see your face! Let me loose, and I'll tear you to pieces! By Allah, you're a dead man. I'm an officer of the Caliph of Aporax, for the Righteous Mokoa." Receiving nothing but a stare from me, he fought his binds some more, and if I wouldn't have shifted one of his rifles to aim at him, he might've managed to break the leather—such was his strength. "Look, you're obviously alone and a stranger in this area. Your actions are forgivable, but only if you let me loose right now. You have attacked innocent travelers on urgent business for Caliph Mokoa. Are you deaf? I'm—"

The other man stirred, groaned, and looked around. His left eye had a twitch that I thought my tranquilizer may have caused, but Patch said nothing about it, leading me to believe the tic was a normal thing for the man.

"Look at this fool, Yahya," Patch said. "He has no idea how many will come for us, or what they'll do to him once he's caught."

I wanted to tell them that stronger forces had tried and failed to catch me, but I was learning more by listening, as is often the case in life.

"Is Ellen hurt?" The one named Yahya strained to see the woman. "Ellen?"

"Her name is Majeda," Patch said. "His Righteous has named her this, so call her by her new name."

"Majeda?" Yahya looked at me, and I saw moisture in his eyes. He was no older than me, but Patch was in his fifties. "Is she hurt?"

"He's a scoundrel, an infidel," Patch said. "What do you think his type do with a woman on the open road?"

The woman's leg moved and she sat up slowly.

"Majeda? Are you okay?"

"Forget about her!" Patch tried to kick his smaller friend, but failed with both ankles bound. "We've got bigger problems than your sister's stolen virtue!"

"What's going on?" The woman named Ellen or Majeda held a hand out to the fire and I saw her shiver, reminding me the desert mountain temperature was definitely dropping. She saw my guns, as well as the captured ones, and the binds on the other two, the smaller being her brother. If I wasn't mistaken, I saw relief in her eyes, but without seeing her whole face—

She tore off her *burqa* and threw it at Patch.

"Why don't you wear it for a change, huh?" She spat at him, spittle drooling down her chin in her fury, which she wiped away with her hand. Probably in her forties, she didn't appear to have the same features as her younger brother. Her eyes settled on my face as she rubbed her chaffed wrists. "Who are you?"

"I am the Serval." Having used my father's old handle in Hawkridge, I saw no reason why I shouldn't keep using it, to hide my true identity. "It seems you're an unwilling citizen of Aporax, Ellen."

"Her name is Majeda!" Patch said. "The caliph—"

"My name is Ellen!" She panted with fury until she focused on me again. "You're absolutely right, I'm unwilling. Ever since Joe converted to Islam, my life has been a nightmare. He thinks I'd be better off as part of some old fool's harem inside Aporax."

"His name isn't Joe," Patch said. "It's Yahya, a name that symbolizes His Righteous' divine choice."

Using the .22, I shot Patch in the chest, and he was instantly quiet—for an hour, anyway. The other two stared at me, as if my brutality shocked them.

"I didn't kill him," I assured them. "He's just sleeping for an hour."

"Joe, I'm not going back," Ellen said. "I can't believe you had them kidnap me again! Besides, I'm past bearing children for anyone now. What are you thinking?"

"Ellen, I never meant . . ." He wept, the rest of his words indistinguishable from his sobs.

"The Serval." Ellen shook her head. "What's that supposed to mean?"

"It's a wild African cat that survives by its wits."

"So, you're witty?" She smiled, maybe a little teasingly. "I don't plan to be added to the next man's bed, Serval. I might be a little old for you, anyway."

"You're not unattractive, Ellen, but no. I need your help in another way. A friend of mine was taken by this Caliph Mokoa's forces."

"A girl? Your girlfriend or wife?"

"No, she's a four-year-old. The daughter of a friend."

"Figures. They start young. They got me last year—that dog." She snarled at Patch, his black beard stirring in the mountain breeze. "I escaped with a few others last month. Ran on foot back to Long Beach. Two died along the way. We were already starving and malnourished. Fathi here is a bit of a sadistic bounty hunter for Caliph Mokoa. A real gentleman, as you've already heard."

"His name is Fathi? I was going with Patch. You know, that little gray patch there."

"That's something you wouldn't live to say again if he heard you. He's probably the most feared man in Aporax. Even more than the caliph."

"You may understand by now I'm not too intimidated by feared men. There've been others before him."

"The Serval always outwits them, huh?"

"How would you suggest I recover my little friend from Aporax?"

She blinked at the fire, and I worried I'd pressed her to remember memories too terrible.

"She was taken recently?"

"Yesterday."

"Then she'll be in the women's dormitory, a horrible, crowded place, as she waits for placement. You have maybe a day or two until she's placed with a faithful family. That could be with anyone inside Aporax, even a butcher. Young girls are cheap in Aporax, and they don't last long. Depending on who wants her, she could go to maybe one hundred different households."

"Then I need to go in tonight."

"You might get in." She winced. "But you'll never get out, not if you steal this child."

"You mean recover."

"They'll see it as stealing. Trust me. Their word is law, always. They're crazy."

"Where's this women's dormitory?"

"You know where the mosque is?"

"In the center of the city? I've seen it through the binoculars."

"The caliph lives in the house south of the mosque. The women's dorm is to the north. They're locked in there and guarded. I was never allowed outside without a guard."

"How'd you get away?"

"I was married to the caliph's cousin. Gag, let me tell you! He's a corpse, as old as Moses. After a few months, I was given the same liberties as his other wives. One day, I put on some men's clothing and snuck outside the wall with some other women. A hunting party didn't notice us riding in the back. As soon as we were clear of the city, we ran for our lives."

"So, it's possible to get away."

"No. They'll chase you down. If not by Patch here, then someone else. Always someone. These people are religious zealots, mister. They don't stop. They think Allah rewards them for their heinous crimes against humanity. They actually believe it! No one can stop them, not even the Serval. Go back to where you came from. That's all we can do now—run."

I helped her onto one of the horses, and she chose to leave without her brother, who continued to cry and beg in words that made no sense. In him, I saw a man whose conscience tortured him, and those who'd been stronger had used him up until he wasn't a man any longer.

Patch woke again, and his first words were curses against me. I let him boast in his false god as I took his clothes. His speech convinced me all the more that I had to go into Aporax and somehow show its people the weakness inside them, a flaw, an error in belief. Perhaps they would find their way to the true God of love and grace if I could introduce a crack into their own hearts that would make them question their false religion. True, I couldn't save them all, but I prayed I could save Natasha Holter. Or die trying.

Chapter Five

My father had often reminded me that we Casperteins have a unique burden to carry—not more or less than others, just different. God had made us strong, and our strength could be abused if we strayed onto a path that was our own rather than God's. Like Adam, as soon as we decided for ourselves what was good and evil, instead of relying on God to direct us so, there would be consequences. As rich as my feeling of vengeance could've been against the evils inside Aporax, I didn't turn toward it. Walking the Christ-like way, the Scriptures teach, is to be both motivated and restricted by love. Any other path, I had to resist.

I left the two remaining horses picketed in the trees on the ridge and walked down to the trail to blend my tracks with the footprints of other travelers. It was after midnight when I reached the western gate to Aporax. The gate was open and manned by two armed men. Their nonchalance regarding my untimely arrival surprised me. They didn't even aim their carbines at me.

"A man convinced me to come here to find myself." I acted curious as I admired their wall of tightly placed logs thirty feet high. Without any handholds, I'd need a grappling hook to get over it. "His name was Fathi Ayyash, and he told me I'd be welcomed at the City of Aporax."

"Fathi Ayyash?"

"Yeah, he was with Yahya, bringing Majeda back for the caliph. I've had a hard ride. Can I stay a night or two, at least until Fathi returns?"

"Travelers are always welcome, especially friends of Fathi." One of the men, his voice oddly high-pitched, turned to his partner. "I'll take him to the Pilgrim's Cottage."

I followed the guard through the gate, realizing this was what Christ had done for us. In a hopeless situation, Christ had put Himself in harm's way out of love. We hadn't known Him when He had died on the cross for us, and Natasha didn't know me. No one would expect a single man to invade a militant compound for a single child.

The lanes of the compound were twice the width of a horse-drawn wagon, and were empty this time of night, so I could observe the structures without distraction. The lanes were carpeted with sawdust, which was another product of the sawmill across the compound. The buildings had no windows, only unpainted wooden doors. Each roof had a metal chimney, and the houses grew in size the closer we came to the tall mosque and minaret tower, of which I guessed was fifty feet high, a dark shadow against the starry sky.

"You'll find other travelers lodging here as well." The high-pitched speaker stopped in front of a long cabin. "Who should I say is with us?"

"My name has been lost, but you may call me the Serval."

"The cat?"

"You know of it?"

"I read a lot, what we have, anyway." He held out his hand, which I thought was strange, since most strangers didn't shake hands on account of old virus fears. But instead, he indicated he wanted my rifle. "I'll need to store it until you leave. Don't worry. We'll return it to you when you want to leave."

I feigned reluctance, then handed him Patch's assault rifle, though I'd scuffed it up a good deal so it wouldn't be recognizable. Under my jacket, I carried my bullpup, indiscernibly hanging on its sling against my ribs. If my ammunition was inspected, he'd find magazines full of non-lethal .308 shells that didn't fit the surrendered rifle, but he didn't ask for my magazines.

Inside the Pilgrim's Cottage, I found a bunk amidst a dozen sleeping men, but I still had no opportunity to sleep. I merely spread my bedroll, which was actually Joe "Yahya" Pensel's bedroll, and laid down. Twenty quiet minutes later, I rose from the bunk, my boots still tightly laced. Unbuttoning my jacket, my short but powerful bullpup barrel poked out.

It was after one in the morning. So far, my plan was working. A religion as strict as Islam offered pilgrims hospitality initially rather than showing their true underbelly right away. Otherwise, the pilgrims would be frightened away by the overwhelming demands of violence that Allah required—if, it was debated, the Quran were interpreted literally.

With no windows in the lodge, I was forced to open the door a crack to see the lane. A man stood guard at the next corner north of me, the direction I needed to go. The moment called for a quiet tranquilizer shot, but the .22 rifle was back on the ridge. The decoy assault rifle and the hidden bullpup were all I had carried under the circumstances.

Silent tranq gun or not, I stepped into the lane and marched straight at the guard. At this point, I was pleased there were no windows in the buildings for my actions to be witnessed. A few paces away, the guard must've seen me in his peripheral vision. Inside such a defendable compound, manned by the strongest force within fifty miles, the guard probably expected a casual early morning greeting. Instead, he received a jab from my fist, and a gel-tranq cartridge from my hand burst on his shoulder. The tiny pin transferred the toxin to the bloodstream as quickly as two heartbeats.

But now, what to do with the sleeping man? I pulled him over my shoulder, took up his rifle, and jogged back to my lodgings. A few men stirred when I entered louder than I intended, but I continued to my bunk anyway. Once the guard was deposited onto my bunk, I returned to the lane.

Dawn was four hours away. The minaret above helped guide me to the city center, where another two guards stood posted, neither facing me directly. The women's dorm was to my right. Hesitation would have drawn attention, so I didn't stop. I had guessed the women's dorm was accessed only by the caliph's approved officers, but I hadn't expected a padlock on the door—in sight of the two guards nearby.

Without another plan at that instant, I shed my parka and held it against the lock. With my other hand, I raised the bullpup and smashed the butt down on the lock. The first strike was a total miss, except for a direct clubbing of my left hand against the lock. Bone and skin seemed to crunch and I barely clamped my throat down before a loud gasp of pain erupted. Instead of standing there in full view, I struck again, this time hitting the lock squarely. It was loud this time since my left hand with the broken flesh hadn't held the parka securely for the second strike. I didn't turn to see if my breach had been observed; I simply pushed open the door and barged into the dark unknown.

If I hadn't been noticed breaking into the dormitory, I didn't want to leave the door wide open, so I closed it, and what little light I'd used to move about the city lanes was now extinguished. Perfect darkness caused me to catch my breath, then I heard the rustling: sheets, clothes, dozens of bodies in the expanse.

"Natasha Holter, come to me," I said firmly into the darkness. "Natasha, I'm here to take you back to your mommy and daddy. Natasha, are you here?"

A candle flickered on, a small flame, but in such darkness, it lit much of the large room. The sterile and windowless exterior of the structures suddenly made sense—about the moment the stench hit my olfactory nerve. Women and girls were stacked four bunks high, from floor to ceiling on straw mattresses. The bunks were built of railroad ties, and the floor here was sawdust, the same as outside.

"Are you with the military?" a nearby woman asked. She seemed to be about my age, but she had no teeth. Her hair was matted and one of her eyes was cloudy white. "Are you here to help us?"

"I'm here for . . ."

Not in all my years in San Diego had I seen such imprisoned humanity—stinking, rotting away, dying without dignity. I'd been naive to believe the situation in Aporax was a city I could run in and out of. Here, many more were in need of rescue.

The nearest woman wasn't the only one who appeared to be maimed. Most of those my age or older, about fifty women, were scarred horribly across the face or had the milky eye of a blind person. From what the woman in the woods had told me, I knew instantly what this was—not abuse but self-mutilation. These women had chosen to disfigure themselves over selection and placement. Men sought women who were beautiful and whole, but these women had scarred or hurt themselves to avoid rape. They were the undesirables, ignored, despised—but I wanted them all! Natasha wouldn't be enough. Here, I would be selfish. Here, I would be a brute. Here, I would be a soldier and not a Good Samaritan. Caliph Mokoa of Aporax would lose his city by dawn!

"Come to me! Everyone, gather to me, quickly!"

The disfigured women closed around me, then came the younger girls who hadn't yet experienced the fear of what lay ahead, to be used, to be cast aside, even to be murdered. Their mothers, if they had mothers, hadn't the courage to scar or harm their own daughters, and I wanted to fix it so they'd never have to.

"Listen to me. We're leaving Aporax right now, but we have to leave it in ashes. Is Natasha here?"

A small girl with curly hair like her mother raised her hand, and she was passed forward into my arms. Kidnapped recently, she appeared healthier than the others older than she.

"Smile for me." I grinned at her. "Show me your teeth."

She gave me an emotionless smile, and I saw her chipped front baby tooth, the mark her mother had given me to accurately identify her. Thank God she hadn't been placed yet!

"All right, listen up!" I swung Natasha onto my back and fastened her arms around my neck. My ammo pouches lined my vest on my chest and ribs for quick access. "How many of those candles do you have?" A box was held up that contained about one hundred candles, each about three inches long—hardly a threat to veterans bent on evil. But I would show this city the wrath Sodom had known. "Give one candle to each person, and light them. Who knows where the sawmill is?"

"I do." It was another woman with a milky eye, but her other eye was clear.

"Pick out four more women. Your assignment will be to go to the sawmill and light the wood around it on fire. It'll ruin the machinery. Who knows where the armory is?"

"I've seen it." This woman had a fresh scab across her forehead which looked like a bullet graze. "It's next door, across the lane."

"Don't try to get inside. Gather four other women. Your job is to burn it down. Use the sawdust in the streets to start fires. Drop the candles everywhere." I nodded, almost breathless at their wide eyes and willingness to live, to fight, to survive. "And this is the most important part—there's a city named Hawkridge a few miles west of here. They are dying for beautiful women like all of you. Each one of you is a precious soul to the God of the Bible, and you will learn to live new lives in another place. Get to

Hawkridge, and tell them everything about Aporax. Tell them the Serval sent you. Now, the sawmill and armory teams, sneak to your targets. Once you light your fires, run out of the west gate. Does everyone understand? The west gate!"

A few heads nodded, and I hoped it was enough.

"Count to twenty, slowly," I instructed, "then the two teams go. At the sound of the first gunshots, everyone else run for the west gate. Who here understands all of my instructions tonight?"

Only two women, older than me, raised their hands.

"Then you two are in charge when I leave. Direct the others. I'll be in the minaret watching over you." I took a deep breath. If they stayed, many of them would die by violent means. But if they left, most of them would live to start over elsewhere. Those who'd been kidnapped could move on from Hawkridge in time. Hawkridge would be overwhelmed with so many women that they wouldn't have to be so selfish of the ones they came upon in the desert. "God be with us all."

The time for silence was over. I imagined my father during his overseas missions for Christians, when he was outgunned and outnumbered, surrounded and doubting survival. But God had been with him, sustaining, protecting, and directing events. That was my God as well—the God who overcame by overwhelming means.

Walking up the length of the dorm room, with Natasha on my back, I kicked open the locked door there, which I hoped led to the mosque. From an open doorway on my right, I emerged into a hallway with light pouring into it. As far as I could tell, by the lack of commotion outside, I hadn't been discovered as missing yet.

At the open doorway, I looked into the candlelit sanctuary of the mosque. Two men who were bowed in prayer raised their heads as I approached, my footfalls sounding heavy on the plank floor. From a magazine on my ribs, I plucked two gel-tranq cartridges. With one in each fist, I slammed each man's shoulder as I walked between them. As if undisturbed from their prayers toward Mecca, they bowed again to the east.

"Are you okay, Natasha?" Her little hands squeezed tighter around my throat. I wasn't disappointed when she didn't respond to me, a stranger. "Hang on. We're going up."

In the forward left corner of the sanctuary, I mounted stairs that spiraled to the ceiling and beyond to the tower where an imam would call for mandatory prayer five times a day. Around fifty feet up, I reached the minaret platform. The wind blew warm as I slid Natasha from my back and studied the angles. Every lane below led to the mosque. The edge of the city wall was three hundred yards away on all sides, which was half the bullpup's maximum range. As long as I was alive, I could command the city.

Far below, five women with burning candles darted from the dormitory and headed toward the sawmill. In a tighter group, the women who were to destroy the armory crowded against its nearest wall and knelt to start little fires against the logs. All day, the wood had been drying from the downpour twenty-four hours earlier; I hoped it would be dry enough to burn.

One guard spotted the women running toward the sawmill. He called to another guard. Instead of firing at the women, they jogged after them, probably guessing the women had nowhere to go.

"I'm gonna shoot the gun now, Natasha," I said. "It'll be loud. Cover your ears with both hands."

She obeyed and sat on the platform at my feet. I leaned toward the west gate. Two men still stood guard at the open gate. The north and south lanes were empty, but I knew as soon as the first shot was fired, the city would become very busy. At that moment, I felt confident I could secure the escape of the women and girls, but my own escape was much more questionable.

The armory's west wall was fully ablaze, and the several women responsible for it looked up at me for guidance. Firelight shimmered on their faces. If they ran toward the west gate too soon, the sawmill team would be left behind, and my job would be more difficult. Cupping my hand, I called down to them.

"Spread out and light more! Wait for the first shot!"

They scattered north and south with more candles, gathering more dry fuel to start fires as they went.

To the southeast, the women reached the sawmill, but the two guards were right behind them. While peering through my scope, I steadied the bullpup and watched for my shot. The guards cornered the women, and the women seemed to recognize their hopeless fate. The two men waved the women away, but two of the team knelt and set their candles to wood anyway.

I could wait no longer. The armory was roaring, and more fires were flickering north and south of me now. Aporax needed to burn, I had decided, to keep their monstrous evils in check, but I never intended for anyone's death. It was time to wake the city.

Exhaling, then holding my breath, I fired at the sawmill guards. As the first one fell unconscious, I shot the next one. The gunfire was so loud, I couldn't imagine a single soul in all of Aporax still asleep.

I swung the rifle to the west and tranquilized both west gate guards, then surveyed the city for anyone with a rifle. Fires leaped by sparks from building to building, and people were screaming and running in all directions. For another moment, the sawmill women were alone, but as soon as their fires were fully ignited, they ran toward me, and I lost them in the stampede. Aporaxians ran toward every gate. An entire city made of wood would quickly become an oven if they didn't flee.

So far, I'd fired only four shots, so no one knew from where the threat originated.

Below the minaret, dozens of women and girls emerged from the women's dorm, ran past the mosque, and joined the procession down the long straight lane to the west gate. I waited for someone to intercept the first women springing for the gate, some of them carrying younger children, but the citizens of Aporax were too frantic trying to save their own possessions from the flames. And it wasn't helping their efforts when the escaping women dropped or threw more lit candles along the lane or onto roofs, lighting other buildings on fire as they went.

The sawmill women reached the mosque and passed underneath me on their way toward the west gate. A volley of gunfire splintered wood behind the slowest runner, and I put my sights on a man with a rifle near the lane to the south gate. The man fell, and two breaths later, bullets cascaded into the minaret framing. I'd been spotted.

Natasha was screaming now, and in my focus, I wasn't sure how long her noise had been audible.

The last of the women reached the gate. I emptied my magazine—twenty-five more rounds—as fast as I could, targeting men with rifles. Before anyone else could manage a shot, I ducked out of sight and inserted a fresh magazine.

"Time to go, Natasha." I scooped her up, and she swung onto my back like she was more ready to leave than I was. Now on the move, she only sniffled, her whimpering at a minimum. "Hang on tightly. Try to be brave, okay? I'm taking you to your mommy."

I started down the stairs. The fourth step shattered from a bullet. From the mosque floor, two men aimed up at me. Skipping the fourth step, I continued down the spiral. As I came around to face the gunmen again, I paused and aimed. Anything careless or hasty would get me killed. Two shots to their chests dropped them, but they'd managed several shots, a couple of which destabilized the spiral stairs.

Only halfway down, the stairwell started to lean. I clung to the center post, a single length of timber, and leapt clear as the whole structure crashed onto the sanctuary floor. To protect us both from the impact and shattered wood, I let go of the rifle to hang from its sling. Landing on my damaged hand, it was my turn to cry out. Natasha lost her grip around my neck and rolled across the floor. Without waiting for the debris to settle, I dove on top of Natasha. More wood pelted my back and head.

Smoke filled the mosque as the fires spread. Natasha and I coughed as we crawled together to the nearest wall.

"Grab on. Don't let go!"

With her again on my back, Natasha didn't make a sound, even though I was gasping through the smoke. The front door of the mosque broke under my boot heel, and we reached what I'd hoped was clean air. Instead, flames and thicker smoke choked the lane. The armory across the way popped a few sparks as munitions began to explode. No one near us was armed. They were all running for their lives, and we wouldn't live unless we joined the exodus.

Halfway down the lane to the west gate, I looked to my left to see an elderly black man running next to me. His face was frozen in terror, and around his neck jangled more gold than I'd ever seen in my life. He suddenly tripped and fell, and would've been trampled if a few men hadn't recognized him as the caliph. They dropped their own possessions to carry him out of the gate to safety. By this act of loyalty from the dark hearts of men who served their evil leader, I knew they would rebuild and regroup. Perhaps I had unsettled their plans and saved a few lives, but evil would be present until Christ reigned on the earth, spanning into eternity.

Behind us, a cache of gunpowder, probably for reloading ammunition, exploded and demolished the entire city center. With no sawmill, no arms, and a weakened presence of people now, I had at least removed valuable resources from this dangerous religious center.

Chapter Six

The next evening, I stood on a low knoll above the birch tree and surveyed the rolling hills and deserted valley below. The remains of the Idaho travelers were a little to the east where they'd been massacred by Aporaxian soldiers when the people had refused to become Muslim. Hundreds of buzzards were circling the sky. From the map in my pack, I knew we hadn't even reached the San Jacinto Mountains, yet. We had a great distance to go. And Jenna Dowler was far, far to the east of us. Was this God's will for me to help so many before I ever reached her, even when I sensed that she needed me right now? All of my planning with Dad hadn't prepared me for the struggling lives I had found in my path so far. It was against my new nature—with Christ in me—to refuse anyone help when I could help them. Jenna, however desperate her situation, would simply have to hang on. She was in God's caring hands.

Our two mares, tethered to the birch tree a short distance behind me, snorted and shifted their weight. Annette and Mia were now rested, while Forest and Sharly were still recovering from their travels and worry for Natasha. The young parents, with Natasha, had slept in Annette and Mia's sleeping bags as I'd slept in my own. For ten hours, I hadn't moved, laying amongst the desert scrub. Since I'd snored most of the time, Mia told me, she had teased me when I woke. After all she'd been through in San Diego, I was thankful her spirits had improved. But our renewed energy wasn't intended to be used for relaxation. I was eager now to get moving. We had several hard mountain passes to cross before reaching Meeker, Colorado.

Distant gunfire made me drop to one knee to offer a smaller target on the knoll. The gunfire was too far to the south for us to be in danger, but I wasn't taking any chances. Annette had heard the shooting as well and ran up the slope to join me where I was scanning the landscape with my binoculars. Burned homes and abandoned cars dotted the desert, but I still searched for movement, gunsmoke, aggressors . . .

"What is it?" Annette crawled the last few yards to sit next to me. "Your friends from yesterday?"

"Probably. Wait." Figures ran into my view, unarmed people in loose clothing. Aporaxians. More gunfire, and one fell, then another. Two Humvees drove into view. "Oh, no. What are they doing out here? Look."

I passed the glasses to Annette as the sporadic gunfire continued.

"Is that the Pacific States' emblem?" She caught her breath. "No, no, no! They're killing the people! Why is Pacific States way out here?"

"This can't be a coincidence." I took back the binoculars and studied the distance the two Humvees would have to cover to reach us. The terrain wasn't friendly for vehicles, so we were safe for the moment. "President Criswell has wanted to recon east of the Rockies for years. Maybe the Brogdons wanted to chase us down, and Galt and Kip sold him on a plan. I see both vehicles are towing fuel tanks. This isn't a short recon for them."

"How far can they go with that much fuel?"

"I don't know, but they can overtake us easily, if they take time to sort out our tracks from the rest." The shooting stopped and the two Humvees drove on, leaving the dead bodies of Aporaxians behind without regard, as Aporaxians had done to others. "But if they run out of fuel, they'll be on foot like the rest of us."

I glanced back at the birch tree, then at the sky to the northwest. The horizon was clear, the day warm and dry in the mountains—perfect weather for traveling.

"What're you thinking, Levi? I know that look."

"We have to keep moving. I hate to do this to Forest, but we're taking the horses for our gear."

"Uh, why would he care about you taking the horses if he's coming with us?"

In my surprise, I almost stood up.

"We can't take a whole family with us. I'm okay helping people along the way, but them joining us? Mom, every single mile will be worse than the last. Every town we pass through will be filled with either cutthroats or bandits who'll want our gear and guns—or Mia and Sharly as wives. And now we have the Brogdons on our heels."

"The Brogdons are killing anyone along the way who's an easy target. We have to take Forest and his family with us or they'll die. Besides, how much gear do you think Forest has?"

We both knew the answer to that—none. Forest and Sharly had run to us empty-handed in the rain.

"Okay, we can leave them at the next town," I said.

"They don't want to be left. Forest and Sharly aren't city folks. He's a hunter—a pretty good shot, Sharly says. And they came from Idaho, so Sharly's shown that she can handle the miles."

"Natasha is only four."

"She can ride a horse with the gear. We did the math. We can cover thirty or forty miles a day like that. Isn't that what you wanted to do?"

"You've got it all figured out, huh?" In the distance, the two Humvees drove east on an old highway. "If the Brogdons are really after us, then they'll double back when they don't find our sign. Eventually, they'll pick up our trail, or up ahead, they'll set up an ambush."

"Then we travel where no Humvee can go. Stay in the mountains, go cross-country, hit the towns on our map only when we need to resupply. We could even make Meeker ahead of schedule, long before winter."

"Maybe." I did my best to form a smile, but I knew the Brogdons. And we'd already witnessed what the towns ahead probably had in store for strangers like us. Afflicted by enemies behind and threatened by the unknown ahead—it wasn't a pleasant prospect. But I'd been critical enough, and it wouldn't help to keep shooting down the ideas the others had already formulated. It was my job to get everyone safely to Meeker, then see to Jenna, if she was still alive. "It ain't easy arguing with you, Mom. I guess all we have left to do then is make packs for the horses and head out. We'll leave in the morning."

Having gotten her way, Annette smiled a tired smile. We were all still a little weary as we were about to start our third week after leaving San Diego. I had no doubt that more challenges were in store for us.

The next morning, I woke everyone early and marched them out of camp before they could eat breakfast. I hadn't slept well, and I was still a little sour about Annette determining the conditions of our traveling party. Once Annette understood our heading toward a distant peak of the Santa Rosa Mountains, I moved off to travel alone.

I left the bulk of my gear on the horse and carried just my rifle and a few necessities into the hills. From a distance, I studied Forest, the tall stranger from Idaho, and Sharly, his short, golden-haired wife. Would Dad have received them so quickly as travel companions? At that moment, Forest aimed my .22 rifle and shot a jackrabbit. Annette had already armed the man!

On the top of a bare hill, I stopped walking to look all around. God had given me so much I didn't deserve, and here I was slow to extend that same unlimited grace to others. As God had held out His hand to me, I was meant to hold out my hand to Forest. In my haste to reach Jenna, I'd forgotten my priority as a Christian—to glorify God. Of course, God would see to my own concerns and Jenna's safety. All I had to do was remain the Lord's faithful servant.

On that hilltop, I talked to God and put my trust in Him not only with Forest and his family, but also with others we would surely meet along the way. Though I was a traveler with no home but heaven, I could still be hospitable. I could offer men and women we came upon friendship and even safety. God had given us Forest, so I had to look at the man as a blessing, even as an asset on our journey northeast. After all, the man had just shot a jackrabbit and provided our dinner! Thus, I understood God intended me to do more than assist strangers. He wanted me to welcome them!

I was ready to descend the hill now to join my band, my travel companions, my family.

Three days later, we set up camp mid-afternoon at an abandoned campsite, and Forest and I set out for a hunt. The heat was taxing, even through the mountain passes. We'd already settled on a plan to rise early in the morning before dawn to travel, then stop before the hottest time of the day. This afforded us twelve hours of hard travel each day, with light in the evenings to repair gear, set up camp, and hunt. Though Forest and I, and maybe Mia, might have been able to travel longer and faster, doing so would've killed our horses as well as wearied Annette, Natasha, and Sharly.

The west side of the Sierra Nevada ridges received more precipitation from the Pacific, and it was there that Forest and I stalked a buck and two does through the lodgepole pine trees. The trees creaked in the breeze, groaning with an eerie sound that left me looking over my shoulder. Forest was below me somewhere, pushing game up to me, if he couldn't get a shot at them himself.

I didn't like leaving the women alone at camp, which was about a mile from the higher timberline. Annette had the second bullpup, and Mia had the shotgun. But even if Forest and I heard their gunfire, we were too far away to arrive in time to help them. From a distance, we'd seen towns and people since the Aporax incident, but they'd been as wary of us as we were of them. Though I was a man of God with non-lethal weaponry to incapacitate enemies, in my wake were indicators of how far I would go to protect the weak, the broken, and the abandoned— including my own family. Hospitable I would be, but careless I was not.

A flash of brown to my left! Too quickly, the deer was gone, but I had its angle. When fleeing, deer run uphill sooner than they run downhill, so I strained to head it off. I reached a clearing and dropped to one knee to steady my rifle. The buck sauntered into the clearing. A high-pitched whistle pierced the air, and the buck stopped, his ears twitching. An instant later, while I was still wondering who had whistled, the silenced click of the .22 rifle made me flinch, and the buck dropped.

Forest had taken my shot, but I wasn't angry. He rose from the other side of the clearing and waved. I stood and waved back, impressed with his marksmanship. With such a small caliber, he would've had to shoot the buck in the head or neck, which was why I'd been the primary shooter with the larger gun, hoping for a chest or lung shot. But meat was meat, and with two more adult mouths in our group, our every resource needed careful maintenance. We hadn't gone hungry yet, but only because we remained vigilant for game.

The woods down the slope to my left became suddenly quiet, although the mountain sounds of bird calls and chipmunk chatter above us had returned after the disturbance of the fall of a fellow creature. That silence below gave me a chill. I realized now that Forest hadn't driven the deer into the clearing if he'd already been at the clearing, having hiked faster toward me than even he probably realized. As much as I wanted to congratulate the young man on his whistle trick and rifle shot, deer didn't usually trot into unprotected clearings by themselves.

It was my turn to whistle, and Forest stopped mid-step in his happy gait toward his kill. There were only thirty yards separating us, but I wasn't willing to yell even then. I touched my eye, then my ear, and pointed down the wooded slope. He nodded and crouched as I angled down the clearing and entered the lodgepole stand again.

Since I'd been raised as a city boy who'd hunted only occasionally, I should've let Forest take point. There was no time to sort that out now, but I intended to strategize with him next time. He seemed the better woodsman, more familiar with plants and animals as we'd walked about. Instead of seeing him as a burden during our trek, God was helping me to see the man's skills.

As I crept forward, I ejected my lethal .308 rounds and took a gel-tranq magazine from my vest. I clicked it into my rifle softly and licked my lips as I anticipated action. My death now would probably mean the death of my mother and cousin as well. Forest had agreed he would use non-lethal ammo if he faced a human enemy, even though he wasn't a believer, but I couldn't be certain he was changing out his lethal rounds at that same moment.

When I finally saw them, I wanted to run back uphill and leave the deer behind altogether. They came in a line, a dozen hunters abreast in full battle gear, an army of gunmen moving toward me, like a line of soldiers assaulting an enemy position.

Glancing uphill, I didn't see Forest, but I was learning to depend more on the man. He was up there somewhere, watching over me, the man who'd risked everything to rescue his young daughter. Prayerfully, I moved to my right and sat down on a deadfall about two feet in diameter. With my rifle hanging on its sling on my right, I set my hands on my knees and waited.

The dozen men saw me and stopped their advance. A few trees remained between us, but from our positions we could size up one another. They were bearded, as was I, unlike most men in San Diego. It was against army regulations for Pacific States troops to wear beards, and I didn't see their shoulder patch or emblem, so I guessed these men weren't Brogdon's troops, who I assumed were still hunting me. More than half of these men carried regular bolt-action hunting rifles and pistols on their belts. A few had assault rifle-style guns.

They grouped up for a moment, several of them keeping their rifles aimed in my direction. When I was certain they all saw me, I raised a hand, a gesture recognized over thousands of years as a sign of peace and greeting. They didn't return the greeting, but two men approached me as the rest fanned out again—in cover formation. Dad had taught me about military tactics more than he'd taught me hunting strategy. These men appeared both cautious and experienced.

The man who I guessed was their leader, larger and broader than me, wore a coat even in the heat. The smaller man at his elbow bore a similar build and beard—perhaps his son. Their eyes were steady and fearless. After all, I was just one man.

They stopped seven paces below me, their rifles aimed at the ground.

"Seems we may have stumbled upon the same deer," I said.

"Seems so." The leader studied the trees behind and around me. "You're not alone?"

"In times like these, it's safer not to be." I imagined it was something Dad would've said. The Serval wasn't known for being direct. "We spotted two does and a small buck enter the timberline an hour ago. We were after them.”

“It’s spring. Bucks don’t run with does,” the leader said.

“Unless the buck was a youngster born from one of the does within the last couple years.” My eyes twitched to the other men down the slope. Two of them had disappeared while we’d been talking. I guessed Forest and I were being flanked momentarily. “Regardless, we got a buck up in the clearing. Being that we’re just passing through and you folks are locals, sharing the kill seems the cordial thing for us to do.”

“Sharing?” The leader frowned. “Since when do strangers share?”

“It ain’t easy starting a new trend.” I smiled and picked at a piece of bark, hoping my nerves weren’t showing through the confidence I tried to project. “Say, three quarters for you, plus the hide. We want only a hind quarter. We’re on the move.”

“We didn’t hear a gunshot. Your people used a bow?”

“Nah. Just a silenced .22. Looked like a headshot. That hunter of mine’s got some aim. A bit quick on the trigger, but he keeps us fed.”

“So, how do you want to do this?” He took two steps to his left and leaned against a tree. “How do we start this new sharing trend?”

“How about two of your men quarter the deer and bring it down here as we wait?”

“What’s stopping them from leaving with all the meat?”

“Mutual understanding.”

“How’s that?” He was amused, and by the appearance of his fierce-looking companions, he was probably more often serious than amused.

“It won’t take more than an hour to gut and quarter that buck. If an hour passes and my quarter doesn’t arrive, we can start shooting each other. See? Mutual understanding."

"Seems fair." He turned to the younger man on his right. "Get Junior and fetch that deer down here pronto. You've got a half-hour. Go."

The man bounded down the slope to the waiting hunters and spoke to a young man. They left their rifles with the others and charged uphill, past me, and up to the clearing.

"So, where're you guys from?" I asked.

"What used to be Escondido. We migrated to avoid the likes of President Criswell. Lost family to him, and figured moving was safer. Hope you're not a friend of his."

"Quite the opposite of a friend." I chuckled. "I grew up in San Diego, so I know his handiwork too well. You should know that his highest ranking general, Galt Brogdon, is up this way, probably scouting eastward for more resources, or somewhere to establish a military base."

"If the general is so far from San Diego, who's keeping President Criswell safe?" The man frowned. "Seems like a situation someone could take advantage of."

"Possibly, if San Diego were on your travel itinerary."

"I've never seen Pacific States military this far inland. Is it somehow connected to you?"

"I wish it weren't. His troops are massacring people along the way. It's part of their strike and submit program to establish dominance, but they seem to be on my family's trail."

"I saw Brogdon's hand in LA years ago. Nobody could stand in his way. We became a tighter force because of them, even though most of these boys were just teens then. We didn't have the arms to put up any real fight." He looked at his men and motioned them up to him. "We've tolerated the Pacific States organizing things on the coast, but if Criswell's troops are reaching inland, he'll meet some resistance. There are hundreds of us mountain hunters up and down the Rockies. Good people who won't stand for mistreatment of their neighbors. I met some last year up north, some sort of coalition called the Kindred."

"The Kindred?" My eyes narrowed. "Not the Kindred of Nails?"

"That's them. Private people, but caring. Helped us after a hard winter, like we were their own family. Taught me something about being neighborly."

"Long ago, I knew a Kindred man—Avery Hewitt. He used to go by the name of Chevy."

"That handle seems familiar to me."

"If you've got enough friends up here, mister, it might be time to put your foot down. Galt Brogdon's scouting east. The soldiers left in San Diego are far from crack troops. They're well-armed, but they're not well-trained. If you had a few resources inside San Diego, and a fair plan to take Coronado, you could bring Criswell to his knees."

"How about you?" He gestured to my bullpup as his men gathered around, men whose fierceness gave way to kinder faces, but with wary eyes. "That's no hunting rifle. A man from San Diego might be useful if a resistance were formed. Sounds like you've given this some thought already. Maybe I'm open to a little government coup. I can field about eight hundred hunters."

I checked my watch, stalling as I prayed to God for guidance. My casual conversation had quickly planted the seeds of revolution. As a Christian, my priorities were heavenly, not earthly, and certainly not for the demise of my enemies, but rather for their salvation.

And that quickly, it all came together in my mind.

"I'm headed east, and I'll probably never come back this way, so let me tell you how to remove President Criswell and start a new government by winning the people. You'll need the Kindred, and you'll need to do it without killing anyone. Only then will everyone from Mexico to Canada see that you're worthy of helping this region find some stability."

"Without killing anyone? After all those vultures have done to my people? Why would we want to keep them alive?"

"Let the new government sort that out. Here's the thing. I'm a Christian, and if the Kindred are who I think they are, they're Christians, too. We're inclined to show mercy where others would be inclined to kill. If that doesn't interest you, then we can part ways right now."

"It interests me." The man nodded and squinted his eyes. "But I'm looking at that weapon that you're carrying, and it looks deadly enough to me."

"Hidden in San Diego, I have five hundred of these battle rifles. President Criswell and the Brogdons have been after them for years. But that's not the best part. I have a quarter-million non-lethal .308 rounds just waiting for the people to take down the bully in his presidential palace. Whatever the future holds, history will look back on how peace was restored to the western half of America, beginning with this meeting. And you and the Kindred can do it without taking a life."

"You forget. They'll be firing real bullets at us. While they're appreciating our mercy, we'll be paying the price in blood."

"Showing grace isn't free, but the rewards are priceless. Besides, with these rifles, you'll move faster and shoot farther. A few hundred of you mountain boys, linked up with the Kindred, who already know how to shoot straight, could take Coronado in one night. I might just be doing you a favor by keeping General Galt Brogdon busy out here in this desert. I'll take him east, but I doubt he'll stay with me through the winter. That means you need to organize and mobilize before winter and hit them at the capital."

"What did you do to these people, Christian, that Criswell is willing to risk his own security to track you down?" He shook his head. "Maybe don't tell me. Just tell me how to take Coronado Island. I've never been there."

For the next twenty minutes, I shared what had been a secret in my family for more than twenty years. I prayed that I was doing what my father would've wanted. He couldn't have intended that I use so many hundreds of rifles for myself, but putting them to use for the sake of rebuilding seemed to fit.

On the ground between the trees, I traced a diagram of the weak points of Coronado Island and the defenses of the Pacific States that could be exploited by the right force. They listened intently, each of them survivors in their own ways, since they were still alive. If they indeed gathered with the Kindred in the north, and found the bullpups where I'd left them, they might just save the countryside from greater bloodshed.

The two hunters returned with the deer, quartered and skinned. Two men were still missing, out there somewhere, but I had someone in hiding, too. Those days, even friends couldn't show their hands completely. But before we parted ways, we shook hands. Though we were from different generations, he and I were cut from the same stock, a mold like my father was. If we weren't the same, the fate of millions couldn't have been discussed so easily. I prayed he used the bullpups for good, not for evil. The weapons were now in the hands of these good men.

"And if I need to send for you, who should I ask for?" he asked, with our hands still held in a firm handshake.

"They call me the Serval. And you?"

"Sebastian Mallinger. These are my boys."

"Which ones?"

"All of them."

I watched the Mallinger family leave with their share of the deer. Forest and I would have to hunt again soon, but giving the meat away had forged a friendship. Even if I never returned to California, I believed God had used me to curb the violence by way of those hard but fair mountaineers.

Chapter Seven

The next few days were filled with such labor, it hardly felt like traveling. As we ascended the steep western slopes of the San Jacinto Mountains, we avoided game trails and hiking paths that might make us visible to the valleys and roads below. The deeper we journeyed into the Rockies, the more sign of survivors we noticed. Several times, the paths we chose were so steep, or on sheer cliffs, that we had to unpack the horses and lead them up one at a time. Precious hours were lost, but we avoided further human contact as we topped a ridge that overlooked the Coachella Valley to the east. Far to the north, I could see the Mojave expanse as it stretched eastward. Our hardships weren't over, but we had come a great distance.

Forest and I sat down on a rock and shared a drink from a canteen. He spoke quietly about the mustard seed, which I'd learned he appreciated for its natural seasoning at a time when spices and seasonings were rare.

"People don't realize," Forest said that day, "that white mustard can be used to treat respiratory infections, even arthritic joints. You can make a tea for bowel problems, the flu, and some colds. Black mustard is a pain reliever, and in some countries, surgeons still use it to disinfect their hands. Early summer is when the plants are in bloom, so we should keep our eyes out for the little flowers. They grow about this high."

He held up his hand five feet above the ground, but I wasn't too concerned about looking for the mustard plant. I'd learned that God had put Forest on this journey to be my companion, and to offer his skills to our group.

Besides, Annette knew plenty of herbal remedies that had helped people all over Southern California.

Below us, Mia, having taken special ownership of the horses, led them up the last stretch of trail. Little Natasha was seated on the first horse, strapped in between sleeping bags, and Annette and Sharly brought up the rear. Annette had been naturally drawn to the other blond, curly-haired woman. Sharly's laugh was always welcome, though it seemed too boisterous to come from such a tiny frame.

That left Forest and me to scout ahead most of the time, or hunt or just talk, when we were certain no danger was present.

"So, you're walking all the way to New York," Forest said, taking a break from telling me about the weak yellow mustards that most Americans ate. "Your mother said you're going to help a blind woman you haven't seen in twenty years. And you're not even sure she's still alive?"

"Well, Jenna is pretty outspoken. Mixed with her courage, that's a potent combination in a new government that's trying to regulate everyone's belief and lifestyle. Jenna is a Christian, so she refuses to call good evil, or evil good. She was raised to exercise covert strategies against the enemy, but I'm not too sure what to make of the Appalachian Federation just yet. She could be in serious danger."

"If it's so dangerous, maybe you Christians should keep your opinions to yourselves." Forest shrugged. "Just a thought."

"Denying the truth never fixed anything, Forest, even if the majority of people still alive are choosing Satan's lie." I loosened the straps on my pack. Even with the horses available to carry most of our gear, I insisted on carrying my own minimal supplies in case the horses ran off, or fell off a cliff. "When I became a Christian, I understood that my opinions about good and evil would need to line up with God's opinions. I don't need to decide what's good and evil. God does that. It's His job to judge people; our job is to love people to the truth of the mercy He provides through His Son."

"Seems you Christians are the ones choosing to do things the hard way." Forest sighed. "But I guess sometimes the hard way is the right way. I see what you're saying. You have to have principles."

"As my dad would say, it ain't easy picking fruit from the Tree of Life."

Mia reached the summit, her eyes on the ground in front of her.

"Swig of water, Mia?" I held out my canteen. Water was scarce in the desert, but I was willing to share with anyone in our party.

But she didn't stop. She didn't even look up. Instead, she plodded past us, the horses weary but obedient as they started down the other side. I noticed Forest watching me, but I didn't share my thoughts. Something was wrong with Mia. Ever since leaving the birch tree where Forest and his family had joined us, Mia had become increasingly distant. She hadn't balked from her duties, but she wasn't being her normal jovial self, teasing me or anxious to chat, anymore.

The laughter from Annette and Sharly was much more satisfying to focus on. They reached us, each with a walking stick and a water bottle. Annette carried the second bullpup on a sling over her right shoulder, her graying hair in a ponytail. Forest threw an arm around Sharly and they followed after the horses, but Annette joined me on the rock to survey the view below.

"It's hard to believe so much beauty out there contains so much danger for us." Annette leaned against me. "Can we pretend there aren't fifty more of these little mountains to cross?"

"If we can pretend there's nothing wrong with Mia."

The light in Annette's face seemed to fade. She looked away, but I saw the worry there. Mia was like a daughter to Annette, and a sister to me.

"It started two weeks ago, that day you came back from Aporax with Natasha. You should've seen her face when I told her the Pacific States were still on the move, maybe even looking for us, and that it could be Galt or Kip. Her face went gray. I shouldn't have said all that. After leaving San Diego, I think she thought the Brogdons were out of her life forever. That's certainly what I wanted."

"But she's safe with us," I said. "She's been so strong."

"Whatever happened to her back in San Diego is on her mind. That's my guess. She still hasn't said anything. What happened there, Levi? I can't help her if I don't know how you found her."

For a moment, I said nothing. I liked to think of us Casperteins as invulnerable, but now I understood that some injuries were deeper than physical. I tried to think about what Dad would say or do at that moment. A leader was responsible for those he led. What kind of leader was I if I had no answer to the question of Mia's health? The Bible taught that there was no peace without justice. But because Jesus had come and received God's wrath for man, man could be at peace with God. Maybe that's what I had to do for Mia—find justice for what had happened. But was that even possible to do?

"If Mia knows she's safe from the Brogdons, will she return to normal? I'll hunt down the Pacific States vehicles and send whatever unit is out here back to San Diego on foot."

"You can't make that kind of guarantee, Levi." Annette frowned sadly. "We have to help her work through this. She can't go around it or avoid it. She has to heal."

"How do you heal in this world?" I felt anger rising inside me and hoped it was righteous anger. Standing from the rock, I gazed south, past the Santa Rosa

Mountains, in search of any vehicles on the desert floor. With a couple well-placed phosphorus rounds, I could end the Brogdons' pursuit. But there were no Humvees in sight. We hadn't seen them for days. "Imagine that she's experienced the worst. How do we help her?"

"We saw it all back home those first years." Annette swiped at moisture on her weathered cheek. "Some people who survived just moved on. Time passed. Others committed suicide. They gave up on life. But others—your dad and I witnessed people who'd been through the worst. They survived and thrived after they gave up their burdens to God. They learned to trust Him through whatever tragedy they'd experienced. God has made Himself available to deal with the worst, even to make sense of it, but some tragedies are too personal to people. They insist on holding onto them, even if they don't mean to."

"Maybe you can get through to her, Mom. You're both, you know, women."

"I wish it were that easy, Levi, but lately, she's avoiding me as much as she's avoiding you."

My own conscience bothered me right then, and if the Holy Spirit had been trying to get my attention, I'd been ignoring Him. But I was listening now, fully aware that I was leader of our small party. My Bible was inside my vest, saved from the bookstore fires after Pan-Day, and it bore Dad's note of dedication to me. Since leaving San Diego, I'd been living as a Christian, but I'd also been selfish. I was learning that my faith wasn't my own; it wasn't meant to be hoarded just for myself. God definitely wanted me to use my role as leader to plant the truth in Forest and Sharly's hearts, even for little Natasha. The last days before Christ's return were upon us. I could be physically brave for anyone, but God had called me to be spiritually brave as well, which I hadn't been. It was time to speak up.

"Tonight, around the fire, we're starting something new." The words felt so directed by God, my eyes watered and my throat choked my voice. "No more just staring at the fire, rubbing our sore feet, and drifting off to sleep. I'll be reading from the Bible for us all. We'll go through the Gospel of John, a chapter each night. And each morning, while it's still dark, once we're packed, I'm praying over us."

"Okay!" She grinned at me, like she expected nothing less from a Caspertein Christian man. "Why don't you pray for us right now as we catch up with the others?"

That night, after we picketed the horses to nip at the sparse deer grass, we ate jerked meat stew, with some amaranth leaves thrown in for flavor and fiber. Annette was saving the nutritious seeds for a surprise, she said, which made everyone curious. But I'd known for years that amaranth seeds could be dried and popped like popcorn. Amaranth grew as a weed along some of the trails, and Annette had been teaching Sharly about other edible plants as they hiked. She'd taught Mia a couple years earlier, and Mia could've helped, but she remained quiet, tending to the horses.

After the stew that night, I noticed Mia staring into the fire. It was a small fire, burning dry roots for fuel since there was no wood.

"From now on," I said as the first stars came out, "I'll read from the Bible each night. If we have open hearts, God's Word will touch us and guide us."

I didn't wait for approval from Forest or Sharly as they sat on a tarp, his arm around her, and Natasha curled up on Sharly's lap. Reading slowly, we finished chapter one of John in just a few minutes. When I closed the cover to pray, Sharly spoke up.

"Read some more."

So, I read some more. We finished five chapters, then I closed it for good and prayed, my eyes turned skyward.

"Thank You, God, for preserving Your Words over the centuries. Help us, Your servants, to listen to Your voice, and trust in Your plans. In Jesus' name, amen."

Annette said amen, but Mia said nothing. Forest and Sharly seemed lost in their own thoughts. I sensed that their lives in Idaho had been void of the Word of God, but I hoped to generate some thirst.

"Early morning tomorrow," I stated the obvious. "We'll be passing Palm Springs, Lord willing."

I left them at the fire, like I usually did each night, taking a small tarp, my canteen, and my rifle up the hill. Thus far, I hadn't set up a scheduled watch amongst us. While Dad had been alive to help us plan the trip, he had figured if our party remained small, and our fire was out each night, we could sleep in relative safety. As a precaution, even planning for just Annette, Mia, and myself, he'd suggested we sleep spread out, able to cover one another. When we were alone, Dad had explained to me how I would grow accustomed to sleeping while sitting up, watching over the camp from a distance, waking at the smallest disturbance.

Thus, above the camp, where I could see the others below, I found a place to sit, wrapped myself in the tarp, and prayed for sleep. The bullpup rested in my lap. Annette stamped out the fire and bedded down amongst the gear. Forest and Sharly shared my sleeping bag, unzipped and laid over them both, nearest to where the fire had been. Natasha lay between them.

Mia usually slept near the horses in her sleeping bag, so I paid her little mind as she stroked the two hard-working animals and spoke softly to them. She'd watered them at a nearby spring that evening, and allowed them to graze on a little grass in the mountain shade. But feed for the animals was scarce. They were losing weight by the day.

But my mind returned to Mia. Somehow, I was losing her. As carefully as I'd guarded us all from harm, there were forces involved within or without that only God could deal with.

I closed my eyes and imagined the map of Southern California. By the following night, we would be across the Coachella Valley and into the Little San Bernardino Mountains. After that, we hadn't planned for a break in our travels until we reached Eagle Mountain, a supposed ghost town. Then on to Cadiz, the home of a large aquifer management corporation. Water would be in short supply until then as we moved through the Mojave Desert. But the trials through heat and sand would be worthwhile, I decided, since other travelers would be using the easier routes, like highways and forested areas to the north or south. Interacting with others would be dangerous, and it would slow our progress. If I'd been alone, I would've sought out other travel companions, but to keep my family safe, I needed to guide them separately from others, when it was reasonably possible.

The horses stirred and I opened my eyes. Mia's bedroll was a dark bundle on the ground at the head of where the horses were picketed. She looked so small lying there, so vulnerable. How could I ever have hoped to keep her safe from—?

Movement to my left! I shifted my eyes rather than lift my rifle. Since I was far above our camp, a predator might not notice me unless I moved. However, this predator wasn't moving toward the camp, but away! The head and shoulders of the shadowy figure disappeared over the trail to the east. Still, I didn't move from my place on the hill. Something was amiss, but what?

Then I realized who the predator was—or rather, who the predator wasn't. Mia's bedroll seemed small and flat because she wasn't even there. She'd left camp! A nighttime stroll was unheard of. Even our camp latrine was uncomfortably but necessarily close in case an enemy lurked nearby.

Heading to camp, I swung my rifle onto my back, and stepped sideways down the slope to avoid the trickle of rocks. On the flat ground, I touched Forest's shoulder. His eyes flashed open, glossy in the starlight. We crept quietly to the edge of camp. Annette, Sharly, and the child didn't stir.

"I need you to keep watch until I get back." I gestured eastward. "Palm Springs isn't far away. There are trails all over these hills. Someone could come upon us by accident."

"Where are you going?"

One of the horses stamped his hoof next to where Mia should've been sleeping if she were there. Whatever she was up to, it was my job to protect her even now, especially now, when she seemed to feel so isolated and alone.

"I want a closer look at the valley ahead. I shouldn't be more than an hour or two."

"Alone, Levi? Let me come with you."

"No. I'd like you to watch over our families. Can I trust you with that?"

"Of course. But be careful!"

Before he could discuss the matter further, I walked down an old trail and out of sight of camp. Where the trail made a sharp bend to the north, I crouched and gazed far below. Palm Springs was still inhabited. Lights, even at that late hour, suggested the town had some kind of power—possibly oil lighting. Would Mia really go into a strange community alone? It seemed an insane thing to do, especially after all she'd been through, but I suspected whatever she was up to had something to do with her recent mood.

As I followed her down the mountain trail, I occasionally caught a glimpse of her far ahead and below. Though I kept hoping she was indeed out for a night stroll, she was headed straight toward the Coachella Valley lights.

Rather than be noticed trailing her, I took a side trail straight to the valley floor and ran out onto the flats to get ahead of her. To remain out of her sight, I stayed in a seasonal run-off stream bed that had only recently dried up.

I was quickly amongst the remnants of old buildings, mostly foundations of houses since the structures had burned on the outskirts of Palm Springs. The walls of the dwellings that hadn't burned had been scavenged for firewood, I suspected. The town itself didn't appear to have a completed wall, but the supports for a defensive barrier had been laid in years past. Walking through those eerie supports, I listened for the smallest sound that would suggest an ambush. There'd been rumors in San Diego of whole towns bent on seizing travelers. Travelers just disappeared—killed, enslaved, or eaten—no one ever knew.

The first inhabited buildings were close to the north end of the old city, where the mountain shadows loomed darkly overhead. Somewhere out there was the once-famous tramway that had spanned the Chino Canyon. The cliffs were steep up there, too dangerous to climb at night. On three sides, rugged hills sheltered the town, and desert spanned for miles to the south, where the Salten Sea had once been. Perhaps a town surrounded by these natural protections had no need for a defensive wall.

"What's your business here?" a gruff voice challenged from the shadow of a building.

I stopped and held my palms open, my bullpup on its sling.

"Just traveling through, trading and scouting along the way."

"You're armed." The man who stepped into view was stocky and bearded. "We're not tolerant of trouble here. Justice will be swift and unpleasant."

"I understand. I'm not a troublemaker."

"You've been warned. You may proceed."

I kept my hands in plain sight as I passed him, then he stepped back into the darkness. Ahead, the lights of the town were burning oil, which I could now smell. Wood was scarce, and the springs nearby had apparently not been capped for electricity, but an oil cache must've been easy enough to refine for fires.

While most survivors of Pan-Day would've been asleep in their towns or forts, Palm Springs was awake and lively. I walked under a string of lit lanterns and two intoxicated men stumbled into me. One belched and the other laughed. In San Diego, President Criswell had sponsored parties, and we even had a Foundation Day celebration where many citizens came into the streets to get drunk off home brews. The Caspertein family had remained separate from those festivities. We took the Bible's warnings about drunkenness seriously. Dad and some of the other church leaders had organized clean-up crews after San Diego's messy celebrations. That memory came back to me now as I observed the deplorable condition of the occupied blocks of Palm Springs.

Garbage was stacked precariously everywhere that lights weren't shining. Looking closely, one could see a continuous pile that stretched down long streets. The rats that scurried there didn't have to fight for food; there was enough garbage to go around. The smell, however, knew no bounds. The two drunks wobbled past me and fell into one of these alleys. It seemed that this city received a continuous supply of food and resources, possibly by trading a resource of its own.

Palm Springs, which was in extreme disrepair, appeared to be on the verge of complete collapse. Their own garbage was slowly burying their town, and as I continued through a small group of chorus singers, I saw the filth had extended into the people's lifestyles, not just into their sanitation system. I turned my head away from the nudity and unnatural acts, the laughter and even a brawl in a storefront with no glass in the windows.

Colorfully-clad women from a balcony waved and called to me for attention, and on the opposite side of the street, young men wearing women's makeup did the same thing, mixed with laughter. Loud, out-of-tune music played from a live band on another balcony.

So brisk was my march through this Babylon that I nearly walked in front of Mia where she'd stopped. I plunged into an alley, feeling guilty for spying on her, and feeling dirty for seeing the things I'd seen there. Up to my knees in rotting produce, I peered around the nearest building corner. Mia was there with a small pack on her back. At least she'd had the sense to bring her shotgun for protection, though it was strapped to her back instead of held in her hands. Her clothes, like mine, seemed drab in comparison to the townsfolk in their bright attire.

Unlike me, she was talking to people in passing, asking directions for somewhere. As she drew closer, I finally heard what she was asking people along the way.

"Someone said there's a doctor here. Which way to the nearest doctor? Can you show me to the doctor?"

Most of the people ignored her. A few pointed in my general direction, then they continued their dancing, laughing, and drinking.

A reveler yanked me from the alley and shoved a large container of smelly brew into my hand. It sloshed onto my chest, and I barely raised the container in front of my face to hide myself as Mia passed by me through the crowd.

"Are you a doctor?" Mia asked an elderly woman who was entertaining three younger men with her stories and touches. Her face was painted and she held a wand with tassels. "I'm looking for a doctor."

"You don't look hurt, precious," the woman said. "Where'd you come from? Across the Mojave?"

"Something like that." Mia slapped at a man's hand as he reached for her. He howled in laughter and danced away. "May I speak to you privately?"

The woman shrugged, turned, then cast her young men a glance that only I could see. She led the way into the nearest building through an open door. The young men seemed disinterested at first, but a few seconds later, after Mia had followed the woman into the building, they entered as well. Since I was taller than most people, I could see the building clearly. Its original billboard had been painted over in white, now reading, "Rooms." It was some sort of boarding house, four stories high.

I entered the establishment after the last young man. He and his companions ascended steep stairs, ignoring me in the rear. At the first landing, a long hallway led into further darkness. Here, the woman and Mia stood. The young men blocked Mia's way to the stairway, and my way into the hallway. I kept my head down and continued up the stairs past them a few more steps, then quietly crept back to the landing to listen.

"I'd like to talk to you alone," Mia said. "Please, it's important."

"It's okay." The woman waved at the three men. "These are my assistants. They help me in the clinic sometimes. Do you need something or not?"

On the stairs, I slipped the rifle sling off my shoulder and held the bullpup in front of me. Though our ages were gapped by eighteen years, Mia and I had lived as family in the same household for years, and both of us were naive to the world's trickeries. However, I had identified the ambush against my cousin as soon as the men had entered the building after her. As a beautiful, young woman, I knew Mia would be more quickly targeted wherever she went. The rules Dad had established for her in San Diego needed to be followed everywhere to keep her safe.

Whatever was happening on the landing, though I couldn't see everything due to the men blocking my view, I sensed that Mia was uncomfortable. The young men had no business being there, not if the elderly woman was truly a doctor, and especially if Mia had asked for privacy. But Mia had come so far, so she relented.

"I need some medicine," my cousin said quietly.

With a puzzled frown, I shook my head. If Mia was sick, she could've told me. I would've gone into any town for her if she needed something that Annette or Forest couldn't gather from the natural elements provided in the wilderness.

"There are many kinds of medicines, precious," the woman said, her voice tainted with teasing. "What kind of medicine did you have in mind?"

"I think I got pregnant," Mia said, but I couldn't process the words very quickly since she was the one speaking them. "It was a few weeks ago, maybe four."

"Are you sure? Four weeks is pretty soon to know for sure."

"I've been feeling nauseous, even throwing up sometimes, and more tired than normal. Please, I can't have this baby. Not now. You must understand!"

"Oh, I think I do, precious. Let them hold your pack for you."

"What? No. I just want the right kind of pill. Or pills. I brought stuff to trade—binoculars, a set of cooking tins, a skinning knife with replaceable blades."

The men barely muffled their snickers, and I flipped the safety off my rifle. I didn't like wicked men laughing at my cousin. A gunshot would probably still be heard amongst the revelers, but none of that mattered now, not with Mia in danger. I had invaded a fortified island for her before. A drunken city didn't frighten me.

"Oh, you are so precious. Honey, we don't want your camping gear. We have everything we want in this city. The only thing missing before tonight was you."

"Please . . . don't!" Mia's voice was strained. "I'm not alone."

"You look alone to me," one of the young men said. "That's why we're here, to keep you company."

I chanced a look around the corner to see one man draw a long knife from a sheath on his belt.

"Please don't. You're a doctor!"

"Hush now," the woman said. "You can help us celebrate the new well where we just struck water. Even more settlers will come from miles around to pay us for water. Don't you want to be part of the celebration, honey?"

"No, please! Let go of me!"

I'd heard enough. Jumping onto the landing from several steps up, I kicked the knife from the man nearest me. Before the others could react, I reached past the other two and gripped Mia's arm. Yanking her past me, I aimed my rifle muzzle at the four of them as they backed farther into the hallway.

"She said she needed help." I walked slowly after them. "And she warned you that she wasn't alone."

"W-we were just playing," said the one who'd held the knife. Now he was holding his fingers.

"It ain't easy getting kicked by a mule," I said slyly.

"What?" He grinned a foolish grin. "I've eaten a few mules, when settlers pay us with livestock for our water."

"When you wake up, you can say you know what it feels like to be kicked by a mule."

The woman seemed to figure out my intentions first. She turned and ran down the hallway. When she looked back, I thought I saw tears on her painted face, but the lighting wasn't good, so I wasn't sure. Regardless, no amount of tears could stop me from shooting her in the backside with a gel-tranq. It knocked her flat. The next one to feel the mule kick was the first young man to swing at me. When he was shot, he flailed into his two companions, which gave me plenty of time to aim and shoot twice more.

Another gun barrel slid past my shoulder in the hallway, but I elbowed it toward the ceiling as Mia pulled the trigger. The shotgun blast rang in my ear, and the birdshot tore into the plaster of the ceiling. Rather than risk Mia killing one of the four already unconscious, I tore the gun from her hands.

"Levi! Give it back!" Her teeth were clenched, her hair a tangled mass across one teary eye. I'd never seen her so mad, so crazed. "Give it to me now!"

"Hey!" a man's voice called up the stairs from the street. "What's with all the shooting? Everyone all right up there?"

I remembered the words of warning from the perimeter guard, so I didn't guess we should stay in Palm Springs and try to explain our situation. The elderly painted woman was liable to have friends and tell a better story than me. It was time to leave this city.

Chapter Eight

Rather than fuss with Mia as we escaped Palm Springs, I used a .308 cartridge and punched her in the shoulder to tranquilize her. Her face was a mixture of shame and fury as she passed out and fell over my left shoulder. With her shotgun sling over my other shoulder, and my bullpup held like a pistol in my right hand, I stepped over the four unconscious citizens to reach the end of the hallway. I climbed out the window onto a flat roof.

At the edge of my brain was the problem Mia had come to solve in Palm Springs. But I couldn't sort it out as I leapt from rooftop to rooftop, then slid to street level. Checking the stars, I found Ursa Major, its cup tip pointing north, and I started hiking east. Though still deep in the city, sand crunched under my boots as I traveled up the street. The trash wasn't the only hazard claiming the city; the desert was blowing in, taking back the land. Somewhere nearby, Highway 10 paralleled my course, but I wasn't about to venture anywhere that would be frequented by the locals.

Winded, I set Mia on the porch of a building with a sign that boasted a robust real estate market. The night was cool, but I was sweating. We were miles away from camp, and I'd just walked farther in the opposite direction in an effort to lead potential trackers away from the rest of my family. By my watch, I guessed the elderly woman and her cohorts were waking up about now. Would a hunting party come after us, even though we'd seriously injured no one? From researching our route east before we'd left San Diego, I knew that many Cahuilla Indians probably still lived in the area. Dad guessed the Native Americans would survive better than most other people groups in America. Such people could now lead to my capture if the citizens of Palm Springs used natives who remembered their ancient skills to track me down.

"I can't believe you tranquilized me!"

Mia rolled over and held her head in her hands. Now being so far from the lights of the town, I could see no other features of her face, but it didn't sound like she was crying.

"It seemed the thing to do at the time."

"And now?"

"I'd rather you walk on your own."

"What am I, your prisoner?"

"Don't make me the enemy, Mia." I passed her my canteen and she took it. "What was I supposed to do, let you kill them? Or let them kill you?"

"They deserved to die, Levi! If anyone did, they did."

I nearly agreed with her, but decided not to fight when she was angry.

"It's four hours until daylight. In two hours, Mom and the others will wake up and expect to continue across this valley. We're on the east side of the valley right now. What do you want to do?"

"What do you mean?"

"I mean, you're my prisoner. You've got a few supplies on your back. What are you going to do?"

"You were there. You must've heard what I told that doctor, if she really was a doctor."

"Yeah, I heard. That's why I'm asking you, what do you want to do?"

"You're giving me a choice?"

"Why would you doubt that I would do anything for you? Come on, Mia. There's no way you can think Mom and I are against you."

"Well, I—" She remained seated on the porch, leaning on her knees, holding her head in her hands. "I'm pretty sure I'm pregnant."

"That's not your fault. And that's not the kid's fault. That's Kip Brogdon's fault."

"Yeah, well, it doesn't matter whose fault it is. It's inside me. I'm not having it. You know how it happened. I can't. Every time I look at it, once it's born . . ."

"Well, you're not helping the situation by calling him or her an *it*."

"Don't act like you could do it, Levi! If you were in my place, you'd kill yourself!"

Now, she was crying in great gasps that shook her body. I sat next to her as she sobbed. Nothing of what lay ahead of her would be easy, but we were family. Casperteins took care of one another. After a few moments, she threw an arm around my neck and wept against my chest. While I held her, I prayed this moment was somehow what she needed to own or bear what had happened to her.

"I feel so dirty, Cuz." She sat back and wiped her eyes. "I tried to pretend I could move on, like it didn't matter, like I was too strong, but now the Brogdons are somewhere out there, coming after me. And I'm pretty sure I'm pregnant. It's a total nightmare."

"It is. No one's denying that. Remember, I found you with that creep. Just about everything in me wanted to put him in the grave, Mia, but I had a choice—to either keep you alive or put him down permanently. Believe me, I thought about it. But I chose life. I can't regret that, because it was the right thing to do. And in time, you'll be glad you chose life, too."

"But every time I look at the baby, if I have it, I'll think of what Kip did to me."

"Taking that kid's life won't take away what Kip did to you, Mia. It won't help. It'll make it worse. There've been countless others. Abortion isn't the answer, even though many have tried to simplify their lives by doing it."

"Aunt Annette is gonna flip out when she sees I'm pregnant. I'll begin to show eventually, you know."

"She's tougher than you think. You are, too."

We sat quietly and watched the stars. Though we were pressed for time, we sat still for Mia.

"Oh, man! I'm really messing up this whole trip for you to get to Jenna."

"No, you're not really messing up anything." I took her hand in mine and squeezed it. "We don't always know why something bad might happen to us. But I know for sure, by trusting God, we'll see a greater good after a little patience."

"You're saying good can come of what happened to me? That's pretty hard for me to believe right now."

"How about we make each other a promise?"

"What do you have in mind?"

"Promise me you'll pray about what good God might produce through this."

"And what will you promise to me?"

"I won't ever abandon you. Not to the Brogdons, not to anyone."

"Well, I think you've proven that. And I can't leave you behind, even when I try."

"So, what do you say? Are we gonna bring another Caspertein into this world?"

"I'm gonna be an emotional mess. I'm just letting you know ahead of time."

"I think that's normal—motherhood and all."

"And I'm already not looking forward to the next eight months. How's a pregnant girl supposed to climb the mountains we have to climb?"

"I don't know. Maybe Sharly can help you more than Mom in that area. Mom never had kids, but I'm pretty sure Natasha will be a good big sister to whomever you're carrying."

"You know, you're gonna make a pretty good uncle, too."

"I look forward to it." I took a deep breath and lifted my head. "On that note, Cuz, let's pray right now, and then we'd better get back to camp. You ready?"

✝

"Get down! Get on the ground!" I ran past Mia who was leading the first horse, and I stopped next to the second mare. Annette stepped past me and, since she was taller than Sharly, and plucked little Natasha out of the seat we'd fashioned for her. "Get the horse down, now!"

I tossed the lead rope of the second horse over her neck and twisted her head around while lifting her foreleg. As we had drilled, the animal no longer fought my touch. She collapsed slowly onto the desert ground and lay still. For good measure, I threw my leg over her neck to keep my presence on the animal's mind.

Meanwhile, Sharly and Natasha lay on the ground behind me, and Annette guided the front mare to lay on the ground in the same way. The desert around us was still except for the wind. Mia, who'd remained vigilant with her shotgun, crawled back to me to hide behind the horses.

"Do you see anything?" she asked.

I used my binoculars to scope ahead to where I'd seen Forest give us the signal to lay low. He was a quarter-mile ahead on a small rise that hindered us from seeing the next basin. Like us, he lay on his belly, watching the area away from us. Forest and I had taken turns keeping point, scouting farther into the desert as we crossed the rocky southern section of the Mojave. It was so flat, we had practiced lying down with the horses. Otherwise, an enemy would be able to spot us from miles away.

"He's just laying there," I reported. "Stay still until he signals."

"Is he hurt?" Sharly cried, which wasn't helping Natasha, who was already on the verge of tears. Natasha had become more talkative lately, especially to the horse on which she rode. "I didn't hear a shot. Levi, please, tell me! Is he okay?"

"He's not injured." I made eye contact with Annette. "Mom, cover the horses. I'm going to Forest. Something's up."

Since Annette had the other bullpup, I counted on her to be my primary backup. Forest, as a crack shot, had permanently claimed the .22 rifle, but it had an effective range of no more than one hundred and fifty yards under the best conditions. If a powerful enemy was approaching or passing by, the situation required a .308 round with its stopping power—or its phosphorus destructive ability.

Crawling forward, I arrived behind Forest, and belly-crawled the last few yards to his side.

"Talk to me." I didn't immediately place my binoculars to my eyes, but rather allowed the landscape ahead to register in my brain first.

"We've reached Eagle Mountain. Look, the railroad tracks led us right to it, like you said."

"Any movement?" The mining ghost town was nestled amidst low-lying hills. Our maneuver to lay on the ground with the horses hadn't been necessary, I saw now, but it was a good precaution. "It looks quiet."

"Look closer." He pointed at the western edge of the town and I gazed through my glasses. The wide paved streets were cracked and grass was growing up through those cracks. An animal was grazing from grass to grass. "That looks like a goat."

"A milk goat." I surveyed the town beyond the goat. Hundreds of single-story houses had been built a century earlier, along with schools, tennis courts, even a pool, to facilitate the miners and their families. A couple houses had blown over, and where their walls had fallen, they lay there still, rather than being used for fuel or for repairs on another house. "Where there's a milk goat, Forest, there's water and probably people."

"I'm telling you, I haven't seen anyone move down there. It's almost sundown, Levi. Someone should be outside. That goat wouldn't be loose like that if there were people around."

"Let me watch the place for a while. Bring everyone up to this point. We're not going into town until I check it out."

"Be my guest."

He jogged back to fetch the others while I studied the town, gradually noting other signs of recent life below—laundry flapping in the breeze, a windmill that was still turning—which would require maintenance in that gritty air. Then I spotted a chicken flap its feathers from shadow to shadow, as if joining other hens for the evening roost. With desert carnivores about, goats and chickens wouldn't survive without human protectors.

I imagined in the days that followed Pan-Day, a convoy from the West Coast had set out and found the old ghost town. Twenty years was a long time to live in isolation, surrounded by immense desert. At least in San Diego, we'd had power and occasional travelers bearing rumors of the world beyond our coastal strip of land. President Criswell had even established some sort of diplomacy with Mexico's citizens, though they'd been similarly impacted by the virus before the border could be closed. San Diego was far from isolated, and far from anything like the ghost town below, which wasn't really a ghost town, I was quickly coming to understand.

The horses seemed mildly annoyed at our caution, but we took no chances, and led them down a dry streambed to hide them better. Annette agreed to stay with the horses and watch over Sharly and Natasha. Forest, Mia, and I left our packs and carried only our water, ammo, and rifles as we advanced on the town of Eagle Mountain. The mountain itself loomed on the edge of town—a rocky, gray contrast to the sand.

I insisted on taking point far out in front. Mia held her shotgun at the ready behind and to my right. Forest shouldered the .22 rifle behind and to my left.

The town was surrounded by a barbed wire fence, rusty and in disrepair, but it was still a perimeter barrier that I guessed would keep horses inside, if necessary. I climbed through the barbs and kept my eyes trained on the rows of houses ahead. The windows were dark, some of them curtained. Most of the curtains were dusty gray, but a few looked white, as if recently washed.

Three days and fifty miles had passed since leaving Palm Springs. If anyone from the Salton Sea area was tracking us, they were far behind. Since we'd scouted for drinkable water much of the second day out of the San Jacinto Mountains, any pursuers would've caught us by now, so I guessed we were now beyond pursuit.

The early morning that Mia and I had returned to camp had raised no alarms. However, Mia's quietness with the horses had been replaced with a casual helpfulness, even a developing bond with Sharly. That made sense to me since I knew Mia was pregnant. Annette had caught my arm the night before and had asked about her.

"Did you say something to Mia? She seems to be doing better."

"I let her know we wouldn't abandon her," I'd said with a shrug. "She agreed to trust God more. She'll share more in the weeks to come. Wait for her. It'll happen."

"Do you know something I don't, Levi Caspertein?"

After smiling, maybe a little sadly, I had walked away. Mia's news didn't have to be terrible when it was finally spoken, even if the man who had attacked her was terrible.

I moved down one lane of Eagle Mountain with rows of houses on each side. Looking closer now, I saw window shutters with cords or straps on them—materials that would've been sand-blasted away over the years for the shutters to flap freely in the wind. Such a detail hadn't been visible from the southern hill, but now I understood why. The residents of Eagle Mountain had wanted the town to appear uninhabited if viewed from a distance. The houses had been intentionally left in disrepair, especially those on the outskirts were left untouched to keep up the facade.

There was a sound in the wind! I knelt on the street, a signal for Mia and Forest to do the same behind me. Motionless, we waited, listening. A dozen armed gunmen could've been behind those curtained windows. Since Pan-Day, for most armed civilians, it was nothing to kill a man or two for a handful of supplies or a bag of food. The truth was, we needed the people of Eagle Mountain more than they needed us. We were out of water and our food was low. Forest had said without water, we would have to butcher the horses and drink their blood, but that would sustain us only temporarily.

Then the sound came again. *A baby's cry!* I expected it to be silenced, but the child wailed and screamed. Turning, I looked back at Mia.

"No one would let their baby cry like that if they knew we were here."

"Sounds like two houses down to the right." Mia waved me forward. "A baby is a good sign. They might be friendly. Go. We'll cover you."

I walked ahead, less nervous now. The baby's wail led me to the front door of a large house. A small garden was sheltered on the lee side of a brick wall. Fresh boot prints had trampled a couple plants, and other plants had been recently uprooted. I recognized the young stem of a carrot, but so early in the season, the small vegetable lay abandoned on top of the soil. A garden definitely meant plenty of water in the area, but uprooted and trampled plants? Maybe the baby's wail wasn't a good sign after all.

Turning the door handle slowly, it squeaked slightly, as did the door hinges when I carefully pushed the door open. My eyes fell on a furnished living room adequate for a large family. Two sofas with well-worn cushions, and a coffee table supported by books under one end. It was someone's home.

"Hello?" I called. "I'm a traveler. I heard a baby crying. We have a child traveling with us as well. Is someone here?"

The baby's voice had quieted to my left down a short hallway. I peered into the kitchen. Plastic jugs sat on the counter, and more gallons of water sat on the floor. It was enough water for us and our horses for several days.

The door that led to the baby was closed. Realizing I was panting, I prayed briefly and steadied my breathing, though my racing heartbeat had a plan of its own. I swung the door wide open and stepped aside. No gunshot blasted through the doorway. The baby jabbered almost curiously. Holding my breath, I chanced a look inside. A woman lay on her side on a queen-sized bed. A man lay next to her, but the woman was staring straight at me, her eyes wide and focused.

The room reeked, more than from just the baby's diaper or body odor. It was the dank smell of disease, of sores and unwashed skin.

I walked past the woman's pale face and threw back the worn quilt to see if her husband was armed, waiting in ambush. He stirred and shivered in the soiled sheets. Afraid of a worse, smaller enemy now, I wiped my hand on my pants and knelt near the woman's face, though out of the path of her breath.

"Can you speak?"

Her mouth worked, and she tried to speak, but only a squeak came out. I glanced about and found clean linens in a closet. After tearing one into strips, I wrapped my hands like a pair of mittens, then picked up a water bottle from the floor. The lid took some fumbling to remove, but once it was off, I helped her take a few sips. Water drooled from her mouth onto the bed, but I wasn't about to risk wiping her cheek.

"Take a moment," I whispered. "I'm here to help you. I'll be right back."

I glanced into the baby's crib and noticed instantly the child's skin color in contrast to the mother's. The baby's face was flushed, his arms waving with a normal color. But the mother's face was creamy, even gray, matted with the dew of death and the patches of shedding skin that I'd seen before.

Outside, I approached Mia first. Forest knelt on the ground across the lane. More and more, I was appreciating the vigilance of the young mustard man from Idaho.

"Don't ask me how," I said to Mia, "but we have a Meridia Virus situation in this house."

"What?" She took a step away from the house. After so many years, the terror of the past still lingered with those of us old enough to remember the chaos and death. Mia had been born after Pan-Day, but even she knew enough to fear the virus. One of her hands went to her stomach, perhaps out of fear, but I understood it was a sign that she was concerned for two lives and not just her own. "This place is so isolated. How could they get the virus here?"

"Obviously, someone brought it to them, and recently." Two houses down the lane, more laundry hung on a line. "Either everyone here has the virus, or those who didn't catch it have run for their lives."

"What should we do? Should we go around Eagle Mountain?"

"No, we need to find the water source here. We won't make it all the way to Cadiz without water. Tell Forest what's up, then go get Mom and Sharly. We'll need their help to look for the well here. There's fresh water jugs in the house, but we probably shouldn't touch anything."

As Mia went to Forest, I watched the town. It seemed haunted, and something bothered me about it that I simply couldn't place at the time. For twenty years, the virus had been non-existent. But in the span of two months, I'd witnessed it kill my seemingly invincible father, and now Eagle Mountain residents were infected. Was there a connection? Was the virus stalking me?

Chapter Nine

Inside the Eagle Mountain residence, I used my sheet mittens to pull the bed quilt back over the man and woman in the bed. The baby in the crib continued to baby talk to me, crawling around in his little cage, but the woman was my focus now. Her fingers moved, motioning me closer. I helped her take another sip of water. Dark-colored tears leaked from her eyes. She was hemorrhaging, close to death, barely conscious.

"Baby . . ." she rasped.

"The baby." I pointed to him. "Yes, we'll take care of him. He's not sick?"

"No. Since my symptoms . . . I didn't touch him."

"Okay." Picking up the infant still concerned me, but the mother seemed to be lucid enough to know when she'd become symptomatic, and when she'd been liable to transmit the virus. "How many are here in Eagle Mountain? Are there others sick?"

"Men came." She took two shallow breaths. "Government checking us. Gloves. Touched everyone. Promised to open trade here."

"They claimed to be government? What government?"

She moved her hand for more water, but before I could get it to her lips, she'd closed her eyes. Caution warned me from checking for a pulse. Instead, I went to the crib and found evidence that the mother definitely knew she was probably infected. Several baby bottles with milk or formula had been left for the baby. And there were a couple of large bowls with the remnants of dried cereal and crackers for him to eat freely from. It was a mess, but at least the little guy hadn't starved.

Leaving the room, I scouted the house. There were more jugs of water stacked in another room. I stared at them, considering the possibility of pulling a wagon with one or both of our horses. We still had a good stretch of the Mojave to cross.

In the bathroom, the toilet had been rigged to flush, utilizing a circular tank of water braced on a shelf overhead. I pressed the handle. The toilet swirled and the tank above gurgled. We'd had the same setup in San Diego, but I hadn't expected to find anything but outhouses in rural areas like this.

As much as I wanted to leave the kid for Annette or Sharly to clean up, I didn't want to put them at risk of contracting the virus inside the house. Using rubber gloves from the kitchen, I carried the baby into the bathroom and set him in the tub.

"I know it ain't easy being bathed with chilly water, kid. Tough it out, huh?"

Nearly retching, like the invincible man I was, I unfastened the washable diaper and threw it away. As if the baby knew the cold dousing he was about to get, he started screaming before I even started pouring water on him. Holding him by one arm as he squirmed, I dumped almost four gallons of water on him. Only then did I dare to apply a thick lather of soap to the shivering little boy. He wailed as loudly as ever as I rinsed him off then bundled him in a half-dozen towels until I located the stash of cloth diapers, rubber pants, and a large package of wipes in the baby room. Still, I didn't take off my rubber gloves. The Meridia Virus had about a three-week incubation period where symptoms could still appear. Guessing by his mother's condition, she'd been sick for about ten days, maybe less.

Ten minutes later, the baby, now comfortable, was more curious about me than fussy, and was bundled in several layers of clothes. I had a packed diaper bag over my shoulder. Holding him at arm's length and facing away from me, I emerged from the house onto the porch to the curious faces of my traveling companions. If the virus situation hadn't been so grave, they would've each probably had a joke about my caregiving skills. The baby looked like a snowflake, limbs stiff and outstretched under all the shirts, pants, sweaters, and a coat.

But the situation was indeed grave. Annette spoke up first.

"Levi, what are you doing?"

"Well . . ." I turned and looked back at the house. Of course, they were concerned about infection. Even Sharly moved in front of the lead horse where Natasha quietly sat like a princess on a pony. "The parents will be dead in hours."

Annette knew better than anyone what the Meridia Virus did to a body.

"We don't have half the protective gear I had in San Diego to deal with this. We can't treat that child!"

"Well . . ." Still, I held the boy at arm's length—not a light bundle, even if he was small at under a year old. "The mother protected him, she said, and hasn't touched him since she became symptomatic. He seems healthy enough."

"Then why are you holding him like that?"

"Maybe that's the way he holds babies?" Forest chuckled.

"Forest!" Sharly snapped. "Not a good time!"

"Sorry, babe."

I appreciated Forest's candor, but Sharly and Annette were right. Maybe I hadn't thought all this through.

"Look, I cleaned him up. I'm the only one who has to touch him for a couple more weeks."

"We're traveling, Levi." Annette glanced at Mia. "How could you let him go inside?"

"The baby was crying. How were we supposed to know the virus was all over this town?"

"You've endangered this whole group." Annette shook her head, hands on her hips. "What're we supposed to do if you get sick? It's hundreds of miles to Meeker still. If we get held up a month or two, treating the sick and dying, the survivors of this family will get stuck in the snow on some mountain pass. Remember your father's words about keeping to our schedule. We're not equipped for snow, Levi. And we're not equipped for Meridia Virus patients in transit."

I was a little shocked at Annette's callousness, but she had loved Dad dearly and she surely didn't want to see another member of the family suffer like that. However, I was a Caspertein, and I had risked my life for less in weeks past.

"Find the water source and fill the canteens," I ordered. "That's what we came here for."

"That's it?" Annette's face reddened. "You're just gonna do what you want? We don't get a vote?"

"There's nothing to vote on, Mom." I looked down at them from the porch. "Not one of you would tell me to leave this child behind. I've endangered myself and risked your well-being. I get it. But if I knew what I know now, coming into Eagle Mountain, I'd do the exact same thing—I'd save this kid."

"I'm okay with it," Forest said. "I've seen the infected. That kid's skin looks normal."

"Forest!" Sharly gasped. "You have a four-year-old daughter!"

"What's the big deal?" Forest shifted his rifle in his arm. "He said he'd be careful for a couple weeks. Nothing has changed."

"Don't touch anything we have," Annette ordered me. "Food, water, gear—we can't touch anything you touch for the next twenty-one days. Can you handle those restrictions? We can't be in contact with you at all. And you have to travel behind us. I don't want to be downwind of you."

"What's going on with you, Mother?" I asked. "You know the Meridia Virus is transmitted only by body fluids."

"Twenty-one days starting today! Got it?"

"Yes, I got it. No touching. I'll travel downwind. I'll keep my distance. What is this, Mom? Pan-Day all over again?"

She turned away, and I regretted my words. Accusing her of panic over a suspected pandemic resurgence wasn't fair. Society had been crippled by panic and the actual pandemic, but I had no right to say she was as irrational as people had become on Pan-Day.

"Can you at least leave me my pack?" I asked.

Without stopping the horses as Mia led them away, Annette pulled on a slip-knot and my heavy pack tumbled onto the concrete lane. Only Forest lingered a moment, as if he wanted to say something, but then Sharly yelled at him, and he jogged to catch up to her.

I carried my pack and the baby back inside the house and set him on his back on the carpeted floor of the living room. From the water jugs in the back room, I selected one with dust on it that appeared to have been filled some time before the virus had arrived. With Annette's words still in my ears, I filled my own water bottles and canteen. Had I signed my own death warrant by saving the baby? I prayed through those confusing moments, not wishing to force God's hand on my hasty actions, but believing I'd acted as Christ would've acted in my place. Hadn't I? In that case, risking my life for another, I was already in God's will. God knew my plight, and if I had the virus now, I was still trusting Him, whether He permitted me to live or to die.

In the baby's room, I found a thermometer and sterilized it with bleach in the kitchen. I wrapped and packed it inside my rigid fly pole case strapped to my pack.

The diaper bag was tethered to the top of the pack with the small tarp, and a dozen rubber gloves went into my cargo pants pocket—diaper gloves.

As for clothing for the baby, I found nothing for him to wear once he outgrew the size he now wore, if we both lived that long. As if my seventy-pound pack wasn't heavy enough, I found a large carton of powdered baby formula in the kitchen, but I was already determined to start the boy on deer meat broth and powdered milk at the earliest convenience. For now, the formula would do. Taking one last look around the kitchen, I saw a bag of dry cereal and a couple boxes of crackers. I figured those would supplement the little guy for a while, and stuffed them into my pack.

Back in the parents' bedroom, I woke the mother by prodding her with my hand wrapped in a table cloth. In the grip of death, she couldn't speak, and I'm not sure she was even coherent.

"I'm leaving now." I touched her cheek through my wrapped hand, hoping she wasn't in too much pain. "I'm taking the baby with me. I'll raise him right, and he'll know his mother's last days were meant to keep him alive. He'll know you loved him."

"Yeah . . ." She smiled weakly, deliriously.

"I'll be raising him as a Christian. He'll know God came as a Man and died for the sins of the world. He'll know that he can be saved from the sin curse by belief in Jesus Christ alone. When we're all in the presence of the Lord in heaven, it would be nice if you were there to welcome us, too. God loves you, lady, and you should know that in a few hours, your next conscious thought will be an awareness of the throne of God. God sent me to take good care of your son. Now you take care of your own soul. If there ever was a time in your life to cry out to God for mercy and rest, it's now."

I prayed aloud for her, with my wrapped hand on her fevered head. By the time I finished praying, her eyes were closed. If my words reached her, I wasn't certain, but I'd gone through the items in that house a couple of times, and I'd found no Bible. It didn't seem that they were a Christian family, but God could reach into the most lost soul and do another miracle, as He'd once done for me.

No one was more unprepared to be a father than I was that evening, but I strapped the boy to my chest and headed northeast, past the shuttered windows and dying families of Eagle Mountain. And though I should've felt abandoned by the family I loved, I had a strange sense of joy. I was dead to my family, at least for a time. But I had saved a life.

✝

Darkness fell that night on Eagle Mountain faster than I could locate or catch up to Annette and the others. In anger, Annette had left me behind, but I had no doubt that she'd intended for me to remain in line-of-sight with them. The risk I'd taken for us all didn't bother me as much as it bothered me that Annette hadn't been willing to take the same risk. We hadn't heard any other crying babies at Eagle Mountain, but that didn't mean everyone else was already dead. The Meridia Virus was transmitted by touch, through body fluids, not airborne particles. We could've checked the other houses for additional survivors, or at least other infected persons who could tell us more coherently how they'd contracted the deadly virus.

As I bedded down in a rocky crevice half-way up Eagle Mountain—with bare rock and steep cliffs above—I considered what the mother had said to explain the virus. Government men had touched them, checking them with gloves. What government? Government people would have helped the people, not made them victims. One thing was sure, someone had brought the virus to Eagle Mountain. However delirious the mother had been, she'd tried to explain something important to me, something that I refused to believe men would actually, intentionally do to a whole community in the desert.

Though summer was nearly upon us in Southern California, the desert was cold that night, since there was no moisture or vegetation across the landscape to retain the day's heat. At least in our rock crevice, we were sheltered from the breeze, and my one-man tarp was enough to contain my body heat for the night. Besides, the baby was sufficiently bundled inside enough clothes for three babies. He drank a little formula and I nibbled on jerked deer meat as I watched the stars and the deserted town below. Slowly, I drifted off to sleep.

I awoke at daylight with a start, afraid I'd rolled on top of the baby in the night. But there he was, sleeping peacefully on one of my down vests. He woke as I threw the tarp off us. The morning air was crisp but it felt good. If I had the virus, I wanted to enjoy every moment of God's gift of creation. Soon, I could be in the presence of my Lord, but until then, I would live to the utmost. How drastically God had shown me fresh humility since leaving San Diego!

"You know today's objective?" I asked the baby as I used rubber gloves to change his diaper, washing him from my water supply. "You and I have to come up with a name for you. Your mother wasn't too forthcoming with your name, not that she wouldn't have said it if she could have. A baby should have a name. Two names, actually. I don't think I'm out of line to say your last name could now be Caspertein. It's got a sound to it, huh? So, what's your first name?"

I rolled up the tarp and wiggled into my pack straps, then saw to a proper carrying system for the baby. Using a carabiner and extra pack straps, I rigged a tiny harness for the child, and fastened him to my breast strap. After checking the straps against his legs, I guessed they weren't too tight and he seemed comfortable enough. He was a little chubby, regardless of the unsupervised feeding the last week or two since his mother had become ill, so he was naturally cushioned against the homemade harness, besides all the clothes he wore.

Using my binoculars, I spotted Annette and the others far out in the desert, moving in a short train in the direction of Cadiz, the next stop on our map. It had been a renewable water facility utilizing a large aquifer underground. We needed to get enough water from Cadiz to make it out of California and into Arizona. The state border wasn't far away from us to the east.

As I was about to start after my family, movement to the west caught my eye. A dark dot in the distance became two and then three dots. Reflected sunlight flashed at me from a windshield. Three vehicles were rolling toward Eagle Mountain! Turning around, I searched for Annette and my company of travelers. No one on ground level, I guessed, would be able to see them now.

I shrank back into my nighttime crevice, and with the sun behind me, I used my binoculars to spy on these visitors. Fear washed over me as I recognized the Humvees. They were dustier now, and one more had joined them since we'd seen the vehicles weeks ago, but they were definitely Pacific States vehicles, with the blue and red emblem on the hood. The front vehicle had a thirty-caliber mounted gun sticking out of its turret, but no one was manning the gun as the convoy turned into the compound below, as if they expected no resistance.

Suddenly, the mother's words made complete sense. Government men had touched and inspected them. And they'd worn gloves. Yes, Eagle Mountain would make a good Mojave base for the Pacific States, if President Criswell was indeed pressing eastward. There was no need for these men to kill the people of Eagle Mountain, but since I'd known the Brogdons, they seemed like the kind of men who would rather kill now and deal with the clean-up later.

Without a careful study of the desert sand, the convoy hadn't noticed the tracks of Annette and her party leading northeast. But I had no doubt that if the perimeter of the town were searched, their prints would be found. Using vehicles, the Pacific States could catch my family very quickly, if they were noticed.

Eagle Mountain was a death zone. It made little sense to me why the Pacific States soldiers would want to inhabit virus-stricken buildings rather than just rape the town of its resources. They had adequately incapacitated any potential resistance. Evidently, killing was easier and faster for them rather than winning the population over to their cause.

The men parked their vehicles and exited to stretch their limbs. We were under two hundred miles from their base in Coronado, a ten-hour drive I guessed, under the current road conditions. From my vantage point on the mountain, I couldn't identify Galt Brogdon or his son Kip, but I was pretty sure one or both of them were amongst the fourteen men who disembarked.

A choice was before me. I could walk carefully away and probably never see the Pacific States personnel again, especially since I was headed into the territory of a completely separate provisional government in the east. Or I could take an extra day to immobilize the three Humvees. Though they had the thirty-caliber with them, and maybe a couple other rifles amongst them that could match or exceed the bullpup's range, the standard weapon of the Pacific States military was an M-16, or some similar .223 carbine. Their troops were generally lazy and undisciplined, relying more on numbers than tactical skill to take coastal territory.

I couldn't imagine myself leaving the troops unbothered just to secure my own safe departure from the area. If they had infected the Eagle Mountain residents, using a type of biological weapon to claim the town resources, they would do so again in another town. It was shocking to imagine that President Criswell had a biological department that, after so many years, had weaponized the Meridia Virus. Hundreds or thousands could be at risk if I didn't discourage them from pressing farther east. Someone had to check their advance. In the least, if I could disrupt their plans long enough, maybe Sebastian Mallinger and his mountain family could organize a resistance with the Kindred.

Deciding to fight, I would be left farther behind by Annette and the others, and if I got into trouble, I'd have no help. With the baby to look after, I couldn't take unnecessary risks. His mother had trusted me, it seemed, but she probably wouldn't want me to run away with her son if I had a chance to bring some justice to her killers. It was a necessary risk.

All day, I dozed, talked to God and the baby, and spied on the soldiers.

"Hazmat suits," I reported to the baby who I'd lain on the tarp, although his crawling and curiosity kept me repositioning him every few minutes. "These guys planned all this. Yep, they're getting ready to burn all the bodies. Uh oh. If they're paying attention, they'll see that you're missing."

But then a worse dread swept over me. It was possible some of the Eagle Mountain residents weren't dead yet, including the baby's mother! Nevertheless, that evening, a heap of bodies was doused with fuel, and I wept at the wickedness as flames leapt at the sky, an ugly stain of smoke in the fresh air.

Suddenly, there were gunshots in the town. It took me a moment to locate the source of the disturbance. Was someone target practicing? No, the soldiers were chasing someone. Someone was alive down there! He hid behind a building and fired on the soldiers, then ran. His weapon sounded like a pistol, in contrast to the soldier's louder rifles.

"I think this is my cue," I said to the little guy, realizing the sole adult survivor of Eagle Mountain was about to be flanked and killed. He had minutes to live, no more, unless I acted now. "Gotta leave you, partner. Shouldn't take me more than a few minutes, Lord willing. Watch over our gear, huh?"

The boy gazed up at me with wide eyes, his mouth open like he wanted to speak, but I didn't have time to coax an intelligible word from him. I checked my ammunition and left the mountain crevice.

Chapter Ten

Because Eagle Mountain had such wide streets, there was little cover for a prolonged gunfight against fourteen armed men. Once through the barbed wire and amongst the houses, I ran in the direction I'd last seen the survivor fleeing. The gunfire alone was misleading since the sound bounced off the buildings and echoed in every direction.

One hundred yards away, the Eagle Mountain civilian ran across the lane I was on. He wore jeans, a blue jean jacket, and a baseball cap. Two seconds later, he was gone, but now I had a fix on his location. I ran to the nearest residence and leaped onto the propane tank. Praying I didn't slip, I vaulted onto the roof. It was steeper than I expected, but I reached the apex and fell onto my elbows the instant four gunmen strode onto the street behind the civilian.

Firing hastily, I shot the lead soldier. My loud rifle had a paralyzing effect initially, since it was such a surprise. They surely hadn't expected resistance in the town. After all, the Meridia Virus had a ninety-seven percent mortality rate, and the three percent difference applied only if the patient received immediate and modern treatment.

Because of their uncertainty, I fired twice more, leaving only one soldier still able to scamper for cover behind a house. Sooner than that man could've radioed for help, one of the Humvees swerved onto the lane. It was the vehicle with the mounted gun, and now a soldier was manning the deadly weapon. Calmly, I ejected my present magazine and slammed home a phosphorus magazine.

The Humvee was fifty yards away and closing fast when I fired one round into the grill of the vehicle.

Smoke instantly billowed as the acid ate everything it came into contact with, and I followed the first round with two more to completely destroy the engine. The driver braked the Humvee, then jumped out to wave his hand at the smoke. The gunner climbed out, and one well-placed round into the big gun's action ruined the weapon permanently.

I changed back to gel-tranq ammo. Since my position on the roof was now known, I slid and partly fell off the far side of the roof. My foot missed the propane tank and I landed on the ground on my shoulder. My gun clattered out of reach, the sling latch broken, and the wind was knocked from my lungs. When I looked up, the jean jacket civilian stood ten paces away. But this was no man! The survivor was an African-American woman, long-limbed and slender, a few years older than Annette, judging by the lines around her eyes and mouth. Her handgun was aimed at my head, and since I'd seen her fire at the soldiers, I knew she wasn't afraid to shoot me.

We heard a soldier running down the lane toward us. By the sound of his boots, he would see us in seconds. I dove to my right, rolled once, and came up holding my rifle. Pivoting, I fired point-blank into the soldier's chest. Two more soldiers down the lane saw me and hid behind the disabled, smoking Humvees.

"Come on!" I called, and ran past the woman. Since she hadn't shot me yet, I guessed she wouldn't shoot me in the back now.

We weaved around the houses, angling toward Eagle Mountain where I'd left the baby. At the last house, I stopped and placed my back to the wall. The tall woman joined me, our shoulders touching.

"Do you have any gear?" I asked. Standing so close, I looked her straight in the face, a determined set to her jaw. She had brown eyes with flecks of gold in them.

"What do I need gear for?"

"You can't stay here." I glanced up the slope. "Let me get to higher ground to cover you, then run when I give you the signal."

"We can't go up there! We'll die out in the desert."

"It's fifty miles to Cadiz. We could be there in two days."

"We can't go to Cadiz. They've been having a water war for weeks!"

She seemed frustrated with me, but now wasn't the time. I had to get up higher. Hopefully, these troops didn't yet know it was me with the bullpup.

"We don't have a choice." I insisted. "These guys'll kill us both if we don't move."

I left the cover of the house and climbed through the barbed wire. Since I'd been a child, hard work and survival had given me strength and stamina, and that afternoon, I needed both. The slope of the mountain began immediately, but I didn't stop to rest until I reached the first rocky outcropping, then signaled for the woman to join me. The setting sun was now in my eyes but I shouldered my rifle as the remaining troops were nearly surrounding the woman and her cover.

When she left her cover and started to cross the fence, they opened fire. As fast as I could pull the trigger, I fired back at them, hitting about half of my targets. The rest moved behind the last house. The woman reached me, though winded, and then she collapsed. Her arm was bleeding badly inside the sleeve of her jacket, and her face was taut from pain and fear.

Below, the two remaining Humvees had driven closer, parked now within my range. I fired four phosphorus rounds, two for each engine, then checked the woman's wound more closely.

"I can't feel my fingers," she gasped.

The bullet had torn through the elbow joint of her left arm. I couldn't think of the woman as a potential virus carrier from the town. She needed help now, or she would bleed to death. Without my gear, I couldn't help her, so we needed to get back to my pack immediately.

Our enemies were now on foot, and that placed me at an advantage with the bullpup and my elevated position. With darkness closing, it seemed a prime time to leave the Eagle Mountain area once and for all. But first, the woman's wound needed to be dressed.

Before she could protest, I used her good arm to pull her over my left shoulder. Her arm was bleeding badly, and since she wasn't speaking, I guessed she'd gone into shock. A few gunshots were fired at us from the town, but we were over four hundred yards away now. Their accuracy was limited beyond three hundred yards.

We reached the mountain crevice and I did my best to set the woman down gently. Regardless of the gunfire, the baby jabbered and yawned next to us, no sign of tears on his face.

"Have a nice nap, little guy? It ain't easy for Uncle Levi out-there dodging bullets while you're up here snoozing."

I drew my skinning knife and cut away the sleeve of the woman's jean jacket. The wound was life-threatening, I judged. A single piece of skin connected her upper arm to her forearm.

"How bad is it?" she mumbled.

"You've lost your arm. It's barely hanging there."

Her head rolled left and right, then her eyes settled on the baby.

"Am I seeing things? Is that a baby?"

I plucked a gel-tranq from my vest and slammed it into her thigh. She jerked, then fell asleep. To guard her from a dangerous level of shock, I elevated her legs and draped my parka over her upper body. Since her arm was bleeding heavily, I didn't have time to explain the situation to her. From my pack, I cut a length of parachute cord and tied a tight tourniquet above her elbow.

Thankfully, the bleeding stopped. With my knife, I cut the attached skin, and the arm fell away. Next, I opened three .308 cartridges and sprinkled gunpowder over the amputated stump.

For the next five minutes, I used a lighter to ignite various patches of gunpowder to seal her exposed blood vessels and arteries. It would've been more practical to light a fire to keep her warm and cauterize the stump with the white-hot steel of my knife, but we were in a battlefield situation.

Annette had packed small medical kits for me and Mia for the trip east, while Annette carried the more extensive first aid kit. The single piece of gauze I had was so small, it barely covered the woman's stump. To supplement the dressing, I took one of the baby's new diapers and safety-pinned it around her stump.

It was so dark now, I could barely see to cut her discarded sleeve into strips to make a rough pocket. She wore a belt, which I removed, then used it to fashion a sort of sling to keep her stump immobile against her torso.

I loosened the tourniquet and prayed that the cauterizing held. Not knowing much about freshly amputated limbs—in the field no less—I was trusting God and my limited training to keep her alive.

We had to leave before the soldiers recovered and prepared an assault on the mountain. However, no matter my determination, I wouldn't be able to carry the baby, my heavy pack, and the woman all at the same time. She was tall and thin, but still weighed about one hundred and forty pounds.

The baby appeared content with another bottle of formula, so I picked up the woman, cradling her in front of me. I figured she had another thirty minutes to sleep on the hour-long tranquilizer. With my rifle over my shoulder, I left the crevice and traversed the mountain to the north. Once beyond the town, I angled down to the desert floor, pausing often to listen for unnatural noises.

The trek was slow, the night dark, and the rocky surface felt strange under my boots.

At the base of the northern side of the mountain, I laid the woman down and ran back to the baby. He kicked and seemed to try to clap as I spoke to him about my plans.

"No crying tonight, little guy, not like when we first met. For one hour, no sounds at all, but once we're out in the desert, you can make all the noise you want. Okay?"

With my pack on my back, I used the carabiner to harness the baby to my chest. I did my best to follow the same route down the mountain, but I got off-track. Looking down at the Town of Eagle Mountain, I saw lights. The soldiers were settling in for the night, I guessed. The lights gave me my bearings and I soon found the woman.

"Who's there?" she called.

"It's me." I knelt next to her. "My name's Levi Caspertein. I know you're in pain, but we can't make much noise. Can you walk?"

"My arm . . ."

"I know. It's bad."

"No, it's just . . . weird. Where's my hand?"

"About a mile south-by-southwest of us, up on the mountain." I listened to the desert and heard no strange sounds, but the soldiers wouldn't broadcast their assault if they were prowling nearby. They already knew now that I wasn't a novice, and if they had a long-range radio, they'd probably communicated to Coronado Island about the gun battle. Only the son of Titus Caspertein would have gel-tranq and white phosphorus rounds. "What's your name?"

"Alice. Alice Prine." Her voice was soft, resigned. "Everyone I knew is dead. We won't make it out here like this."

"How are you not infected like everyone else?"

"I was up in Cadiz with my husband when some government visitors came two weeks ago. When we returned, everyone told us they'd made contact with a government from the West Coast. But then they started getting sick. The visitors had infected the whole town. Everyone died quickly. I was careful not to touch anyone. Reminds me of Pan-Day, except this time my husband got it. He must've touched someone who had it, even though we were gone during the visit."

"Well, you're not the only Eagle Mountain survivor."

"The baby?"

"Please tell me you knew his parents. I'm having a hard time coming up with a name."

"Everyone knew one another in Eagle Mountain, but I don't remember his name. His mother's name was Leslie—a lovely woman who taught the children in the town English and mathematics."

"Then I guess it's still up to me to figure out a name for him." I placed my hand on the head of the baby as he jabbered something to us. "Eagle Mountain is just over that hill behind us. The Pacific States soldiers are camped out there. I destroyed their vehicles, but if they have a radio, there'll be reinforcements here by dawn. I know you're in pain, Alice, but we have to keep moving."

"I think I can walk, if I can lean against you." She reached for me to help her stand. "I'm a little light-headed."

"You lost a bit of blood, and your blood pressure is probably high because of the physical shock. Hold onto me, but we have to head out."

"We're still going to Cadiz?"

"That's where my family went."

"Well, I'd better tell you what is waiting for us when we get there, and you'd better tell me who in the world these Pacific States people are."

We started walking slowly, Alice Prine on my left so I could hold her good arm. She had a gentle way of talking, and the baby was quiet as I listened to what was happening at Cadiz. Fresh water had been a resource in high demand all over the country, and though there wasn't a short supply of water in Cadiz, those who controlled the well weren't willing to share. San Diego had remained pacified under President Criswell partly because Coronado Island controlled the desalination system. He pumped just enough fresh water into the city to keep civilians dependent on him. But Cadiz was rich in fresh water from the large underground aquifer. The Colorado River Aqueduct thirty miles southeast of the aquifer had been diverted years earlier, but the aquifer remained an oasis of water for potentially thousands to survive for perhaps decades.

"The battle lines in Cadiz are drawn by race, believe it or not," Alice said. "Blacks and Hispanics. If there are Whites around, they want nothing to do with the situation. When my husband and I visited last month, we expected to find things as they had been—functioning and civil. There was talk about getting the railroad up and going again. The tracks should be right over there, to our right. Anyway, we found a battlefield instead. The Hispanics weren't giving enough water to the Blacks and the Blacks weren't paying enough for their water rations. Most of Cadiz has been demolished. It was such a mess, my husband and I left after only one day—after we heard the water pumps were being sabotaged. So no one was getting any water at all when we left. Since my husband was Hispanic, we weren't sticking around to be forced to pick a side in the conflict."

"So, what are travelers like us supposed to do?" I yanked Alice upright as she tripped and started to fall. Falling on her stump would've been horribly painful. Even keeping her upright had made her gasp. "We won't make it to Arizona on the amount of water we're carrying from Eagle Mountain, and I'm carrying an unusual amount to keep this baby in clean diapers."

"That's why I think this is a bad idea. If they couldn't get a pump working in Cadiz, it might be an empty town when we get there. How far ahead are your people?"

"A day, and they have two horses to carry their gear, so they're moving quickly. Thirty miles a day at least."

"Horses? I haven't seen a horse in years. But a horse out here will never survive. You'll need too much water. If they've reached Cadiz, and anyone is left there, your horses are already on the barbeque."

"They won't hurt my family, will they?"

"How attached are they to the horses?"

Our pace across the desert floor was miserably slow with Alice in her condition. As I supported her in her weakness, my own energy waned after a couple hours under the added strain and weight of my pack. The important thing was to put some distance between us and Eagle Mountain, but a little was all we were able to manage.

I shared with Alice what I knew of the Pacific States and why they were coming east—to chase me, to claim Mia, and to recon for more territory and resources.

When we stopped before dawn, Alice nearly collapsed in exhaustion. The temperature had dropped through the night and she was shivering as I helped her into one of my coats. I laid out the tarp so she could rest, and I changed the baby. When finished, I lay next to Alice, the baby between us, and covered all of us with the rest of the tarp. The ground under us was covered in gravel, yet we were too tired to care.

The baby and Alice were asleep in seconds, but I lay awake and prayed for God's protection for us and Annette's party. We'd barely escaped the Meridia Virus, then the Pacific States killers, and now we were approaching another battle zone, it seemed. Would it be this way for me all the way to New York? If I survived, and suffering produced endurance like the Bible said, then I'd be one enduring traveler by the end of my journey!

Alice Prine fell to her knees for the third time in the last mile, except this time, she shook her head at me.

"I don't know what's wrong." Her good hand touched the stump of her left arm, a fresh dressing on it that morning. I'd let us sleep until after dawn, and even that was a risk in the open desert with Pacific States troops nearby.

Several paces ahead of Alice, I went ahead to gaze over the next rise. The only objects ahead were a dozen boulders half-covered by blown sand. A dim line far to our right marked the remnants of a railroad line from Eagle Mountain to Cadiz, but I was avoiding anything where others might frequent or even leave tracks for someone else to see. We had over forty miles still to travel to reach Cadiz, where I suspected Annette and Forest would be trying to get water. As much as I wanted to be at their side, they didn't particularly want my company right then, and I had my own company to take care of.

Then I looked south, and it's a good thing I did, because I saw movement in the growing heat waves.

"Brogdon," I whispered, which kicked off a fresh string of chatter from the baby strapped to my chest. He hadn't so much as fussed once since I'd rescued him from his mother's room. Any other baby would have whined at the wind and sand and all-around discomfort of a desert journey, but not this Caspertein. A first name for him began to develop in my mind.

Only one of Brogdon's men would've been so persistent to come after us on foot. They had to know it was me by now. And they would know their lives weren't at risk by hunting me, because we Caspertein Christians didn't believe in killing our enemies or taking vengeance into our own hands. But that didn't mean I would make their attempt on our lives especially comfortable.

The longer it took us to reach Cadiz for more water, the more water we would use in the desert. With Alice holding us up, we'd definitely need more water. I'd brought more than I expected the baby and I would need to cross the next stretch of desert, but not enough for two adults for several days.

I moved down the ridge of the small rise and found its highest point, which provided a view of over a mile southward. After three giant steps down the north side of the hill, I reached the bottom of the shallow rise. Here, I unclipped the baby, took off my pack, and jogged to Alice. She was still on her knees with her head bowed. Before she could object, I scooped her up in my arms and carried her back to the baby.

"You can't carry me all the way to Cadiz. Take the baby, Levi. I'm all finished. Maybe whoever's back at Eagle Mountain won't even come after us."

"I'm just keeping us all together, not carrying you to Cadiz." I set her at the baby's side. "And as far as those friends of ours at Eagle Mountain—it looks like they're on our trail already."

"They're in sight?"

"Yep." I readied my rifle and binoculars, and gave each of my non-lethal ammunition magazines a couple taps to dislodge any dust that might've settled in them. "Nice of them to bring us some water, huh? Right when we were wondering how we'd make it to Cadiz without more water, too!"

"Water?" She craned her neck, trying to see over the rise. "Oh, you're being funny. This is a time of humor for you? Do you remember what they did to my husband and the others?"

"This is how God works. Our enemy is bound to be burdened with too much water from Eagle Mountain. And look, we're in need of water!"

"Maybe you should drink a little water. You're talking like a man on the edge. You can't take them alone. That's insane."

"I know what they'll do to me when they catch me." I crawled to the top of the shallow ridge. "You probably have a good idea of what they'll do to you, too. We don't have a choice but to shoot it out. Keep your head down and pray."

"I'm not praying!"

"Believe me, lady." I glanced over my shoulder at her. "You're better off in God's hands than mine. I'd pray if I were you."

"The gunfire will terrify the baby!"

"It's not his first gunfight, but if he starts crying, you can comfort him."

The infant was already crawling into her lap like the explorer he was.

Laying prone over the hill, I studied the advancing party through my binoculars. Six or seven men walked in a straight line, approaching us directly, following our tracks. They were still a half-mile away, I guessed, but they were closing rapidly, traveling as fast as I would've trekked on foot alone. What crack troops had the Brogdons brought in?

When they were at seven hundred yards, I flipped off the safety of the bullpup.

"How certain are you that this'll work?" Alice asked. "Maybe I should take the baby and—"

"No," I said without turning my head. "They're almost within range. Let me focus."

The baby seemed to scold her anxiety as well, and I smiled with a calmness that defied the situation. This was why God had guided me east—to rescue people like Alice and the baby. God was with me. I was His ambassador.

When the enemy was inside four hundred yards, I could see them easily. Seven men, now in my range, but I was beyond their general range. None of them seemed to be carrying a large gun—nothing over a seven-millimeter or a .223 rifle.

I managed two well-aimed shots before they scattered and dove to the sand. Mentally, I marked the first two I knew had been tranquilized, and checked my watch. In one hour, those first two would gain consciousness and rejoin the fight. That left me one hour to tranquilize five more gunmen who almost certainly had orders to kill me.

Chapter Eleven

Striking a target at a quarter-mile is no easy task, but four hundred yards was easier than six hundred, so I intended to incapacitate the soldiers before they could withdraw beyond my range altogether.

As soon as the five remaining men rose to their feet a few minutes after the first two shots, I hoped they believed I'd moved on. Four of the five men checked their unconscious comrades, and the fifth used a spotting scope to search for me. That's when I aimed and fired at the fifth man. While that gel-tranq round was still in the air, and before the first gunshot could've reached their ears, I fired again at another soldier. Almost simultaneously, two more men went down. Three left.

After I'd recovered from the second shot's recoil, I had trouble locating all three of the remaining conscious soldiers, even though my scope was magnified. One was hiding behind a sleeping man, another was pretending he'd been shot . . . but where was the third?

If the third man had run or crawled off down a ditch, I couldn't risk him finding a defensive position to shoot back at me. I rose to my feet and dashed directly toward them. Because of desert run-off, the ground dipped a few times between me and them, but the third man couldn't hide very well if I was standing over him.

Bullets whipped past my ear. I stopped suddenly and fired at the two men in sight, while they both continued trying to kill me with automatic weapons. When I hit one, the other hid more carefully behind one of the unconscious men. Instead of advancing head-on now, I circled to my left. The closer I drew to flanking him, the more dangerous this man's lethal rounds became. He tried to pivot around his cover, but once I was within two hundred yards, I dropped to one knee and gazed through my scope at one of his exposed legs.

When he felt the round hit his calf muscle, he jumped upright, as if in protest, then fell flat. Nobody likes to be bested by a lesser force. But my safety was still in jeopardy. Where was the last man? I didn't approach any closer; I only waited for some glimpse of movement. As the seconds ticked by, I first doubted there was even a seventh man, and then I feared he'd somehow used one of the shallow gullies to flank me. If I were shot now, all seven men would end up taking the baby and Alice. What a fool I'd been to leave the cover of the small ridge! The gunfight hadn't gone perfectly, and I was stranded without even a rock to hide behind.

Crouching, I finally advanced on the six unconscious men. The desert ground was easy to read, the tracks of men disturbing what patterns the wind had made. No gunshot was fired as I prowled amongst them. They'd traveled light, which explained how they'd traveled so swiftly. But I still saw gear I could use, particularly water containers. None of these men were Galt or his son Kip.

The rifles scattered about were standard M-16s, a reliable carbine, deadly and accurate in the right hands under three hundred yards. Hardly trusting my eyes, I counted seven rifles! The missing man had scuttled away and left his rifle behind. Each of the six men around me had sidearms as well, so the seventh couldn't be counted on to be weaponless. He was definitely out there somewhere.

On the west side of the group of six, I found a trail in the sand. Someone had crawled away. And the ground was low there, hidden from my previous vantage point where Alice waited.

Walking into the desert, I searched the bare landscape to the south. Nothing moved but heatwaves.

West, nothing. East, the train track and a couple granite hills in the distance. What about north?

I started running as I realized my amateur mistake. Focused on a bold offensive, I hadn't considered any sort of defense for my companions. Alice didn't even have a knife!

The struggle was over by the time I reached them. Kip Brogdon was standing over Alice. He held a skinning hatchet under her chin. His sidearm was drawn and aimed at the baby. I froze, my rifle aimed at his chest, and prayed for a safe end to what seemed an impossible situation.

Sand was matted on one of Kip's cheeks where he'd crawled low, like a snake, against the ground to reach the baby and Alice. His hair was tousled by the hot breeze, but his eyes were steely, daring me. The rest of Galt's troops from Coronado may have been common soldiers, but Kip had led his father's assaults for some years now, and to catch us on foot proved that I'd underestimated him.

"Drop it, Levi!"

His trouser knees were torn and his knee was bleeding from crawling over rocks. He was more slender than the last time I'd seen him, but to catch me unaware, he was obviously the better tactician. The snarl on his face told me he wouldn't hesitate to kill one or both of my dependents. Saving one wouldn't be easy, but both was unthinkable. Did I dare a shot? If he fell, Alice was dead, and if his hand jerked, the baby was dead.

Alice's eyes seemed to beg that I would choose her, which would mean sacrificing the baby. Her amputated stump was dripping crimson again onto the thirsty ground.

And that's when an idea hit me. It had to be from God, so I blurted it without hesitating another second.

"Kip! Your hand! She's from Eagle Mountain!"

The only thing worse than losing to me, in Kip's mind, would be the possibility of contracting the virus from Alice. Kip gasped and stepped back. In his reflexive repulsion, he raised his hands. It was the edge I needed. My muzzle barked and Kip was thrown backward. The hatchet and gun flew from his fingers before he landed hard on his back.

Alice fell free, then crawled on her three limbs to the baby, whose eyes were wide. His little mouth was in the shape of an *O*, as if surprised. But he still didn't whimper, and I counted him worthy to take our family name, for us Casperteins aren't known for our whining.

I went to Kip and checked his pulse. He'd taken the gel-tranq point blank and high in the chest. Such a mule-kick could sometimes cause injury, even break a bone, but under his shirt, he seemed to have only a welt.

"Don't ever leave me alone again!" Alice hissed at me, fire in her eyes. "He could've killed us!"

"I know. I'm sorry." I picked up Kip's handgun, a semi-automatic .45 caliber, and disassembled it. After I threw the components in several directions, I pocketed the trigger mechanism to toss somewhere up the trail. "We have to plan more carefully for this type of situation. One thing for sure, I'll be glad when we get out of this desert!"

"You don't really think I have the Meridia Virus, do you?" She rocked back and forth, cradling her stump. I wished I had a shot of morphine for her pain. "I was around my husband a lot toward the end."

"I don't know, but if you become symptomatic, that means the baby and I probably will, too." Before she could voice any more of her fears, I helped her drink from my canteen. "All the more reason to consider what awaits us in the afterlife."

"You want me to pray and you want me to consider the afterlife? What are you, some kind of religious wacko?"

"Depends on who you ask." I chuckled. "Listen, before these guys wake up, I have to collect their guns and water. If I leave my rifle with you, will you be okay?"

"I don't know. It's a big gun. You think I can shoot it with one hand?"

"If you had to, I have no doubt."

Rather than leave Kip there in plain sight, I threw him over my shoulder and carried him halfway back to his unit. I stuck his hatchet in my belt. The tool was razor-sharp, used for skinning big game like bear or elk. No doubt, Kip had used it to shed the blood of people he and his father were meant to govern for President Criswell.

Each soldier had a canteen or two. Since I had no wish to see them die of thirst in the desert, I left three canteens for the seven of them, and I took the rest. Three canteens would sustain them for their march back to Eagle Mountain, but they wouldn't be able to continue without more water.

Alice and I needed only three additional containers for her and the baby, so the rest I split open with Kip's hatchet, and allowed the contents to soak into the sand. There were several dried food pouches I took from them as well, thankful for how God had provided for our needs even through my enemies. Without food and water supplies, Kip and his men would be forced to return to Eagle Mountain rather than pursue us.

"How do you feel?" I asked Alice once back in talking range.

"My arm is throbbing. I can feel my fingers, but they aren't there anymore."

"Phantom pain. I've heard it wears off when you stop thinking about it so much."

"Easier said than done." She stared at her red stump. "Not in my wildest dreams did I ever imagine I'd be in this situation. Eagle Mountain was safe, quiet, far away from all violence. I've never even heard gunfire there before."

"Safety can be deceptive." I shouldered my pack, then picked up the baby. "When we're comfortable, we get complacent. Can you manage a couple more miles?"

She gave me my rifle, then I helped her to her feet. When she swayed against me, I steadied her, then placed her hand on my pack frame.

"Hang onto that, okay?"

"No, you're carrying enough."

"We don't have a choice. Kip Brogdon's dad will come this way with armored vehicles as soon as he gets word of this mess. We've all got to push ourselves and get to Cadiz before we're caught out here in the open again."

We started northeast at a slow pace.

"So, how much longer are you going to call that kid 'the baby'?"

I told Alice the story of Caleb from the Bible, who had spied on the Promised Land with Joshua. When others had cried in fear about the difficulties of conquering the land, Joshua and Caleb had remained faithful. They hadn't whined.

"That's what I thought of when I noticed that this baby doesn't seem to whine too much. Caleb. Caleb Caspertein."

"What about a middle name?" she asked. "Kids won't tease him unless he has a middle name. It's an American rite of passage."

"What did you have in mind?"

"Really? You'll let me pick something?"

"I'd say we're the closest thing to relatives he's got left."

"Then, I pick Marciel. It was my husband's name. He can live on, in a way."

"Caleb Marciel Caspertein. Yep, he'll definitely get teased."

Two days later, I licked the moisture from the opening of my empty canteen. Our water was gone. Caleb had received the last of my water, and Alice had finished hers off that afternoon. With five canteens apiece, we should've had enough to cover the last forty miles to Cadiz inside a day and a half, but Alice was still recovering her strength, and I had refused to leave her behind.

Though nearly sixty years old, Alice seemed to be in excellent physical condition. However, her loss of blood and continued pain had broken her spirit. She didn't object to my prayers over her, but she hadn't been receptive to the gospel message yet. She struggled to keep walking, losing ground even though all I could manage myself was a shuffle, barely lifting my feet a few yards in front of her, mile after mile.

The sun was merciless. Though our heading was northeast, I had trudged sideways with my back to the sun much of the day, intending to give Caleb shade from the exhausting heat and burning rays.

A shiny black object reflected sunlight in the sand in front of me. I sat down cross-legged and unhooked Caleb to set him in my lap. Despite my attempts to shield him from the sun, his lips and nose were still sunburned. If we didn't reach Cadiz by dawn, we would be dead.

Flicking the sand off the shiny object, I picked up what I discovered to be a smartphone! As a teen, a similar gadget had been my obsession, like it had been for everyone else in half the world. But now, it was an eyesore in the desert, a worthless piece of plastic and technology that symbolized America's materialistic and moral decay before Pan-Day.

I cast the smartphone aside then noticed something else in the sand—tracks! Annette and the others had left a trail easy for us to follow. Except now those human and horse tracks veered to the left.

"Levi." Alice caught up to us and dropped to her knees beside me. "Cadiz. You hear it?"

Turning my head, I listened to the evening breeze. In the span of the coming hour, the heat would be replaced by a chill that would mean dressing Caleb back into all the clothes I had for him. But in the air there was more than a chill. There was the sound of rocks clacking against one another. No, those were gunshots. It was far away, but a battle was being fought. A battle meant people. People meant water. Water meant life.

When I stood with Caleb, my eyes fell again on the tracks that had turned. Now I understood why those tracks had turned north—to avoid Cadiz altogether! I said as much to Alice.

"How could they have enough water to keep going?" Her voice was raspy and her words slurred. "Whatever your family is doing, we need water now. You've kept us alive this far, Levi. You can't let us die now!"

"No one's going to die." With strength I didn't think I had, I drew her upright to hold her at my side. "Whatever's happening in Cadiz, we need access to their water, right now!"

Annette and the horse tracks faded away to the north, but we continued at a slow pace toward Cadiz. Behind us, the Pacific States troops were certain to be mustering. In front of us, we faced a battle that raged louder by the minute.

As we walked on, I searched my memory of similar circumstances in the Scriptures. God's people were often caught in the middle between two warring or disobedient countries. Ultimate invincibility wasn't always awarded to God's dutiful people, but ultimate usefulness was given to obedient men and women of God. I figured I'd rather be useful to God as we walked into Cadiz, rather than invincible and unusable by God. With this in mind, I prayed for direction. How could I be useful? In every regard, we were refugees and fugitives. What would I have to offer either side in a water dispute, made worse by racial animosity?

The tan, infertile desert had claimed the foundations of buildings at the edge of Cadiz. I couldn't imagine how Cadiz might've once appeared, but now the inhabited sections were surrounded by barricades, two forts inside walls of debris and trash. Seen through my binoculars, I wondered if wars one thousand years earlier had been fought this same way—two sides launching attacks at one another, neither willing to back down.

Between the two forts was a wasteland—a demilitarized zone of sorts—of about one hundred yards. I stared at this wasteland and prayed. Where was God in these badlands? Was He missing from the Mojave altogether? No, I decided, and let my binoculars hang from the strap. The rejection of God didn't mean that God was absent.

"I have a plan," I said as we stood a safe distance from the wasteland zone. "For this to work in our favor, we have to show each side that it's in their favor to meet with me. I have to go to one fort, and you have to go to the other fort."

"Naturally, I'll go to the Blacks, but what do I tell them?"

"Tell them the Serval is an ambassador come from the coast. We'll all be dead in a month from the Meridia Virus unless we meet in the demilitarized zone at dawn tomorrow. Three leaders from each side, besides you and me. They have to come and hear what I have to say. And no one is to bring any weapons."

"Why do I have to be there? I don't want any part of this conflict."

Though I'd only known Alice under duress, she appeared worse now than I'd seen her. Exhaustion and dehydration had bowed her tall frame and paled her dark skin. Of course, she probably thought I'd never looked worse, either.

"This last week hasn't been kind to either of us. Dawn will come early. Get your fluids. Have a real doctor look at your arm. Before I continue on to Colorado, we should see this thing here in Cadiz to a sound conclusion. That's why I want you there. Then, we'll say our goodbyes."

"No. Wait a minute. You're not leaving me in this dump! I'm not staying here. I don't know anyone here, even if that eastern half of the city has the same skin color as me. Eagle Mountain was my home, not this place. Levi!"

"I think once you have other options presented to you, Alice, you'll reconsider. There's nothing but hard travel in front of me, more of what you've gone through the last few days."

"Listen to me!" She stepped so close, Caleb's feet kicked her belly. "You saved my life. You cut off my arm. We crossed a desert together. I may be old enough to be your mother, and we may not have known each other before last week, but you and that kid are the only people I have in my whole life now. I promise you, I'll get fixed up and once we get out of this desert, I won't slow you down."

"Alice, I'm going to Colorado to find my family. This is a Caspertein family trip."

"Don't you want me to come?" She raised her dust-coated eyebrows. "If you want to ditch me here in Cadiz, California, just say so. Otherwise, add me to the Caspertein clan, and let's get moving."

Her legs seemed to fail her for a brief moment, and with my free hand, I held her upright by her good arm. But her face was as determined and challenging as ever. No one could blame her for her failing body, not after all she'd been through. If she was as tough on an extended journey as she'd been the past miles since Eagle Mountain, she wouldn't be a burden again. I believed her.

"Fine. Rest up. I'll see you at dawn."

Chapter Twelve

The world has always offered many obstacles for Christians. The day I walked into the Hispanic side of Cadiz, I walked the path many other Christians had walked before me. God had directed me to leave San Diego, but that didn't mean my life would be tulips and butterflies. Ever since leaving San Diego, God had moved me through the lives of various people, and I knew I was meant to touch their lives for Christ's sake. Dad had taught me that a Christian who doesn't touch his neighbors as Christ did—that Christian should question if Christ is in his life at all.

When the Hispanics opened the gate to their fort, it wasn't simply because I wore a wide-eyed baby on my chest, for I carried a snub-nosed rifle as well. "I'm a messenger from San Diego," I'd told them, and they'd opened their tall gate out of curiosity, I guessed.

Weapons were aimed at my head and at Caleb as I did my best to walk stoically through the entrance. My tongue was swollen and my feet felt heavy, but I held my head up, intent on finding Caleb and myself water and safe passage, by way of an idea I believed God had brought to mind.

A short man with no shirt held a handmade sword and waved it at my head.

"You in the wrong city, *hombre*." His mustache still had that evening's meal on it, as did the hair on his tattooed chest. "Why're you bringing a baby to a place like this? Can't you hear there is a war happening?"

The fort's wall was thirty feet high with shaky scaffolding supporting a line of riflemen on top who were trading shots with the other fort. The top of the wall appeared to be plated with steel, but sections of the wall were only tin, and bullet holes peppered the thin metal. The man's sword was fashioned from discarded steel, and other soldiers' weapons nearby proved to me that ammunition was getting low. When both forts were out of ammunition, I guessed they would turn to fighting with their primitive weapons in hand-to-hand combat, and a greater number of lives would be lost.

"A military force is on their way here," I said. "I crossed the desert a couple days in front of them to warn you. They'll kill everyone here and in the other fort to get your water and any other supplies you have."

"Do you see a city of dogs here, *vato?*" He sneered at me. "We are a military force. I have two hundred fighting men and women inside these walls. No one will take our water pump!"

He used his sword to point at a contraption on which several women were filling jugs with water from a spigot. It must've been the last working pump in the city. The whole battle had shifted to gain ownership of it, and the Hispanics obviously had it now.

"The force I'm talking about is several thousand strong," I said. "They have a limitless supply of ammunition, vehicles, and modern equipment. They'll follow the rail from Eagle Mountain to Cadiz. They've already slaughtered everyone in Eagle Mountain. Cadiz is next. Unless you listen to me."

This lieutenant wanted to challenge and intimidate me, but the concern on his sweaty face was telling. He and his soldiers were watered, but weary. A man in a distant shelter screamed, perhaps from shoddy medical attention to his wounds. I hoped Alice was receiving better treatment for her arm. Though she had no real investment in the Caspertein family, I was happy that she had insisted on continuing the journey with us.

"You should talk to Medina. *Vamanos.*"

I followed him as he turned away. Several soldiers fell in behind me. The shanty huts of the survivors—barely more than metal roofs on poles—stood beyond the fort's first structures. Children sat in rags and women labored over sizzling grills. My stomach rumbled, but what Caleb and I needed was water. When we passed the pump, I unclipped my main canteen—dry for hours—and held it up.

"Wait," I said. "We just crossed a desert."

My escort glared at me. Surely, with an underground reservoir, they could spare a single canteen of water!

"Hurry up."

I handed my canteen to a woman on the pump platform, and she submerged my container into a jug. When she gave it back to me, I held it to Caleb's lips first. It spilled down his chin as he slurped at the moisture, then I took a few swallows. If we drank too much too soon, I knew we'd get sick, but it seemed now that we wouldn't die of thirst.

We weaved through more huts until a cellar door was thrown open and we descended into the dimness. I hoped we'd left the filth of the fort's ground surface behind, but the smell worsened below. Sewage was backed up somewhere and the stench of unwashed bodies was just as suffocating.

My escort stopped me before a thin Mexican man at a desk. He was older than me, had a shaved face, groomed hair, and a firm gaze. Unlike his men, this soldier maintained a disciplined appearance. He didn't rise when the shirtless man spoke to him in Spanish, explaining why he'd brought me down to him. My Spanish was fair, but I didn't let on that I understood.

"I am Jose Medina," he stated to me, then gave orders in Spanish to a woman in the corner. She approached me, motioning at the baby. I surrendered Caleb to her without hesitating since it seemed I was being treated as a guest by this man. But my right hand hovered over my rifle on its sling, in case I needed to respond. A metal chair was offered to me, which I accepted after freeing my shoulders from my pack. I collapsed with relief onto the chair, my legs begging for rest. "You say an army comes? Peacekeepers?"

"No." I shook my head. "This is no peacekeeping force. Have you heard of President Criswell of the Pacific States?"

"Rumors. Some politician who plays president in San Diego doesn't affect us here."

"His territory spans from Canada to Mexico. Now his military is pushing east, taking control of resources as they travel. They have modern weapons and a massive arsenal. In Coronado alone, he has five thousand men."

"Five thousand? Really? You know this for a fact?"

"Yes, I lived there. And another five thousand at posts up and down the coast. No one is able to stand against him, although some men in the mountains may be organizing a resistance. You won't be able to stand against the Pacific States military. You have only two hundred men. With the incentive of water, women, and children, they'll be merciless against you whether you surrender to them or not. They'll kill you all, unless they want to keep some of the women and children for other reasons."

"We could fight. You've never seen us in battle. What's your name?"

"I'm called the Serval, a desert cat." Glancing at Caleb, I saw two women now tending to his diaper and feeding. "You can't fight against the weapon they're using to destroy their enemies."

"What weapon?"

"I didn't want to say before now." I rose from my chair and leaned over his desk to whisper into his ear. "The Meridia Virus."

As I sat back down, he couldn't hide the fear on his face. In a matter of two weeks, everyone in his city could be on their deathbeds, and he knew it.

"He's this evil? This President Criswell?"

"He is, but his top general, General Galt Brogdon, is worse. His son, Kip Brogdon, was spotted in Eagle Mountain three days ago. They killed everyone in Eagle Mountain, all while acting as if they were a friendly government force. Those who were barely still alive, they burned with the dead."

"Three days ago? They could be here any day!"

"I came to warn you as soon as I could." I paused to pray in my heart before I continued, though my body was exhausted and my mind was struggling to function. "I know how you can stop them, but you can't do it without the other fort helping."

"They won't help. The Blacks care only for our water. If we stood on the wall together against this threat, the blacks would take the first opportunity they had to kill us and take our pump."

"Unless you convince them to work with you, President Criswell will own the pump in a week, and you'll all be dead."

He thought about this for a few moments. The men who'd escorted me to the basement stood against the wall behind me, offering no word for or against my warning. This told me they trusted their commander, and for such hard men to trust Jose Medina, he must've earned it with courage and sincerity.

"We can't work with the Blacks. Tell me how to defeat this force, and I'll do it with the men and women we have here."

"Impossible. The other fort is only one hundred yards away. That's too close and affords too many blind spots for an advancing military. Both forts have to stand together, or they'll fall together."

"You don't understand. We have too much history—years of atrocities since Pan-Day. On both sides, I'm ashamed to admit. We're fighting for our lives, our pride, our futures."

"How many fighters do the Blacks have?" I asked.

"A few less than we have, but they have ammunition. We have the water. It's an odd relationship. We give them water for ammunition, then we continue to fight."

"We men have made many such foolish arrangements throughout history," I said, "but someone has to end this, or everyone dies. It ain't easy making hard choices to offer peace, but you must."

"They won't listen to me! I'm the face of the devil to them."

"Well, they don't have to listen to you. They have to listen to me. You simply make sure they believe you when you agree to survive with them. Survival is often based on mutual concessions. This decision must be made—join forces or die."

"What do you gain by this?"

"All the water I can carry as I leave and—"

"And?"

"And the knowledge that I provided the way for peace between neighbors. The Bible says to love one another, and I can't love your people without offering them safety. Jesus Christ offered us safety from evil, but that love He offered must be received, stood for, and shared."

"You're a Christian?"

"I am, as was my father. Beside him, I witnessed many great men like yourself stand for numerous principles, but the only principle that mattered in any of those men's lives was the principle of the cross. To live, we must love. To love, we must sacrifice. We can't love our neighbors while we love ourselves so much."

The commander looked away and seemed to study the dark recesses of his bunker for a moment.

"Perhaps we could fight with the Blacks for a week, but we're a long way from reaching a lasting peace."

"At dawn, we find out. My partner is in the other fort right now. If you trade water and ammo occasionally, you must have a signal between forts to draw a cease fire."

"We do."

"Then set up a meeting for dawn."

Dawn came too early for me, especially since after my meeting with Jose Medina I'd spent a couple hours trading bullets for supplies. Only a half-dozen .308 rifles existed in the Hispanic fort, and bullets meant so much to them that I was given enough food provisions to last another two weeks with Caleb. I had traded only my lethal rounds, of which I had many more, and I kept my non-lethal gel-tranqs and phosphorus rounds a secret.

Word spread quickly after my meeting with Medina that I'd brought news of pending doom. But as an outsider, I had other news they wanted to know, however small. As I bartered with men and women over smoked meat—which may have been dog—I was asked questions by the gathered crowd: had any communications been set up between the larger cities yet? Had Los Angeles been destroyed by fires and earthquakes as rumored? Was there a safe way to the West Coast I could recommend?

As I spoke of the continued dangers in California, a young Indian woman tended to Caleb at my elbow. She was about eighteen, I was told, and spoke neither English nor Spanish. Her name was Vorca, one of the Hispanics said, and he explained that she must've been born in isolation after Pan-Day to speak only a mountain Indian dialect from the old days. Whatever her history, Vorca was pleasantly plump and friendly, and I was thankful for someone to care for Caleb while I haggled on prices.

When I'd bedded down in a community bunker that night, Vorca was at my side, with Caleb between us. Oil lamps burned on the fringes of the musty room, and the snores and stirrings of soldiers couldn't keep my weary body awake. A few minutes after lying still, I opened my eyes to see Vorca watching me. She smiled and closed her eyes to sleep. God immediately touched my spiritual senses regarding this young woman. She was an outcast in Cadiz, a potential caregiver for Caleb, and she seemed to have a thing for me. As far as I was concerned, I wasn't interested in romance with her or anyone else, but I did pray about my growing Caspertein band taking on another life.

Vorca was the first thing on my mind at dawn when I met with Jose Medina at the southern perimeter gate.

"You have a Native American woman named Vorca," I said to him. Two other Hispanic Cadiz leaders handed their rifles to other soldiers since I alone was to be armed for the meeting. "You know her?"

"The mute? She's done nothing but mope about and drink our water. She hides when there's gunfire, so I haven't put her on the wall."

"Then you won't miss her if I take her as a nurse for my kid." I glanced toward the pump where Vorca and Caleb sat on a bench with my pack. "She doesn't belong here."

"You have a tongue that dictates, Serval," Medina said without much favor in his eyes. He licked his thumb and smoothed down his eyebrows. "Let's see how the next few minutes go, and then we'll talk about what or who I let you leave here with."

The three Hispanics filed out the door, then I joined them in the peaceful desert air—fresher than anything I'd been breathing inside the fort. The night before, Medina had seemed reasonable, but now I understood why he was the leader of this rabble. He had the mind of a tactician, careful and alert, but also decisive and assertive when needed. I was glad I hadn't been disarmed, in case he had an aggressive plan for me after I presented my idea to him and the Blacks when they were all together.

Though Alice Prine, my traveling companion, appeared weary and gaunt, her face brightened when she saw me. If she hadn't shown up, I would've been worried, since the day before she'd clearly expressed she wanted to move on with us. It seemed that her stump had been properly dressed. She also brought extra bandages, which were evidently for her departure. A small pack with a canteen fastened to it was hanging over the shoulder of her good arm.

Three men accompanied Alice to the middle of the demilitarized zone. One of the Blacks stood out more prominently than his two junior officers. He had a speckle of moles across his cheeks, and gray sideburns colored his otherwise dark hair.

"Medina," the black man greeted coolly and held out a duffel bag.

"Rawls." Medina thrust his hands in his pockets as one of his lieutenants set a heavy jug of water in front of Rawls, the black commander. "Seems we have a pending threat."

"I have heard it."

Rawls' junior officers worked together to move the water jug behind them. With this simple transaction completed, both sides crossed their arms and faced one another with a look I can only describe as unmasked abhorrence. These men had killed each other's families and neighbors for months or years, and now I expected them to work together to survive? By God's grace . . .

"May I begin?" I asked, intent on leading, but realizing submission was the key to victory. Alice moved to my side and nudged me gently. The desert and tragedy we'd survived was an experience that bound us together. "Just so we're all up to speed, the Pacific States military is on its way to the east, expanding their territory. They used the Meridia Virus to wipe out Eagle Mountain. The baby and Alice here barely survived."

"We know all this," one of the junior Blacks said. "How do we stop them? Why do we need to join these baby killers?"

He snarled at the Hispanics, and Medina and his men snarled similar looks and sentiments that grew in volume until I shifted my rifle in my arm. They reluctantly shut their mouths and waited for me to continue.

"The Pacific States soldiers need to make physical contact with your skin to transmit the Meridia Virus. They can't advance on Cadiz without their armored vehicles, so if you stop their vehicles, you stop the soldiers. If you don't allow them to touch you with their gloved hands, you stop the virus. They won't fight you head-to-head, rifle-to-rifle, man-to-man."

"So, how do we level the field?" Medina asked. "Neither of us has heavy artillery to disable armored trucks."

"Yeah, 'cause you already used it on us!" Rawls spat, and the verbal fighting started again.

Alice and I turned away from the delegation.

"You're ready to head north after this circus?" I asked her.

"Not only ready," she said. "I'm desperate. This isn't going to work, Levi."

"Give it another minute." I crossed my arms and prayed for what was left of Cadiz. Instead of peace, they had accusation. Instead of help for one another, they had bullets for one another. But one-by-one, they saw me waiting once again, and they hushed themselves for me to continue. "The makings for peace are difficult to envision without looking into the eyes of desperation."

"There can be no peace between us." Medina shook his head. "For every wrong we may have committed, they've committed a dozen. You cannot have peace with butchers."

"Then you'll die horrible deaths inside a month. Less than ten days after exposure to the virus, your symptoms will start to show. It'll begin with a fever. You'll shiver and sweat uncontrollably. It'll feel like the worst flu you've ever had—times ten. Then your kidneys will shut down. No one will help you as you beg for mercy, because no one has the medical training to treat a highly contagious victim. All it will take is one person to get infected, and then your whole fort will be finished. I've seen the way you all live.

"The Pacific States will stand back and watch you suffer for days, or maybe they'll enter your forts once they see that you can't lift your arms to defend yourselves. They'll throw your bodies into a pit like they did on Pan-Day, the dying still able to call for help until other bodies fall on top and suffocate the living. But the Pacific States won't be content with infecting you. Once you're disabled enough, they'll walk easily through your city and kill whomever they want. Anyone who survives the virus will be murdered, raped, or enslaved. So, by all means, continue to quarrel over the past as that army draws closer. Seriously, they could be here any minute. Look at you. So full of hatred, you haven't even deployed scouts to the south to give you an advance warning. You don't want to live. You just want to hate, then die with your hate."

"You care more about your pride," Alice said, "than your own people. They're looking to you guys to keep them alive, and here you're about to lead them right to their deaths—deaths that are preventable."

"What do you expect?" Rawls kicked at the sand. "War is all we know."

"You're fighting the wrong enemy," I said, "with the wrong weapons. You're right, there won't be any peace between the two of you. Not until there is justice first, with a gesture of justice that's mutual. I can't even tell you how to defeat the Pacific States until you want to live more than you want to die hating each other. How will I know you want to live? You'll make a move toward forgiveness."

"What're we, school boys?" Rawls scoffed. "Are you telling us to shake hands and be friends?"

"Well, I suppose I could shoot the six of you now, "I said, shifting my rifle to aim in their general direction, "then find leaders in your forts who actually want to save your people. Peace or death. The next words out of your mouths had better convince me to stay, or Alice and I are walking.”

“Who do you think you are?” Medina said. “We gave you shelter. You are our guests in Cadiz! Now you talk to us like children?”

“Okay, have a nice death. I hope you’re at peace with God even if you’re not at peace with one another.”

I marched briskly away from the middle of the party. There didn’t seem anything else I could say or do. Alice jogged to catch up, then together we headed toward the Hispanic gate.

“Where’s the baby?” she asked. “I’m surprised you left Caleb alone.”

“He’s not alone. We may have found him a nurse— and an additional companion to our party.”

“In one night? You don’t waste time, do you?”

“Peace!” a voice boomed from behind us. We stopped and turned. One of Rawls’ men stepped away from the rest. He appeared scarred and battle-weary in a blood-stained flak jacket. “I move for peace. No one more than me has reason to keep fighting. I’ve lost both my daughters this year. No one else should go through that. I’m tired of this fight, if I can be met halfway.”

Everyone was still for a moment—even the wind, as if the whole demilitarized zone waited for a final word.

“Medina?” I called.

“If it’s really mutual, we can try.”

“That might have to do,” Alice said to me. “You may not get more than that out of them.”

“I agree.” Alice and I walked back to the group. “This has to be unanimous. No one can leave this morning and undermine the decision made here. Everyone has to speak up and commit for this to work.”

One at a time, the other four spoke for peace. They indicated they were ready to fight together, and ready to live together if they survived what the Pacific States was about to throw at them.

Chapter Thirteen

We were several miles north of Cadiz when the battle began behind us. My small band of two women and a baby stopped and gazed south toward the gunfire. I raised my binoculars and searched the desert town for signs that my plan for them had worked, but we were too far away now, and the Pacific States troops had attacked from the south, so I could only hope I'd saved lives.

My plan for the town of Cadiz, once they'd agreed to pursue peace, was to give their riflemen just enough phosphorus rounds to stop the Brogdons' armored advance. I'd given them only twenty rounds, but each round had the potential to destroy an entire vehicle engine, if fired accurately. They had wanted all my .308 shells, but I had stood my ground on only twenty. It was enough. The Brogdons probably wouldn't advance with more than ten vehicles across the desert, since they didn't know what kind of resources they'd find along the way. Twenty rounds was enough for a decisive win against a superior force—with a few rounds left over for another battle. Most importantly, the phosphorus rounds had been meant to destroy vehicles, not people, so lives would be saved, I hoped, even if the Brogdons were forced to retreat across the desert on foot.

My band and I continued after a few minutes, our pace urged faster than normal by the threat of an enemy close behind us. Our footprints across the pebble-strewn sand made obvious impressions, as easy to follow as it was for us to follow Annette and the others now several days ahead.

Alice led the way, a pack on her back with supplies from my pack, as well as a little gear she'd picked up from Cadiz. In her only hand was a steel staff that may have once been a pry bar for heavy machinery. She'd turned it into a walking stick, and probably a weapon if an enemy or wild animal were to prowl too closely. The rod was heavy, and I'd thought she would drop it by the second mile, but she hadn't grown weary. With just one functioning arm, I guessed that arm would become stronger than it ever had been. Her right arm would compensate over time. She walked with her head up, planting her steel scepter and swinging it forward at intervals, like a determined ruler leading her people to safety.

Vorca, our young, plump Indian addition, carried a knife on her left hip, a canteen over her right shoulder, and Caleb on her back. Though Vorca's legs were short, she still seemed to be strong. She had no pack of her own besides Caleb. I followed a few yards behind her, intent on gauging our pace and stamina for the coming days. But I doubted we would catch Annette and the others now, unless they were held up at one of the places on our map where we'd planned to stop for food and supplies.

As of yet, I'd shown no symptoms of contracting the Meridia Virus. The thermometer I'd taken from Eagle Mountain provided an accurate way to check my temperature periodically. There was no sign of a fever yet, so I knew I wasn't transmitting the virus. I wanted to make sure I was symptom-free for Oatman, Arizona, our next stop on my map. Since Vorca knew no English, and seemed unable to communicate by sign language, I'd given up in frustration when explaining how she should watch Caleb for virus symptoms. She seemed capable on her own to tend to the infant, so I let her remain the silent member of our little group, which she seemed quite happy to be.

"Buzzards ahead!" Alice announced, then ran ahead to a dark form on the desert floor.

My heart sank in fear of what we would find. Annette had passed by Cadiz, avoiding the conflict there rather than refilling their canteens, but at what cost?

The stench of death reached my nostrils before I arrived at the corpse of one of Annette's horses we'd procured outside Aporax. The mare lay on her side, legs outstretched over a swollen belly. Alice and I stayed a few yards back and studied the sign on the ground.

"They camped here." Alice pointed with her steel staff at a small circle of ash. "About five days ago, you think?"

"About that. We lost four days between Eagle Mountain and Cadiz, then another day or two at Cadiz. With only one of their horses, they'll be carrying more, moving slower. If we keep moving, we might catch them in the mountains, if not before."

Silently, I prayed for my family's safety. I missed them terribly, even though we'd parted after harsh words.

Caleb jabbered a complaint at the odor, then sneezed. I glanced at him in time to see Vorca draw her blade to cut off the horse's tail and hang it on her belt. She checked the horse's tongue and eyes, where bugs were nesting, then stabbed into the hindquarter on the right side of the animal. Alice and I watched with disgust as Vorca cut deeply into the muscle of the hind leg, where no rot had reached yet, confirmed no doubt by measuring the rate of decomposition of the eyes and tongue. This woman was already proving herself useful by skills and knowledge I didn't have.

Vorca held up three enormous slabs of meat, as a fisherman holds up his catch, then she tied the meat to her belt, using the horse's tail. When she'd washed her hands in the sand, then wiped them on the mare's coat, Alice started northeast again, following the tracks from Annette that the wind hadn't blown away. Cooked well enough, the horse meat would be safe to eat. I began to search the ground for twigs and sticks to collect for a fire that night. All of us were ready to leave the empty desert behind.

Though Annette and I had parted ways under strain, I was eager to rejoin her and Mia. Thankfully, Forest Holter was a competent hunter and provider, so I wasn't too worried about their safety. But I would breathe easier when again at their side, if they would have me, once Annette's imposed quarantine time was finished, which I still thought was unnecessary.

Behind us, the gunshots of Cadiz faded, and the buzzards overhead settled onto the horse. The mare's death felt like a sign—death haunted us; life was fragile. We had to continue to trust the Giver of life for direction and protection.

Tucked into my pack strap was Kip Brogdon's hatchet. Nothing spoke of the danger that haunted us more than that deadly blade. I didn't wish him a good journey.

Nearly eighty miles northwest of Cadiz, we reached Oatman, Arizona, on an early morning. In the distance, we could see desert hills and low canyons, but the ghost town had the feel of a prairie settlement with the landscape covered by brown grasses. We followed Annette's obscured tracks down Main Street, paved, but now covered with sand and a few scrub plants.

Vorca stopped walking and adjusted Caleb on her back. He hadn't been cared for better since we'd adopted him. A mile outside Oatman, we'd made camp the night before. The young Indian woman continued to impress me, finding us food, shelter, and water in the most obscure places. Her stamina, even that third morning in the cool dawn, seemed untapped.

"This place isn't totally abandoned," Alice said, poking her steel staff at a pile of horse manure. "Think it's your people?"

"It's not necessarily Annette." I recalled the research we'd done in San Diego for this trek. "There's supposed to be wild burros around here. It was a providential advantage in coming this way. I'd hoped to catch a pack animal for us."

"Unless they really are wild." Alice gazed up at the dark windows of the forgotten buildings. As many abandoned neighborhoods as I'd seen over the years, I still got chills, imagining the lives that had once called these places home. "I'm not leading a wild horse."

"They're the offspring of pack animals from a hundred years ago." I shifted my bullpup in my arm, remaining vigilant, ready to fire my non-lethal rounds. "Maybe they have some of that domestication still in their blood."

"How long do you want to spend corralling a wild animal?" Alice moved her handless arm, as if she wanted to rest it on her hip, but then remembered she had no hand. "This is your journey, Levi, but I have no interest in losing more ground in finding your family."

"Take that side of the street. I'll take the left. If we see nothing by the end of town, we'll move on."

Alice took one step to the right, and a bullet burst through the manure at her heel. She froze and I dropped to one knee, my rifle at my shoulder. Vorca jogged to the nearest building, which had a half-collapsed wooden balcony.

"You're not welcome here, traveler!" a man yelled, presumably at me. Whoever he was, he had ducked out of sight now, perhaps somewhere inside one of the second floor windows of the adobe hotel. "Get out of town!"

Since I had no visible target, and the speaker could've killed us already if he'd wanted to, I let my gun hang at my side as I rose to my feet.

"We're just passing through," I hollered. "Tell us where to fill our canteens, and we'll gladly be on our way. We're heading east."

"East?" Movement in one dark window caught my eye. A man's head and shoulders appeared. "What kind of fool are you? People are coming west by the droves, if they can travel. You don't want to go into the Plains Zone, traveler!"

"The reasons they're leaving is the reason I've got to go." I stepped closer to the hotel. "I have a friend who needs me. Have you been as far as the area under the control of the Appalachian Federation?"

He leaned out the window, a slender bearded man clothed in desert fatigues, an intimidating silver-colored assault rifle in his hands still aimed at me.

"You best forget anyone you ever knew under the Appalachian Federation. That zone is like East Berlin, if you're old enough to know what I mean."

"A police state. I've read books about it. You made it out. I can get in to do what I have to do."

"I shot my way out and lost a lot of friends in the process." He pointed down at the first floor. "Come on in. The town water's in here."

He left the window, but I didn't move right away. My eyes surveyed the other buildings, then stopped on Alice's face. Her eyes were hard to read since she seemed so calm. She was nothing like the frantic survivor of Eagle Mountain I'd rescued many days ago.

"What do you think?" I asked her.

"He shot at me." She shrugged. "But who doesn't nowadays?"

We walked together to the front of the hotel. Vorca must've seen our guarded advance and moved from her hiding place to join us. Caleb mumbled in rhythm to her jostling gait.

The front of the hotel was missing, including the door. A battle had been fought there in years past, and it appeared an RPG had made a final decision to the conflict. In the dimness of the hotel lobby, a tail swished at a fly and another burro groaned over what I guessed was a belly full of water.

A pool of water bubbled in the center of the lobby. There seemed to be no distinguishable outlet until I noticed a horizontal pipe that led somewhere under the floor. Thus, the water level remained constant rather than flooding the lobby where six more burros relaxed in the accidental stable.

"I saw your rifle and thought you were the enemy." The man, maybe in his mid-forties, spoke in what I guessed was a Boston accent. He hopped down a flight of stairs against the wall, half the railing missing, his left leg held aloft. It was bandaged and stained with blood. "As you can see, I'm in no condition to host anyone who wants to stick around."

Vorca went to the first burro. It hardly flinched as she lifted its foreleg and checked its hoof. I guessed she was seeing if the animals were lame or able to pack gear for us.

"Bullet wound?" I used my foot to slide a rickety chair toward the stranger, his silver rifle now slung over his shoulder. "I was hoping we'd left gunfighting behind us for a few days."

He eased into the chair, sweat on his brow. I flipped over a useless water bucket with a bullet hole in it for him to elevate his foot.

"It was this little jerk I was traveling with. Picked him up in Kansas. Knew he was no good, but traveling alone can be reckless, too." He sat up straighter as Vorca left the burros and knelt to unwrap his leg bandage. "Did she wash her hands? Did you see her wash her hands?"

"By the smell of that wound . . ." I touched my nose. "I'd say she couldn't add more deadly germs than what you're already growing there. Don't worry. She knows her stuff."

"I think I'm done for, anyway." He cursed in pain as Vorca prodded him. "Hey, are you sure she knows what she's doing? She's not exactly being gentle!"

"Honestly? I've never had a conversation with her." I waved at Caleb, and he giggled and slapped the top of Vorca's head. The Indian woman ignored the infant's antics and continued to work on the stranger's leg. "She doesn't speak English as far as I can tell."

""But she's with you, right?"

"She's carrying my kid on her back." I grinned. "I think you can trust her. I do."

"Somebody's coming," Alice announced from the gaping hole in the front of the building. From her position, she was looking east, the morning sun in her eyes. "Looks like four on horseback. Maybe more."

The man with the leg wound slipped his rifle off his shoulder, but I rested a firm hand on his arm. He was in no position to fight since his bandage was unwrapped and under Vorca's care.

"I've got this. Just guard my people in here if these travelers come in for water."

I bolted upstairs and found the second story room where the stranger had been sleeping and guarding his water hole. I suspected he'd relied on the animals downstairs to help warn him when travelers came through, since he'd probably been feverish from his leg wound, and prone to sleeping.

Through the window, I spied four horsemen and two pack horses in tow. As they drew up in front of the hotel, I noticed the second person was a middle-aged woman. They saw me and each slipped a hand to their rifle scabbard, but I didn't react by aiming my rifle at them. Someone in this untamed land had to break the cycle of violence and actually be hospitable.

"Howdy, there." I touched my brow as if I were tipping my hat. "We've got water and shade inside, but nothing else to spare at the moment."

The lead man had an unruly beard, but there was no hostility in his eyes.

"I thought Oatman was uninhabited, just animals roaming free."

"Give us a couple days, and I'm sure the town will return to the burros."

"We won't be sticking around, either. Headed to Oregon."

"The Pacific States are regulating their own type of martial law along the coast," I shared. "A mountain family led by Sebastian Mallinger and a coalition called the Kindred may be leading a much-needed revolt for independence. The Mallingers are much farther south than Oregon, but the Kindred might be ranging north along the Rocky Mountains, around Yosemite Park. They're good people. Christian folks."

"Maybe California would be more to our liking, then." The man glanced at his wife. "We just want to go someplace where we can live life fairly around honest people. We know it'll be hard anywhere we go. You're the first to give us any meaningful direction."

"If you go to Southern California, you can find the Mallinger family, or in Central California, look for the Kindred. Tell them the Serval sent you. You'll be welcome among them." I gazed over rooftops from my vantage point and checked what I could see of the desert for movement. "Just avoid Cadiz and Eagle Mountain. Come on in and we'll look at the map." I went downstairs to the lobby.

Friendly words didn't automatically make for relaxed nerves, but I tried to settle our guests' anxiety about meeting strangers by hanging my rifle sling over my shoulder. Though I'd recently arrived at Oatman myself, I played the part of host and dipped a bucket deeply for the first horse. Vorca seemed not to notice our visitors, and the man with the leg wound was in too much pain from Vorca's working on him to offer any assistance. Only Alice remained vigilant with her staff as she stood at the gap in the wall. Even with only a staff, it was an advantageous position that caused our guests to glance at her more than once. A single swipe with that staff could break one or two horse's legs. No one accustomed to riding wanted to walk in that desert.

The semi-wild burros crowded to the back of the lobby on the opposite side of the pool from the saddle horses, and once everyone had their water, Untamed Beard and his wife spread their map on a broken table below the stairs. I explained the situation southwest of us, and about the Brogdons' tactics in the name of the Pacific States.

Considering my advice, they changed their route and now planned to go due west, then south once they reached the mountains, avoiding Cadiz, Eagle Mountain, and the heart of the Mojave.

"With any luck, we'll find these Kindred people," the man said. Though I'd shared my handle, he offered none. "We're from Texas, the Gulf Coast. Nothing but drought for ten years. Couldn't go east, so we figured we'd go northwest. Find a valley and plant some crops. Farming's in the family."

Less than an hour after the horsemen had arrived, Alice and I stood in the hotel entrance and watched them leave. While it was still early, they wanted to cover more miles.

"You make friends too quickly for my comfort," she said, reminding me that she and I had much different priorities in life. "What're you thinking?"

"I'm just wondering why God brought those people through here at this time," I said. "They came and went for no apparent reason."

"Normal people don't wonder about those kinds of things."

"Well, there's no waste with God." I checked my rifle and placed it on my back again. "Maybe it was to guide them around danger ahead, or send them to the Kindred who'll need them. It's interesting to imagine all that God might be doing, but our job is to imitate His Son, Jesus Christ."

"There were Christians at Eagle Mountain." She twirled her heavy staff. "They wouldn't have shared their water with perfect strangers like you just did. You risked everyone's lives, even Caleb's."

"I was thinking about how God's love can be expressed to people because they need it, not because it's safe." I smiled at her. "God likes to prove His Word to be true. We just have to be willing to step out in faith."

She stared after the riders for a moment, and I prayed for her open heart. Then she turned to me.

"What do you want to do about the wild burros?"

"See if Vorca can pick out two of the healthiest ones. We'll need a couple lead ropes. You might have to scavenge the town. Watch out for rusty nails. I'm gonna see if our host has more news from the east."

Inside the hotel, I found Caleb kicking and waving, laying on his back in a patch of wild grass nearby. A burro stuck its nose right in Caleb's face to inspect the wiggling creature. Vorca was making up a bed next to the pool for the wounded man. She had fetched his belongings from upstairs. I helped Vorca carry the wounded man to his new bed and knelt next to his fevered head. He told me his name was Brian Steelman.

"How come I felt better before she did that to my leg?" His face was yellow.

"That wound was poisoning you slowly. I don't know what she did for you, but I think you'll be better off."

"How can you say that? I can't stop shaking!"

"Well, knowing Vorca like I think I do . . ." I eyed the wide woman as she changed Caleb, using a discarded flower pot to pour water over him. "I think if she found your leg real bad, she would've already amputated it."

"Amputated?"

"She knows about things like that. Once you're able to hobble around, catch one of these burros and continue your journey. Your leg can continue to heal as you ride. While you're weak, you need to be down here rather than going up and down those stairs."

"I have to keep a watch for bandits. They'll ruin the pool and kill the burros for meat."

"You'd best do what Vorca's set you up to do, and trust God about the rest. You won't survive this otherwise." I chuckled as Alice semi-patiently communicated with Vorca about the burros. "What do you know about the northern region of the Appalachian Federation?"

"It's a paradise." The man laughed, but then it faded to a choking cough. "It's paradise for Conformists. They're the party that controls new policy. But it's the radicals that get the baton. Non-conformists are hunted down and killed."

"Christians?"

"There aren't many of those left, I think. They were rounded up pretty regularly years ago. Conformity and tolerance is some sort of state religion. Anyone who's intolerant or voices an opinion is arrested. Most aren't warned. They just disappear. I was just tired of all the state regulations in the name of freedom and peace. Maybe I'm running from a little of a past I'd rather forget, too."

"My friend is in upstate New York. She would never renounce her faith or conform to something false."

"Then she's probably not alive. Sorry. Everyone has to pass the Citizenship Entrance Exam—the *C.E.E.*, pronounced *see*."

"The *CEE*?"

"Only tolerant religions are legalized, but you can be a Christian if you confess that all religions have equal value. Some do that."

"What would they do to her if she didn't pass this *CEE*?" I frowned and looked away. "She's blind. Do they have prison facilities or what?"

"A blind Christian?" He took a deep breath. "There were facilities, yeah. But there were a lot of executions—so many that they stopped making news."

"What about checkpoints?"

"On highways, yeah. That's why I've been on foot for two years." He gripped my arm. "You can't go over there, man. They'll kill you. You can't help people like that anymore."

"We helped you, didn't we?"

"Yeah." He released my arm and closed his eyes. "I guess we'll see about that. Are you guys taking off?"

"If you'll be okay."

"You can't take me with you. And I'm not going east again. Just promise me this." He suddenly opened his eyes and stared hard at me. "Kill that little rat who shot me—Monty Ashlaw. He's two days ahead of you, chasing a couple pretty girls."

"Did they come out of the desert? Had a horse and a young man with them? He had a little peach fuzz on his cheeks."

"That's them. I've never seen a more miserable group of travelers, even myself when I was at my worst, even now."

"They were injured?"

"No, just dying of thirst. For two days they recovered right here. That's when he devised his plan, I suspect."

"Who?"

"Monty Ashlaw, the rascal. I should've left him back in New Mexico. I knew he wasn't right in the head."

"What did he devise?"

"Those girls—he went after them after they left here, leading their tired horse."

"Describe this Monty guy to me." I felt anger rising in my chest. Forest could defend Annette and the girls from a distance. No one could shoot straighter than he could. But if a traveler snaked his way into their midst under the guise of being a friend . . .?

"Blond. Freckles. Shorter than you and younger. Complains all the time and eats more than his share. Good enough picture of the scoundrel for you?"

"The women were okay when they left here?"

"Fit enough to walk, until Monty catches up to them. No telling what he'll do. It's my fault, really." He clutched his midsection and shivered from his fever. "When he went on and on about wanting to be with them, I shut his mouth with the back of my hand. But he had his little revolver."

"A little revolver?"

"It's in his pocket. Shot me on purpose in the leg just so I'd die slowly. I'd chase him down if I could, even going east, but I suspect he'll be sorted out by you sooner, if those people are with you. Am I right?"

"Will he hurt them?"

"Well, he won't be nice to them."

I looked up and saw that Alice had returned, and she'd heard the last bit. Though she'd never met Annette and the others, by the look on her face, she seemed to want justice as if she were family.

With so much violence and death in the world, we didn't need another reason to follow suit, but it seemed this Monty Ashlaw fellow had a Caspertein confrontation in his future. I was worried less about what I'd do to him when I caught him than how Mia, in her pregnant condition, was dealing with him right now. It was time to leave Oatman.

Chapter Fourteen

We left Oatman and the man named Brian Steelman before noon. We were carrying more water than we could drink in five days, and traveling faster than ever with two floppy-eared burros in our employ. I had tried to place Caleb on one of the narrow backs of a burro, but Vorca had insisted on carrying the child on her back. She'd also taken the lead ropes from my hands to lead the beasts of burden herself. The stubborn animals were surprisingly cooperative, at least for her.

This left me nearly without anything to carry, besides my rifle, canteen, and Kip Brogdon's hatchet. The first burro carried my pack and half the water. The second animal, a little smaller than the first, carried Alice's pack and the rest of the water containers—an assortment of bottles, jugs, and canvas. First, we would drink from the containers that leaked, and there were several of those we'd found at Oatman.

Alice took the lead, having become familiar with the locations on my map, as well as the prints of Annette and the others ahead of us. I brought up the rear, chewing on a length of grass and humming a hymn, trying to settle my nerves about Monty Ashlaw. Occasionally, I saw his boy-sized boot prints in soft soil, and my heart skipped a beat at what justice God might want me to exact in this environment. The young man had left Brian Steelman for dead. What would he do to my family?

As a Christian, my eyes were to be focused on eternal matters. God had established human government in Noah's day to keep sin in check as well as to teach society His justice. I didn't believe my journey as a Christian had equipped me to perform the governing duties of maintaining justice beyond the spiritual preservation of His people. As a man of mercy, I was more inclined to forgive and seek a gracious path rather than condemn a man to the finality of death. Carrying non-lethal ammunition declared the truth I believed in my heart—how I was to love even my enemies. That's not to say I wasn't tempted that day, or any other day, to swap my non-lethal rounds for my lethal rounds to silence certain dangers once and for all.

That evening, we camped in a wooded box canyon surrounded by low cliffs twice as high as I stood. While Vorca tended to the packs and animals, I collected firewood. Alice climbed up a flood-carved gorge and stood on top of the cliffs.

"Those dogs we saw outside Oatman are out there," Alice said. The barks and yips of a pack of wild dogs could be heard in the distance. "After everything we've survived, I'm not dying by some wild beagles!"

We built the fire extra-large that night, though I knew half the dogs out there had probably been domesticated at some point. They didn't have the same fear of fire and humans as a true wild canine might have, and now that we had the burros, I was more concerned about their safety than my own that night. The pack animals didn't mind the nearness of the firelight or our company as I tethered them close to our bedrolls.

Without asking permission of my fellow travelers, I read from the Psalms that night, loud enough for Alice to hear while on guard above us, and for Vorca, who stared into the flames, though I doubted she understood a word. The burros hung their weary heads as if they knew the dangers of the hundreds of miles before them. Caleb slept on a full stomach as the desert chill swept over us. We all went to sleep near the fire. I dreamed of catching Monty Ashlaw and tying him to a tree for the wild dogs to devour. It was a terrible dream.

It took two more days to reach Peach Springs—double the amount of time it should've taken since we went farther to the south to avoid travelers and canyons. We even lost Annette's trail a few times, so when we spied the town of Peach Springs from a hilltop, we weren't certain if Annette and the others had entered the ghost town or not.

"I don't see any sign of life or water." Alice used my binoculars as I watched with the naked eye for movement, then she handed me the glasses. "We're okay on water. Let's just go around. It doesn't look right, like it's been intentionally left to fall apart. We did that at Eagle Mountain, so people from a distance thought the place was uninhabited. I know the signs."

"I have to track my family."

"We can pick up their trail on the east side."

"This is my chance to gather a little intel on Monty Ashlaw. A settler here might be able to tell us if he's traveling with Annette and Mia."

"Forget intel. Let's just keep moving and catch up to them tomorrow night. Whatever's going on in this town, they don't want to be sociable."

"My family could be down in that town, Alice." It didn't seem likely, but something was drawing me to Peach Springs. I prayed silently for God to confirm His direction—a strong sense I couldn't explain to Alice. "We've seen enough travelers coming from this direction lately that there must be a trading post down there."

"You're taking unreasonable risks." She slammed her steel staff into the dry dirt. "If you're going down there, I am, too!"

"Can you help Vorca understand to wait here? She listens to you better."

Alice left my side, and I continued to watch Peach Springs. Darkness settled on us, and there was no visible light coming from any of the buildings. It seemed unlikely that the town was completely uninhabited with so many travelers migrating westward, cutting through the remnants of these very buildings. Commerce was always a reason to settle even in the most obscure town.

When I'd left San Diego, I could count on two fingers the lives that directly depended on me. Now, I needed two hands to count those lives, not to mention Jenna Dowler and the danger for which she summoned me eastward. So what was I doing walking into a ghost town that most likely wasn't truly uninhabited?

As Alice followed me down the slope to Peach Springs, I felt fear of the unknown, but I did my best to trust God. Nothing was unknown to Him. He guarded my daily life, and my eternal life, as I'd entrusted my soul to Him. Though I continued through the edges of that small town, I didn't feel like a courageous Caspertein this time. There was something eerie about this place.

Like other settlements we'd passed through, Peach Springs had many houses on the outskirts of the town that had been stripped of paneling and window glass, even some framing and roofing. Near the center of town where the buildings were spread apart, I suddenly crouched low. In silence, Alice touched my shoulder with what I knew was her stump, to let me know she was near and was following my lead. As an older woman surviving her family in Eagle Mountain against all odds, though with only three functioning limbs, her presence still comforted me.

Something moved out there in the darkness—something human rather than the wild dogs abandoned from countless homes nationwide.

Alice whistled through her teeth as quiet as a whisper. I narrowed my eyes to see what she saw. There—a piece of clothing, white in the sea of blackness! It moved off the street, past buildings, and out of town. Following anyone at night in a strange land was a recipe for discovery, but we couldn't lose our only lead to the mystery of Peach Springs. How could a frequented town become such a ghost town? And since I knew Annette had passed this way, I was about to discover what Annette may have come upon or traveled through.

"Come on," I whispered to Alice.

We tracked the person from a distance, pausing often to listen. When we halted, our ears strained for sound. Alice remained close enough for me to feel her shiver, maybe from the desert chill, but probably from fear. She wasn't the only one.

"We're following two or three people, I think," Alice said after ten minutes of stalking. We were far out of town now, weaving down a trail into a deep gorge. I smelled vegetation and wet earth. "No fire? Not even a torch?"

"I know. Either these people are afraid, or they have something to hide."

That's what elevated my concern. The farther we went from the town, the more likely those we followed would light a torch or flashlight—unless absolute secrecy or danger were present. Some areas of the trail were perilous with a cliff on one side, but the dangers I sensed were manmade more than geographical, though we were careful to plant our feet only on solid ground.

"There." Alice pointed her staff.

I saw what she was pointing at—a light, or at least the glow of a light source somewhere deeper in the gorge, farther ahead. And the sound of water, lots of water.

"The river is very near," I said, then continued forward. My bullpup remained against my shoulder at the ready, the scope an inch from my eye.

The trail narrowed and the river grew so loud, I knew we were near a waterfall. Light, by oil, I guessed, lit up the gorge now. We edged around an earthen corner and shrunk back. Two men with rifles on slings stood guard across the canyon trail that hugged the mountainside. I peered into the gorge, then up at the slope—they were too deep and too steep. We couldn't go around. The hidden community ahead was well-defended. Though suspicion permeated the world, I fought the urge to believe we'd stumbled upon anything but a paranoid river town. Perhaps during Pan-Day, they'd been victims, and a law of secrecy had been enforced. Peach Springs above had probably become off-limits, except under extreme circumstances, like for fetching supplies or building materials.

Entering a hidden community was dangerous, even if its citizens seemed peaceful. The risk of further exposure to the outside world could turn a gentle housewife into a raging killer. I'd seen it before. But now I was curious, and I hoped my Caspertein wit could convince my unsuspecting hosts that I wasn't a danger to them.

Alice nodded when I held up my hand for her to stay back. I took a deep breath, slung my rifle over my shoulder, and stepped around the corner into the guards' sight.

"Excuse me," I said.

They both jumped in shock and leveled their rifles at me. I was already holding my palms wide, showing that my hands were obviously empty.

"Where'd you come from?"

"Peach Springs."

"How'd you find us?"

"The waterfall is on my tourist map," I said, suddenly remembering that fact. "I'm a peaceful traveler, a God-fearing man in search of friendly people to trade with."

"You'd best head back the way you came." The speaker was clean-shaven and older than I was. He glanced at his partner, a short, hairy man. "Or should we take him to Tasker? He could be with us."

"I'm definitely with you," I blurted, not certain what I was committing myself to.

"Are you alone?" the clean-shaved one asked. "You have any belongings?"

"Why don't you take me to Tasker?"

"Do you know Tasker? How'd you know to ask for him?"

"You said his name a minute ago," his friend said accusingly. Their rifle muzzles dropped a little. "He heard you say Tasker; he doesn't know Tasker!"

I stepped closer and squinted in the dimness at the rifle the hairy one held. It was a small .22 bolt action rifle. By the shape of it, I could see it was a Savage—*my* Savage, with the 3x scope I'd sighted for hunts since I was a boy! It was the .22 Forest Holter had used since his family had joined us after Aporax had fallen. The muzzle had its short sound-suppressor—custom-made and rare.

While the men discussed who'd mentioned the name Tasker first, I drew out two non-lethal cartridges from my vest, lunged forward between their rifle barrels, and stabbed a cartridge into each man's ribs. Both tranquilizers burst. The struggle was muffled by the dull roar of the waterfall. Alice must've been watching since she was at my side as soon as the men fell.

"Are you sure that was necessary?" She set her staff aside and picked up one rifle as I picked up my .22. "These could've been peaceful people."

"They could've been, but now we know for sure." I checked the .22's ammunition. It was still loaded with non-lethal rounds, which meant it probably hadn't been checked too thoroughly by the thieves. "This has been my rifle since I was a kid. Forest was carrying it."

"The married guy who was with your mom?"

"The same."

"Maybe he traded it."

"Not a chance. Mom would never allow it. Besides, as a hunter, Forest cared too much for it to trade it away." I licked my lips and gazed toward what was the community proper, clouded by waterfall mist. "Annette must be here. They probably wanted Mia and Sharly to bear children."

"That's sick." She checked her new rifle in her one-handed way, but I took it from her. With a toss, I watched it disappear over the ledge into the river. "Why'd you do that?"

"You're traveling with me. No killing." I gave her my bullpup, its compact size better suiting her one-armed frame. "It's a semi-automatic. Just aim and fire. But it's got a mean kick. Wind your stump in the sling like this."

"You can't go in there alone."

"This fires silently." I patted the .22. "I'll get my family. You just keep this trail open. We'll be leaving in a hurry. If you run out of bullets, use that thing." I gestured at her steel staff. "I'm counting on you, Alice."

She held her chin up proudly, seeming to appreciate that she was needed, and not viewed as an invalid.

"Don't make me come in after you." She grinned, her teeth white in the strange lighting. "Vorca, Caleb, and I aren't exactly Casperteins without you."

I searched the unconscious men and found two more non-lethal magazines, all that I'd given Forest from my pack. The magazines felt full, which meant I had ninety rounds to battle my way to my family—using a rifle I knew as well as my own hand.

Rather than lurk ahead, I walked up the trail as casually as possible, like I belonged. The smell of oil lamps seemed denser in the humid air. Gradually, the scaffolding of the community took shape, lamp light illuminating the structure that hugged the cliff straight up and straight down to the river. And then a shadowed presence loomed behind one wooden ramp into the cliff itself—a cave.

As quickly as I identified the cave, I spotted an armed sentry on a platform at the mouth of the cave. But I didn't shoot the guard. Instead, I paused on the trail, stretched, and studied the area for other guards. The rest of the community seemed to be asleep. For years, they'd probably been safe, and now they'd grown complacent, not imagining an invader could so easily slip past their two gatekeepers on the narrow trail.

The ghost town above now made sense. It appeared uninhabited, so travelers kept moving, but just a few minutes' walk away, Peach Springs had been reborn in the mist of the waterfall. Except they didn't only hide. Apparently, they shanghaied unsuspecting travelers, too. Annette would never have abandoned her trek toward Colorado to join such people as these. Something had gone terribly wrong. In the back of my throat, I tasted bitterness. Monty Ashlaw had done something to hurt my family, and I was too late.

Confident that there were no other guards on duty, I raised my rifle, aimed, and shot the sentry on the platform in front of the cave. Before anyone else could discover my assault, I climbed a short ladder, then bounded up the ramp to reach the cave platform where the sentry now slept. I knelt and disassembled his rifle and tossed his ammunition toward the river.

Not far away, someone sneezed. I stood and assumed the position of the sentry. I realized whoever had sneezed was in the cave, but it was pitch black down there. Stepping closer, I smelled the odor of human bodies. A complicated pulley system descended into the shaft, and the bucket attached to the pulley was in the raised position, hooked securely to my platform. People were in the shaft, in that stench and darkness, and the bucket was raised?

Someone coughed, and another spoke something. Voices echoed from the depths of the cave. I frowned at the scaffolding of the waterfall community. An entire fort system of comfortable living structures clung to the cliff. Why live in a damp, dark cave . . . unless it was by force?

Whatever my next move, it was a risk. I could hunt through the community for whoever this Tasker was, or I could start with the cave.

I moved to the edge of the platform, my foot next to the bucket, which was large enough for two people to sit in, and I cupped my hand.

"Hey, down there," I called. There was a hushed silence. Was I dealing with friends or foes? "Need anything?"

There was no immediate response.

"What're you willing to give us?" a clear, strong voice said back, I guessed about thirty feet down.

"What do you want?" I glanced at the cliff shelters, hoping the noise of the waterfall covered our voices.

"Got any food? Dinner was a little light. We've got some young ones down here."

I didn't have time to gradually explore exactly what was happening. One thing for sure—whoever was in the cave didn't want to be there. It was time to put all my cards on the table.

"Listen: I just took out three guards up here. Tell me what I'm dealing with."

"Levi? Levi, is that you?" another voice asked.

I knew that voice!

"Forest! Is Annette down there with you? And Mia?"

"No, it's just me—and some other people. Everyone, quiet! Let me talk. He's my friend. He'll help us."

"I'm here, Forest. Quick!"

"I've got sixteen people down here. Drop the bucket and pull us up."

"Okay, but I need you up here first to keep guard."

I turned and waved at Alice to join me, though I couldn't see her on the dark trail. What we had to do outweighed the risk of leaving our route unguarded. As she came out of the shadows, I unhooked the tram-bucket and, hand-over-hand, lowered it to Forest. Alice joined me, needing no explanation, and freed me of my rifle so I could work easier.

The tram hit rock below, and the ropes wiggled as the car was weighted by a body.

"Pull me up!" Forest ordered.

The pulley system was complicated and slow. I was sweating in the damp air when Forest's hand reached out and gripped the wooden platform before I'd raised the tram all the way up. He climbed up beside me, wearing no shirt since it was wrapped around his head, which had been bleeding. Reaching back, he held out a hand to someone else who'd been in the tram with him.

"All's clear," Alice announced, standing closely.

Forest yanked a young black girl out of the tram. She landed on bare feet, her trousers torn off at the knees.

"Down," Forest guided, helping me with the ropes so we could work twice as fast. "They actually keep slaves here. The slaves work the mines until death."

"What about Annette and the others? And Sharly?"

The tram reached the bottom and we drew it back up seconds later.

"Best I can figure, they're on the road still, thinking I'm dead." He chuckled. "Hey, want to know how I stayed sane the last few days?"

"How?"

"By praying. And now you show up? I'm a believer, Levi! Somehow, I knew everything would be okay. I kept telling these people that God was with me in that hole!"

The next two—two black women—reached the top and unloaded. One of them the mother of the girl already on the platform. I wiped my brow and lowered the tram.

"I was doing my best to catch you guys," I said, panting as I strained on the ropes for the next load. "Had some worries about a Monty Ashlaw. You cross him?"

"In person." He touched his bandaged skull, then continued to heave. "Ambushed me up the canyon when we were hunting. When I came to, he was talking to these canyon jackals like he knew them. He just wanted me out of the way to get at our families."

Anger raged through me, and I used the adrenalin to work the ropes. Two black men hopped out of the tram next.

"Forest, get on the rifle," I said as the two men took over the strenuous work for us. "Alice, meet Forest."

"Pleasure."

Alice gave me my rifle and Forest aimed the .22 at the cliff shelters of the townspeople.

"I'll guard the trail," Alice said, and took the hand of one of the young women. "Send them to me."

She disappeared with the girl and women to keep our escape secure—and to fetch her steel staff, no doubt.

"All blacks?" I asked as another tram unloaded two teenage boys.

"And anyone else they wanted to kidnap to work their mine."

"They guessed we wouldn't be missed," one of the black men on the ropes said. "I've been here for two years."

"Well, they guessed wrong." I shook my head. "I can't wait to catch up with Monty!" I looked at our black companions. "What kind of mine was this?"

"It's a gold mine." Forest shivered and I gave him my outer shirt. "But the last I heard, it wasn't worth anything."

"So, what do we do about this place?"

"We know what to do," one of the men said. A few more crept down the ramp to where Alice waited. "The river was diverted so they could build here. And there are three support timbers that hold their houses in place. It'll all come down in an instant."

"Just make sure you give the people warning before you destroy the place," I said. "You don't want to treat them like they've treated you."

No one responded. My opinion had been voiced, but it wasn't my place this time. These people had a plan for justice already in place—to flood the community with water.

The last tram of people arrived, and I received several embraces—my brothers and sisters caught in the same struggle to survive. Then, Forest and I joined Alice to slip into the night. Peach Springs was a place I didn't want to see in the daylight, nor meet its inhabitants. Some people were better left alone, passed by in the night, left in God's sovereign hands. They would reap what they'd sown.

Chapter Fifteen

Somewhere east of Peach Springs, Vorca stopped our burros and we set up camp in the rain. Dawn was two hours away, and we hadn't covered many miles since breaking Forest out of the slave cave, but we were exhausted. I used Kip Brogdon's hatchet to collect firewood from a small stand of trees, then we huddled around a smoky fire, too soaked to sleep, too weary to talk right away.

Over the flames, I watched Forest's face as he stared at the fire. They'd beaten and starved him for two days. His lips were cracked and his cheeks appeared hollow. Though he would physically recover soon, he appeared haunted by the experience.

"Annette's tracks will be washed away in the rain," Alice said. With her staff in her hand, she crouched with me as we shared the cover of a tarp.

"She'll stick to the route we planned," I said.

"If Annette gets in Monty's way," Forest mumbled, "he'll take her out of the picture to get to Sharly and Mia."

Vorca, without cover from the rain herself, tucked a rain slicker around Forest's shoulders. She had built a small lean-to out of our gear for Caleb, one side open to the fire. I still hadn't heard the child cry. He only wriggled, kicked, and jabbered, brightening our gray-weather moods.

"At dawn, I'm going ahead." I glanced at Alice. She'd become quite attached to me over the past two weeks, as any two people would who'd survived the threats of death several times. "I need you to keep this party moving. Stick to the map. Forest knows it, too. Can you do it?"

"I'd rather go with you." She looked away, into the dark rain. "But I'll do it."

"You don't know Monty," Forest said. "I swear, if he touches—"

"I'll deal with Monty Ashlaw." I set another tree branch on the fire. "He won't know what to expect when I show up. If he's hoping to take advantage of the women, he'll try to take me out secretly, like he did to you. But I'll make my move first, right away. Brian Steelman in Oatman said he has a pocket revolver. This kid is dangerous. I'm not taking any chances."

"When will we see you again?" Alice asked without looking at me, as if she felt abandoned.

"As soon as possible, I'll stop Annette and the others to wait for you all to catch up. We'll be safer traveling as one party, even if we're a little slower and we require more supplies."

"I'm trusting God about you," Forest said, his eyes flooded with tears. "Sharly and Natasha are my life. You helped us once, Levi Caspertein. You can do it again. If I had the strength to move like you right now, I'd go myself."

"God is with the Casperteins." Alice nodded at the fire, her statement confirming to me that prayers were making an impact. "We are the Casperteins."

I smiled weakly, wondering if she was confusing the word Christian with the name Caspertein, but as long as she understood the God of the Bible was real and trustworthy, it didn't matter what earthly family she felt she belonged to.

Two hours later, I collected an extra tarp and a small pack, and walked into the growing light of dawn. I'd slept only an hour that night, but the danger I sensed for my family urged me onward. Our food stores were low, so I'd taken only a little jerked meat, hoping to come upon something that day. If I jogged for one day, I would catch Annette, unless she'd diverted from our plans. Cameron,

Arizona, was one hundred and ten miles away, her next scheduled resupply town and old tourist entrance to the Grand Canyon. Unless I hiked into the canyon, water would be scarce. I would need to depend on what I had in two canteens, and pray Annette had some to spare when I caught them. Since they still had one pack horse, I guessed they were well-supplied. As dangerous as Monty was, he'd been this way before, even if as a predator, so I hoped he was guiding them to occasional water sources.

My pack was high on my back and my boot laces were tight as I set off at a slow jog. The rain stopped and the sky cleared. I was expecting a hot day. The rust-colored landscape was bathed in golden rays and I felt as swift as a man should who is marching to rescue his family from the hands of a dangerous foe. I prayed it wasn't revenge I sought, but merely my family's recovery. As yet, I hadn't determined what to do with Monty Ashlaw, but one thing was certain: what I did to him could impact the rest of my trip—my conscience, my relationship with the Lord, even my leadership in the family. Monty had shot Brian Steelman, a man who'd been hospitable to us, and Monty had literally sold Forest into slavery. How was a Christian to react with grace and mercy to such evil?

The wind began to blow mid-morning, covering my perspiring skin in fine, red dust. Around noon, I slowed to a walk, climbed a treeless mountain, and sat down on a ledge with my binoculars in hand. Looking over the canyons and cliffs, ridges and dry stream beds, nothing stirred as far as I could see. Rock formations stood everywhere, like ageless monuments to those who'd perished without water in past days. And maybe I would even join those who had died if I failed to find Annette's tracks.

After careful hydration, I back-tracked to avoid a deep fissure, then I continued at a jog directly north. The hard living for the past twenty years had conditioned my body to withstand being pushed to the limit, and I thanked God I was healthy enough to respond to the present need.

Before sundown, I skidded to a stop, my feet sweaty and sore from the unforgiving, sunburned grit under my boots. But I didn't care about the sand under foot at the moment because the narrow valley in which I now stood had a smooth floor, as if from an ancient glacier flow. Though the rain had done its job erasing most sign, a few soft spots still bore the indents of footprints. I knelt there, breathing hard, careful not to conclude that the markings meant something that they didn't.

However, the tracks seemed to be from Annette and two other adults, plus a larger circular set of prints every few feet—obviously from a horse. And they were headed in the right direction.

"Please give me speed, Lord," I prayed. "And give me light."

I started on my second canteen as the sun set and I plodded on. But the sky became overcast and I smelled rain in the air again. Though it didn't rain on me, the clouds above were enough to block out the light of the stars and moon, making it unsafe to travel. I'd prayed for light, and God was telling me I needed darkness. He wanted me to rest, I sensed. Without complaining, I curled up under a boulder where rattlesnakes may have nested, but I no longer cared. Sleep came quickly, once I pulled the tarp over me.

Hours later, after midnight, I woke to the laughter of coyotes. The sky had cleared. The shapes of the rocks were visible enough to travel, so I headed out, sucking on jerky as I walked, stretching my tight muscles and sore joints. Without the ability to see far ahead, I couldn't determine whether I was entering a box canyon or even if I was still on Annette's tracks. As long as I didn't step off a cliff, distance was my goal, and locating the tracks again was a matter I had to leave for dawn.

But I collapsed as the sun rose. My body was in excellent condition, but even a machine has its limitations. On my hands and knees, I prayed for a little more. My food was gone, and my canteen was nearly empty. When I'd left a whole day earlier, we'd been two days behind Annette. Had I traveled two days in one? I thought not, but once I found her tracks, I'd know for certain how close I was.

Still bowed to the ground, I prayed for guidance to deal with Monty Ashlaw, a rogue, a villain, a predator, which was saying a lot since the law of the land seemed so primal. But there was still a code among travelers, especially among friends. Monty had violated the final code when he'd left his companion, Brian Steelman, for dead. And then he'd gone after my family.

In the Pacific States, as militant as President Criswell had been through General Brogdon, criminals were still apprehended and sentenced to labor or execution. From the sound of the Appalachian Federation, basic law and order prevailed in its police state, even if its regulations had targeted Christians in some way.

But in the lawless land between the Pacific States and the Federation, every man determined what was right for himself, like in the biblical days of the Judges. I was tempted to do the same, but I was a Christian, and I knew Christians have a new nature whereby we are supernaturally guided by the Holy Spirit. God's Word was revealed inside us to discern good and evil. I didn't determine my own version of right and wrong. I was to guard God's Word and uphold His judgements. So what did God want me to do about Monty Ashlaw? Still, I received no clear message from God.

Confident that God would guide me, I rose to my feet and shielded my eyes against the eastern sun. There were hills ahead that would make for vantage points to search for my family. But that meant I would have to climb those hills. Walking had become a challenge, let alone climbing.

Thinking back, I had covered sixty miles in twenty-four hours.

A horse whinnied. I chuckled and glanced skyward, thanking my Lord for a little comedy along my route, even if that comedy pertained to my questionable sanity. Now, I was hearing horses out in the desert!

The horse whinnied again, and this time I wondered if the sound was real after all. Startled, I turned around. Fifty feet behind me, a horse stood gazing at me! Near the horse were four bulky shapes in either sleeping bags or tarps—Annette, Sharly, Mia, and Monty, I guessed. Little Natasha was sleeping with her mother, no doubt.

Their fire had smoldered to glowing coals by the time I walked into their camp. Since my exhaustion had bordered on delirium, I had actually walked past their sleeping camp in the dusky light!

"Levi!" Annette sat upright, her hair matted and her face slimmer than I'd ever seen her.

I reached for a metal container in the coals and felt the weight. It was full. After pouring some hot meat broth into my canteen, I sat back as the camp came to life.

But they didn't all clamor to hug me. Annette backed away from me, abandoning even her sleeping bag. She was still in her stocking feet. Sharly held Natasha protectively in her arms, and Mia looked to Annette for instructions. Monty, blond and freckled as described, appeared startled, but his face quickly portrayed a crooked smile, as if he'd already anticipated cutting my throat or shooting me in the belly.

After guzzling from my canteen, I wiped my mouth and held out my arms. Already, the nourishment of the broth was coursing through me, reviving my muscles and mind.

"Really? You're still clinging to some notion that I have the Meridia Virus? I continue to be symptom-free, you should know."

"It hasn't been twenty-one days, Levi!" Annette glanced at her rifle, which was closer to me than it was to her. "You've endangered us all!"

"You need to check your hysteria, Mother," I stated. "I've sucked on a thermometer four times a day since Eagle Mountain, and I still have no sign of a fever."

"Then where's the baby you had?"

Mia tugged on her boots and backed away from me, too.

"The baby's fine—further evidence that I'm no carrier, because if it hasn't been three weeks for me, it has been for him."

"How do you know? When did you last see him?"

"I'm not going to argue with you, Mother." I jutted my chin at Monty. "Who's this? And where's Forest?"

"He . . . fell off a cliff a few days ago," Annette said, still not moving any closer to me. "Hunting. There was a cliff. We . . . couldn't even get down there to find his body."

"Forest fell off a cliff?" I frowned at Sharly. "That doesn't sound like Forest, does it? I was on your trail for days. Didn't see any buzzards overhead that always indicate something like that."

"Monty saw it happen." Mia approached the fire and picked up the container from the coals. Annette was visibly protesting as her niece touched what I'd touched, but gave up when Mia ignored her. "God sent us Monty. He's been helping us, even scouting ahead some."

"A real godsend, huh?" But I was watching Sharly's downcast face, her eyes on the ground. Tension permeated this camp. Clearly, Sharly had her doubts about Forest's accident. Mia seemed to think Monty was a blessing from above. And Annette was torn between shooting me and probably keeping Sharly from running back down the trail in search of her husband. Then I held out my hand to the new face. "So, you're Monty, huh?"

"That's right." He grinned with too much enthusiasm for such a somber moment.

Rather than drag out a confrontation, I gripped his hand firmly as we shook, then pulled him into a left-handed punch to his jaw that rocked him on his heels. He didn't go down since I still held his hand, but he was stunned enough for me to draw the small revolver from his pocket and take a hunting blade from his belt.

I tossed the revolver to Mia for safekeeping and threw the knife into the fire. Only then did I release his hand. As he scampered away, I kicked him in the seat of his pants to send him sprawling in the dirt at Annette's feet.

"Levi!" Annette shouted, and set a protective hand on Monty's head.

"Don't you Levi me!" I boomed back, hearing my father's authority in my own voice. "Shame on all of you for allowing a coward and a killer to travel with you! He shows up and Forest goes missing? What's wrong with you, Mom? You haven't even sent word back to me, left me a message, or anything in days. Just running away, are you? Is that all you can do? And you talk about me endangering everyone! You lost a horse in the desert and you almost died before reaching Oatman. It's time this family squared things away!"

"You came through Oatman?" Monty asked as he stood up, rubbing his jaw. He shook off Annette's touch, as his true character began to reveal itself.

"That's right. I came through Oatman! Where you shot Brian Steelman and left him for dead—because he knew you were a cutthroat and a predator after the women here!"

"Levi!" Annette gasped. "How dare you accuse him of that!"

"Did he really kill Forest?" Sharly asked me, then stood with Natasha in her arms to face the devil himself. "Did you kill Forest, or did he really fall off a cliff?"

"No, I swear it." He cast me a look like he feared me now, which was wise for him. But his evil didn't stop. "He really went over that cliff, tripped on a rock or something.

I tried to grab him. He died bravely, though, just like I said. Didn't scream or anything."

"He's lying." I sighed and rooted through Annette's pack for dried fruit. My teeth felt numb, I was so hungry. "That's not what happened to Forest. Go ahead, Monty, tell them. Tell his wife what you did to him."

I stuffed my mouth with dried banana chips and apricots—a feast! Monty stammered a few words, repeating what he'd said already, when suddenly a gunshot made us all jump. Mia held the smoking revolver, tears in her eyes. Monty fell over clutching his stomach.

To this day, I think back to when I'd tossed that revolver to her. Wanting my own hands free to deal with Monty, I had put it into her hands, rather than trust Annette or Sharly with a loaded weapon under the tension. But it had been Mia who hadn't waited for an explanation. It seemed she'd begun to care for the criminal in those few days, his charm certainly giving her false hopes for closeness. Now that his sin was exposed, she was unwilling to be merciful.

Before she could fire again, I grabbed the gun from her hands and emptied the shells onto the ground. Annette was kneeling over the dying man when I reached him. He was gasping his last breath, staring at the sky with seconds left, the bullet having punctured his diaphragm.

A moment later, he was still, and I brushed his eyes closed with my fingertips.

"He lied to us!" Mia's voice was high, defensive and nervous at the same time. "He killed Forest. You said, Levi!"

My ruse to intimidate and provoke Monty had actually incited Mia, leading to Monty's death. I was as much to blame as she was. A man was dead because of me. Blood was on my hands, and I wanted to vomit.

"Can you get my shovel?" I asked Annette softly. "I'll bury him in a minute."

She didn't respond. Tears filled her eyes. One of her hands still hovered over the dead man's bloody torso. In her mind, I guessed she saw only how our trip was unraveling in death and bloodshed.

I stood and took Mia by the hand and led her out of the camp.

"What are you doing?" She struggled uselessly against me, her weeping turning to choking sobs. Though she was a tough young woman, and a Caspertein through and through, I was two decades older than she was, and heavier and stronger. After a few steps, she stopped resisting and allowed me to lead her.

Fifty yards from camp where no one could hear us, where the ground rose to a natural pillar of rock, I drew Mia into a fierce embrace and held her as she fought me. My reaction to her killing a man—justifiably so in her mind—surely made no sense yet, but I chose this method to tell her the full story.

"Monty was a bad man," I began, squeezing her so tightly that I felt her exhale. "And he planned wicked things for you and Sharly, probably after he killed Mom and Natasha. But back in Peach Springs, I followed a trail into a canyon . . ."

As I spoke, she resisted me less, and her small fists closed against my torso. Her sobs turned into a wail against my chest when she heard that Forest was still alive, that she'd killed Monty before the man could confess his other crimes or intentions.

"Now, this is what's going to happen." I released her from my embrace to hold her by her shoulders. Her tears had mixed with the red dust on her cheeks to look like a smear of paint on this bloody morning. "Forest and some other friends of mine will be joining us in two days. Killing, even for this, is not our way. Tell me you understand that."

"I know." She didn't wipe her eyes. "I just wanted him to pay. He said things to me. Private things. I believed him. I just . . ."

"We don't kill people, Mia. For any reason."

"I know." She took a deep breath, but her hands continued to shake. "I can't believe this. It was in my hands, and I just . . . What should I do?"

"Well, there's nothing to do about Monty. And out here, there's no law but the law we hold ourselves to."

"But I killed a man I thought was a murderer."

I nodded and prayed for the right words. Monty's final fate by God's hand hadn't been given to me, and I certainly had no authority to judge my cousin's future.

"Are you really pregnant? Do you know for sure yet?"

"Yeah. For sure."

"Then, you'll be a mother in a few months. Take today to pray and wrestle out with God about what's happened, why you did what you did. Even if you thought Monty killed Forest, it must be dealt with before the throne of heaven."

"I'm a . . . *killer!*" she blinked fresh tears away, and I saw the terror in her eyes. "My life—as long as I live and afterward—will always be one of shame."

"Or of motherhood," I reminded. "Does Mom know yet?"

"I didn't have the nerve to tell her after we left you at Eagle Mountain. I don't deserve to be a mother now."

"Sin isn't something we erase. There are consequences, but sin isn't something we cover up, either." I thought of my own transgressions, and where I'd found relief. "Christ calls us to believe in His gift for us. He's the only one who can cleanse us from shame and guilt. We're inspired to come to a place of repentance and change. He restores us as sons or daughters. This day isn't your legacy, Mia Trimble. God will take you further. It's not His will to leave you in shame. Leave your shame where He's already done the work—at the cross."

She took a deep breath and wiped her nose.

"When did you become so wise, Cuz?"

"I've made a lot of blunders, but I try to learn from them. Besides, we both know Dad never stopped teaching us these things."

"Aunt Annette is watching us."

"It's to be expected. There's still gunsmoke in the air."

"Right."

"Stay here for as long as you need to. Talk to God. And listen to Him. I'm going to bury Monty."

But Monty's body would have to wait a few more minutes. Annette stood bewildered as I passed by her and knelt in front of where Sharly sat. In the two weeks since I'd seen her, she'd ceased to care for herself, it seemed. Her blond curls were tangled and greasy-looking. The clothes she'd worn and cared for since Idaho were torn and stained, and they'd not been patched or washed. Natasha was filthy, her face crusted with dust, and her fingernails too long and dirty. Mother and daughter looked up at me with sadness and confusion.

"Sharly, are you listening to me?"

"I'm not sorry she killed him. You can't ask me to be sorry she killed him, Levi!"

"Well, that's between you and God. I found Forest almost two days ago. He'd been sold into slavery, but I was able to free him. He's behind us a little ways. They'll probably catch up with us by tomorrow night."

"What?" She lifted her chin. "He's alive?"

"Yes, he's fine. Natasha here could use some attention, before Forest sees his daughter like this. And maybe we could clean ourselves up some, too? Forest will be bringing other company as well. Do you hear me?"

"But Mia—she shot Monty."

"Yes, she did. Maybe when the time is right, you can help her heal from that. Monty didn't kill your husband after all. Now, can you pull yourself together, clean up, and care for Natasha?"

"Yeah, but we're low on water."

"I'll take care of that. Use what you have."

Annette still hadn't moved, so I went ahead and fetched the entrenching shovel with the folding head. I found Monty's few belongings and wrapped his bloody corpse in a pair of pants and a shirt from his pack. Only then did I pick him up—as light as the young man had been—and carried him one hundred yards east to the shadow of a boulder. The parched soil wasn't packed there, and I dug the grave deep enough to keep the coyotes away. Before dragging Monty into the hole, I took his boots off him, which were new enough to suggest to me that he'd stolen them. His feet were about the same size as the women's feet, but I thought of Vorca, who had worn-out, patched boots, probably taken from one of the dead in Cadiz.

With the body covered, I stood there for a moment. My father and I had buried others in San Diego, but in recent years, they'd been Christians mostly, and their passing had been a matter of rejoicing and even comfort. But I'd seen no evidence that Monty was a man of God, nor had he been given the gospel message, at least by me, before Mia had shot him. So this burial was one of mourning, a reminder of the fate of wicked people.

"Let's move camp into the shade of that rimrock," I instructed Annette back in camp. "It'll protect us from the heat of the day while we wait through tomorrow for Forest and the others."

"What others?"

"More people to add to the Caspertein clan." I chuckled, though her face remained somber. "God just keeps bringing them to us, so I guess we just keep taking them in, right?"

She turned away without answering and began to pack their belongings. The horse groaned as his back was loaded once again.

Chapter Sixteen

Using my binoculars from atop a bluff, I studied the landscape to the southwest. It was still a little early to get a visual on Alice and the others, but I was hopeful.

With the empty canteens around my neck, I swung the field glasses to the north, peering at a shadowed gorge where I'd seen small birds darting in and out. Surely, it was a water source and possibly a little vegetation. It seemed it hadn't been a waste bringing the containers with me up to the bluff.

Behind the rimrock, I found a dry creek bed bordered by short cliffs where I climbed down to reach a spring and a sliver of meadow. I startled a jackrabbit and it disappeared down a hole. Birds chirped as I invaded their secret habitat. The water bubbled from deep underground, ran for only twenty yards, then trickled back into the earth.

I sat on a rock and sipped the cool water. The jackrabbit peeked his head out of the hole and sniffed at me, probably the first human he'd ever crossed. The hidden paradise was a sanctuary for me for an hour as I prayed—confessing my sinful thoughts and selfishness, and seeking the Lord to point my way toward His path even more. My attitude regarding Annette had been one of rebuke. Sure, she'd allowed herself to become undisciplined as a leader, and it had nearly cost her life and the safety of the others. But perhaps I'd been too firm with her.

Smiling as I filled the water containers, I anticipated Alice's arrival, as well as seeing Caleb's perpetual smile and fascination with life. Vorca would be a most welcome spirit among us, hopefully setting an example of service and responsibility for the other women. We all needed to do our parts.

Above, at the rimrock, I found the new camp taking shape. Annette avoided eye contact with me, but she took the water I brought her. The horse gladly accepted two handfuls of grass I'd brought from the paradise, and a gallon of water, then I returned to the spring. But this time, I'd come for more than just water. I stretched out on the grass where a single dandelion grew, and I slept. Around midday, the sun reached the spring and grass where I lay, but all I did was roll over and fall back to sleep, recovering lost hours from hard travel and toil that no one else could do.

I returned to camp before sundown. Annette was standing watch, but when she saw me, she immediately turned to see to the fire. Mia ran down the slope a short distance to meet me, a sheepish smile on her face. She took several containers from my shoulders to help with the final delivery.

"We thought you'd continued without us, you were gone so long," she said jokingly. "Did you see any game?"

"Nothing that would feed us all." I kept my two canteens on my belt and gave the rest to Sharly and Annette at the small fire. The horse took more water and grass, but now I was thinking about the arrival of our friends and their animals. "How are the food stores?"

Mia inventoried their packs aloud as Annette continued to cook. We were only halfway to Cameron, and I knew Alice and the others were low on food. Forest would have to take the .22 and scout far and wide for game in that lonely wilderness. I was hopeful my jackrabbit friend in the gorge wouldn't need to go into the stew pot. We needed a small deer at best, or a couple of dogs, at worst. But meat was meat when you were starving, though we weren't to the point of eating desert lizards yet, in my opinion.

That night, when I sensed everyone was about to bed down without prayer or chorus or reading, I stood over the fire and adjusted my rifle over my shoulder.

"That's the first thing I've had in weeks that I can call a real dinner. Thank you." It had been a delicious pot of wild cabbage, grouse meat, and corn tortillas. "Mom, could I have a word?"

Without waiting for her to respond, I walked out of camp toward Monty's grave. When I reached the boulder, I leaned against it and crossed my arms. Annette didn't leave camp for five minutes, maybe out of protest, but she finally came. Since I'd been back, she'd been hard to read, but the sourness between us had to be confronted before the night passed. Regardless of my list of complaints about her leadership in my absence, now was a time of reconciliation, especially before the others joined our party.

"Thanks for coming down." I watched her body language—avoidance, loneliness, guilt. "I wanted to talk to you alone. It's been a tough few weeks on everyone. How're you holding up?"

"How do I look like I'm holding up, Levi?"

"You probably look better than I do." I chuckled. "Taking this rest will be good for all of us."

"Yeah, I guess so."

"Remember when Dad was dying, you insisted on being at his side, regardless of the danger of contracting the Meridia Virus?"

"I'll never forget it."

"That's what came over me at Eagle Mountain. I just had to help that baby. I took precautions, but I knew right away it was reckless. I should've waited for your guidance to approach the whole issue the right way—once I discovered the virus was all over town. I'm sorry. I learned from it. Will you forgive me?"

"Forgive you?" She scoffed, and I saw her guard evaporate. "I'm the one who's been in a foul mood since that day. I abandoned my son with a baby, killed a horse crossing that desert, and left Forest for dead when he was really alive. I just got so focused on Colorado, you know? And I was mad at you for putting me in that position to lead without you. You're a natural, Levi, like your father. People follow you because they know you're safe, and they know they're safe following you. It's not like that for the rest of us. Look at the mess I've made of things."

"We can afford to lose a few animals. Everyone's still alive. Well, Monty excluded. He reaped what life he lived, but that's not on you."

"Mia's taking it better than I thought. Whatever you said to her right after the shooting must've been something important. Again, just like your father."

"She has a few burdens to carry." I gazed at the first visible stars. "She'll need you a lot in the months to come. We all will."

"I can mother these kids just fine, Levi. If you lead us. We're still trying to beat the snow, right?"

"Right." I thought of Jenna, still months of travel away from me. The snow would stop a family caravan from traveling, but not me. I wouldn't wait for spring to continue to New York. "Our party's larger, but with pack animals, we'll keep a healthy pace. We picked up two of those burros in Oatman. They eat less but carry the same load as the riding horses. Once we get out of this desert, travel will be different, though still a strain. Water and game should be more plentiful, but so will people."

For a moment, we stood quiet. The renewed peace between us was already tangible. She placed her back to the boulder next to me, and I relaxed my arm as she hooked hers around my elbow.

"So, tell me who to expect in this second wave of Casperteins you've picked up. You haven't made me a mother-in-law yet, I hope."

"Not yet, Mom. Still waiting on the Lord for that one." I felt my face warm at the mention of romance. There'd been a couple young women over the years who'd caught my eye, but nothing had lasted. We Casperteins were a high-profile family, and few could handle the pressures of leadership and responsibility that seemed my family's calling. "Well, there's a woman named Alice. You could call her Alice the Amazon, I suppose."

"An Amazon?"

"About your age. She's from Eagle Mountain, too. Got shot there. I had to amputate her arm at the elbow, but she handled it well."

"And without an arm, you still consider her an Amazon? You mean like a warrior?"

"Oh, you'll see. Then there's Caleb, the baby."

"Caleb?"

"I named him."

"It's a good name."

"He never cries or complains. It's amazing. I like to think he'll follow in the footsteps of us Casperteins."

"Caleb Caspertein." She nudged me. "Has a ring to it. Your first son, huh? And who else?"

"Vorca, Caleb's nurse. This short lady doesn't speak English, but she's sort of a medicine woman, cook, and horse whisperer all in one."

"Vorca. Does she speak another language?"

"Well, I've never heard her speak. And when I try to talk to her, she acts like she doesn't hear me. She sort of listens to Alice, though, so we function somehow." I turned sharply toward her. "Oh! And Forest is a believer now!"

"Forest is?"

"It was about the first thing he had to say when I freed him from the Peach Springs cave."

"Wow. So, all these people aren't just traveling with us. God is really in this."

"Definitely. He's reaching them through us." I grit my teeth and winced. "The Brogdons aren't letting up, though. At least a week ago they hadn't. I think they lost their vehicles crossing the dessert, but there are other highways they could take to try to catch up to us. They're out for blood, it seems."

"It's almost supernatural, their hatred and hunt for us."

"Yeah." I figured she'd understand more after Mia told her what Kip Brogdon had done to her—and why he wanted her back—but Mia would have to tell her about that. "This valley is easy to miss. In the morning, I'll head out to intercept Alice and the others to bring them back here. After a good night's rest, we'll leave the next morning. We're a good forty miles west of Cameron still."

I told her about the hidden gorge where they could find water. We watched more stars come out and identified a few, which my father had taught us. Then, arm in arm, we returned to camp, and I praised God that we were a happy family once again.

The next evening, I escorted Alice, Forest, Vorca, and Caleb into camp against the rimrock. Though everyone was tired to the bone, Forest still found the energy to run the last few yards into Sharly's arms. The young mother had somehow washed her hair, anticipating her husband's return.

Annette greeted Alice with a canteen of cold water, and since the two ladies were nearly the same age, I hoped they would become friends. Alice had become tough and warrior-like, and Annette still retained some of the grace from her modeling days, but I believed God would help them find some commonalities.

Mia went immediately to Vorca, taking the burros as the woman eased the baby and pack to the ground. Vorca looked more weary than I'd seen her before. As soon as Caleb was off her back, the young Indian woman sat on the rocky ground and checked the soles of her boots. No doubt her feet were in pain. Not only was she hefty for her height, the ground that day had been especially scorching hot from the sun, and her soles had worn thin.

Before Vorca could know what was happening, I unlaced her boots and tugged them off, along with her socks, to check her chubby feet for damage. There were a couple heat blisters under the toes, but I could see nothing serious. For once, I had this woman in a position where I could serve her. Annette had extra water already in camp for the additional pack animals. I poured one bottle over Vorca's feet, rubbing them gently. When I looked up at her face, she had tears in her eyes, but her mouth was in a wide grin. She was wiggling her toes as I left her with Monty's boots. A quick foot rub was the least I could do for the woman who'd been as much a part of the family as me or Alice, since leaving Cadiz.

That night, over cabbage and mashed beans, Forest recounted his story of survival in the slave cave, including his profession of faith in Jesus Christ. Alice shed tears as she spoke of losing her husband in Eagle Mountain, and her arm later that night. But it was Caleb who stole the show with his squirming, jabbering, and smiling antics, rejuvenating us all with youthfulness we no longer felt. He seemed to know he was the center of attention and took full advantage of it. It felt good to laugh again.

The next day, we were two hours into our journey, the beasts and humans laden with water and packs, when Forest held up a trophy from his morning hunt. He stood on a high rock above our path. It looked like a small coyote, or maybe a wild Spaniel dog by the color, so I couldn't help but joke about it.

"Excellent!" I yelled at him from the middle of our caravan. "We'll have gopher meat for dinner!"

"It's not a gopher!" Forest eyed his trophy twice. "It's not!"

"Prairie dog stew!" Mia whooped.

"Why don't you leave the desert rodents alone, honey?" Sharly said, unable to resist the banter.

Ten miles from Cameron, we made camp. The coyote made a delicious feast. Using a poncho and a few sticks, I placed the remainder of the strips of meat into a makeshift smokehouse. Drying by smoke overnight, the meat would be preserved for a couple more days without spoiling. Not that anyone wanted to eat coyote for a few more days, but it was seasoned by Vorca and smoked with hard wood, so it was more than edible. And it was nutritious.

The next morning, while the camp was being packed up, Forest scouted the trail ahead and I hiked a ridge south of us. This close to another town, we intended to stay together, for protection as well as a show of strength. We needed to be vigilant of anyone around us.

From the ridge, I looked toward the growing morning sunlight. Cameron wasn't in sight, but at least two roads were visible ahead and north of us. They were empty, and oddly, I saw no one guarding them. At least at the moment, no one seemed to be traveling in our direction from the town, either.

Through my binoculars I scoped our backtrail to the west. It seemed clear, and I started to leave the ridge, when something registered late in my brain. I peered west again. What was that dot? A shadowy tree perhaps? An oddly shaped rock? No, it was moving. It was larger than a dog, but too thin to be a horse. A person all alone out there? No, whoever it was had to be with a larger party.

I wouldn't have been so concerned, except the person on our backtrail was following our exact tracks. We were being followed on foot by someone, but who? The immediate answer that came to me was that it was Brian Steelman from Oatman, but his leg wound was probably still healing in the hotel. Besides, he would've had a burro to ride and carry his supplies, if he'd decided to come east again.

As we'd traveled, I may have underestimated the impact we'd had on those we crossed. Someone could've been trailing us as far back as Aporax. Or was it an enemy from Palm Springs? Mia and I had left quickly, leaving ruthless people in our wake. Eagle Mountain had seemed like a dead community, but Caleb and Alice had escaped alive, though not completely unscathed. Perhaps this was another survivor. A fighter from Cadiz was possible, where Alice and I had spent the night and given hope to many in the midst of a hopeless conflict.

Below me, Annette shouted for the order to march, and I waved at her to lead away. But Alice was already in the front by twenty yards. Then came Annette, Vorca with the three livestock, and Sharly and Mia in the rear. Forest, far ahead, carried his .22. Annette carried the other bullpup on a sling, and Mia had the shotgun. Caleb waved his arms at the horses, while he rocked to Vorca's gait, and Natasha had bonded with one of the burros enough to speak sweetly to the sweaty animal. We were a battle-weary party who'd survived a dozen threats, and we were only a few weeks into our journey.

I chose to hike south on the ridge, rather than join my family. The lone pilgrim on our trail didn't worry me as much as it made me curious. In an age of hostility, I fought with my flesh to show hospitality, instead. Christ had called His people to be neighborly, not just to whom we chose, but to all who needed to be treated as such. Many, many miles ago, I'd given up trying to keep the Caspertein travelers totally isolated from the rest of the world. God knew Jenna Dowler's status of persecution in the east, and I prayed I would reach her eventually. But I couldn't ignore the needs of others along the way. Perhaps I was more wary now, and maybe not as naive as when we'd started out, about what might await us along the road. With God's wisdom, I would remain open to aiding those who had need of help.

When next I spotted the lone traveler, he was on his hands and knees. He was close enough now to identify through field glasses, but not to speak to just yet. The person I saw made me recoil and search the plain for more danger. *It wasn't possible!* Not here. Not now, when my family was still learning to work together and travel in peace!

It was Kip Brogdon.

I swung my bullpup to my shoulder and aimed to the south, west, and north. Was I being set up? My heart pounded as I waited for a sniper bullet to slam into my body. But no bullets flew at me.

Kip Brogdon climbed to his feet again and continued following my family's tracks. He appeared to be injured, or maybe dehydrated. Both were possibilities in that desert. He'd never catch up to the Caspertein convoy at his pace and condition. He had no pack on his back, no gun sling, no gear—only a canteen on his belt.

He was ten yards away when I stepped out from the rocks. I did my best to watch him as well as keep an eye out for the glint of reflection off a rifle scope from an elevated height somewhere around me.

Kip stopped and swayed on his feet. He lifted a hand.

"Stay back, Levi." He was panting, and his words were slurred—a symptom of a swelled tongue from dehydration, rather than drunkenness. The canteen on his belt was evidently empty. A man needed twenty liters of water a day in that heat. His container was only two liters. "I have the virus."

I continued to aim my rifle at him. His wasn't a family I trusted or favored, but his skin did look wrong—pale rather than burnt.

He fell to his knees.

"Where's your dad, Kip?" I turned my head in all directions, but there was no one that I could see. "Huh? Where's General Brogdon?"

"Decimated . . . in Cadiz. He retreated to try another route." His eyes drifted closed. "Our bio-weapon container broke open. Dad returned to Coronado for reinforcements."

I crouched low to make a smaller target for any ambushers.

"Where are your men? You had a few last time we talked, remember that? You aimed a gun at an infant and held a blade on a friend of mine! Where are your men, Kip?"

"Dead. All dead. A faster strain of Meridia. Thought I was in the clear. Got it from one of my men. I knew . . ."

After all my neighborly thinking and designs for hospitality, I couldn't yet run to this enemy's side. *He had raped Mia!* He had hunted us with his father, even murdered little Jose Hernandez on the bridge in San Diego. Aporax refugees had been gunned down by this man, and in Eagle Mountain, an entire town had been infected. And those were just the atrocities I knew about.

"Yeah? What do you know, Kip Brogdon?"

"I knew . . . you would help me if I found you."

"Help you?" I scoffed through clenched teeth. God certainly knew how to show me exactly where my flesh was still a problem in my walk with Him. "There's no antidote for whatever Meridia Virus strain you've got?"

"No. Not antidote. Other help."

"Other help?" I shook my head and checked the wind direction. The Meridia Virus was transmitted by contact with bodily fluids, but I wasn't taking any chances. "Toss me your canteen. I'll pour some of my water into your canteen, but if you have the virus, you're a dead man walking, Kip. Fluids will only prolong the inevitable."

"I don't want to die." He weakly tossed his bottle to me. It tumbled across the sand. "You can help me, and you know it. Don't deny me, Levi Caspertein. You can't. You're a Christian. Please, help me. . ."

From my day pack, I drew out a pair of socks to use as mittens and picked up his canteen. Wiping it thoroughly, I unscrewed the lid. Careful not to touch openings, I poured a few cups into his bottle and threw it in front of him.

"The only help I have for you is the gospel of Jesus Christ, Kip Brogdon."

"Yeah, that." He fumbled with the canteen lid. "You gotta tell me, Levi. Your dad would have. He tried many times, even before he died, but I wouldn't listen. I don't wanna go to hell."

He hung his head and sobbed. *This monster was actually crying!*

"When did you talk to my dad before he died?"

But the answer came to me all at once, and I wanted to pull the trigger on him right then. I would put him to sleep and drag him into the rocks. He was done. The birds and coyotes could clean his bones. No one would know or care.

The evidence had been in front of me for weeks. Since Pan-Day, the Meridia Virus had had no resurgence. Suddenly, my father had become infected, then the virus was being spread by the Pacific States? Dad hadn't stumbled upon refugees with the virus. *The Brogdons had assassinated him!*

"You killed my dad." I stood and took a few steps away. *How could God want this?* A cold-blooded, mass murderer didn't get the gospel for free. He had to pay! "No. No forgiveness for you, Kip Brogdon!"

Again, I aimed my rifle at him, now at his face. At that close range, the impact might've killed him, even with a gel-tranq. I squeezed my eyes shut, blinking away sweat. No, they were tears.

Lowering the rifle, I shouted incoherently and kicked at the ground, sending dust and rocks flying yards away.

"How can you be sorry now?" I yelled, my voice echoing off the rocks and canyons. "There's no God for animals like you! No Savior!"

I crumbled in the dirt, weeping, my own words like poison to my ears. Who was I to condemn a man—any man—to eternity without the simple truth of the cross? Was the gospel not for the broken, the fearful, the despised? Was I really any better of a man than Kip Brogdon?

"Please, Levi . . ." He wailed a dying man's wail, something from deep in his soul, the torments of guilt from a lifetime of wickedness and victimizing. "Don't leave me. You're my only hope. No one else . . . Tell me, and let me die. Just tell me what to do. Please."

"God!" I screamed, punching the ground. "How could You? This isn't fair! Not this man! *Not this man!*"

But there was no voice from heaven, no vision to guide me or confirm my selfish words. Only the morning breeze. Dust settled where my fist had disturbed it and the sand soaked up my tears. The world didn't care.

My objections were fruitless. The life in me, the undeserving life I'd been given by God, spoke to me as loud as thunder. As powerful of a man as I was, I was no match for the Holy Spirit as He touched my heart, broke my resolve, and whispered to me of my own hopelessness without God.

Broken, I crawled over to Kip Brogdon and sat cross-legged an arm's length in front of him.

Chapter Seventeen

"We're a sad lot, you and I," I said to Kip Brogdon as he sat slowly dying of the Meridia Virus. The minutes ticked by, and my family traveled farther away from me, but this man was my burden at the moment. It would've been unbearable to my soul to leave him without sharing the gospel message, for which he begged.

"Just tell me, Levi. Is there any hope?" Still, he wept, hands in the dust, head down. "Is there anything that can be done for me? I can't die like this."

"We all die. But God's Word says we don't have to die estranged from Him." I took off my day pack, then found and opened my pocket Bible. Before me was just a man. No longer was he my enemy, but a lost soul. While he pleaded for life, I couldn't give him death.

Verse after verse, I read and explained. When I asked periodically if he understood, he said he did. Even then, he didn't lift his head. I continued. The deep wounds done to my family by this man were no longer as significant as the glory God would receive by him coming to the cross.

"Today, you must decide if you will be your own master, or if you'll trust God to cleanse you from your sins. Christ Jesus died for you, knowing the sins you would commit, and He offers you life eternal right now. If you repent from your sins and unbelief, and place your trust in His saving hand, you will die physically only, knowing He will receive you as His child. The message is the same for us all. The things we do may differ in this life, but we are all born cursed, and our nature itself needs to be regenerated by God Himself. By believing, He will resurrect you to be with Him."

"I believe." He nodded. "I'm scum."

"Do you deserve the gift He offers you?"

"No." He moved his head slightly from side to side. "Not even a little. I hated Christians. I deserve nothing good. The things I've done . . ."

"Despise all of that horror, Kip. Look only to Jesus now."

"Yes, I have no one else."

"Will you turn from your ways and follow in Jesus Christ's way?"

"As long as I live. I don't know a lot about His way, though." He lifted his head and I saw him take a breath. His bloodshot eyes met mine for the first time. "He's forgiven me. I know it, because you read it to me. I can die now. You didn't have to tell me the truth, Levi. You could've let me die without knowing all those things about God. I wouldn't have had the opportunity to believe, but you showed me mercy."

"Believe me, Kip, I was tempted to walk away, because I'm still just a man whom God is working on."

"This is God's justice, I guess. I'm dying by what I used to kill others."

"We reap what we sow. Always."

"I accept it. It's okay now." He lifted a hand and touched his chest. "He's given me peace. Do you think I'll see any of the people I killed in heaven?"

"It's probable." I thought of my own father. "But they'll just praise God that His truth broke through your hate and stubbornness. God will receive the glory."

"Not everyone would be so forgiving if I stayed on earth. Mia—"

"Mia's moved on. That's the past."

Telling him about her pregnancy would've placed undue weight upon his new heart, so I held my tongue."

"Okay." He drank a little water. "What now?"

"You see that hill with the rimrock around its base?"

"Yeah, I see it."

"Circle it to the right, along the base, and you'll find a creek and a little grass. It's the only water within miles of us. I can't carry you, and you're in no shape to travel farther. You can crawl that far, if you can't walk. It'll be a nice place to die. We're a little light on hospice care out here."

"Thank you, Levi. It sounds perfect. Water and grass."

"I'm glad you came to God, Kip," I said. And I meant it sincerely.

Before I left him, I tucked his hatchet into his own belt. It was his, and even if he were close to death, I thought maybe he could use it to dig at the ground or fend off coyotes if they crept near. In a perfect world, I would've left him with a Bible, but I had none to spare. He was in God's hands now.

I caught up with my family two miles before entering Cameron, Arizona. The town had been founded on the Navajo Indian Reservation, but there was no sign of Native Americans as we walked that morning down the center of the bustling town. Hundreds of people drifted up and down the street, which was choked by scrap-board trader booths. Many cast us curious glances, or maybe they were envying our pack animals, but we kept moving until we reached an open stretch of the wind-swept street and stopped at the curb.

"Tour down the Little Colorado River Gorge!" a man yelled from the back of a wagon as it rumbled past. He had a cardboard bullhorn, and like many men, he carried a rifle across his back. Others had semi-automatic sidearms on their belts. "We leave in ten minutes!"

"Gun show!" another called from across the street "Shoot your best and pass the test. Get your tickets here!"

A group of prostitutes welcomed other new arrivals into town, arrivals from the east. Two of the women called to me and blew me kisses. Alice stepped protectively close to me and planted her steel staff firmly on the pavement. The prostitutes understood the message, and turned their advances elsewhere.

"Oh, look, honey!" Sharly tugged on Forest's arm. He appeared as unsettled by the festive atmosphere as I felt. "They have kids' clothes! Natalie's already bursting at her seams. Caleb will need new clothes soon, too."

I followed Annette's eyes to a storefront that advertised spices, and Mia gestured at a booth that sold ammunition, which we could use for hunting, especially for her bird gun. They all looked to me for direction.

"This place is full of cutthroats," I said, not caring who of the townspeople heard me as they wandered past. "Nobody go anywhere alone. Don't trade away anything we need for the journey. We leave at noon."

It seemed understood that Alice and I would remain with the horses, along with Vorca, who tethered the horses individually to three different rusted handicapped parking signs. Before I could stop her, Vorca, with Caleb still on her back, marched away out of sight in the crowd behind several booths.

"Maybe she's gone to change Caleb," I said.

"You want me to go with her?" Alice asked like the lieutenant she'd become at my side.

"Yeah, and keep an eye out for a horse stable. We can't be the only pack train in town."

Annette and Mia had already headed toward the spice shop, with orders from Forest to keep an eye out for mustard seeds. Forest and Sharly had entered the store that advertised kids' clothing, among other essentials. I didn't see anything of interest until I spotted a sign that boasted electronics. Radios, walkie-talkies, and an assortment of digital music players were inventoried on a large chalkboard. A boy walked by me carrying scavenged boards and nails for sale to set up new booths. It had become a boom town.

"Hey, kid," I called. "Can you see if the clerk of that electronics store will come see me? I can't leave my horses."

"What's in it for me?" he asked.

"What do you want?"

He craned his neck as he looked over our gear, then settled his eyes on my gun vest.

"Three shells."

"Four," I raised, since I had ammo to spare. "Two as you go, and two more when you bring him back."

He held out his palm, and I gave him two regular .308 rounds. When he scampered off, I turned around to see three men smoking rolled cigarettes while eyeing our gear. Most of the menfolk in town wore beards like me, and jeans and flannel shirts, or army surplus jackets, regardless of the growing heat. And all men and women carried water containers with them—bottles, canteens, and rifles.

"You come from the west?" one of the observers asked. "Everyone is trying to go there. Why you leaving?"

"I'm joining up with family," I said, tucking my thumb under the sling of my rifle. In a breath, I could swing it into action. "You boys heading to California?"

"We hear it's settled along the coast, organized-like," one man with yellow teeth said. "Do the Pacific States really have an army?"

"Yep, and they're coming this way." This made them raise their eyebrows, so I kept talking. "President Criswell is wiping out anyone who doesn't submit and give them all their gear. Cadiz just fought a battle with them. It got ugly. I met one of the survivors yesterday."

"Cadiz?" Another man spit on the ground. He had greasy hair and acne. "I was gonna go through there along the rail line. Rumor is they have water to cross the Mojave."

"I'd choose another route," I said, "but maybe they'll share their water if you have something to trade.

Ammunition will be a big sell to them, after all the fighting they've been doing."

"So, you don't recommend meeting up with the Pacific States government?" another asked. He had old food stains on his shirt front.

"President Criswell and General Brogdon are interested in control. They confiscate whatever they want, and they have the power to do it with their thousands of troops. But they have a weakness."

"What is it?" They all leaned in closer.

"Greed. The more they take from settlers and travelers, the more enemies they make. I guess that's why a revolt is being organized to set up an honest and just government, something that a citizen can count on in a time of crisis."

"A revolt?"

"You guys have families?" I asked.

"We all do."

"West of Palm Springs, up there in the mountains, you'll find a family called the Mallingers. They'll see that you get established in a good settlement and get started with the new government about to be set up. The Pacific States have had their day. People are tired of the killing and the conditions. They're done hiding."

"I'd fight for a cause." The stained teeth one nodded. "Thanks, stranger."

They wandered off, considering my words. I hoped I'd sent Sebastian Mallinger and the Kindred more family men to back their efforts. If anything, in the bazaar that the town of Cameron had become, rumors would prevail and the whole town would know what the west really held—danger, possible revolt, and warfare, with the option of freedom if they worked with the mountain family of Mallingers.

"You the guy who wants to see me?" a balding clerk asked. He wore glasses and a baseball cap turned backwards. His apron bore the remnants of charcoal and glue.

"Tell me about your walkie-talkies." I paid the boy who'd brought the clerk over.

"Line of sight and range of about five miles. Maybe more on a good day. For the right price, I'll throw in the headsets. They mean nothing to me if I sell the communication sets."

"You have two?"

"Yep. That's all I could fix with the solar recharger so far. I guess I could include two extra batteries, too. The ones in them now should last a year or two on trickle-charge every day the sun is out. Even on a cloudy day, keep the solar patches aimed toward the sky, like on your shoulder."

"So what does an electrician want that a drifter like me might have?"

"I don't do guns." He walked amongst the horses and opened a pack, like it was common practice to search through another's items for something worthy of trade. "Got any fruit?"

"Just the tail-end of some dried assortment."

When he reached one horse where my pack was strapped, he studied my short crossbow, then set it aside. He unpacked my parachute cord, aluminum cutlery, extra pants, and a water filter.

"You really don't have anything. Even if you did, dust has caked everything you have."

"I just crossed the Mojave. How about the riding horse?"

"Seriously?" He repositioned his glasses and checked the beast's hooves like he knew what to look for. "This is a good horse. A little worn out, but nothing a little grazing won't cure."

"That's true."

He returned to stand in front of me.

"Well, now we've found something I want from you, but the horse is worth far more than the radios."

"You're an honest man," I said. "What else do you have for a traveler?"

"Hmmm. You hunt, too?"

"Yeah, all the time."

"I have a wind-direction indicator for shootists. It's digital, but it runs off its own charge like a windmill. And I'll throw in a couple waterproof watches, like the one you're wearing. And two flashlights with rechargeable batteries."

"How do I recharge?"

"Same as the comm sets. I make everything interchangeable these days."

"You've got yourself a deal, electrician." I offered my hand.

"Okay, traveler." He smiled and shook my hand. "I'll get your stuff and show you how to use it all."

Ten minutes later, I gave him the riding horse from Aporax, and he gave me my electronics, the most valuable being the two-way radios. Forest would appreciate the wind indicator for shooting game, and Alice and Sharly would like the watches. Everything seemed to be coming together for the remainder of our journey.

"Levi!" Annette called with a strained, high-pitched voice. "They have Vorca!"

Annette and Mia emerged from the crowd. Mia held her shotgun across her chest and Annette showed panic on her face. They'd known Vorca only a couple days, but family was family. And Vorca had Caleb.

"Which way?" I shoved my electronics into one of the burro packs. "Where is she?"

"Behind the saloon, there!"

"Stay with the animals!" I started away, then turned back. "Don't leave the burros!"

I pushed through buyers, sellers, and browsers to reach an empty alley, then came upon a courtyard packed with a press of bodies. Holding my rifle high, I squeezed through the bystanders to the center where I found Vorca on her knees and Alice standing protectively over her. Vorca's head was bleeding from the temple, and Caleb's baby pack had been torn from her shoulder. Caleb lay on his stomach on the ground, scooting forward on his belly, squealing with delight at experiencing pavement for the first time.

"What's going on here?" I aimed my rifle at the crowd that encircled them. If they all attacked at once, we'd be mauled, and Caleb would be trampled. "Who's responsible, Alice?"

Alice jabbed her staff at a bearded bunch of men in sharp suits. These were townspeople, not travelers. One with a gray beard wore a gold chain on his breast pocket.

"You hurt my son's nurse?" His watch made for a nice target for me to aim at. With my left hand, I reached for Vorca, touched her shoulder, and tugged at her arm. "Vorca, can you walk? Come on."

"She's an Indian." The gold watch man puffed his chest and lifted his voice for the hushed witnesses to hear. "We all know what Indians did to us two years ago—the massacre!"

"This is Indian land," I said. "We're on the Navajo Reservation."

"This woman was with those raiders!" the man accused. "Our town charter says that no Native American scalp-taker is welcome in Cameron ever again."

"This is my family's nurse!" I fired back. "Her name is Vorca. We just crossed the Mojave from California. She's no raider or scalper. She cares for my son like her own— my white son. Who hit my nurse while she carried my son?"

"I say she was with the raiders two years ago." The man raised up on his toes and lifted his chin to seem taller than he was, but he only reached my nose. "Some of us recognize her as one of the raiders, don't we? Massacred all those travelers on the road, killed them as they begged for mercy. You all know the names on the memorial, and the graves of so many who settled this town. She's responsible. Don't listen to this sympathizer. He's probably a spy for them, planning another attack, worse than the first!"

"That's ridiculous!"

"Are you calling me a liar, son?"

"Are you calling all of us liars?" another man at his elbow challenged me. He held a metal baton. "You call a man a liar, and you'd better be prepared to kill or die."

"Death doesn't prove the evidence one way or another," I said. "Life does. We're leaving town. Vorca, come on."

Still, the young stunned woman didn't climb to her feet.

"You're not taking her!" Gold Chain pointed at Vorca like he was the hand of death. "Indians are hung. She'll be hung now from the bridge. Her friends will see and stay away."

"You won't hang an innocent woman!" I made a show of sighting down my rifle. "You're the first to get it, old man."

"And then you," Alice stated, pointing her staff at the one with the baton. "Hit me with your little club and see what happens."

"The law says she dies!" Gold Chain shouted. "If the law isn't followed, then we have anarchy. Without the law, we lose our haven of trade and pleasure. Without the law, we are dead! What say you? Do we follow the law? Do we punish those who raped our women and ate our children that terrible day?"

The crowd was stirred and angry. They cheered and shouted, and in their midst, they closed on me and Alice, jostling against us. Alice swung her staff, but they surged anyway. Someone kicked Vorca and she fell over. It was insanity, and I couldn't win against such mindless reasoning and irrational prejudice.

"You want to hang her?" I shouted. "Then hang her at the bridge! Justice, you say? Let justice be done. Who am I to stand in the way of the law? Take the Indian!"

I snatched Caleb from the ground by the back of his layers of shirts and coat.

"Levi!" Alice gasped.

"We're done here!" I yelled over the uproar as they swept Vorca to her feet. With Caleb held high, I waded through the people, hoping Alice was staying up with me. She couldn't swing her staff in that press of fury, but I still wouldn't have wanted to cross her rage.

We reached the clear alley with Alice on my heels. Though the staff was in her hand, I gave her Caleb, who she clutched awkwardly with her stump. As we marched back to the burros, I reloaded one of my bullpup magazines, alternating between five non-lethal and five phosphorus rounds. Then the last twenty shells of the thirty-round magazine, I ensured were gel-tranqs.

"Where's Vorca?" Annette took Caleb from Alice.

"Get across the bridge north of town. Go now. Run! Mia, take Caleb. Mom, load your rifle with tranqs. Alice, get them moving. I'll find Forest and Sharly. Go!"

Alice and Mia loosed the lead ropes and led the two burros away. We hadn't resupplied or even watered the animals yet, but we didn't have a choice.

I found Forest indoors at the head of a long hall set up as a shooting range.

"Serval!" Forest laughed when he saw me and held up a jar of brass bullets—his winnings. "Look who's the mighty hunter! Five little rubber ducks at fifty paces—"

"Listen! Family emergency! Come now. They took Vorca!"

"Vorca?" Forest whistled for Sharly, who sat across the room from the shooting, ear-protectors over Natasha's young ears. "Vorca's in trouble!"

Sharly jumped to her feet and joined us. The mob who had Vorca had a head start, but I didn't believe the town's bloodthirstiness was as strong as our familial bond. The town of Cameron had picked a fight with the Casperteins!

Chapter Eighteen

We beat the town to the bridge, which spanned the canyon north of Cameron—a two-hundred-yard expanse of terror with danger nearby.

Annette had waited at the bridge for me, Forest, and Sharly, but Alice had responsibly taken Mia and Caleb across and out of sight. Now would have been a great opportunity to test my new comm-sets, but they were in my pack on one of the burros.

"Mom, cross the bridge and find a hidden firing position to cover Vorca once the shooting starts. Go!"

For once, the strong-willed and opinionated woman my father had married didn't share her point of view. She ran, and a moment later, I saw why—the crowd of townsfolk was approaching, a mob with hanging on their minds.

"Get below the bridge," I told Forest. "When I start firing, you free Vorca. Mom and I will cover you. Get out of sight."

I didn't have time to run the length of the bridge to hide, but I didn't want to hide. For my phosphorus rounds to be effective, I wanted to be on the bridge to place them perfectly. Halfway up the bridge, I dropped to my belly on the eastern side, against the vertical steel trusses. There were two suspension towers that stabilized the bridge with thick cables, one tower on each end of the bridge. Aiming at the one nearest the town, I imagined they would use the lowest cross beam as the hanging beam. One hundred yards away, I waited.

Forest was somewhere out of sight below the bridge when the first of the mob stepped foot onto the bridge.

The noise, even from my distance, was sickening. No one voice could be distinguished from another. The attitude seemed the same—crazed fury. I guessed four hundred people had gathered for the lynching.

Vorca was easily identified, her short, round shape wider than most of the others. These people didn't care that they were about to murder a loving, gentle woman who'd cared for an orphaned infant across the dangers and heat of a desert. And yet, these people weren't really my enemies. They were in sin's bondage, and in their refusal to repent from their unbelief, their lives served only death and the prince of darkness who so blinded the hearts of this world.

The end of a rope was tossed over a horizontal beam. I aimed carefully at the man's chest who held Vorca. The man seemed to be lecturing and spitting at her simultaneously. Her hands were tied behind her back, and she was crying. My heart nearly broke, and I prayed that she didn't think I'd truly abandoned her.

"Protect Vorca, Lord," I said aloud, knowing it would take little effort for one of the gunmen to shoot the bound woman, once the shooting began.

My first round found its target, the lecturer. My next bullet was phosphorus, so I aimed at the suspension cable on the tower, where its tension was tightest.

Annette fired from behind me, so far away that she was probably invisible to the naked eye. Like me, she was intent on releasing Vorca of her captors, and another man fell.

My next shot took out the man with the gold watch, an easy target as he backed away from Vorca. She took two steps back herself, then seemed to understand she was being rescued. Before Forest could get to her, she started running toward me where I lay on the bridge.

I guessed the sheer idea of gunmen firing indiscriminately into the crowd sent them stampeding over one another as they retreated from the bridge. A few riflemen tried to line up to return fire at me, or perhaps to shoot Vorca in the back, but every time they leveled their weapons, a fleeing observer or a round from Annette knocked them over.

Meanwhile, I concentrated on destroying the bridge's stabilizers. Forest emerged from under the bridge about the time Vorca trotted up and flopped down next to me. Since I had nearly no cover, except for a few narrow steel trusses at my elbow, this was no place to stop!

I drew my skinning knife and cut her hands free from bailing twine.

"Get out of here!" I yelled at her. For once, she listened, and jumped up and ran.

My phosphorus rounds were eating the bridge quickly. Cables creaked and steel groaned loudly. Part of the suspension tower collapsed as Forest dashed past me. From what I could tell, he hadn't fired the .22 in his hands, but he didn't need to. Annette was doing enough shooting for a whole unit.

The rest of the tower tumbled inward, loosely blocking the other end of the bridge with oozing steel, and a putrid smell that made me gag even at that distance. Bullets could fire through the carnage, but no one would pass through the barrier. Yet, I wasn't finished securing our escape.

When I ran out of tranqs, I slammed in a phosphorus magazine and placed three rounds spaced evenly across the surface of the bridge, firing at a distance of twenty yards. Since I was in the middle of the bridge, the whole span would collapse into the river gorge, and me with it, if I didn't move.

As I raced to catch up to Forest and Vorca, Annette continued to fire. Passing under the northern-most tower, I shot one round into each of the tower's two supports. The town of Cameron had lost its traveling privileges to the north. A bridge that had stood for decades had been brought to a steel heap in ten minutes—over an innocent woman the town had wanted to hang. I hoped the bridge they lost was a source of shame as well as repentance for the people of Cameron.

One thing was certain: with no bridge, the town couldn't be resupplied from the east. In a year, I guessed the town would be uninhabited.

That night, we camped east of Tuba City. Though it was inhabited, we wanted to mingle with no one who could later identify us, so we steered clear of the residents. It was ninety miles from Cameron to Kayenta, our next scheduled resupply and possible refuge from the high elevation and dry desert. In a week, we'd be through the corner of New Mexico and into Colorado.

But the anticipation for the end of the journey for many in our party didn't bring wings to our spirits. Cameron had been a lively treasure trove of both supplies and information. But we had run away without receiving much of either.

Worry had beset me in a fresh way. What if Uncle Rudy and my cousin Rex weren't in Meeker, Colorado, anymore? What then? How could I tell my travel companions that for me to reach New York by the following spring, I would have to abandon them once we found our Caspertein relatives?

Natasha cried in her weariness and Sharly didn't know how to comfort her. Forest seemed too tired to scout ahead or hunt, and I didn't force him. Mia seemed distracted, glancing often at Annette, who'd spoken hardly two words since leaving Cameron. Only Alice seemed her usual self, marching proudly at the front, swinging and planting her heavy staff every two strides, never looking back, expecting that we were keeping pace.

Not even Vorca was her normal self. *She was talking!* We didn't know what she was saying, but she was talking. Her native words were usually directed at me, or sometimes at Caleb, who yawned at her speech while I scratched my head. Vorca didn't seem daunted by her capture or by her swelled scalp, which she hadn't allowed Annette to inspect or stitch.

"The people of Cameron may send trackers after us," I told Alice outside camp that night. We'd stepped out under the guise of searching for firewood. There was none in the desert, only old roots and dried weeds that had blown perhaps hundreds of miles in the wind. "Just because we tore down one bridge doesn't mean there weren't others."

"What do you want me to do?" She shared my canteen, filled from a muddy water stream a mile back. If Mia was like a little sister to me, Alice had become my older sister, loyal and without complaint. "You want me to stay behind?"

"Forest needs to hunt tomorrow. Annette is too worn out. Mia is—you might as well know—expecting."

"She's pregnant? By whom?"

"A long, secret story. My point is, it's down to you and me. If a Cameron posse comes for us, they'll probably be on horseback, led by people who know this land better than us. You won't be able to beat them back to us to warn us when they're coming."

"You want me to use one of your radios?"

"No, you'll be too far away. If you see people coming after us, I want you to start two fires. Space them about fifty yards apart and make them real smoky. I'll see them from ten miles away or more. If danger is expected, then we can prepare."

"You really think they'll come after us?"

"We fired non-lethal rounds into that crowd, and we stole their prisoner. Just because we didn't intend to hurt them, that mob probably won't take their defeat too well." I exhaled through my teeth. "Altogether, we fired about one hundred rounds, I think. We shot gel-tranqs to save lives, but I have a hunch that a lot of angry people woke up an hour after we left Cameron and still want blood."

A commotion in camp drew our attention. Annette had spilled over Vorca's cooking pot as she stepped over the small fire.

"Aunt Annette!" Mia called after her as Annette marched directly at us in the dim lighting.

Annette stormed straight up to me and slapped me hard on the side of the head. She'd aimed high, maybe to make sure I felt it, instead of landing the blow on my unruly bearded cheek. My ear rang as she continued off into the darkness, away from camp.

"What was that for?" Alice asked.

I wanted to rub my stinging skin, but I didn't.

"It could be that Mia just told her she's pregnant."

"I thought you and Mia were cousins."

"We are. The kid's not mine."

"Then why'd you let her slap you?"

"Maybe she just needed to slap someone." I grunted, defeated in an effort to understand Caspertein women. "Or maybe she blames me for not getting to Mia faster after she was kidnapped."

"That's one reason my husband and I moved to Eagle Mountain. We saw one raid for child-bearing brides, and we packed up and left the next morning for the desert. But that was years ago."

"You never had kids? You never said."

"I can't have kids. But those raiders probably weren't about to listen to me explain why before they would've killed my husband."

Alice bedded down near the fire while I remained alone in the dark. Vorca had given up on cooking after the incident with the spilled beans, and had passed out smoked coyote meat and dried apricots instead. She even brought me a portion, declaring the menu in words that sounded like Dutch before she waddled back to the fire.

The night was cold, but I didn't move. Praying for safety over my expanded family, I gazed at the blanket of stars above. My God had made those awesome lights, and He was even more amazing than the stars. He could certainly keep a few of us wandering numbskulls on a summer trail to our destination.

"You should've told me," Annette said from a few feet behind me. I hadn't heard her approach in the soft sand. She stood next to me, watching the stars over our camp. The two burros nuzzled Mia as she unrolled her bedroll where their lead ropes were anchored under a heavy rock. "I knew something was up, but I had no idea it was this."

"She's a tough girl, like her aunt."

"This explains why she's been asking Sharly so many childbearing questions lately."

"You know, it wasn't for me to tell you, Mom." I put my arm over her shoulders. "This is part of her healing, finally talking about what she couldn't before."

"But a mother needs to know these things. By that, I mean me, Levi! It makes me wonder what else you're keeping from me."

I hoped she didn't feel me tense against her at the thought of Kip Brogdon. He'd committed unspeakable acts. Had Annette figured out that he and his father, the general, had killed Dad? And now there was Mia, and the child she was carrying—a constant reminder of her violent night in Coronado. But to me, her pregnancy would still represent a miracle of life—for her child and for Kip Brogdon. He'd come to Christ. Surely, he had died from his infection by now, even if he'd reached the hidden spring behind the rimrock.

"Cameron folks may be sore about our departure." Changing the subject was better than lying to her. "We have a low mountain range between us and New Mexico, then we can focus on heading straight north into the mountains of Colorado."

"What do you think they'll do to us if they catch us?"

"They only got a good look at Alice, me, and Vorca. But they'd probably treat us all the same at this point, so we won't let them get close enough for us to find out."

The next morning, we started early, staying south and parallel to Highway 160. Alice was already gone as we set off in the dark. Regardless of the previous evening's angst, Sharly and Annette had only smiles and attention for the expecting mother. Though I'd never been the head of a family before this trip, I understood the burden of secrecy regarding Kip Brogdon. To protect them all, Mia especially, I wouldn't tell them about his probable conversion. As far as anyone knew, we'd left the Brogdon enemy on the other side of the destroyed bridge.

I walked at the rear of our group that morning, so no one would notice how concerned I was about a possible signal from Alice. Seeing me turn every few minutes and scoping the area southwest of us would've been unnerving to everyone, even though they all knew Alice was watching our backtrail.

Meanwhile, Forest agreed to scout ahead, a walkie-talkie clipped to his jacket and a headset over his dome. As he hunted, he could call back instructions to Annette to go north or south as we progressed through the thousands of canyons that made up the greater Grand Canyon territory.

"*Vlat coren-son choh-neh.*" Vorca laughed and pointed at Caleb. She stopped and adjusted a burro's pack cinch.

I had no idea what she'd said, but Caleb seemed thoroughly amused, grinning and talking, kicking his loose legs against the air. His new position of being strapped on top of a burro's pack was working out well. Tears nearly came to my eyes, so thankful was I for my expanded family. My desire to keep them safe had become my obsession, but deep down, I knew only God could do that. My God was in control. I had to trust Him in all things.

For two days, we trekked toward Kayenta, moving onto the sand-choked highway on the occasions that we couldn't pass through a gorge or cross a ravine. Forest reported many travelers on the highway, moving usually in small groups, but always heavily armed with rifles. We wouldn't have hesitated to interact with these pilgrims, except for their safety and ours. It was beneficial that we remained separate after what had happened in Cameron.

Outside of Kayenta, we made camp early, planning to enter the town the following morning. Our water supply was low and our energy was lower. As Vorca, Mia, and Forest set up camp, Annette and I bowed over our map in the fading sunlight.

"Three hundred miles to go." Annette sighed heavily. "At least it won't be in this heat."

"That's true." I glanced at the others to ensure they weren't listening. "But it'll be the most dangerous terrain we've covered. We'll be on mountain highways that haven't been maintained, with cliffs and rivers to cross. Some bridges will be washed out. Suspicious settlers will shoot us on sight. Predatory animals have probably experienced a population explosion. Lions will be after our burros, and bears will be curious about any food containers we have."

"You're not exactly comforting me right now, Levi."

"You have to know the score as we're coming into the home stretch. It won't be easy getting everyone all the way to Meeker."

Forest whistled and pointed to the west. A lone figure jogged in from the desert dusk. It was Alice. She reached our small fire and sank to her knees to drink from a water skin Sharly gave her. Alice had been gone almost three days. She was coated with sand that had been kicked up from the desert, plastering her sweaty skin. She had the appearance of an aboriginal native, her heavy staff and muscular limbs making her look like a fierce character to behold on the open range.

"Bad news." She wiped her mouth, then focused on me. "Pacific States forces have regrouped in armored vehicles in Cameron. The whole town welcomed them, it seemed. It's no wonder, though. They have a mutual enemy—us."

"Even by truck, they're still at least a day's travel behind us," I said, "especially since they have to drive around the river gorge to another bridge."

"Yeah, except they're rebuilding the bridge." Alice accepted dried meat from Forest. "Some sort of suspension bridge. They know their town is finished without a bridge there."

"There are other routes east," Annette said, "but the Brogdons are staying on our trail. This is personal, Levi."

No one said the obvious—that Mia and I were a driving force for the general. Kip Brogdon's death wouldn't necessarily help us, I privately considered, especially since his disappearance would probably be blamed on us.

"Once we get to Shiprock, New Mexico," I said, "we'll be turning directly north. To chase us will take General Brogdon too far off the path President Criswell probably sent him to follow to blaze eastward. We'll resupply in Kayenta tomorrow, then it's ninety miles to Shiprock. Figure four more days, and we'll be on the western slopes of the San Juan Mountains."

"So, how do we stay alive for four more days?" Forest asked. "The Pacific States and our Cameron friends are less than a day behind by vehicle."

"We'll just have to get creative." I smiled. "The Bible is full of creative ways to stay out of harm's way."

"So, . . . that's our plan?" Mia asked, glancing nervously about. "Keep moving and be creative? We have an army behind us, and who knows what's ahead?"

"If everything goes perfectly, we could be in Meeker, Colorado, in a month." I paused to look them each in the face, except Vorca who was feeding Caleb and Natasha.

"This trip hasn't gone perfectly yet, so I really don't expect it to go perfectly now. But God has preserved us. We've gained some scars and enemies along the way, but we're still alive. Forest, Annette, and I have plenty of ammo, and anyone who doesn't have heavy artillery, we have them outgunned. I've learned—perhaps the hard way—that unexpected things may happen, but God remains present with us. So, as we move forward, don't trust in me or our guns. You can't see God, but He's as real as you or me. Focus on Him."

As everyone returned to their personal tasks, Alice signaled me with her eyes and we stepped aside into the scrub brush that covered the desert floor. As exhausted as I expected her to be, she appeared energized, with wide eyes and an erect posture.

"Where's the hatchet you took from Kip Brogdon?" she asked. "You've kept it in your belt since before Cadiz."

"Huh. I haven't had it for a few days now." I frowned. "You know something about it?"

"I saw it on Kip Brogdon yesterday. He walked up on me suddenly while I was scoping the western skyline looking for vegetation that might identify a water source." Her voice was low, but she glanced at the others to ensure we were far enough away for her words. "Just a couple weeks ago, I could've sworn this guy was trying to kill us! You gave him back his hatchet, Levi?"

"I gave him his hatchet to die in peace." I frowned and gazed at the setting sun. "How is he still alive?"

"He says you saved him by some miracle from God. God forgave him and healed him." She crossed her good arm to her stump and scowled. "I couldn't find any water for two days, not like I'd hoped, so I was low. He wandered up to me and had only one canteen himself, and he shared it with me. I probably wouldn't have made it back tonight without his help. Our worst enemy may have saved my life."

"That's . . . amazing, Alice." I chuckled at the wild turn of events. "Why are you angry?"

"Well, we have it in our minds that this guy is our enemy, and then it turns out he's not. All he used his hatchet for was to chop a little kindling for a fire."

"I don't know what to tell you. We're running from these people because they want to hurt us. But we don't need to be disappointed when God softens their hearts toward us. This is a moment to praise God, Alice."

"I'm not sure I share your enthusiasm."

"So, where is he now?"

"I told him about his father's forces coming up behind us, and that Mia is barely grasping what's happened to her, what he did to her. It's not time to welcome him into our clan, Levi."

"It may never be time." I sighed. "He's a man banished by his own past crimes, I'm afraid. He may be forgiven, but the wounds he's caused are deep. Sadly, he'll probably rejoin his father's forces."

"No, he said he's going down to Second Mesa to search for a Bible. He doesn't want to run into any more people without being able to tell them more about the God who saved him, the God of the Bible."

"So, he's out of the chase?"

"I didn't know whether to hit him with my staff or to hug him. What a jerk."

"It sounds like God has set him free." I muffled my laugher in my cupped hand. "How is he a jerk?"

"Because one minute he's a creep who about killed me and Caleb. He's probably even responsible for killing my husband, Levi! And the next minute he's saving my life by offering me water and sharing some jackrabbit meat over a fire."

"So, why didn't you hit him with your staff? I know you've been itching to prove yourself."

"It's that obvious, huh?" She shook her head at the staff in her hand. "I can't put my finger on just what it is, but you said God forgave us. The cross, right?"

"Right. His forgiveness is applied to us when we receive that truth by faith."

"Well, I guess I believe now."

"You guess you do?"

"No, I do believe." She growled under her breath, which made me laugh more. "Quit giggling, Levi! I'm struggling here!"

"My apologies. You're experiencing God's Spirit in you. You're a believer now. It changes the way we behave and think."

"It gets worse."

"What do you mean?"

"That jerk may have been the one who shot off my arm. He said he's not sure. But he gave me this." Alice held out her right hand. There was a diamond ring on her ring finger. "When you left my left arm behind, you didn't take off my wedding ring. He's been carrying it since he found my arm, he said."

I had no words as the sun disappeared. We stood there together, a few yards from camp, until I pulled Alice into an embrace. She was reluctant at first, but a breath later, she let her staff fall to the sand. I squeezed her tightly, wrapping her thin frame in my arms as she shuddered and finally wept against my shoulder. They were cleansing tears, I knew—tears of pain, and release, and faith, and newness of life.

Then I cried with her.

Chapter Nineteen

We entered Kayenta, Arizona, in two groups. I'd even shaved my beard, knowing that whoever populated the town would be questioned by the Pacific State troops once they rolled into town. Forest traveled with Sharly, Vorca, and the kids. I escorted Annette and Mia into town soon after.

Regardless of Kayenta being a town on the old Navajo Nation Reservation like Cameron was, I still saw no Native Americans as we walked in front of Basha's Diner. It was a quiet trading town, with dozens of armed people about. A movie theater stood down the street, now advertising an auction for townspeople and travelers alike. Evidently, word hadn't yet reached Kayenta that the bridge to Cameron was down, so several separate caravans were preparing to leave as we arrived. Across the street from where I stopped with Annette and Mia, Vorca tied the two burros to a lamp post. Forest kept his hand on his rifle sling as I had instructed him to do, in case these citizens didn't welcome Vorca, either.

A water hose extended from what was once a fast-food restaurant. A sign read, "One gallon = one bullet, or equivalent." We needed a lot of water, but I wasn't about to pay anyone with my phosphorus or gel-tranq rounds. Twenty-two-caliber shells were easier to come by, and Annette and I had more .308 hunting rounds than we needed.

Annette and Mia bought dried oats, fruit, hardtack, and jerked horse meat while Forest and Sharly focused on loading water onto the burros.

About this time, Alice drifted into town, also disguised in a hood and an empty sleeve hanging to give the appearance of being a two-armed woman. She looked to be unarmed, since her staff was strapped to one of the burros. As Forest and I avoided one another, Alice also moved about the town independently. Her assignment was to gather intel about the road ahead, both north and east. We were headed north, but I also longed for news about the Appalachian Federation and of the Christian persecution Jenna Dowler was enduring. Meanwhile, Forest and I dropped misinformation about traveling to Texas and the Gulf.

An hour later, Forest and I were both ready to leave, communicated by a mutual nod from across the street from one another. But Alice was nowhere in sight. Vorca began to lead the burros down the street out of town.

"Did you see where she went?" I asked Annette. She and Mia both shook their heads. There seemed to be no commotion in front of the dozen stores in town. The two-dozen people in sight drifted from shop to shop without interruption in their own supply hunts. There seemed to be several hundred citizens from the town. I figured they occupied the many houses on the streets behind the main thoroughfare.

Annette and Mia started to leave town, a couple hundred yards behind Forest. With my family on their way, I walked in front of each of the stores, shops, booths, and trading posts, but still, I didn't find Alice in any of them. How much trouble could a one-armed black woman find in a quiet town? I turned back to check the stores again, praying for my new sister in the faith.

When I got back to where I'd started, I noticed the movie theater-auction house was the only place I hadn't checked. I walked through its open double-doors into a dark interior. As my eyes adjusted to the dim lighting inside, I heard a clang and cursing in the auditorium directly ahead. My rifle was still over my shoulder, but my thumb was under the sling, ready to swing it into action.

"We're closed!" a man with a pointy-face yelled at me. He lifted an overburdened rack of clothes from the floor and balanced it upright. "Didn't you read the sign outside? The auction isn't for three more days."

I stopped in the center aisle. Half the theater seats had been removed to accommodate heaps of gear, most of it necessities for travelers rather than for settlers in town. But I did notice books and lamp shades, stoves, and vases as well—items from a past civilization, it seemed.

On the stage of the theater, two more men, stripped to tank tops, carried a bundle of tarps across the expanse, and dropped them onto the floor.

"Looks like you guys had an earthquake in here." With the toe of my boot, I nudged aside a metal barrel. Water canteens lay strewn across the floor in my path. "What happened?"

The pointy-faced attendant, about my age, wrestled the clothing rack into a better position, then cursed as he stacked two rolled-up sleeping bags against the rack.

"What happened was a thief made a mess of my inventory!" He scowled at me as he knelt to collect the canteens. "I told you, three days until auction. We won't be ready until then, especially now that I have to clean up this mess."

"I won't be here in three days." The men on the stage had stopped working to talk quietly between themselves. Their attention was obviously on me, since they were watching me none-too-covertly. "A thief knocked over all your stuff here?"

The man roughly positioned the metal barrel to the side of the aisle and took a moment to study me. Something had definitely occurred recently in the theater. Suspicion toward strangers was standard operating procedure in those days, but this was something else.

"Yes, a thief resisted apprehension and caused what you see here. Thieves come through town all the time."

"How do you know they're thieves?"

"Because they have nothing, so they come here to take what's not theirs. They carry nothing, so naturally, they come to carry away my merchandise. They prey on other people by taking what doesn't belong to them."

"Looks to me like you have enough junk to share with needy people," I said, holding up an umbrella, then dropping it into a burlap sack which held an assortment of other wet-weather gear. "But thieves are a different story. No mercy for thieves, right? I mean, anyone who even looks suspicious should be— What do you do with thieves when you catch them?"

"When we catch them?" Pointy-face glanced at the two men on stage. "They have to pay for what they've done. Naturally."

"Of course." Drifting down the center aisle, I passed the attendant and approached the stage. I picked through a rack of baseball gear and selected a wooden baseball bat and three balls. In high school, I'd been a football player, but the feel of a bat was natural to me as well. My hand was off my rifle sling now, but none of the men were visibly armed with anything more than pocketknives. "Do you catch many thieves in here?"

"A couple times a month."

"That's a lot of thieves." I reached the bottom of the aisle and looked up at the two workers. Both men were built like bricks, maybe brothers. "Let me guess: these thieves travel alone and have no real threatening weapons?"

"Yeah, you know the type, huh?"

"Yeah, the type easy to take into custody."

"If they weren't trouble, they'd be traveling with others." He shrugged. "We know they're trouble because they're alone, drifting, looking for trouble."

"Of course." I scoffed. "And you can probably read these kinds of people before they ever actually steal anything from you, right?"

"What do you want? What's with all the questions?"

"Let's say I'm not interested in buying any of this junk, but I'm interested in what you do with the thieves."

"Why? They're good for nothing but a leather strap, until they're broken."

"Good for nothing? No, everything has value." I held out my arms. "Look at me. I'm a hunter. Do you think I want to carry my own gear? I'd rather some good-for-nothing do the hard work for me."

"What're you asking, mister?" one of the stage hands asked.

"What's the value of a thief in this town?"

The three men appeared uncomfortable, but their greed was winning them over.

"What do you have to trade?"

"Guns and bullets." I held up the bullpup. "Look at this ugly beast. A .308 battle rifle with an eighteen-inch barrel. It's not for weak men. Are you weak men, or men of strength?"

"How many rounds do you have?" the attendant asked. He seemed to be the boss, but the Brick Brothers worried me more if it were to come to a scuffle. "Three mags. I'd want no less."

"Three magazines? That's ninety rounds, plus a state-of-the-art weapon." I clucked my tongue, hefting the baseball bat in my hand, appreciating its balance. "You must have some real fresh merchandise to ask for that much. I don't want anything used up or crippled."

"I guess that means he doesn't want today's catch." The Brick Brothers laughed together until Pointy-face glared them to silence.

They were obviously laughing at Alice's expense, since she was crippled, in their eyes. It had been a mistake to send her scouting the town without her staff.

"I won't buy anything blind." I said and tossed the bat and balls aside. "You show me what you've got. You want to be the envy of the town? Look at this rifle. It's a gem. But you'd better make it worth my while."

Pointy-face and one of the Brick Brothers led me out a back door of the theater to a Quonset hut that smelled like wood chips and dung. The Brick Brother turned on a light and I braced myself for what I might see. But the scene was too horrific to prepare myself for.

My eyes moved across several people lying on the floor and chained by the neck. I spotted Alice Prine immediately. Her eyes were closed, and her limbs lay in awkward positions. Her lip was swollen and bleeding, the blood still wet since she'd been taken only thirty minutes earlier. The floor was covered with soiled wood chips, except where steel posts were anchored into cement blocks. The prisoners' chains were attached to the posts.

"This one's probably the best buy." Pointy-face kicked the shoeless foot of a young man who sat up suddenly. His face was filthy, his eyes daring. "He's just a teenager, but he'll work for his freedom, won't you?"

The young man lunged for Pointy-face's leg, but he reached the end of his chain, and his head snapped backward, followed by the rest of his body.

"Everyone else is female?" I walked past three prisoners, one older woman on each side of Alice. "They're all thieves, huh?"

"They wandered into town alone, and we just knew they'd be a problem. Someone has to protect the town. Everyone in town expects it."

"What about the black one here?" I tapped my boot on Alice's bare foot, her boots probably back in the theater, up for auction. "A thief, too? She has only one arm."

Alice stirred and rolled over. Her eyes opened and registered on the ceiling, then her hand went to the locked metal ring around her neck. I imagined it was cold against her skin and threatened her larynx.

"The cripples are the worst. They expect handouts. Found this one going through a sack of buck knives. Just looking at her, I could see she had nothing to trade. When I talked to her, she said she was traveling alone."

"Fair game, huh?" I did my best not to sneer. Pointy-face was much smaller than me, but I was certain Brick Brother would need to be tranqed before I had to physically grapple with him. "I don't want the kid. He'll cut my throat the first chance he gets. The two old ladies? I don't need housekeepers. But this one-armed woman, she can still haul my pack."

Alice sat up and blinked, everything coming into focus by the look on her face.

"Nah, she's not for sale." Pointy-face kicked wood chips at Alice, making her flinch and snarl. "She's too new. She hasn't been broken yet. That takes a couple weeks on the chain, no less."

"Broken or not, I'll take her." I tapped the bullpup. "You want this, don't you?"

"Sure, but you're not listening. She's not for sale. They have to submit before they can be sold. It's for your own sake. Look at her eyes. That woman's got something wild inside her still."

"I'll break her on the trail. Unlock her. I'll throw in an extra mag of ammo." I made a move to draw a magazine from my vest. Alice met my eyes, and her mouth twitched—the makings of a smile that I hoped only I had noticed. "A good beating now and then might be just the attention she needs."

"Leave her alone!" one of the elderly women said, but cringed away as Pointy-face loomed with a raised fist, his shadow over her. "She's done nothing, and you know it!"

"Shut up, you old bat, or you'll die on the chain!" Pointy-face jutted his chin at me. "So? You ready to deal? I usually don't sell to strangers, just the citizens I already know, the ones who want an extra hand around their homes, if they can support the extra mouth to feed. We look out for each other, you know? It's my job to chain up the trash, and we all work together to recycle it."

"You mean there are others around town you've sold to people in the town?"

"Oh, yeah. Probably about thirty are still alive. A couple died through last winter, but we got a little labor out of them first."

I avoided Alice's eyes, knowing they would be filled with both fury and pleading. It was one thing to buy back Alice, or even the three others in captivity. But thirty more in slavery? The whole town was justifying this brand of oppression!

It was moments like these I hated being a leader. One wrong move, and I could get us all killed. And if I took too long to make a move at all, General Brogdon would be rolling into town with the Cameron citizens ready to hang me.

The Brick Brother drew a ring of keys from his pocket and looked to his boss for instruction.

"Give me your one-armed new one," I said. "She'll learn her place."

Pointy-face nodded at the Brick Brother, and he bowed over Alice.

"Hold still! If you run, we'll shoot you. There's nowhere to run to, anyway. Desert all around us. Besides, you got no shoes."

I'd heard enough. As soon as I heard Alice's neck ring click open, I slid gel-tranqs into both my fists. One, I slugged into the Brick Brother's shoulder before he stood upright. Pointy-face started to turn toward me, but I slammed one tranq into his chest. Both men slumped to the ground. Alice leaped to her feet, then instantly wavered.

"Easy there." I held her arm as she gained her equilibrium. "Can you watch the door? Make sure this big guy's brother doesn't catch us in the middle of our break."

She leaned against the wall nearest the door, and I knelt in front of the other three captives to unlock their chains.

"They call me the Serval. I don't stand for this kind of treatment of people God has meant to be free. But if I let you loose, you'll have to help me free the rest of the captives in the town."

"I'm not sticking around this town for anything!" the young man with the filthy face said.

"If you don't want to help the others," I said, "then you're no better than these two. I see no reason to even unlock your neck." I turned to the two older women, giving the teen a moment to think about the cost of his freedom. "How about you two? I'm new in town, and I have an idea to free the whole town, but I'll need your help."

"I'll help however you think I can," said the first.

"Me, too," the other said, trying to straighten her soiled blouse. "It's about time someone stood up to these people."

"Hey, Serval?" Alice called. "You sure about this? Your mom may not want another town hunting us down."

"They left town an hour ago, and even if she were still here, this is Peach Springs all over again." I felt my nostrils flare. "Dangerous or not, this little enterprise at the expense of innocent lives is getting shut down! I'm not moving until something's done."

The women held their necks for me to unlock them, both with sores where the unwashed metal had rested for days or weeks.

"Wait!" The teen scooted closer, his tone much more humble. "I'm sorry. Please, I'll do whatever you want if you take me with you."

"Levi! Someone is coming!"

Alice moved aside so I could flatten myself against the wall beside the door. The two elderly women stood frozen as the door opened. I jabbed the second Brick Brother in the gut with the bullpup.

"Get in here!" With my free hand, I drew a gel-tranq. I wasn't keeping the big brute conscious long enough for him to attack us. As soon as he was inside, Alice closed the door and I tranqed him in the shoulder. To the women, I smiled. "Well, ladies, lock 'em up."

I unlocked the teen and we crouched in the middle of the floor as Alice continued to keep watch.

"First rule," I began, "I don't want any killing. I'm a follower of Jesus Christ, and God frowns on killing. Second rule, now that you're free, don't go west. Go any direction but west, which is full of conflict and evil for days."

"I know people in Albuquerque," one woman said. "There's a small government established there, I heard."

"That's a couple weeks of walking," I said, "but that's a good plan. Get these people out of Kayenta with you, if you would welcome them. Tell all the slaves we're about to free them and to travel south. But first, everyone will need to stock up on water and gear. What's your name, son?"

The teen snapped to attention.

"My mom called me Gilly. That's all I remember before she died."

"Gilly, you're in charge of supplies. Gather stuff all these people will need to travel—shoes, coats, tents, canteens, knives, cooking gear. Everything in that theater is up for grabs." I focused on the two elderly women. "You two will help Alice and me separate the slaves from the civilians, and then equip them to leave town on a southern route, assuming they want to leave."

"What if the, uh, owners of these people put up a fuss?" one of the women asked.

"Then I'll tranquilize them, or Alice will thump them on the head. Alice, find something sturdy to use. Sorry, but your staff went out with the pack animals."

"That theater is full of provisional clubs." She flexed her muscular right arm.

With the slave trader locked up and unconscious for the next hour, we left the hut and entered the theater. Gilly took his orders seriously and began to inspect a bag of canteens. While walking through the theater, Alice found my baseball bat and tested its weight in her firm arm. She and the two older women followed me out of the theater.

"Spread out across town," I told them. "Tell everyone we have a town meeting in twenty minutes. Have everyone come to the theater. That's where we'll reveal our intentions."

"Why would they come?" Alice frowned. She shoved her feet into a new pair of boots, which I stooped to tie for her. There were boots without laces which Alice could fit on herself, but only laced boots were sturdy enough for walking. In time, she'd learn to tie them with one hand. "Nobody knows us here."

"Tell them I have a Meridia Virus emergency bulletin. They'll all come."

The two elderly women split up and walked up the two sides of the street. One of the women limped, possibly from abuse while in captivity. She would never last a lengthy journey on foot to New Mexico, but those who'd been targeted as thieves simply had to leave town. I prayed for guidance in sending them on their way in peace and safety—but first I needed to set them all free.

As I waited for the townspeople to gather, I selected an elevated perch above the street by climbing onto the roof of a parked RV, which sat next to the theater. The vehicle's paint had long since disappeared from the wind and sand, but it showed signs of being lived in. The roof flexed under my weight, but it would work for a brief speaking platform—or shooting perch, if it came to that.

From my position, I gazed west across the brown landscape covered with dry grass. No sign of General Brogdon's forces, yet. Was he hunting me as much as he was in search of Kip? I tried to imagine Kip, recovered from the Meridia Virus, now shining Christ's light wherever he wandered, carrying a Bible as he traveled. He was the most unexpected convert I'd ever crossed, reminding me of the greatness of my God and His love even for the lowliest soul.

"What's this about?" a man with a leather apron yelled up at me. "Something about the Meridia Virus?"

"I'm a messenger from out west," I said, my hands on my hips, my rifle on its sling over my shoulder. "I'll make the announcement as soon as everyone is gathered."

They came from all over town, several hundred of all ages, carrying in their hands whatever they'd held at the moment they'd been called to attend the meeting. Such was still their concern about the virus, even after twenty years. One woman held a paintbrush. A man carried a rake. Their haste was to my advantage: very few brought firearms. Those who did, I recognized them as strangers in town, travelers stopping for gear or staying temporarily before moving on. Everyone wanted news from the west, from where so few, it seemed, ever came.

The crowd reached almost three hundred by the time Gilly pounded on the side of the RV to get my attention. He'd washed his face since being released from his chain, and now he appeared even younger than I'd thought. His hair was light blond, and whether from being on the chain or not, he looked as thin as a pole. But he seemed able and willing to continue performing his duty of supplying what his fellow captives required.

"All the stuff is ready. See?" he pointed at the theater. Against the outside wall to the right of the door was a pile of gear. "Packs, canteens, extra boots, knives, tents, and sleeping bags. There's hardly any food, though."

"That's okay. Good man. One more thing. In the back of the theater, there are hundreds of old bicycles. See if you can find a few that will work for the people who can't walk too far."

"Are you going with us?" He shielded his eyes from the mid-morning sun, and I could read worry on his face. "I don't want to go to Albuquerque. I want to go with you."

"I'm going to northern Colorado."

"Colorado." He looked down at his feet for a moment, then turned his eyes back to me. "Does it snow there?"

"For a few months out of the year."

"Then I'll get us some better boots. And the bikes you want." With that, he jogged away.

I chuckled as I watched him depart, reminded of how much my trip to reach Jenna had been out of my control. Why would I expect to control who joined me now?

At the back of the crowd, Alice raised her bat in the air, a signal to me that she and the other women had gathered everyone from the town who wished to come. From my shoulder, I slipped the bullpup into my right hand. There were a few firearms visible in the crowd, but my elevated position offered me a firing advantage. I raised my left hand to silence the crowd. They hushed themselves.

"They call me the Serval!" My voice was loud and full of authority. While growing up, I'd witnessed my father make public declarations to organize or inform neighborhoods of survivors around San Diego. "I have come from the west where great conflicts are raging. Those conflicts are moving this way. In just a day or two, a military force will reach Kayenta. Your very souls depend upon your immediate reaction. Listen carefully to me!"

The murmur of concern died down as I waited, then continued.

"Kayenta has become a town of shame. You've shed blood with the auctioneer and the two men who've kidnapped those who traveled alone. Perhaps God has sent me here to warn you to turn from your wicked ways. The military force that will arrive in town soon has been exposed to the Meridia Virus. Quiet now! You're a town in need of repentance. The slaves you've bought need to be set free. You'll have your hands full staying alive in the coming days. Right now, don't hesitate—who's been a slave in this town? Raise your hand. Quickly!"

Hands began to shoot up. Some were more reluctant.

"There!" I called, pointing with my left while keeping my right on my rifle. Alice squeezed through the crowd to separate the slave—forcibly, if an owner stepped in to stop them. "And there! And you—I see you."

The elderly women did their part as well.

A pregnant red-headed woman about my age didn't raise her hand, but she started after Alice and the others, who were being directed toward the front of the theater. An aging man grabbed her arm and smacked her. The crowd pulled back from the couple. The woman cried out under the blows from the man. The distance was only thirty yards. I angled my rifle downward with one hand and fired one round into the man's ribs. Whatever the circumstances of these people, I wasn't tolerating the captivity of anyone who was being held against their will. The redhead had opted to leave.

"Don't worry, he's not dead. He's just sleeping for an hour. Now, don't ruin your opportunities for redemption!" I shouted, my tone a little fiercer. "Look around you! These are your neighbors. You've bought slaves and acted like you're guiltless. But in your hearts, you've known this day would come. Today, you're being set free. The people you've kept are free to leave, and you yourselves are free of your burdened consciences. Start over. Prepare for the enemy who will soon drive into town. Will you join their evil tactics, or will you turn from your wicked ways altogether? Is there anyone else?"

"Who do you think you are?" A heavy-set man with glasses shook a smoking pipe at me. I'd noticed that a middle-aged woman had left his side faster than he could stop her. "You can't come into this town and change what we've determined to—"

I tranqed him in the chest, shutting off his counter-accusation.

"You can't spread this poison any longer!" I shouted. "You don't determine right and wrong. Right and wrong have been written by God, in your hearts and in His Word, the Bible. Some of you will turn, but many of you won't heed my warnings. A day is coming soon when judgment will be upon your heads. The kidnappers from the theater are being punished. Think of the new strain of the Meridia Virus that's in the wind. I am the Serval, a servant of Jesus Christ. A spiritual war has been raging for a long time across America. It's time to make sure you're on the side you want to be on for eternity. Now, go to your homes and prepare for the worst."

The people appeared shaken. Instead of rushing away as I'd hoped, they gazed at one another as they mulled around, asking each other questions.

"Meet at the school in one hour!" a man with a cane bellowed. "Go home, collect yourselves, and get to the meeting in one hour!"

My speech was finished. I climbed off the RV roof by way of its rusty hood, and started toward the building. Alice approached me, the weariness of her own violent captivity evaporated from her posture. We marched together to the front of the theater.

"Thirty-four people, mostly adults," she reported. "Even with the bikes Gilly found, some of the women can't travel more than a day or two."

"If they can get to the next town south of us, it'll be an improvement for them," I said. "They have nothing else here. Those who can need to travel farther away and start over."

"Levi, listen." She stopped me in front of the crowd of liberated people as Gilly equipped each refugee with various items. Several of them had hurried back to their old residences for other possessions and returned. "Some of these people have been captives for years. Who's going to get them safely to the next town? Who's going to speak for them and keep them together when there seems no hope? Gilly can't do that."

"Right. Gilly's coming with us."

"I'd like to go south as far as they need me." She looked away, her eyes wet. "You've rescued me again, and I think it's so I can do this. You have your calling, to reach your Jenna in New York. This may be my calling, to help these poor people."

"Alice, you don't need my permission." I smiled and set a hand on her shoulder. "I'm proud of you. You're one of God's children now. You're caring for people like Jesus wants us to."

"I don't know if I'll ever see you again." She tucked her baseball bat under the stump of her left arm and held out her right hand for me to shake. "You're something special, Levi Caspertein."

Instead of shaking her hand, I embraced her with an intensity of emotion that I hoped she felt as well. We'd become like family, like brother and sister, in a few short weeks. But God had purposed in her heart to part ways, and I wasn't about to change her new heart of compassion.

"I'll pray daily for your safety, Alice."

She backed away and swung her bat onto her shoulder.

"This doesn't mean I'm not part of the Caspertein family anymore." She grinned. "If I feel like wintering in Colorado, I'll find your mom in Meeker, right?"

"She'd be happy to have you."

Thirty minutes later, with full canteens and canned food from the theater, the freed captives left me and Gilly standing in the street.

"You know how to use that thing?" I nodded at a compound bow and quiver of aluminum arrows Gilly had strapped to his back.

"I'll figure it out," he answered smartly, then reconsidered. "Can you teach me?"

"I'd be glad to. You're joining the Caspertein family now. What we have and what we know—it's yours to have and know."

We walked out of Kayenta before noon, smoke from the theater beginning to billow from the fire I'd started on the stage. The victims who'd passed through the town had surely not all been accounted for, but repentance had been preached. True reconciliation with God through the cross was up to the people now.

Chapter Twenty

We hid below a rocky ledge, clinging with our fingers and toes to the slippery boulder beneath us. The compound bow on Gilly's back poked me in the neck, and my own gunstock jabbed me in my gut, but we couldn't adjust our positions. Twelve marauders were above us.

Two hours outside of Kayenta, the two of us had climbed a bluff, gazing ahead to see Annette and the others. Instead, we'd stumbled upon a motley band of cutthroats. I knew they were cutthroats since I'd been close enough to one man to see the necklace of human teeth around his neck. Before he screamed to warn the others, I'd grabbed him by the necklace and hurled him off the ledge. But he'd screamed anyway, my impulse reaction to silence the man having failed. Now, Gilly and I were trapped.

"There's no one here," one man said somewhere above us.

"When have I ever been known to fall off a perfectly good mountain?" another argued and cursed. "Look around better. He was as big as a bear. There's nowhere for him to hide. Look at my leg! I think it's broken in two places. He's somewhere around here!"

Pebbles trickled over the ledge above us and dropped thirty feet to the desert floor. From my point of view, we couldn't jump that far or climb down the sheer face. Climbing back up was impossible as long as the cutthroats were there. Even if I did have superior firepower, a face-to-face fight with a dozen gunmen would be suicide. We would have to wait it out.

I gazed out across the brown landscape. The sun was on its downward arc. Even if we did survive the jump down, there was no cover for one thousand yards around the bluff.

"I'm slipping!" Gilly whispered.

In my crouched position, I leaned back on my arm and kicked out my right leg to bar the teen from hurling over the edge. He came up against my leg, a delicate balance for me since I could begin to slip as well. Squeezing my eyes shut, I tried to focus through my strained muscles and cramping limbs. Death was above us, and death was below us, just different methods. Which did I prefer? I preferred a fighting chance, which was to fall below and run for it. If we could get far enough away without being shot, I could defend us with the bullpup.

Darkness would be our friend. Somehow, we had to stay in our hiding place until the sun set.

"Move back and sit down," I whispered, but it felt like begging since my outstretched leg, holding my weight and his, was already trembling. "Push the pebbles aside. Quick! I'll hold you."

I braced myself for his movements. He trusted me and leaned against my leg to turn and clear loose shale away. As soon as he sat down, bowed over on behalf of the low ceiling of our crag, I gasped in relief.

"Take my rifle."

Balancing on one arm at a time, I helped him take the sling off my shoulder. Finally, I was able to move farther away from the edge and rest my legs. Sweat poured off my nose and chin. Though my pack was with Annette, I carried a canteen on my hip. It was nearly full of Kayenta's water, but that wouldn't last long, even on the north side of the outcropping where we were in the shade.

"Conserve your water," I instructed quietly. Men were moving above us, mumbling as they continued to search their elevated hideout for a bear-sized man. "It'll be a long afternoon if we wait until dark."

"I don't have any water."

"What?" I frowned at him. "We just came from—"

He pointed downward. His water bottle had fallen when we'd climbed off the ledge above.

"Well, it's a nice view, at least." I took my rifle from him and kicked more rocks away from my heels to give me more traction on our angled perch.

But then another threat came to mind. As soon as the bandits had thoroughly searched their small mountain, they would check the sand for sign around the rock. If they walked below us and looked up, we'd be spotted.

"We can't stay here," I said. "They'll find us. We'll be trapped."

"What do you want to do?"

"If I hold you by your belt, can you lean out and see if there are any footholds to climb down?"

"Okay."

This youth's willingness and courage was already making me proud. It took five minutes to ease out of his compound bow and quiver, which we stuffed behind us where the horizontal rock was smallest. I set my rifle with the bow and planted one foot on the ceiling to keep my body wedged in place. With a firm grip on the back of his belt, he moved toward the ledge.

"Look!" He pointed straight out into the desert. "Someone's out there!"

I looked up in time to see the sun's reflection off glass. Yanking Gilly back to me, I clawed for my rifle. Using my scope, I peered directly north.

"It's my family," I said, barely making out three heads over a bump of sand one thousand yards out. "Wave. Wave something, Gilly. Let them know we see them."

When in Kayenta, I hadn't needed my binoculars, so they were with my pack. Mia, Annette, or Forest were certainly using my stronger field glasses to search for me.

Gilly tugged a faded baseball cap from his pants and waved it vigorously. The reflective signal from afar ceased, but not soon enough.

"There's people out there!" one of the brutes above warned.

"It could be a posse from Kaibito. We hit them one too many times."

"They're a hundred miles from us!" A blow landed on flesh. "Shut up! It's no posse. Whoever threw Vic off the rock is still out there. If they're sticking around, I smell competition. Someone's moving in on our territory."

"Competitors?"

"They want what we got."

"We don't have anything. We're even low on ammo."

"They don't know that. We can flank them. Send four east and four west. We'll have them by nightfall. Take the nets and bolos to get them alive."

"What if they have guns?"

"Guns or not, no one has much ammo these days."

They strategized more, but I started to do my own planning. In the distance, I was probably seeing Annette with her bullpup, Forest with his .22, and Mia with the shotgun. Vorca and Sharly were probably on the other side of the bluff with Caleb, Natasha, and the burros. But at a range of one thousand yards, no one was shooting anyone, not even with the bullpup. Annette needed to come closer to make a difference for me, and also so I could cover her.

As if she could hear me, a lone figure stood and walked toward us into the desert. Then, off to the side, two other figures moved forward—I guessed Mia and Forest, in cover formation. They were thinking ahead, not spreading out beyond Forest's one-hundred-yard range, so he could cover Annette. And Mia could cover and spot for Forest.

"They're coming right at us!" A cutthroat cursed from above. "What're they doing? No way are they attacking us with only three men. Call everyone back in, now! They're assaulting us straight on while others are probably approaching from other directions. Get eyes on the other side of the hill. Something just . . . doesn't feel right about this . . ."

Instead of making an assault on Annette's position, the crooks withdrew their plan to flank her, and prepared to defend themselves against their unseen enemy.

Annette kept approaching. I guessed she wore one headset, while Mia and Forest shared the other radio. They were spaced about eighty yards apart, walking steadily toward us.

They stopped inside six hundred yards. Annette commanded the desert now, and waved confidently at me, now easily identifiable in my scope.

"Wave at them," I told Gilly, and he did.

"That's your family? The Caspertein clan?"

"That's them." I chuckled and watched Annette spread a blanket out, set her ammunition magazines on the blanket, then lay on her stomach. Though she had no cover, lying prone at nearly a half-mile away, she would be safe from anyone firing at her. I doubted any of the cutthroats were snipers, even if they did have a couple long-range rifles. "Alice and I were supposed to be a few minutes behind them. When we didn't catch up, they obviously came looking for us. Seems we're acting more and more like a family."

"Nobody ever came looking for me," Gilly said. "Not for anything good, anyway."

"Well, you're with the Casperteins now. We've got our share of problems, but we find our way along the path of love more often than not, because we keep our hearts on God's love."

I reached over to nudge his shoulder, like a father might sincerely do with his son. But that movement was all it took to shift my weight the wrong way. Turning to my right hip, I fought for traction as I slid forward. Clawing with my fingers for a purchase didn't help. There was nothing on the bare rock to hang onto.

When I went over the ledge, I was immediately worried about hitting rocks on the way down. Harder than necessary, I shoved my body backwards off the perch. My body turned as I fell. Rock brushed my back, flipping me forward. Pawing the air, I realized I was about to land face-first!

My foot touched the rock wall, somersaulting me to an upright stand an instant before I collided with the ground. My forward momentum didn't stop as my legs buckled under me. I pitched forward and landed hard on my left arm. Sharp rock sliced through my flannel shirt above the elbow and my arm was immediately wet with blood before my body settled into the orange sand.

"There he is!" someone above me yelled.

A bullet slammed next to my head. The report of the rifle brought me to my senses. But then another rifle boomed, farther away, and I glimpsed a body collapse on the rocky ledge.

Before I could be targeted again, I lunged to my knees and dove closer to the base of the rock. Gasping from the impact of the fall and the pain in my arm, I struggled to recover as the gun battle raged above and across the desert.

"Serval!"

"Stay back!" I yelled to Gilly as men blindly shot down at me. They couldn't possibly see me, but an instant later, their attention seemed to swing toward Annette. No doubt, she would fire only when she had a sure target. And she'd already fired five times, if I could trust my ringing ears and rattled brain.

"Gilly, drop my rifle!"

I stared at the sky, waiting for my gun, not sure if Gilly had heard me, doubting I could lift my injured arm to catch the heavy rifle. An instant later, it dropped outside my safe cover, but I dared bullets rather than risk damage to the scope and chamber. With one strained arm, I caught the weapon, then backed up to the rock again. My foes were torn between Annette, who was out of their range, and me, who was out of their reach.

Above, it seemed the enemy had retreated for cover from Annette, and I was given a reprieve from gunfire. Holding my rifle between my knees, I found it to be functional and undamaged. But my left arm was nearly useless from pain. Blood dripped from my numb fingertips. Shooting the bullpup with one hand and hoping for an accurate shot was out of the question. I'd only waste our bullets.

Suddenly, Gilly dropped from the perch. He grunted loudly, landing awkwardly on his feet, then toppled over, and lay still. I set my rifle down and dragged the boy by his arm to the safety of the rock face. He stared wildly at me, his chest heaving, until he gasped. His diaphragm recovered from the shocking impact of his drop, and he began breathing normally. As soon as he sat up, he examined my arm.

"This might hurt," he said.

I clenched my teeth as his fingers tore something from my arm. The nerve was immediately relieved, but the throbbing agony of the injury only worsened. Gilly opened his hand, full of my blood, and showed me a sharp rock the size of my thumb.

"That definitely didn't belong in my arm." I grinned at the boy, intending to calm the worried look on his face. "Carry my rifle and start walking."

"Walking? Where?"

"Out there." I nodded at the expanse between us and Annette. "We'll be okay. My mom will protect us."

"Yeah, but . . ." He frowned at the distance. "There's nowhere to hide!"

The cutthroats fired at us with automatic weapons, probably hastily, and Annette answered with one shot. We heard a man grunt and a rifle clatter.

"It's like trusting God," I said, taking my belt off. "We have no cover for the messes we might find for ourselves, until we trust God to heal us and protect us. We trust God to make us right. There's no other cover out there, except the cover of a single superior weapon. Come on. We'll walk together, but I can't walk for you."

Gilly adjusted the compound bow and quiver on his back, and cradled the bullpup in his hands like he intended to sprint rather than walk. The instant I thought he would go with me, his shoulders slumped, and he shook his head.

"No way. They'll pick us off out there."

"They'll pick us off easier if we stay here, Gilly. All they have to do is find a way off their ledge and creep around the hill to shoot at us." I tightened my belt around my arm wound. "Tell you what: you walk in front of me, my hand on your shoulder. If they shoot at us, I'll take the bullets first."

He stared at my face, blinking a few times.

"Why would you do that for me?" He looked away. "I'm usually the one who gets treated the worst."

"Not here. Not with me. Let's go." I turned him to face the desert, my good hand on his right shoulder. "Walk quickly. Change directions often, like every ten steps."

"Zig-zag?"

"You got it. I'm right here with you."

He took a deep breath and we left the cover of our rock wall. In two steps, we were in potential view of the killers. Annette's rifle barked more rapidly. I heard the tranquilizers slapping stone behind us. The gunmen were sure to be confused at the type of ammunition we were using, since it wasn't ricocheting off the rock.

Gilly angled to the right, then swerved left for a dozen paces. When he zagged back to the right again, a bullet popped sand a few feet away. My hand guided his shoulder. He trembled, but kept walking. My pain was such that after those first few yards, I focused only on following Gilly. We were trusting each other, moving left and right, as the gunmen behind us tried to anticipate our erratic trajectory, while Annette maintained pressure. With every step we took, we made it harder for the killers to hit us.

Finally, we reached Annette.

"Keep moving straight ahead," I told Gilly.

Annette remained prone, the rifle no longer barking, but her eye still on the scope. I noticed she was responsibly collecting all her brass shells for reloading later. We had a couple hundred rounds of gel-tranqs between us still, but once those were gone, we'd be left to reloading lethal rounds into the shells.

Up in the hills, Gilly and I found Vorca, Sharly, and the kids. Gilly helped me sit on a horse pack that Vorca had set on the ground. Sharly offered Gilly water while Vorca chattered her disapproval of my field dressing. She unwound my belt and tore my shirt to examine the wound. Soon after, Annette, Mia, and Forest hiked into camp.

"Where's Alice?" Mia asked. I guessed my cousin had appreciated the one-armed Amazon more than anyone else. They had moved about camp the same way, never shirking from duty.

But I couldn't immediately answer her question while I was in the throes of pain. Vorca wasn't being too gentle as she cleaned and stitched the hole in my upper arm.

"She's taking the slaves south," Gilly said. He shied away from Annette as she reached for his bruised and battered face. "What are you doing? I'm fine."

"What happened to you?" Annette asked as she wiped her cheek, leaving a smear of gunpowder smoke. "How is it that every town we go through is either kidnapping or brutalizing its people?"

"It's like the Book of Judges that Levi read to us," Forest said. "When people are left to do what they think is best only for themselves, they'll always end up hurting others."

"Alice is trusting God," I finally said. "She found her purpose when a bunch of people needed to be guided to New Mexico. She'll keep them alive. They had no one else. When she's not needed anymore, she'll track us down and join us again on the trail to Colorado."

"Levi, you've got to quit scaring me like this." Annette and Forest packed up the gear. They tightened the cinches, making the burros groan. "It'll only take one bullet."

"We were trusting God," Gilly said, "and you. He said you'd cover us."

"Let's talk on the road." Annette took my rifle from Gilly and slid it into a pack strap on the lead mule. "Come on, young man. I want to hear your story. You can walk in front with me."

"Me?" Gilly appeared startled. "You want to talk to me?"

"Knowing my son like I do, I'd say God has brought you to us for a reason. We have a long walk so you can tell me your life story."

Annette started walking. Gilly raised his eyebrows at me, and I nodded my approval for him to fall in order. He smiled, obviously not familiar with a mother's attention, and caught up to Annette. Vorca used her knife to cut the horse hair stitch as Mia tugged the burros ahead.

"Go now! Giddy up!" Natasha said, raising her arms from atop the second burro, as if she were a princess commanding the entire procession. "Faster! Go!"

Forest and Sharly walked off to the east to scout for game. He had one radio headset on one ear to communicate with Annette, who wore the other one. Vorca waddled away, Caleb waving and jabbering at me from her back.

For a few minutes, I didn't move. I stood there admiring my family. We'd lost Alice, hopefully only temporarily, as she sought her own path for Jesus Christ, but we'd gained Gilly.

"Thank You, Lord," was all I could say—thanking Him for the pain, and the trials, and the miles, and the tears, and for . . . family. Yes, we'd begun to act as a Christian family, rather than merely as a group of people on a trek.

We reached Highway 191 that night.

The next morning, two columns of gray smoke rose far away to the southwest.

"I thought you said Alice was going south. Isn't that her signal?" Annette brushed her tangled, graying hair as camp was being packed up. Somehow, she remained a beautiful woman through the heat, dust, and toil. "What do you think it means? Is it for us?"

The location of the smoke was north of Highway 160, the opposite direction from where Alice had headed with the Kayenta refugees. As I studied it, I felt in my gut that it wasn't from Alice, yet it was the two-column smoke signal I'd told her to use if danger was closing on us. There was only one other person it could be: Kip Brogdon. After he and Alice had shared a meal and water days earlier, she must've explained the signal to him.

"It's for us. Vorca!" When she looked at me, I waved northward. "Take us north."

"Annette, look what I found." Gilly approached us, oblivious of the danger. He donned a black motorcycle helmet too large for his head. "How do I look?"

Annette flipped the helmet visor down over his face.

"I think you're the only one of us who'll come out of this desert without a sunburn." She laughed, much to his approval as he flipped the visor back up. "Go help Sharly with the packs, would you?"

He immediately obeyed.

"You have a new fan, Mom," I joked, stretching my stiff arm muscles.

"You're the one who keeps bringing me more family." She smirked at me, but without the harshness. "I think I'm learning to roll a little better with God's curve balls on this trip. And your shenanigans."

"If we skip a resupply in Shiprock, it's two weeks to Norwood." I eyed the columns of smoke again. "But we don't have a choice. General Brogdon must be on our trail. We figured it would be close, but we're still two days outside Shiprock."

"You didn't answer my question. If that's not Alice, who's signaling us?"

"I can't say for sure."

"Levi, don't hide stuff from me." She forced a smile. "Just tell me who our friend is out there. No big deal."

I couldn't lie to her, but I definitely couldn't tell her it was probably Kip Brogdon, participant in Dad's death, assaulter of Mia, murderer of dozens, if not hundreds.

Forest saved me as he communicated on the headset in her ear. Annette pressed the ear piece into her ear to hear more clearly. We both peered up at the nearest ridgeline where Forest had run the instant we discovered the smoke signal.

"He says there's a column of trucks!" Annette reported. "And they're just fifteen minutes back! Everyone, we've got to move out now! Go, Vorca!"

Gilly and I remained behind with two tarps, beating the ground to cover our tracks, especially those closest to the highway. Gilly swung his tarp left and right with great effect. But I feared my injured arm reduced my movements to a one-armed twirling action, kicking up more sand into my face than covering our tracks.

Fifty yards off the highway, Gilly took our tarps into his arms and we ran after the others. The spine of an ancient lava formation provided adequate cover, but only if we crouched low. The burros were hastily unpacked and forced to lie on their sides. Gilly covered the eyes of the first animal, and lay over its neck. Mia handled the second burro.

Forest ran from his lookout and skidded into our hiding place next to Sharly.

"Here they come!" Annette shouted. "Everyone, stay down until I say. Don't even look up!"

We panted with our cheeks against the lava. Sharly lay with Natasha on the ground with Forest, who checked his rifle chamber in preparation to fire. Caleb was lying on his back next to Vorca, enjoying his opportunity to kick and wave freely.

The rumble of engines made the burros' ears twitch, but the rest of us remained frozen in place. If one of our footprints was noticed in the sand, we were dead. General Brogdon would send waves of soldiers against us, knowing we wouldn't kill them. In minutes, he would overwhelm us. Annette and Forest were the only two who would be effective shooters. Mia had the shotgun, but I didn't want her in a place where she might kill again. Since Kip Brogdon was no longer with his father, the general might assume the worst about his son—and blame us for his disappearance. This certainly intensified his search for us. But I didn't blame Kip. God had given life to a dead man, in more ways than one. Kip was now walking for God, and it seemed we were being chased for it.

The engines faded without changing. I disobeyed Annette's command, and raised my head. Before the vehicles were too far away, I studied the convoy. Eight Humvees and two tanker trucks with fuel trailers. With so much fuel, I guessed they could cross the Mississippi and keep going. Unless they were stopped. Licking my lips, I wondered if I should go on the offensive again. A couple phosphorus rounds on the tanker trucks would disable the whole convoy. At least, until others arrived from San Diego. Chances were, however, that the Pacific States were setting up depots and field bases along their route now. There would be no stopping General Brogdon. In the ten vehicles, I guessed they carried a total of close to fifty men—only a fraction of what they could muster if the call went out for reinforcements.

"We really needed to get to Shiprock before them," Annette said. Still, no one else moved. "How are we supposed to get ready for the mountains?"

"There'll be plenty of water in the mountains," I said. "Forest, food will be our biggest problem until we reach Norwood. That's two weeks away. Meeker is two or three weeks beyond that. There are more towns along the way, but none that we planned to visit."

"We'll ration the dried fruit and beans," Annette said. "You say Vorca knows vegetation, so she can help me collect greens along the way. All right, everyone. We can get up."

Annette checked Vorca's handiwork on my arm, while Forest, Gilly, and Vorca repacked the burros.

"I'd sure like to know Vorca's story," Annette said. "These stitches are perfect. You're the only one besides Caleb that she talks to in her own language. Any breakthrough?"

"Nothing yet, but at least she's talking."

"We were interrupted earlier," she said. "You were about to tell me who is watching our backtrail with smoke signals. We'd be prisoners or dead right now if we wouldn't have been warned."

"I think we can chalk it up to the work of God. Turning north will get the general off our backs now. We're on the final stretch to Colorado."

"You're avoiding the question again. Enough with the mystery, Levi. Who's back there?"

Chapter Twenty-one

Everyone in the Caspertein caravan gave me reasons to continue north with them, but I insisted on remaining behind at the volcanic formation. I told them I had to see for sure who was behind us. If it was a friend, as I guessed it was, then that friend needed to know we had departed our eastern heading to now march north.

Reluctantly, Annette shoved my bullpup into my one good arm, and Mia gave me my pack and enough food to last three days, if I rationed carefully. Sharly topped off two canteens for me, and Vorca checked my healing wound. Gilly shook my hand like the man he was quickly becoming, and Forest waved from afar as he watched over our flock like the shepherd he'd become.

I relaxed against the formation and watched my family grow smaller in the distance. It was several miles before they disappeared over a gradual rise, then I saw them no more.

Flexing my bad arm, I tested the stitches, knowing I would use it in an emergency, pain or not. A permanent and ugly scar was of little concern to me, but deeper tissue damage was still a danger if infection set in. Unless a situation arose, my left hand would remain in my jeans pocket to immobilize the limb.

Anticipation kept me from resting comfortably that sunny morning. I pondered the ways of God. Ever since leaving San Diego, God had caused me to cross paths with specific people for specific reasons. Whether I realized the reasons at the time or not, looking back now, I more fully grasped God's mighty hand in every skirmish or conflict or meeting. On the night Mia was assaulted by Kip

Brogdon, God's hand seemed very small. But I still knew God's hand never caused evil. He even permitted man to go his own course, though always showing His might and goodness by allowing a glimmer of good to blossom for those who would seek His face. I considered what the Apostle Paul taught—that even in darkness, the Lord leaves a witness of His goodness and light. It was that glimmer and witness I was eager to see now.

I would've enjoyed a moment with my family to celebrate Kip Brogdon's miraculous conversion, but I believed their wounds were too fresh for them to see God's hand from sin's wicked assault. Like in any tragedy, a rainbow accompanies rain in the daytime, but we have to look up from the right position. Annette and Mia were still learning to look up. Though my protectiveness for my family was intense, I was still learning to trust God to work in my enemies as He worked in my loved ones. My carnal mind had disapproved of caring for Kip Brogdon, but the Spirit in me rejoiced in his new birth. Who could make sense of the eternal within the temporal?

Throughout the day, I read my Bible and tried to doze. Every five minutes or so, I turned and rose to my knees to check the highway in both directions. Twice, around noon, I saw a small group of travelers, heavily armed, moving east, but none heading west. Though I'd expected more westward-traveling pilgrims, I guessed word had gotten out about the Pacific States movements in the region. No doubt, General Brogdon had crushed many people's dreams of going to the West Coast. Every corner of the nation was locked in its own variation of oppression. The grass certainly wasn't greener in California.

In the afternoon, I saw another party walking eastward with a horse pulling a cart of belongings. I scoped their faces with my binoculars, as I had the others, but saw no one familiar. Perhaps the two columns of smoke had been a coincidence? Maybe Kip Brogdon wasn't behind us at all.

But then I saw him minutes later. His Pacific States crimson jacket was faded from sun and dust, and the curls on his head were more prominent as his hair had grown longer, but it was him. As he drew even with me, I saw he wore a meager pack on his back now, and he held something in front of him. He was reading aloud. It was a Bible! His voice reached me and I frowned at this mad man as he traveled alone while talking to himself.

Rising to my feet, I whistled three times before he heard me and stopped walking. I waved and he left the highway to approach me.

"What kind of a lunatic travels alone in this land?" I asked with a chuckle.

"Do I look like I have anything to steal?" He laughed back, the laugh of a man at ease. His face, with bright eyes and a wide grin, was barely recognizable from the militant crook I'd known for years. "Seems I'm not the only lunatic alone out here."

"We got your signal. The family headed north." I held out my hand. He shifted the Bible into his other hand and shook my hand firmly. "You saved my family, Kip. That Pacific States convoy roared past here this morning, just thirty minutes after we saw the smoke."

"I've shed enough blood in my lifetime." He sighed, and we both checked the highway for travelers. "Until I die, by man's hand or by the elements, saving lives is my only way now."

"That's all you own now, huh?" I gestured to his hatchet tucked into his waistband. "It ain't easy making sense of how God inspires us to let go of this world, is it?"

"Yeah, it's pretty simple for me now—a Bible, a tomahawk, a canteen, and a bedroll." He didn't seem able to stop smiling. "Hey, this is good timing. Help me understand this King Melchizedek thing in the Book of Hebrews. What am I missing?"

"Can you stand some dried jackrabbit meat while we talk?"

"Beats raw pigeon eggs." He touched his gut, then laughed.

We sat on the north side of the lava spine and nibbled smoked rabbit as we opened the Scriptures. He had many questions about the Bible, and since I'd lived in a Christian home since I'd found my father twenty years earlier, I could answer most of his simple questions. We were shivering in the darkness before we realized how much time had passed. Side by side, we unrolled our bedding, and I shared my tarp over his thin blanket. Bowing under a starry sky, we prayed and wept together. Such was our joy for being saved from our old natures of corruption, and our compassion for souls still in terror of judgement. I'd never prayed with a man in such anguish for the unsaved, or in such jubilation for having been saved from eternal hellfire.

Before we slept, I called him my brother, and then we fell silent until morning.

✝

"How did I let you talk me into this?" I asked Kip Brogdon the next evening. Side by side, we approached the town of Shiprock from the northwest, having made excellent time across the grassy landscape. "I should be on my way to catch up to my family."

"You said it yourself: you guys had planned to resupply here." He lifted a waist-high strand of rusty barbed wire, a remnant from the days of property owners. "Knowing my dad, he'll leave a couple Pacific States reps in town, then keep moving east."

"Yeah, except he'll double-back any minute, as soon as he realizes he missed us somewhere on the highway." I ducked under the wire and readied my rifle for use. "Besides, neither one of us has anything extra to trade for the kind of supplies my family needs."

"So, it's like we're the Israelites on the edge of the Red Sea." He laughed far too casually for the danger we were walking into. "We're moving forward, trusting God to provide a way."

"When did you get so bold for God?"

Ten miles to the southwest, the Monadnock Rock Formation rose fifteen hundred feet, a lonely piece of backdrop to the quiet town as we walked down one street. Remnants of houses to the left and right of us revealed that they'd been reduced to ashes years earlier. Green grass now grew in patches where floors used to be.

In the center of the town was an elementary school, but we'd seen no life.

"Something's wrong." I tightened my grip on the bullpup. "This is supposed to be a thriving religious center for the Navajo People."

"So, where is everyone?"

At that moment, a man on horseback, accompanied by two youths with rifles in their hands, rode into view. They passed an unmanned trading post and approached us. I glanced at Kip in his barely-recognizable, worn-out Pacific States jacket, except for the identifiable patch on his shoulder. Faster than he could stop me, I reached out and tore the patch off his shoulder.

"What'd you do that for?"

"Trust me." I stuffed the patch into my pocket. "Like most towns your dad visits, you don't want to be known as a Pacific States soldier here."

"I'm AWOL, anyway."

Raising my hand at the three strangers, the man reined in his horse and stopped ten yards away.

"By the look of you two," the horseman said, "you're not from around here, either."

It was then that I noticed their horses appeared weary, their heads hanging, with mud on their legs from crossing a river somewhere.

"We came to town looking for supplies." I gestured at Kip. "But we'll be rejoining our companions sooner than we thought, since no one's here."

"Oh, they're here, just out of town burying their dead."

"Was there a gun battle?" Kip's hand went to his hip where he'd once worn his sidearm. "Who was it?"

"Those Pacific States raiders." The man shook his head. "The town put up a good fight, but they would've been slaughtered if we hadn't been coming into town. The Pacific States military retreated to the east. Maybe they'll think twice about forcing a town to resupply them at gunpoint. But a lot died on both sides today."

"That's the strike and submit campaign." Kip nodded, but only he and I understood how personally he knew his father's tactics. "How many were lost?"

"About a dozen from this town. Plus some injured. We didn't lose anyone in our group. That's one advantage to having a handful of grenade launchers."

"RPGs?" I whistled. "Yeah, I bet ol' General Brogdon would run from that kind of response."

"Knowing him, though," Kip said with a serious look, "he'll take it out on the next town."

"How many in your group?" I asked.

"About fifty. We're from Southern California, followers of the Serval. My name's Fritz Larskell, and my boys, Craig and Clint."

His boys nodded politely, but I didn't know how to respond right away.

"Did you say you're followers of the *Serval?*" I barely held back a laugh at the name I'd been using since leaving San Diego. "What's a Serval follower?"

"The Serval is a Christian soldier who's sweeping the country of oppression, from coast to coast. Half the people with me have been touched by his life one way or another. Loved ones have been brought back to their families. Lost souls have been found. Hope is being restored. We crossed

Arizona on Highway 10, then cut north to arrive here, trying to get ahead of him. Everywhere we go, we run into people on the move who know about him. I came from Hawkridge, but there's other Servalites with me from other towns—Aporax, Palm Springs, Cadiz, and a dozen other places."

"Servalites?" I frowned now, growing more concerned as the man spoke.

"Yep. He's got people on the move. Some of us have lost our homes or never really had one. The Serval has a purpose. We're looking for him to join him and serve God. He'll tell us how." He studied my face, then Kip's. "You two have a seasoned look to you. You heard of the Serval or if he's come through here yet? Wherever he's headed, we'd like to know."

"Give us a moment, Fritz." Kip grabbed me by the shoulder and turned me away with him a few feet. *"Really?* You've been using your dad's old handle?"

"I thought it was a harmless nickname." I gasped, still not completely grasping what I'd heard Fritz Larskell say. "How was I to know this would happen?"

"My dad won't tolerate an armed band like this as he tries to expand the Pacific States' territory. He's trying to settle the Plains Zone before the Appalachian Federation does."

"You heard Fritz. These boys forced your dad to retreat to the east."

"He'd retreat only temporarily so he can radio in two hundred troops to deal with this! Dad's group is only a scouting party, like I was. No one can stand against him. And remember, if he really wants to, he can unleash the Meridia Virus and just wait it out as it kills everyone. No, these Servalites can't stand against Dad."

"I think you're wrong." I glanced back at Fritz Larskell. "These people are tough. Listen to them. They're just looking for a leader, and then they'll know how to stand the right way. Fifty people is quite a force for your father to deal with.”

“Levi, if Dad hears you’re leading an armed band of tough soldiers, he’ll go after you specifically.”

“He’s already targeting me, Kip. We’ve been running for our lives for weeks.”

“Well, this could get worse for you and your family real fast!” He surveyed the Larskell men. “Are you willing to lead these fifty people, keep them alive, and be the answer to their lives?”

“Of course not. I have to get to New York. These people just need some direction and protection. It sounds like they might even have some Christians among them.”

“Are you going to teach them what they need to know to survive my dad? Or rein in their zeal to become Servalite missionaries across America?”

“I told you, no. I can’t stick around.” I grinned. “But I do know someone who would make a good Serval.”

“I don’t know . . .” He frowned. “I suppose . . .”

“They need to know about the gospel,” I said.

“The words you shared with me in the desert were plain enough. They brought me back to life. Is there more to salvation besides believing in Jesus Christ for forgiveness of sins and deliverance from the old nature?”

“No, that’s the gist of it. And you have your Bible to guide you through the rest.”

“Your dad left a legacy, Levi. I’ve read Dad’s intel reports on him.”

“So, can you do this? Can you lead these people?” I lowered my head. “Kip, it ain’t easy being the Serval, but that’s who they need right now.”

“Well, if you’re not going to be, then I don’t see any way around it. I have to be. I’m the Serval.”

“Okay.” I turned him by the shoulder. “Follow my lead.”

As we drew near to Fritz Larskell again, his sons were smiling like they already knew our secret.

"Which one of you is the Serval?" Fritz asked. "Craig here said he remembers that rifle from Hawkridge. The Serval had it."

"My name is Levi Caspertein," I said. "We had to discuss how meeting you may change our forward momentum."

"We won't be a burden at all, I promise!" Fritz climbed off his horse and tossed the reins to Clint. "We're all survivors, hunters, and veterans of a hundred battles."

"In Hawkridge," I said, "the Serval passed through your town after meeting your founder. In Cadiz, he neutralized the conflict between Zareen Rawls and Jose Medina. The Serval has repelled the Pacific States troops and routed Mokoa, Caliph of Aporax, freeing hundreds from bondage. Gentlemen, meet the Serval."

I nudged Kip toward the man.

"It's an honor, sir." Fritz shook Kip's hand. "This is a day I've hoped for weeks to live to see. Boys, in the rebuilding of America, this man will be a legend! Imagine what he's already done. God is with you, sir, and now we are, too. We're at your service. Tell us what to do."

"The honor is mine." Kip placed his hand on Fritz's shoulder. "Before Christ saved me from condemnation, I was a filthy, rotten sinner. I'm not worthy to be called a hero by any name, but I would enjoy meeting your people. Maybe we can put together a plan to reach out to the rest of the country. After all, we do have a message."

"So, you'll continue east?" Fritz asked.

Kip glanced at me, and I shrugged, as if to say, *"You asked for it."*

"I don't see why not, Fritz. Craig, Clint—those rifles you have there better be for hunting. The Serval doesn't kill people. Non-lethal weaponry only, except for hunting game. We're only here to express the love of God."

They continued to talk as Fritz led them through town, and I was forgotten in their wake, happy to follow them from the back and glorify God at the miracle that had occurred in Kip's life. The man he had been was dead and gone.

Kip Brogdon was now the Serval!

The members of the Caspertein family are natural leaders, but that night in Shiprock, I was a spectator. I watched from a nearby bonfire as Kip "the Serval" Brogdon carefully balanced the celebrations of the Servalites in finding their leader, and the townspeople mourning over their losses. The Servalite energy was so infectious that the people of Shiprock, even with their fresh wounds, were singing hymns to God an hour after sundown. Kip himself knew none of the worship songs, but musicians with instruments materialized, and the celebration began. Shiprock's residents had fought and won a battle, with the aid of the Servalites, and the Servalites weren't about to think lightly of this day when God had brought them to the Serval. God had shown them victory, and they were learning that He had eternal victory in store for them.

In his presidential-like status, Kip passed me several times, escorted by some father, or a child pulling him by the hand to meet someone or to explain the gospel to a relative. When our eyes met in the firelight, I noticed the seriousness in his face. He wasn't being swept up by the attention. The people could celebrate, but he was now burdened with their safety, their hopes, and their futures. He had led military men for many years, raised amongst the ranks of his father's wicked but committed soldiers. The Servalites needed a leader, and I believed God had given them the right one.

For a moment—and just a moment—I viewed Kip from a worldly perspective. My father, the mighty Titus Caspertein, the first and real Serval, had been murdered by this man and his father. Now, he bore the name of my father, the name that was mine to wield in the face of my exploits and enemies.

But it wasn't a name or a work meant for me, and the Holy Spirit inside me quickly set the life of Christ before my spiritual eyes. I could make no claim on a mere human title.

That night was one of rejoicing for the people, but I was melancholy. I belonged with my family. Though Kip was assuming leadership of a missionary corps to reach the nation, it wasn't my calling, even though I wanted to be effective as I knew he would be. Rather, God had another calling for me, one in the east, and along the way, to touch others with the life of Christ in me. Although my journey had a goal of reaching Jenna and ensuring her safety, the journey thus far hadn't been limited to her alone. It had been meant for many others whom I couldn't yet fathom in number.

The next morning, before the sun rose, Kip walked with me a short distance to the north. The energy I sensed from him was electrifying rather than exhausting. He'd been up all night, sharing his plans with Fritz Larskell and other Servalite elders, and he wasn't the least bit tired. All of America awaited their message.

"I will never forget you, Levi," he said to me as we reached the outskirts of Shiprock. "When I deserved your hatred, you showed me compassion. When you had every right to kill me, you kept me alive. I understand the message of Jesus Christ in His gospel much more clearly because you showed me God's love. Having said that, because we're parting ways, I need to say something that is weighing on my heart."

"I'm listening."

"Before your father got sick, Dad sent us to confiscate all the shortwave radios. Remember?"

"I remember. You and some soldiers showed up at our house and took our radio and antenna."

"Dad also sent me there with my gloved hand smeared with the Meridia Virus, the strain we had weaponized. I shook your father's hand that afternoon. He was hospitable even when we meant him harm. I touched everything I could in your house. I tried to kill all of you. But only your father caught the virus. *Levi, I killed your father.* It was me."

I was silent for a time as he waited for my response. What he'd said wasn't exactly news to me, but it would've been wrong of me to speak carelessly or lightly of what had been his burden for many weeks. This was an important moment for us to both grow, and I couldn't miss this opportunity, even though it was making my knees weak from anguish. Now I knew the details of my father's murder.

"There are no words to express how much you took from me, Kip. You may have been following orders, but you had a choice to kill or not. You chose to kill. We all have to live with the memories of what we did before coming to Christ, but because of Christ, we don't have to live with that guilt any longer. It means a lot to me that you told me. And you were risking a reaction from me just by telling me. Regardless of my loss, I'm a Christian, and my response toward you must be the Lord's response. He has forgiven me. He has forgiven you. You're leading a lot of people now, people who need you. Your conscience needs to be clear about this, so please know that I also forgive you. I forgive you fully. I am that certain that you were in the grip of sin when you killed Dad, but now you are in the palm of Jesus. You are one of His sons. That makes us brothers, even through heartache."

"I'm not worthy of being called your brother." He wiped his face in the dawn's light. "It doesn't seem right that I'm now the Serval. I didn't realize until now just how much this all means to you."

"No, I see it as God's plan. You'll lead them in ways I couldn't, if I'd assumed the role as Serval."

"But I don't know the Bible too well."

"You'll learn. We all learn. And you have some other Christians in your band of Servalites. They'll help teach the others as well as you."

We embraced, shook hands, and embraced again. When I walked away, I looked back several times, and he remained standing there, waving, for a long, long time.

Chapter Twenty-two

Though I anticipated catching up to my family, hiking alone had always appealed to me, especially since I'd learned how to pray. In this sense, my time alone wasn't spent alone at all, but with my Father and Friend, the Lord.

I crossed into Colorado and spent the night on a ridge that overlooked the western landscape—the terrible and unforgiving desert that we'd traversed. If not for the curve of the earth, I imagined I could see all the way to Eagle Mountain, where both Alice and Caleb had joined my side. Thinking of them, I prayed. My fire crackled as I prayed for Alice, who'd become the leader of an exodus in her own way, and for Caleb, who would soon realize he was part of a unique family of stubborn survivors and uncompromising Christians. He would, as a youth, choose his own path, and I prayed for his spiritual guidance even now.

The next morning, I came upon a muddy river flooded with spring runoff. It was impossible to safely swim across because of logs and other debris flowing down the boiling waters. Since I was east of where my family had turned northward, I followed the river to the west along its southern bank. For a day and a half, I picked my way along the bank, steep and slippery in many places, where mist and moss clung to boulders and branches. No map I had with me showed this river, or a potential bridge from before Pan-Day, and I began to doubt I'd chosen wisely by heading upriver at all. Since Pan-Day, landslides, earthquakes, and broken dams had diverted whole tributaries. Now in the mountains, I had to adjust for unexpected terrain.

Then, on the third day out of Shiprock, I emerged from the forest to stumble upon the cracked pavement of an aged, shadowy highway. The road led to the river gorge a stone's throw away where there was an old bridge. It wasn't made of steel as from the days of cars and trucks, but it was made of rope and timbers. Giant tree beams suspended this wagon-wide bridge a few feet above the flowing torrent.

However, the bridge was occupied, and before I could dive back into the forest, I was noticed by people who turned in my direction. My left arm was still healing, so I was certainly in no condition for conflict, if I were attacked. In an instant, I prayed that friendly diplomacy would prevail here. Chances were slim that there was another adequate river crossing, or another bridge where my family would've been able to cross. They must've come this way.

Instead of unslinging my rifle, I raised my right hand to wave. About fifteen men, women, and children saw me now, and two children waved back at me, but were quickly reprimanded and restrained by their mothers. The four men in the group moved to the front. Two carried fishing poles and sidearms, but I saw only one rifle—an old lever action. This wasn't a clan of warriors or military people.

"Hi there!" I approached and stopped a few feet from the bridge, which was much cruder-looking up close. It seemed reasonable that they had built it themselves, and a settlement was probably nearby. They studied me, their faces somber and afraid. The children shyly peered at me from behind their mothers. "It ain't easy trying to cross this river without my own bridge. Perhaps I could use yours for today?"

Except for me and the children, no one else was smiling, and my own smile was beginning to cramp my cheeks.

"We're peaceful folks here," one man said. He held an axe over his shoulder. "We don't want any trouble."

"I'm not looking for any. I just want to—"

"We know who you are." The man tightened his grip on his axe. By the size of his shoulders and arms, I guessed he'd spent hours each day chopping wood. "Your people came through here a few days ago. Shot my son and two of our huntsmen. They said you weren't far behind them, and if we weren't hospitable, we'd regret it. We've got no conflict with you, mister."

"My family doesn't shoot people without reason." I now rested my hand on my sling, ready to swing it into action. As skilled as this man was with his axe, he would be no match for a gel-tranq in the leg. "Besides, if it was my family, your son and the huntsmen are perfectly alive today, right?"

"True. They're just bruised a bit."

"There probably shouldn't have been any shooting at all," I stated. "Likely just a misunderstanding. Were any of my people hurt?"

"Not on account of us. We didn't get off a shot."

I chuckled.

"Your family camped near us," another man said. "We were all friendly enough, but in the night, two of our boys snuck into their camp and stole the livestock. Six winters ago, we lost all ours. The boys acted on their own, and we've punished them, but your family assaulted our settlement to get the animals back. We thought a whole military unit was attacking us."

"Yeah, that sounds like the Casperteins." I grinned. "But I figure everything is patched up now, right? We don't have to be enemies just because we had a rough start."

The adults glanced at one another with uneasy looks.

"Your family said we'd sown the wind," the axe man said, "and that you'd arrive like a whirlwind. What does that mean? Those were their last words before they left—after they shot us and got their burros back."

"It's a quote from the Bible," I said. "They were telling you that you reap what you sow, and the reaping will be a disaster."

"Like I said, we don't want any more trouble."

"Well, I've been known to overwhelm foolish people who mean my family harm, but it seems you and I intend no injury to one another. Since I'm traveling through your land, I'm obliged to request passage through here. My pack is full of supplies, so I need nothing from you. On the other hand, if you want to get ornery with me—"

"Oh, stop it!" a woman stated, elbowing her way past the man with a fishing pole. She wore a parka, which seemed more appropriate for winter than for spring time. "If you boys are done posturing, we can at least feed the traveler. Your name's Caspertein?"

"Yes, ma'am." I stood up straighter, recognizing a matriarch when I heard one—reminding me of Annette, though this woman was years older. "I'd be thankful for a warm bite, and maybe I can share what I have."

"What do you have?" the axe man asked, craning his neck for a better look at my heaping pack.

"I have news. The country is being reshaped. A lot is happening that you folks should hear about."

I crossed the bridge with them, and whatever initial reluctance the men had in receiving me, it was replaced by the wide-eyed friendliness of the women and children. I walked at the front of the group with the axe man and the rifleman. Two dogs ran up from the river's edge and several children dashed ahead of us to announce our arrival at whatever settlement awaited.

The axe man's name was Lewiston. He offered no first name, but his sideburns reminded me of old Wolverine comic books I'd discovered in a box back home in San Diego. The gunman's name was Dwight Thall. He was older than Lewiston, and had a more pleasant disposition.

They led me up the highway a quarter-mile, then turned off to the left onto a worn trail. The trail angled down a steep slope and opened into a clearing where a log settlement had been erected in a soggy bowl of earth with hills on all sides. Three dozen more people of all ages and races came from the cabins. By the time introductions were made by Lewiston, his hand was on my shoulder, claiming me as if he were entirely responsible for my existence. Forty names of adults and children were given. I shook twenty hands and received numerous food gifts before I was offered a resting place for my heavy pack. People laughed and cheered, as if I were a long-lost son returning home. At some point, a garland of wildflowers was even set on my head. I took a bite of a slice of honey-sweetened bread, and tried to express my thanks and approval with a full mouth, which brought more laughter.

But I'd learned to see beyond what seemed warm and innocent. Two men stood guard with rifles on the hills above us. Mud underfoot told of either a sewage or a flooding problem. The cabins were as roughly constructed as the bridge had been, with gaps and twigs hindering seamless walls. Recent rains had washed away whatever mud had filled the log gaps, and I guessed wintering in the mountains was a bone-chilling experience for these people who seemed to have been there for years.

Finally, I was shown to a cabin where a couple bachelors—hunters for the settlement—cleared off a bunk for me. If the town knew how far I'd dragged my weary body that day, they would've let me rest, but it was only mid-afternoon, and Lewiston had further plans for me. He shooed others away—though many young women and children still lingered at a distance—and took me on a trail west of the settlement. The ground dried out as we climbed the hill, then I heard the roar of the river's headwaters ahead.

On the ridge of the forested hill, we stopped to admire the river on one side of the hill and the settlement on the other. I was still reeling from being treated like an honored guest rather than a lonely traveler, especially since my family had left a threatening mark on a people who seemed to be barely surviving in the wild.

"See the ditch we dug for fresh water?" He pointed at the river, its bank interrupted by a trough and gate for water management. "We're never short of water. One of the men even built a plumbing system that flushes our latrines. We have a septic drainage field downriver, just off the highway."

"Very ingenious." I gestured at the gunmen. "What's with the sentries? Expecting trouble?"

"Always." He scowled and shook his big head. "Got them Roan boys across the river. They raid a few other settlement in the mountains, too. Some say they're ex-cons, freed from unguarded prisons years ago. They've hit us twice for food and took a couple of our women. See that one there? Her name's Loreen. Not pretty enough for the Roan boys, I guess. They let her go and she wandered back here. Too bad, too. She was already an orphan. Now, nobody wants her and she'll never find a husband. She just wanders around like that, leaving flowers around the cabins. Only God knows where she picks them."

We watched the woman set wildflowers along the base of one cabin, then she moved through the mud to the next. I took off the garland from my head.

"Did she make this?"

"Yeah, she must've picked those. Strange she'd approach you. She usually stays away from most people, especially strangers."

"She seems likeable enough."

"Too skinny. Crooked teeth. Doesn't talk. Everyone gives different reasons for not including her in settlement activities. It's all very sad."

"These Roan boys are south of the river, you say? Why don't you tear down the bridge?"

"The woods around here have been hunted out. The only game around is across the bridge. That's why we built it. We need it to eat, but now we live in constant fear of more raids."

"Well, that's no way to live." I frowned at him and he nodded. "The Roan boys have taken some of your people. You never tried to get them back?"

"How? We're not soldiers. We have five rifles, and enough ammo only for hunting. The Roan boys are heavily armed. We wouldn't stand a chance. The best we can do is try to keep a lookout and defend ourselves when they come. If they come again."

"Oh, they'll come again. Their kind always does, Lewiston." I studied the settlement a moment longer, fully aware that I wasn't there by accident. God wanted me to help them, to ensure their safety, or to help them develop their skills in some way. And as quickly as I recognized God's involvement in my being there, an idea came to me. "How far south of the river is the Roan boys' camp?"

"I snuck up on them once while hunting. Their cabin is about ten miles from the bridge."

Sticking my thumb under my rifle sling, I sensed action. My pack was in the bachelor cabin, but I didn't need my pack to deal with predators. I needed only my rifle.

"How long since the last raid?" I asked.

"Just before Christmas. You have something in mind?"

"I have a lot on my mind, Lewiston. The question is, can you handle what I've got to say?"

A moment passed. Birds were fighting over seeds above us. It was truly a peaceful place. If I were to settle in the forest, this would be an ideal place to settle.

"I was a psych major in college when Pan-Day hit us. Most of the people here were classmates and their families. I convinced them to leave Denver with me. We all lost a lot of family from the Liberation Organization rampaging through this area years ago. Some of us have married, raised kids. But we've barely survived. Between you and me, I know it sounds cowardly that we can't do anything about the Roan boys, but we're not that kind of people. We've never killed anyone."

"How many other settlements in the mountains around here?"

"About six that we know of. They're private, but friendly. A couple of our kids have inter-married with the others. We talk a couple times a year. Whatever you need to say, just say it. I can handle it."

"You can't live in fear."

"We don't have a choice, Mr. Caspertein."

"Yes, you do. Everyone does. You're just focused on the wrong things. Don't you believe in God?"

"Everyone here has their own beliefs. No one is too pushy."

"I'm not asking about everyone else. I'm asking about you."

"God and I have an understanding—we leave each other alone."

"That's just plain ignorance, Lewiston." I shook my head. "I know God well enough to know He'd never make such an agreement. You wouldn't be in such a desperate situation if God weren't trying to get your attention. I guess that's why I'm here."

"What do you have to do with this?"

"God sent me to tell you to pay attention to Him." I turned from him and gazed northward, at the nearest hills. "And I'm here to show you how to live without fear. You interested?"

"Sure, I'm interested!" He flapped his arms against his sides. "I'm out of ideas, and no one else is having any great epiphanies."

"Well, let's get started then." I knelt on one knee and gestured that he join me, like I'd seen my dad draw people in to his plans for them. Lewiston dropped to a knee and swept the ground clear of pine needles, as if he expected me to draw with my finger. Instead, I lifted my sore arm and set my hand on his shoulder. "Lord God, we are ignorant men. We have gone against You in our thoughts and actions. But we need Your help. Guide Lewiston, Lord. His people are suffering and he is fresh out of ideas. I may be able to make some suggestions from You, but Lewiston's got to follow through. Father, You sent Your Son, Jesus Christ, to die for us, cleansing us of our sin so we could speak directly to You. We need You now."

A moment passed.

"Is that it?" Lewiston asked.

"I think you should say something."

"Like what?"

"God only responds to the prayers of a humble man. Have you lived a perfect life?"

"Not by a long shot."

"Tell Him that, and then ask Him for what you need."

"Okay, um, God, I've never prayed to You. Uh, I guess You know I'm a sorry excuse for a man, and an even sorrier mayor of this settlement. I'm . . . sorry for, uh, being selfish and ignoring You, and for sleeping with Weston's wife before he died. I've never felt good about that. We really need help here. I don't know what to do. Give us some ideas, like Your guy Caspertein said. Is that it?"

"Do you believe He heard you?"

"I thought that was the point. Don't you?"

"Oh, I know He heard us, but prayer and obedience work by faith. Are you open to His direction?"

"Absolutely. I'm desperate. I can't remember the last time I wasn't worried about our safety."

"We're ready to get to work then." I began to draw on the ground where he'd cleared. "Just make sure you pray to God as often as you can. No one needs to know, but they'll know soon enough when they see you're making confident and wise decisions."

"I don't really feel any different."

"Faith isn't an emotion; it's an attitude, like confidence. Faith comes from knowing the truth. I've spoken the truth to you, and to grow in faith, you'll need more truth, to study it, after I'm gone."

"How do I do that?"

"Do you have access to a Bible in the settlement? You said some of the people are religious."

"Yeah, a couple of the families on the north side have a Bible. They're kind of strange, though."

"So you've never gotten to know them?"

"No."

"Sounds like it's time to. Now, listen. The settlement's position is all wrong. You've done well all these years, but with the threat of the Roan boys, and low morale right now—you have to make some changes. First, your settlement is in this bowl. You have this canal that brings in river water, but your only drainage that I can see is your sewage system, right?"

"Yeah."

"All the ground around your cabins is a perpetual bog. It's always muddy, unless the ground is frozen, right?"

"Yeah, but we'd rather have our plumbing work right than have no mud outside."

"We'll get to that. Next, your defenses are all wrong. If you're attacked, the settlement isn't defendable. Sure, your sentries up here on the hills will be safe, but all they'll do is watch the raid. You have to relocate the settlement to higher ground. You'll be drier and strategically safer."

"What about running water? There's no water up on these hills."

"That's what water wheels are for. I helped my dad construct some for growing crops down in San Diego. They'll work here, too."

"Water wheels can make water run uphill?"

"A river this size and a couple water wheels along the way—you could pump water to the top of the San Juan

Mountains. I've seen what water pressure can do. If you put the settlement in the right place, water won't be a problem."

"So, how far do we have to move everyone?"

"That hill, there. It's broad enough. Excavate the top. Make a plateau and a water reservoir. Rebuild the houses around the hill on wooden foundations, stepped down from the top. The reservoir can have spillways on all four sides of the hill, providing fresh water and plumbing for each home. Then you build a wall above the base of the hill."

"Okay, I can kind of envision this. As long as the water is set up, I can sell this to the counsel."

"I'll draw it out for your builders." I rose to my feet, and he joined me. "But there's still the matter of the Roan boys."

"I haven't heard anything from God yet."

"Judges Seven might be a start."

"Judges Seven? I told you I was a psych major, not a lawyer. I don't know legal jargon."

"No, it's a Bible passage. A farmer named Gideon used three hundred men and a little strategy to destroy an army of thousands."

"Three hundred? We only have forty-six people here, and two-thirds of them are women and children."

"You'll need to send secret runners to the other mountain settlements. But study Judges Chapter Seven first, then improvise and trust God."

Side by side, we admired the settlement. Loreen carried her basket of flower stems and continued from cabin to cabin. She was an outcast in the settlement, despised and scorned, so I was naturally drawn to help her.

"How many stolen women do the Roan boys have?"

"If they're still alive, two of ours. More from the other settlements. I don't know how many exactly."

"We'll have to get the women back before the Gideon strategy."

"We?"

"I'll help you get them back," I said, "but it's up to you and the settlements to run the Roan boys out of business."

"Well, this oughta be good." He crossed his arms and smiled. "How do we get our women back?"

"Loreen knows." I nodded at the young woman below.

"She doesn't look too forthcoming. I mean, when she's not spreading flowers all over the place, she's off picking them from somewhere."

"Leave her to me. Who's your best marksman with a rifle? Your best huntsman?"

"Dwight Thall. You met him at the bridge."

"He and I will go get the women tonight. You and the others get started with the other plans."

"The council will have to be convinced this is worth all the work."

"So? Convince them." We walked down the trail to the settlement. "And trust God in things that you know He inspired. He goes before us to fight our battles."

"You take this God stuff pretty seriously, don't you?"

"Once you start reading the Bible, you will, too."

Chapter Twenty-three

Dwight Thall touched my shoulder to wake me. He withdrew against the bachelor cabin door as I sat up. I wasn't used to sleeping indoors.

"Lewiston said you needed me for something." His lever action rifle was slung over his right shoulder. "I'm part of the council. Whatever you need me for, I hope it's worth missing all that Lewiston is proposing tomorrow morning."

"Lewiston says you're the best shot around."

"I don't know about that. I just bring in the most meat, when it seems safe to track game south of the river."

"You'll do." I appreciated a modest man. "You don't hunt with a scope? What's the farthest you've dropped a deer?"

"Just under two hundred yards, I figure."

"Ever hunt with a scope?" I held up the bullpup. "The barrel is as long as your rifle barrel, but the weapon's overall length is shorter since the chamber and barrel start back here in the stock. The ejection is forward and to the right. It's a .308, called an NL-X2, designed for Christian Special Forces who needed a compact, non-lethal weapon for extractions. We also call it a bullpup."

"Non-lethal?"

"Gelatin tranquilizers." I handed one cartridge to him. "Range is six hundred yards. I can drop a running deer at five hundred."

"Impressive. But I still like my open sights." He gave back my bullet. "I hope you don't want me to use your bullpup to hunt with. If you're comfortable with it, you should keep it."

"Oh, I'm not giving it to you. I need a man who understands the flight of a bullet to trust me tonight."

"Well, Lewiston is wound up about something. And he's a hard one to get excited. I supposed that means something. What do you have in mind?"

"You knew some of the women taken by the Roan boys?"

"Sure, we're only a few families here. It hit us all pretty hard."

"You'd recognize them if you saw them again?"

"The women? Yeah, it hasn't been— What're you getting at?"

"Come on." I led us out of the bachelor cabin, my day pack on my back, my heavier pack left behind. The afternoon nap had revived me. It took me two seconds to spot Loreen with her flowers. As we approached, I heard her humming to herself. "Hello, Loreen. Do you have a minute?"

She stopped humming and hid her hands behind her baggy jeans. I held up the garland she'd given me earlier that day.

"Thank you for this." I set it back on my head, which brought a little smile to her face. But when she noticed Dwight, her face darkened and she moved to the side, which left me directly between the two of them. "I have to talk to you about a difficult subject."

"The Roan boys," she said, again revealing her hands full of flowers. Kneeling, she set several blossoms against the nearest cabin. "Did they take someone from you?"

"No, but they hurt you, and that concerns me. And they still have a few others about your age, I understand. I need to ask you some questions about the Roan boys' camp."

"The dungeon?"

"That's what they call their camp?" I plucked a few flowers from her hand and joined her in pressing them into the mud at the base of the wall. "The dungeon?"

"No, that's where they kept us during the days."

I glanced at Dwight, my eyebrows raised. He shrugged and shook his head.

"I've never heard any of this before. I didn't even know she could still speak."

"No one ever asked me." Loreen's hands were empty of flowers now. She turned away, perhaps to fetch more, but I took her muddy hand in mine. For a moment, she didn't move. She only stared at my hand. I thought she might shrink away, but instead, she dove into my arms, her face against my chest. "Please, take me with you! I can't stay here any longer. They think I'm going insane. They talk about how dirty I am all the time. I'm nothing to them!"

Two young women walked past us right then. They snubbed their noses at us, particularly at Loreen.

"Keep walking, ladies!" Dwight said. "Loreen, why didn't you tell us about this dungeon place?"

With some prying, I held Loreen at arm's length and looked into her eyes. She wasn't an ugly woman, just plain. If I were staying at the settlement, she might've been the type of woman I could've made a home with, but my focus was on taking care of the settlement, then moving on to catch up with my family. The only kind of romance I could imagine was one that took time to build in one place, and I wasn't interested in staying in one place.

"Tell me about the dungeon," I pressed. "Please? Dwight and I are listening very carefully."

She wiped her eyes and nose and tucked her hair behind her ears. Her hands had been grimy with mud, so her face was now smeared with the same.

"It's deep in the ground. They put us in there before the sun rose every morning. We slept all day in the dark."

"It's a hole in the ground?" I asked. "How big?"

"Like . . . there." She pointed at the dimension that was between the nearby cabins. "And the top has a cover. But it's always cold."

"I'm sure it is. How many women were in the dungeon when you left?"

"Ten, I think, but one died. Nine now. Unless they got more. They were always talking about getting more."

"Why did they let you go?"

"They didn't let me go. I pretended to die." Fresh tears streamed down her muddy cheeks. "I did good, right?"

"Oh, yes. You did good. You're a hero. You've been through a lot, and people haven't known how to help you, but all that is about to change." I faced Dwight, Loreen's hands clinging to my left hand. "You have a family, right? A wife?"

"Yeah. So?"

"Where's Loreen been staying?"

"In the feed barn . . ." He pointed, then immediately lowered his head. "Never mind. I'll take her to my wife, to our house."

"And get us some dinner," I said. "We'll eat on the road. Loreen, go with Dwight. You'll be staying with his family for now."

I walked to the east side of the settlement to wait for Dwight. Lewiston emerged from a cabin I guessed was a meeting hall. He jogged up to me with a grin on his face.

"While you slept all afternoon, I've been giving my presentation to the council. I've begun to explain parts of your plan to them. Everyone is excited about the water wheels. Some of them have other ideas how to use them, too."

"Good. Listen, make sure no one else goes south of the river until Dwight and I return."

"You sure? Maybe you want some of the others to back you up?"

"No, Dwight and I have this. And, just so it's not a shock to you later, as Dwight and I retreat with the captives, we're destroying the bridge."

"*What? No!* It took us a year to build! We need it to hunt. I told you that!"

"Lewiston, you need to build a drawbridge. Lower it when you need it; raise it when you don't. You said the raids didn't start until the Roan boys had a nice bridge to cross. So, we remove their access. Easy."

"Oh. A drawbridge! Of course! Maybe I shouldn't tell the others until after the bridge is destroyed."

"That's your call."

"Hey, I read Judges Chapter Seven. It's inspired some talk, but we want to meet with the other settlements first. We won't stand for the Roan boys any longer!"

"That's the attitude!"

Dwight joined us.

"I'll pray for you both," Lewiston said as we walked away. "Show 'em we're done getting pushed around!"

I wasn't sure Lewiston was a true believer in Jesus Christ yet, or whether he'd simply been restored some dignity. But he was on the right track, reading from the Bible and praying. It was a start.

Ten miles south of the river, after three hours of hiking, Dwight and I reached the Roan boys' camp. Most of the way, we used the forest highway, but for the last mile, we crept through the dense forest, using hunting stealth. Dwight had indeed been the right choice as a companion for this task. In the dark trees, by the light of the moon and stars, he tested each foot placement before stepping forward. The keen ears of deer had trained this woodsman to be extra cautious as we eased toward their camp, which we heard long before we saw it.

Dwight had avoided their camp during hunts, he admitted, so he knew the location well enough. We discussed my plan while on the highway, so now we were silent, two creatures of the night intent on catching unsuspecting prey at their weakest moment.

When their camp finally came into sight, I almost felt foolish for all the caution. It didn't take a Panamanian jaguar to sneak up on a drunken party, for that's what we found. A bonfire burned in the midst of three small cabins with canvas roofs. Men and women were dancing around the fire, drunkenly yelling, singing, stumbling about. A woman screamed from somewhere, maybe from one of the cabins, but we couldn't see enough to respond quite yet.

"I count eight," Dwight said aloud, since there was no reason to whisper or signal with all the noise. "There must be one or two more inside."

He was counting the Roan boys, but there seemed to be an equal number of young women as well.

"I agree. Any idea where the dungeon would be?"

"Maybe in that open ground on this side of the fire. Impossible to tell until they put the women in there." He leaned his rifle against a fallen log and set his pack on the ground. With binoculars in one hand, he waved at me with his other. "Go ahead. Make your circuit. I'll keep watch."

As previously agreed upon, I began to prowl through the trees around their camp. I needed an adequate shooting platform from which to cover Dwight when he went in to recover the women. Dwight was remarkably calm about my plan to put him in harm's way, yet I had selected a marksman on purpose—because he understood perfectly well the effectiveness of a precision shooter. From the right vantage point, I could cover him. And with a calm head, which he seemed to have, he could direct my shots.

Since the women were all in one place only during the daytime, our operation was limited to a daylight raid. I preferred darkness to blanket us, but the circumstances couldn't be changed. Rather, I had to appreciate what daylight would offer us. In the light, I could see better to shoot better, and when escaping, we could all travel faster. Of course, the Roan boys could shoot and travel, too, but they didn't have a bullpup. And they would be hungover.

On the far side of their camp from Dwight, I noticed the shadow of a tall tree on the south side of the tree line. At about three hundred yards out, I thought it might make a proper shooting stand. The mountain ridges were too rolling and gradual, and the forest too thick, to merely set up on high ground for cover fire.

The tall tree to the south, when I reached it, was a dead pine that had been struck by lightning and charred. A split halfway up its center provided a route to climb to the lowest branches, which were as thick as my arm and forty feet high. The lower, smaller branches appeared to have been burnt away in the strike. With my rifle on my back, I reached the lowest branches, then continued to climb higher, using the thicker branches. I knew of a boy in San Diego who'd fallen from this height and been paralyzed, so with that in mind, I tested each handhold and foot placement before shifting my weight. The dark of night was no time to be climbing dead trees—if ever there was a time for climbing them at all.

Soon, I was above the other treetops, and the clearing in front of their site afforded me a proper line of fire. Dwight was somewhere in the bushes northeast of me, and his camp was almost perfectly north of where we were. As the sun would rise in the coming morning, and as the prisoners would escape, any of the Roan boys would have the sun in their eyes during a gunfight. The sun would be behind me and to my right. All I had to do now was anchor myself appropriately to the tree trunk to steady my rifle.

Returning to Dwight, I found that he had a little to report.

"A few of them have fallen asleep. The fire's burning out now, too. From what I could see, a couple of the women were led to that open space and disappeared. The dungeon's got to be in that area. It's just too dark to see more."

"Well, it'll be light in a few hours. I found a high perch that'll work well, three hundred yards out. I'll be due south of you."

"How's the line of fire?"

"Clear, unless you step in my way. You have the hand gestures memorized?"

"I point and you shoot." Dwight grunted. "Not much to memorize. But I don't like going in without my rifle."

"You'll need your hands free in case you need to carry one of the women. Besides, we're not here to kill anyone, even if we think the Roan boys deserve it. If the local settlements want to set up some sort of governing system, you can deal with them accordingly. But as far as I'm concerned, we're here only for the women."

"It's your call. You're the shooter."

"We'll rest here two hours, then I'll get into position." I sat down, my back against a log. "Wake me in an hour to spell you. Unless I start snoring. Then you can wake me earlier."

"You can joke and sleep at a time like this?"

"When you know your life is definitely in God's hands, and when your conscience is clear, peace of mind isn't hard to come by."

I drifted off to sleep with those words and a smile on my face. Dwight had tolerated a prayer I'd spoken for us at the bridge, but he wasn't too open quite yet, it seemed, to believing in a caring God.

An hour later, Dwight nudged me with his foot.

"It's three-thirty. They're all asleep."

I rose and crouched behind a tree. The camp bonfire was barely glowing now, and nothing seemed to be moving in the clearing.

"We could go now," he said, "before dawn."

"Were all the women returned to the dungeon?"

"You're right. We'll wait, just in case someone's missing."

"Sleep if you want."

"I'm too excited." He sighed. "I've hunted deer and bear, but I've never done anything like this."

"Deer and bear don't shoot back. That thought's liable to boost your adrenaline. Just so long as you keep a calm head. We're not leaving any of the women behind."

"They're going to be steaming mad—those Roan boys. They might chase us all the way to the bridge."

"We talked about that. I'll cover your retreat for as far as I can see you. You just keep those women moving. Ten miles is a long trek, but everyone can rest once you make the settlement."

"You're some kind of daredevil, Mr. Caspertein."

"We do what's right. That's all. And trust God with the consequences."

An hour later, I prayed aloud for our safety and the women's well-being. Dwight was more receptive to this kind of prayer. He didn't say amen, but he did say, "Good," at the end, as if he approved. Some men, God hit with a bolt of lightning, like the pine tree. And others, He reached them with a gentle lead rope, like our burros needed in the hands of Vorca.

Dawn began to touch the sky as I climbed the lightning-struck pine. When I reached the intended height, I took off my belt and flung it around the trunk, which was thinner than my waist at this point. If I slipped from the branches on which I stood, I didn't expect the belt to hold me, but I slid it through three loops on the front of my jeans to at least stabilize me. Shedding my pack, I fastened it to the tree about head level, then hooked my left injured arm through its straps. Since the bullpup was so short, its barrel didn't need to rest on anything to steady it. Rather, I braced myself, and pressed my body and the gun against the trunk to steady my aim.

Waiting for a gunfight was never easy. I did my best to pay attention to the shrinking shadows, my eyes on the distant camp through the scope, and occasionally through the binoculars. But restlessness was beginning to prod me. Annette and the others were almost four days ahead of me now. Their supplies would be low since they hadn't been able to enter Shiprock as Kip and I had. My pack held additional gear, what little I could carry. Forest was probably hunting often, leaving Annette and Mia to defend Sharly, Natasha, Gilly, and Caleb, if anyone attacked. If they kept moving, they were potentially a week away from reaching Norwood, a town with an elevation of seven thousand feet. A few hundred people had lived there before Pan-Day. We expected such people to be survivors, and perhaps willing to trade with us.

And yet, every time I thought of family, I also thought of Jenna. Over the years, she'd become like a sister in the faith to me. We'd been teenagers the first time we'd met. I'd been orphaned when I was in high school, but after finding the father I'd never known, I was introduced to the Dowler family about the same time. Since Jenna was blind, I'd once guided her with my arm when we'd spent a few days together at a COIL training compound. Maybe those days had born within me the protectiveness that I felt even as an adult to see to Jenna's safety.

Because I knew what it meant to need others, I had believed that Jenna needed me, because of her blindness. But I hadn't become the rock in her life that I'd wanted to be. Christ had become her Rock. And the infirmity she had was her strength that had actually brought us together over the years. No doubt, having a father like Corban Dowler had contributed to her stubborn confidence and independence.

Jenna was family, and so I would go to her—not because we were lovers, and not because she was blind, but because she was a sister in Christ and she'd asked me to come.

However, Jenna was still one thousand obstacles away from me—one thousand towns of suspicious people, a hundred highways of treacherous travelers, a dozen regional militarized zones between me and her. I prayed for God to give me the strength to endure through it all, because at this pace, I wouldn't reach New York until the following spring. Winter wouldn't stop me, but it would certainly slow me down. If we could find Uncle Rudy and my Cousin Rex, I guessed they would have cross-country skis I could use to continue east alone.

Alone. It was a sobering thought. Meeker was three weeks of hard travel away. The companions I'd gained thus far couldn't be expected to continue the journey—my journey, my quest to reach the blind woman who'd called for my help. I would go alone, and face whatever God set before me. He would fight for me, and I would bow to His command. After all, I was His traveler, His pilgrim, His son.

Sunlight touched the right side of my face. At the same instant, two men emerged from one of the cabins, each man roughly holding onto the arms of two young women. Through my binoculars, I watched them pull the women along and stop on the span of clear ground. With the toe of his boot, one of the men flipped up a trap door. The way it flopped open on the hinges indicated to me that it was a heavy door. It surely had a lock of some kind on the outside.

Both men shoved the women toward the shadow in the ground. Obediently, as if they'd practiced the routine a hundred mornings before, the ladies climbed down what I guessed was a ladder. One of the men bent to hook a latch, then they both went into another cabin. A moment later, they exited the cabin with three more women, and led them to the same hole in ground. This time, when the men returned to the cabin, they didn't emerge again.

So, these were the men in charge of morning security. My eyes burned from little sleep, but I couldn't imagine the Roan boys being too energetic after a wild night of partying.

I swung my gaze to the bushes where I knew Dwight was hiding. In the morning light, I figured he'd discovered where I was at almost a quarter-mile away, high above the other treetops. Sure enough, he stepped from the foliage, crouching low. If the Roan boys had thrown a couple women into the dungeon overnight, and seven more this morning, that made nine. Were there more?

Allowing my binoculars to hang on my neck, I raised the bullpup scope to my eye. The magnification wasn't as strong as the field glasses, but the lack of magnification through the scope gave me a broader field of vision all around Dwight.

His first steps out of the tree line were hesitant steps of caution, but then he started to run, crouched, his arms held out wide as if he were trying to keep his balance over uneven ground. Soon, my field of vision encompassed the cabins as well as Dwight. A few seconds later, he knelt at the dungeon door. This was too easy, I thought, and Dwight seemed to sense the same thing as he hesitated to open the trap door. He checked the cabins for movement, then glanced in my direction.

"I'm here, Dwight," I mumbled, my scope centered on the doorway of the middle cabin. "What are you waiting for?"

He lifted the trap door. Still nothing from the cabins. For a moment, Dwight hovered over the hole in the ground. When he pointed to the east, I knew he was giving instructions to the captives.

Suddenly, the women emerged. Dwight hauled each of them up the last few steps. They clutched blankets, but no coats—and no shoes! Of course. Their captors had discouraged any attempts to escape during the winter by taking their footwear. But it was nearly summer, and barefoot travel wasn't impossible.

Nine women came out of the hole in the ground, huddled together briefly, then ran toward the eastern tree line. I watched them go—without Dwight! He was signaling me. Switching to my binoculars, I caught some of his gesturing in time to make sense of his change of plan. There was one more captive. He was going after one more woman. The others must've told him that someone was still missing.

The women reached the trees and passed from my sight. If one or two of them were from Dwight's settlement, then they knew to head north once they reached the highway.

In all my imagining, there was no way Dwight could rescue the last captive without attracting attention. She'd evidently been added since Loreen had escaped.

"Bring them into sight, Lord," I whispered to the morning air, and switched back to my rifle scope. "I'm ready."

Chapter Twenty-four

Dwight seemed to understand the same thing I did: to rescue the remaining captive woman or women still in the hands of the Roan boys—stealth was no longer an option. At the door of the western-most cabin, he gripped the door latch, then swung it smoothly open. I clenched my teeth the instant he disappeared from my view. Anything could happen in there! He could be cut by a knife or shot point-blank as the intruder he was.

But there were no gunshots.

A moment later, a woman passed through the door, with Dwight reappearing behind her. In her hands she gripped a pair of boots, probably stolen from one of the Roan boys. Smart girl! Dwight closed the door slowly, apparently intent on letting everyone sleep, as the woman tugged on the boots. She wore belted trousers and a flannel shirt. Maybe she'd stolen the clothes as well, since the other captives had worn tattered dresses.

She and Dwight were on the move, but not quick enough. The door of the eastern-most door opened and a man emerged, adjusting suspenders over his bare chest. He yelled, being unarmed, I noticed, but Dwight took the hand of the woman and led her away.

However, the rest of the Roan boys were alert now. One of the men fired into the air to stop Dwight at the edge of the smoldering bonfire. He stopped, released the woman's hand, and raised his hands. The woman didn't seem as compliant. She glanced east and south. I doubted Dwight had gotten a chance to advise her of his plans to flee eastward.

One of the Roan boys dashed to the dungeon, its door still ajar. The criminals didn't all have rifles, but a couple carried drawn handguns. Ten men were in view now, all facing Dwight. It would've been a hopeless situation, if I hadn't been there to even the odds.

"Whenever you're ready, Dwight," I said, my trigger finger twitching in anticipation.

The men were talking to Dwight. *Which settlement was he from? What was his name? Why was he alone? How many had come for the women?*

Dwight's hands were raised. Three raised fingers on his left hand were a signal to me. His right hand pointed awkwardly to his right, at a man with a large gun, maybe a shotgun. Of course, Dwight wanted the scatter gun taken out first. His left hand signaled with two raised fingers. Then with his right hand he gestured to a man on the left. Another rifleman. Since Dwight was on the scene, he had to be the one to point out the greatest threats. As a rifleman himself, Dwight knew what to look for—cold eyes and men who carried their weapons like an extension of their arms.

Lastly, Dwight signaled with one finger, and pointed out a heavyset man who seemed to be doing all the talking. He moved close to Dwight, behind him from my point of view. The man pulled his arm back to strike Dwight.

Then, Dwight's raised left hand clenched into a fist. My first shot hit Mr. Shotgun in the chest. Before I guessed they'd heard the report of my rifle, I adjusted and fired at the second man. Dwight crouched and dove to the side, clearing my line of fire to put a third tranquilizer into the gut of the heavyset talker.

After that, I had my pick of the seven remaining criminals. Four dropped flat on the ground, trying to locate me by the sound of my rifle. I shot two more before they realized they needed cover. Two disappeared into a cabin, presumably for rifles. The other three hid behind the middle and eastern cabins.

They finally spotted me. To them, I was a silhouette far away, like a sailor clinging to a ship mast. But I was three hundred yards away, far too distant for the likes of these scoundrels. They did try a few shots, which required exposing themselves from their covers. One rolled away from his cabin cover, and in a prone position, aimed and fired hastily at me. As he lined up for another shot, his first having fallen short in the trees below me, I shot him over his head and into his backside. He jumped upright, then fell and lay still.

Another, from a cabin doorway, fired a semi-automatic at me, but his aim was so frantic, he had no idea his rounds were also falling far short. He fell asleep with a gel-tranq to the shoulder.

That left three more, and they weren't in sight. I looked up for a moment to see Dwight sprinting for the eastern tree line. He was safe! But the woman had taken off in a different direction—to the south, toward me. Perhaps she'd heard my rifle and knew this was a safe harbor.

A flash of movement behind the cabin! One of the men—no, two!—slipped into the forest before I could fire a shot at them. Maybe they'd gone out a back window. The third man also reached the forest to the west before I could fire. I wasn't about to waste gel-tranqs on hasty shots, just to bite the heels of men I couldn't target well. It was better to let them think they'd escaped undetected. For a moment, I watched the trees for them to reemerge, but they were already behind green boughs and spring bushes.

"Hey!" a woman's voice called at me.

I was too busy releasing myself from the pack strap and belt to try to spot her below.

"Yeah?"

"Are you coming down?"

"On my way."

It took me five minutes with my small pack and rifle to reach the lowest branches, then to carefully descend the charred trunk. Winded and feeling a couple slivers in my hands, I hopped down the last few feet—into the arms of a wild-haired woman with piercing gray eyes. Her black, wavy hair hadn't seen a brush for days, I guessed. Her lip was swollen and she had dried blood on her chin.

"Are you injured?" I asked.

"Nothing serious." She was at least my age, almost forty, with a fierceness to those eyes that I hadn't expected to find in a victimized woman—and I'd seen many. But she hadn't been broken like Loreen. No, not this one. She'd fought, and her battered face proved as much. "Which way do we go?"

"East." I led the way, gauging the risks ahead, thankful the gray-eyed woman had grabbed boots, or our journey straight through thick underbrush would've been hampered greatly.

The noise we made was significant, but speed was necessary at this stage. Having seen where the last three Roan boys had gone into the woods, I guessed they weren't near us. Besides, they'd probably go after the nine women with Dwight sooner than the single one I had.

We reached the highway sooner than I expected. I knelt and leveled the bullpup northward, up the quiet and straight two-lane highway, now littered with leaves, pine needles, wind-blown branches, and the occasional deadfall. The woman caught up to me and fell to her hands and knees.

"Sixty-second rest," I said, glancing at her. "Are you good? We almost left without you. We were told there were only nine women still being held."

"They got me just last week. Killed my brother. They stopped putting me with the others. Said I was teaching them bad manners." She smiled, showing good, straight teeth. "I didn't make it easy on them."

"Good for you. Ready? We have to move quieter now, but just as swiftly."

"Lead away."

We crossed the highway and entered the woods on the east side. Forty yards into the trees, I turned north to parallel the highway. Now, I ran ahead in short bursts, then paused behind mossy trees to study the road. The woman with me was louder than I'd hoped. At one pause, when she'd caught up to me again, I knelt in front of her and pushed her onto her backside. Before she could resist, I'd untied one of her boots and retied it much tighter than she'd had it.

"No noise as we run," I said, moving to retie her other boot. "Tighten up your belt and tuck in your shirt. Nothing loose. You need water?"

"No, I'm good."

"What's your name?"

"Lyla."

"I'm Levi Caspertein."

"Pleasure."

"Our plan is to travel ten miles north to a river. Dwight and the rest of the women are ahead of us, so far. But the rest of the Roan boys are probably out here now, too, maybe setting up to ambush us. They could be anywhere on the highway. That's why we're not taking the easy route."

"Makes sense."

"If we're noisy, they'll hear us coming."

"Got it. I'll try not to stomp."

"Can you whistle, like a short, high whistle?"

"Yeah." She showed me.

"Good. If you need my attention for anything, don't yell or call me. Just whistle like that, and I'll stop to talk. You need water or a break, whistle."

"I won't need anything." She was wide-eyed and eager. "Why are you looking at me like that?"

"You almost seem to be enjoying yourself."

"If there's only three of them left, then you took out seven already, right?"

"So?"

"So, I think I'm on the winning side. Why can't a girl have a good time while we're winning? I just kept praying in that place. This is better than I could've imagined, just like the Bible says."

"You're a Christian?"

"Reborn and baptized." She smiled again, which I was beginning to enjoy. "Don't worry about me. God never promised a path of daisies. I've lost a lot in my life, but I know this isn't how it ends."

"You sound like someone I know."

"Who?"

"Me. Let's move."

It seemed our talk was effective. Lyla stomped a little quieter in her oversized boots, and I focused on the hunt. Indeed, it was a hunt, since my prey was hunting Dwight and his party of nine. My left shoulder wound felt wet with blood from the movement, but I didn't stop to examine it.

Suddenly, I saw movement ahead and dropped to my belly. Lyla was two paces behind me, and collapsed at my elbow. Her fingers tapped my canteen, and I unclipped it for her. We'd been running in short surges for thirty minutes, and she was surely thirsty, but she took only a couple swallows. Discipline. I liked her even more.

"We caught up to somebody," I whispered. "Can't tell if it's Dwight or the jackals."

"Jackals. Good name for them."

"Don't move until I signal you, okay?" To give me freedom of movement, and assure her that I wasn't abandoning her, I shrugged out of my day pack. "Bring this with you when you come."

I ran ahead, leaving her behind. Without the twenty pounds on my back, I felt like a deer, light and mobile, leaping easily over logs and dodging moss-covered branches. When I saw unnatural color on the highway ahead and to my left, I halted and brought the scope to my eye, the stock to my shoulder in a ready position.

My field of vision through the scope was of a face I didn't recognize—a man's face, looking in my direction. He was sixty yards away, but he'd probably heard me coming. His mouth moved and spoke words that I couldn't hear, but he was speaking to someone. Then, he moved into the woods toward me. Now I saw all three of them, with rifles leveled, bodies crouched, eyes like, well, jackals. This was their mistake, to come after me. They surely thought the noise they'd heard was their prey, hiding from them. But I wasn't hiding as their prey. I was hunting as a predator.

Staying low, I eased to my right so I wasn't meeting them head-on. I took a piece of dead wood and tossed it into a bush on my left. They were near now, and moving almost past me. If they stayed on their heading, they'd find Lyla, but I wouldn't let them get that far.

All three were in sight now. My body was partially concealed behind a tree, the bullpup peeking out, tracking them. I shot the nearest one first, in the hip. The second turned to locate me and I shot him in the upper chest. He was a smaller man, and the punch of the gel-tranq threw him backwards, causing his heels to fly up. The third man ducked out of sight, but his cover was limited to tree roots, exposed from a past storm.

I gave him no chance to find better cover or gain his nerve to face me. Setting my rifle down, I snuck up to the root system. With a lunge, I hopped onto the tree. For an instant, I gazed down at my trembling prey, then I fell upon him. We rolled over once, but I was much heavier and stronger, even with my injured arm. When we settled, I was on top. With ease, I plucked his rifle away and tossed it into the bushes. Straddling his torso, I withdrew a semi-automatic handgun from his shoulder holster. He was a wiry man in his forties, sneering as he squirmed underneath me.

"Hold still. Don't make this harder than it needs to be." From his belt, I took a hunting knife, with what appeared to be blood and deer hair still on the hilt. "Didn't your daddy ever tell you to clean your weapons before you put them away? This is disgusting."

"I killed my daddy. Let me up and I'll kill you, too!"

I placed the blade to his throat and he stopped moving. The edge was sharp, regardless of its filth, and a thin line of blood appeared on his skin.

"We're tired of you jackals. Death is on your heels. Change your ways or die. No one else will show you mercy. Repent or die. Those are your choices."

"Repent?" he asked.

Maybe he didn't know the word, or he was confused that he was being given an option. Whichever he chose, I wasn't about to tempt my self-restraint against his mouth. I drew out a gel-tranq from my vest and stabbed it into his chest, hard enough to give him a deep bruise to later reflect on his evils and God's mercy. After all, he would live because of Christ, for I was just a man, more inclined at that moment to serve vengeance than reprieve.

"We're clear, Lyla."

My pack was on her back as she jogged to me through the undergrowth.

"You killed him?"

"Maybe I should've, and he probably deserved it, but no. Just tranquilized him for an hour. We'll be far away when they wake up."

"Do you mind?" She gestured at his body.

"Be my guest."

"My brother's belt." From the wiry man, she whipped off the belt made of horsehair, then exchanged the large boots she was wearing for the smaller man's boots. "Much better fit."

We collected their firearms, and Lyla kept a .9-millimeter with a shoulder holster. The other weapons, we disassembled and threw all over the forest.

"So, we're in the clear?" she asked. "That's all ten men?"

"For now."

"You're not one of the mountain people from around here, are you?"

"No." We walked to the highway. "How could you tell?"

"You think and move like a soldier. Most of the civilians out here are hiding out. For twenty years, they've been sneaking around, avoiding everyone, barely living. So, if you're not from around here, why come and rescue a bunch of local girls?"

"Remember in the Bible when Lot was captured? Abraham chased down those kings and recovered everyone. Maybe that's my inspiration."

"Oh, you're a Bible reader as well, huh?" She grunted as she swiped at a low branch. "I thought my family was about the last of the Jesus freaks from before Pan-Day."

We reached the highway.

"Reborn and baptized, as someone once said."

"That's original."

"I thought you'd like that."

By the time we reached the bridge, Lyla Grady and I were pretty well acquainted. She had an uncanny way of saying things that I often said, or believed, yet I liked her way of saying things better, for they were more refined and gracious. Her ability to see God's hand through her most recent afflictions gave me pause. To myself, I kept thinking, *"If only Annette and Mia could touch this woman's spirit!"*

Lyla was the daughter of a Nebraskan corn farmer. He'd raised Lyla and her recently-deceased brother on Bible principles, but they'd remained covert Christians. The Mid-West was a place of superstition and fear nowadays, and with rumors of the Appalachian

Federation territory spreading westward, Christians continent-wide were turning more underground.

Bandits had burned their fields and killed Mr. Grady, so Lyla and her brother had run for the Rockies. Here, they'd found only more heartache. Just recently, Lyla had been taken hostage, so her health hadn't yet experienced the normal effects of captivity. She was nearly as tall as me, her posture straight, and her shoulders broad and squared. I was left with a yearning, wishing I'd met her brother, a gentle but courageous man, she'd said, who'd died unafraid by one of the Roan boys' blades. He sounded like the kind of man I would've liked.

At the bridge, Lewiston and ten men revealed themselves from behind trees.

"Dwight came through thirty minutes ago," Lewiston said. He held his axe. The others had pistols or hand-to-hand weapons, which wouldn't have stopped even three of the Roan boys, but at least they were beginning to stand together. "It took us a year to build this bridge, but I decided to talk over the drawbridge idea with everyone. We're ready to burn this bridge as a symbol. We owe you, Caspertein."

"You don't owe me for telling you the truth. The truth is always free." I browsed the faces of the men who'd come out to greet me. "You'll have hard times ahead, so it'd be good if you remember this day, when evil was defeated against the odds and without bloodshed. Lewiston, if you keep your faith in God close to your heart, you'll continue to lead these people well through every potential disaster. It's not about what we do. It's about what inspires us. Now, I didn't bring any food to barbeque, but I'd sure like to see a bridge burn!"

The men laughed, and Lyla and I moved to the north side.

"You're kind of an inspiring speaker." Lyla elbowed me playfully in the ribs. "You sound like you're not going to hang around much longer. Is that true?"

"My family is a few days ahead of me." I tried not to sound regretful about leaving, but I was. This amazing and forceful woman could only be a passing soul in my life since I was called elsewhere. "They'll be worried if I don't catch up soon. You'll be in good hands here. Lewiston is on the Lord's path, I think. These people need a firm Christian hand. God will use you here."

She smiled at me with what I guessed was understanding, then we both joined the cheering as flames licked at the girders. The roar of the mighty river below was helpless to extinguish the flames. More of the settlement citizens joined us to watch the smoke rise and timbers crumble. Even Dwight returned and we embraced over our successful mission.

"When will you leave?" Lyla asked with what seemed like dejection in her voice.

"In the morning." I smiled and put my arm around her, my spirit feeling a kinship with her familiar spirit. "I'm sorry I have to leave after we just met."

"You haven't said—will you be coming back this way? We talked about everything else on the road here except what happens next. You said you have family in some place called Meeker?"

"It's in Colorado. After that, I go east." I nodded, feeling the uncomfortable silence. Goodbyes were never easy for me. That's probably why my band of travelers had gained so many souls since leaving San Diego. "A friend in New York is in trouble."

A couple of the younger girls from the settlement dragged Lyla away right then. Laughing, she went with them without looking back at me, and I felt I'd done something wrong. The bond we'd developed in half a day seemed not to matter, now that I was leaving. I wasn't a man to remain in one place when I felt the tug to move on. Would I deny Jenna Dowler my attention just because others were attracted to me?

"The settlement relocation has been approved, Caspertein!" Lewiston announced. "And we already sent runners to the other settlements in the mountains with the news of the girls' homecoming. You've changed our lives!"

"No, no. God gets all the glory, Lewiston. He's my motivation for helping others. I'm as thankful as you are when I see His blessings."

"What're we gonna do without you?"

"You'll lead and everyone will grow. There'll be heartache and struggle, but when Jesus Christ is given room in a man's heart, even the valleys are places of growth."

"Say, some of the people are worried about the returning victims. We were gonna have a feast tonight, but maybe a celebration isn't what they need most."

"Oh, you should celebrate! Celebrate them. I've known victims of this kind of assault my whole adult life. Their greatest fear is that they'll be rejected and shamed. They may carry scars, Lewiston, but a leader needs to show that people with good hearts look not at the flesh, but at the spirit. Celebrate in mourning and joy. Let them know they are loved. Love is always the channel for healing."

"Maybe I should make a speech." He rubbed his jaw. "Most of the returning women are from other settlements. They may not be as caring as we are of victims like this. We should send them home with a real message, but I'm not one for sermons."

"While you're thinking about what to say," I said, my voice low, "don't forget about Loreen. She's the real forgotten hero in all this."

"How so?"

"She escaped by pretending to be dead, made her way back here, and gave us the intel we needed to bring the women back alive. Without Loreen, Dwight and I wouldn't have been able to locate the captives so easily, if at all."

"You're right. We've kind of shunned her." He shook my hand with a grip only loggers have. "That settles it. We celebrate the girls tonight, including Loreen. It's a new day for us all!"

Chapter Twenty-five

Two deer on a rotisserie fed the settlement by torchlight that night. Mayor Lewiston made such a fine speech, he decided to make a speech every hour throughout the evening. Someone produced a horrible-tasting brew, of which I drank a small amount, though I'd never drank alcohol before. And Lewiston was toasting everyone, including the recovered girls, and me, and the burnt bridge. It's possible by that late hour, when he toasted the bridge, that he was too intoxicated to recall that he'd actually burned it down. But everyone was in such a festive mood at that hour, they didn't care. I passed my cup of grog off to someone who seemed to appreciate the taste, and I settled for honey-sweetened water the kids were drinking.

Between handfuls of roasted deer meat—for there was no silverware except for knives—Lyla approached me for the first time since the bridge burning.

"So, you're still leaving in the morning?"

She knew I was, so why was she torturing me again? Someone had given her a flowery dress that made my collar seem tighter just by looking at her. A man with a fiddle danced past us, the noise buying me more time to think of a proper answer.

"I have a lot of ground to cover before the winter drops a blanket of snow on everything."

"Since my brother and I recently arrived around here, I really don't know anyone at any of these settlements."

I cleared my throat, uncertain and terrified at the same time over what she might have been suggesting.

"You have a natural way about you," I said, doing my best to pay her a compliment. "Wherever you settle, everyone will benefit."

One of the other recovered women curtsied before me, and I danced a few spins before twirling back to stand and clap next to Lyla. A man with slicked-back hair and a Bowie knife on his hip approached Lyla and asked her to dance, but she declined—while glaring at me. The man walked away downtrodden.

"Why did you do that?" I asked. "It took him half the night to gain the courage to ask the prettiest girl to dance with him."

"Levi Caspertein!" she yelled over the music. "You're the dumbest, most ignorant and selfish man I've ever met!"

With that, she slapped me hard, then stormed away. My face was still burning when Lewiston walked over, his wife on his arm.

"What was that about?" Lewiston asked. We watched Lyla pull Mr. Bowie Knife into the dance with her. He was all grins and blushing. "I thought you two were hitting it off."

"That's love for ya," Lewiston's wife said, pinching her husband's cheek. "You should've seen me land this lumberjack. Had to drive a few wedges into the ol' stump before he started tipping over my way."

"My family's spread halfway across Colorado, and I'm needed out east for other reasons. I can't stay here. She knows that. I've told her I can't stay."

"You know you've always got a home here when you do return, Caspertein." Lewiston nodded at Lyla. "But don't expect that filly to remain available. Of all the women who returned, she's the one who I'd wager suffered the least."

"I'll be leaving before sunup." I happily changed the subject. "These last couple days have been a bright spot in my journey."

"You changed a lot of lives here, Caspertein. You know, some of the women have even proposed we name the town."

"Guess what name keeps coming up," his wife said. "Caspertein!"

"I've been here for two days! Pick a name that means something or relates to the land—Riverside, or New Bridgetown."

"The name Caspertein means more to us than all that." Lewiston shook my hand again. "Whatever we decide on, you have a good journey."

I found it hard to get to sleep after eating so much, but by praying my thanks to the Lord for a providential impact on the settlement, I drifted to sleep in the bachelor cabin. My pack was ready for marching, with three days of smoked food for eating on the go.

"Levi Caspertein! You get out here this instant!"

My eyes flashed open. I knew that voice. But I only knew that voice as a pleasant one, not an angry, harsh voice. Where was I? What was happening?

"I'm coming!" I yelled back, before I completely realized where I'd lain my head for the night. As I shoved my feet into my boots, the last two days came back to me. The river settlement. The Roan boys. And that was Lyla Grady's voice, demanding my presence.

With my rifle in hand, I wasn't yet fully outside when Lyla lit into me.

"How dare you treat me like this! I don't shack up wherever someone might abandon me! I'm a Christian woman! You don't have the right to leave me behind! Do I look like the kind of girl who carries another man's pack?"

"Carry another man's pack?" Half the settlement had been startled awake. A few men and women stood in their night clothes in their doorways to see what the commotion was about. The more committed celebrators were still sipping grog at the smoldering fire pit.

"Well, I'm not that kind of girl! Yeah, you saved us. But it doesn't end there. You're a coward, Levi Caspertein, and I don't mean the kind that's scared to face an enemy. Oh, no! The great Levi Caspertein will single-handedly defeat a whole army, I'm sure! But a woman drops a few obvious hints, and you run for the hills. Obvious, I say! I couldn't have made it more obvious, you coward! So you better get used to the idea, Levi Caspertein—Lyla Suzanne Grady is no coward! I'm leaving with you because you're too pig-headed to invite me yourself. You're taking me . . . because I don't belong anywhere else!" Now, there were tears in her eyes as she took a breath after a sob. "Nobody tells me where I gotta be anymore. I'm going with you. I am. And don't try to stop me."

For a moment, I stared at her, blinking, as she waited for me to respond. No one in my life had ever spoken to me that way. In high school, I'd been a football player, strong and tall as a teenager, and no friend or foe had called me a coward since I could bench press almost twice my body weight. But this woman in front of me . . .

"Okay." I set my rifle down, still feeling the shock of her words, and recalled an important lesson from my father. In such moments, especially with women, he had counseled me, unless there's a sound biblical reason not to, it's best to concede. "Fine. You're coming with me."

Lyla left the pack at her feet and fell into my arms. I held her as she mumbled incoherent apologies into my shirt. My watch said it was an hour until dawn.

She pulled away without meeting my eyes, and shouldered her pack.

"I'll grab my stuff," I said, which took less than a minute to throw on my ammo vest and heavy pack, then grab my rifle as I walked through the settlement. Lyla was ahead of me with Lewiston's wife, saying their goodbyes.

"I guess she's going with you." Lewiston chuckled at my expense, but I wasn't sore.

"I guess so."

"We helped her pack."

"I'm sure you did!"

I didn't know whether to be embarrassed, angry, or elated over the way I'd been drawn from my slumber. Until I decided, however, I figured I'd just remain neutral. Perhaps I'd treated Lyla like she was fragile. For however long we were together, I prayed I didn't make that mistake again. What needed to be said, I'd say. And why hadn't I invited her to come with me to begin with? Possibly because I foresaw in Lyla more than a traveling companion. Maybe I was afraid of commitment. Ever since coming to Christ in my late teens, I hadn't seriously focused on chasing down a wife, even though there'd been a couple of compatible women over the years.

"Lyla has your breakfast, Mr. Caspertein," Lewiston's wife said, patting me on the shoulder. "You two be safe, and stay together. Lyla, you take care of this one. He's a catch."

A few of the other men, including Dwight Thall, were there to bid us farewell. I almost felt like I belonged there, and if others hadn't been expecting me, perhaps I would've lingered longer with them in this peaceful place by the river.

We were silent the first few miles, using the highway to head north in the growing light. The woods were beautiful with the sun peeking through in dusty rays across the treetops. I'd been in other forests in the west, but nothing like what the Rocky Mountains had to offer. What diversity, variety, and abruptness!

Still without talking, Lyla passed me a biscuit with leftover meat sandwiched between. It was dry, but good.

Lyla's pack was nearly as bulky as my own. Since the women had had nothing when they'd been rescued from the Roan boys, the whole settlement must've come together to gather supplies for her. As a practical woman, she had no doubt packed only what we would need on the trek, but I was still curious at what they'd given her.

An hour after dawn, we waded across a small stream, took a break to refill canteens, and shed layers of clothing as the day warmed.

"Lewiston said they didn't have any Bibles to spare," she said suddenly while sitting on a river rock. Taking off her boots, she examined her bare feet. "You have to share yours with me."

"No problem." I pulled it from a vest pocket, suddenly aware of how wrinkled and sweat-stained its pages had become. "You want it now?"

"Do I look like I want it now?" She winced as she poked at a blister on the side of her foot. Or maybe she winced because of the bite in her voice. "It's those boots I wore yesterday, the ones that were too big for my feet."

I knelt in front of her.

"Give me your foot."

"There's nothing you can do."

"Give me your foot."

Reluctantly, she gave me her left foot, which appeared to be the worst. I took her ankle firmly in one hand and planted her foot on my knee as I inspected it.

"This blister is fixing to pop," I said, and leaned over to dig through my kit. "A blister this big is like an open wound if it pops."

"Yeah. I get it. But it's not my fault."

I raised my eyebrows at her tone. Words came quickly to my mind, but I prayed through what needed to be said, either now or later, but they needed to be said.

"If I leave you here because of your mouth, will that be your fault?" I shrugged, holding her captive by her foot in my grasp. "You can limp back to the settlement for all I care. Don't think your little display back there means I won't dump your attitude here or at the next town. Do you want to test me? This is just you and me right now. If you can't get along with me, then I'd rather not have you mingle with my family. It's your call."

"You can't just—" She stopped herself, checking her tone by clenching her teeth, then sighed. "I don't want to be with anyone else. I want to go with you."

It was a long way from an apology, but I smiled, anyway. I took her words to mean that whatever she was upset about now—she'd work on it or explain it to me when she was ready.

"Here, cut that and thread the needle." I held up a piece of thread. "Give us about six inches."

She accepted a spool of thread and my smallest sewing needle.

"I thought blisters were supposed to be left closed."

"They are, but only to protect against bacteria. If you keep walking on this, it'll pop and rub the skin off. We have miles to go each day. Keep your feet clean and dry. Change socks every time we stop, at least until you get used to these new boots that fit your feet a little better. Hold still now."

She leaned over to watch me run the needle and thread through the worst blister, from side to side. I clipped the needle free, leaving the thread trailing through the blister.

"The thread will absorb the fluid, and the skin will remain intact to protect against bacteria."

"Where'd you learn that?"

"Wait. We're not done."

From an extra shoe sole, with pieces already cut out, I cut padding for her blister, like a donut to protect the skin in the middle. Using one strip of medical tape, I taped it into place.

"We'll go through tape too quickly if we change this each time you swap socks. Tonight in camp, you need to fashion a strap to keep it in place, with a hole cut out."

"Okay."

"Watch these other red spots that're developing. And these men's socks you have won't work. You need to wear socks that fit your feet."

"I thought all socks were the same. My brother and I never had these kinds of problems when we were hiking."

"Were you covering forty miles a day at the pace we're moving?"

"Probably not."

"That'll be our pace. It won't be too much for you, as long as you take care of your feet."

"Got it. Thank you." She clasped my hand as I started to draw away. "Thank you, Levi. And I'm sorry. I was wrong to call you a coward and talk to you that way."

"I can be clueless sometimes. I had presumed wrongly that you didn't want to come with me since I'm traveling to somewhere far away."

"I guess cluelessness isn't cowardice." She smiled. "You're the most courageous man I ever heard of or met. If my brother . . . He would've loved to meet you. What you did in the woods yesterday—no one would believe it if I told them. Outnumbered ten to one, you beat them all. And you didn't even kill anyone. You risked your life against theirs. That's not a coward. Have I embarrassed you enough? Do you forgive me?"

"Under one condition," I said with a straight face, then smiled. "You take care of these feet, huh?"

"I will." Her face glowed anew, like the morning I'd rescued her and she'd fled to me. "You have to teach me all your travel medicine tricks."

"Oh, that's really my mom or Mia's area of expertise. Mia's my cousin I was telling you about. Those two could make a sling out of a blade of grass, then boil the root to cure a fever!"

That night, Lyla laid the contents of her pack on the tarp, and I inventoried our resources. Sometimes survival depended on what a person had at hand, and that included what everyone else in the party was carrying, too. I could see she'd brought several practical items. But then I noticed that the flowery dress from the night before wasn't among her gear. Evidently, that had been a borrowed dress, maybe worn just for me. I had to pay closer attention to this woman!

We repacked for the next morning. After eating biscuits and meat, I drew out my Bible. We were two hundred yards off the highway, isolated from civilization it seemed, so I'd built a medium-sized fire.

"Look after your feet," I said, "and I'll read to us."

"How about I read to us?" She plucked the Bible from my hand. In the same motion, she leaned back and kicked her stocking feet onto my lap. "And you look after my feet."

"What are we?" I joked. "An old married couple?"

I had said it without thinking, but I couldn't take it back now. Heat burned around my neck and ears.

"You said it, not me." She stifled a giggle, then let the awkward moment pass. "Where am I reading from?"

"Let's start in Genesis and see how far we get."

"How far we get until what?"

I looked up from her feet.

"What?"

"You said, see how far we get. I know we're going to Meeker, but the way you said that, it sounded like there's an end to us reading together. In Meeker, do we split up? Do we have to go through this all over again?"

"Lyla, we've known each other for two days. This is our first full day together. I don't know what else the Lord has planned for us, but it does seem Meeker will be a crossroads of some sort, which we'll have to discuss when we get there."

"Because of your friend, Jenna?"

"Yes, because of my friend, Jenna." I gently removed her socks and examined the skin by the light of the fire. "Now, will you read, please?"

She read, and I prayed. Oh, did I pray! Though she'd marched as hard and as far as I would've, had I been alone that day, she wasn't the company I had anticipated. What a distraction she was! I was certainly attracted to her in a variety of ways, but my mind had been on survival and safety for so long, I didn't know anything about how to act with a woman. If the situation had been to my choosing, I would've preferred that a third party had been along with the two of us. That wasn't because I didn't trust Lyla, or didn't desire her—but because I was attracted to her and I didn't want to be careless with the responsibility that God had given me as a man. Even as disciplined and well-intentioned as I was, I knew the flesh could cave-in to temptation if I wasn't very diligent.

I tended to Lyla's feet that night, and she read from the Bible, through Genesis ten. When we went to sleep, it was on opposite sides of a dying fire. She snored lightly and I listened to the coyotes not far away. What was God telling me? Jenna was a world away, and here was Lyla— a fierce, dark-haired Christian woman who seemed to have fallen into my life so naturally. What was happening?

"Yep, those folks passed through here two, no, three days ago." The toothless man leaned on his rake in front of a general store. I could see through the windows that the shelves were empty. "Nice folks, they were. My wife had a rotten tooth. That woman with the big smile had a pair of pliers and handled it right there on the porch where the light was good. Sharona's been as happy as a peach since."

"Sounds like Mom," I said to Lyla. "You'd be surprised how many tooth extractions actually happen in a city in a year. Seems like everyone in San Diego stopped brushing their teeth after Pan-Day."

"We had a hard winter, so we couldn't help your people out." The old man gazed at the passing clouds over my head, as if he were remembering a long past event. "Seems to me they helped us out more than we helped them. Visitors now and then come for honey or vegetables. But we got neither right now, just some canned food for ourselves."

We left the man and his gap-toothed wife, who lived alone on the side of the highway. Their carefree presence of mind gave me hope that we'd left the sunbaked lunacy of the desert far behind. I anticipated seeing friendlier mountain people now, like these folks.

The highway ended abruptly at a ghost town. We spent two hours searching the houses, which had been looted already, until we found socks that fit Lyla's feet. Her sores were healing even as we made good time, gaining on or staying equal distance behind my family.

There was little that Lyla and I didn't talk about—except what would happen after Meeker. We spoke of politics in the Pacific States and corn farming in Nebraska. She'd been a young teen, a couple years younger than I, when Pan-Day struck. Her parents had homeschooled her on the farm after that. Her mother had died of appendicitis a few years later, and Lyla had become the homemaker of their household by the age of seventeen. For years, she'd cooked, sewn, and laundered as her father, brother, and the neighbors exported corn to buyers linked to the Appalachian Federation. Only in the last couple of years had they become aware of the injustices and persecution against Christians in the east.

"There's the Lone Cone." Lyla pointed to Norwood, Colorado's signature landmark in a field of green grass and orange flowers. The steep north face of the abrupt peak bore a hint of white as we passed it. "Uncompahgre

Plateau is to the north. Are we going straight across it or along Highway 141?"

She was becoming more familiar with my map as we went. Her late brother had drifted west more than he'd followed a map. My father would never have permitted a journey without careful preparation and planning.

"Depends which way everyone else wants to go. Water is scarce on the plateau. So we'll probably go by way of Grand Junction."

When we reached the top of Wright's Mesa, we walked down the quiet street of Norwood. It proved to be a small town of friendly people as they came out to greet us. They didn't carry guns, and I was tempted to conceal mine under my jacket.

"Don't worry about a room!" one woman said. She wore a Christmas sweater even in the warmth of spring. "We've got several bed and breakfasts for married couples to choose from."

"Oh, we're not married." I leaned closer. "Can we still find a couple of rooms?"

"Of course!"

"Word has it," an elderly man with a pipe muttered, his pot belly peeking from under his shirt, "the military is moving up from the south. You heard anything?"

"Oh, don't listen to him!" A middle-aged woman waved her hand at him. "My father and his radio. Always mumbling about some nonsense that has nothing to do with Norwood. It's either something on the East Coast happening, or something on the West Coast collapsing. Just a bunch of irrelevant nonsense!"

"You come over to Stacy's Diner right there." A young woman pointed to a green framed restaurant that looked to have been freshly painted. "Stacy'll feed you enough for two meals. I know because she's my mom."

People came and went, drifting away after welcoming us, some leaving hints for business. A couple youths on bicycles rode ahead of us down the street. I marked them as the culprits responsible for the attention we were receiving. As they rode, they tooted their bicycle horns, no doubt a rehearsed signal to announce that strangers were in town.

Suddenly, I saw a familiar face.

"Forest!" I waved and tugged on Lyla's arm. "That's Forest!"

We embraced like brothers and I introduced Lyla. Since Forest had been with us for so long, he didn't seem surprised that I'd picked up another straggler to join our trek.

"Your mom and Mia are staying over there. Sharly and I put up in that white house back a couple streets. I already traded some of that mustard I've been mixing up! Some older couple took in Vorca, Gilly, and Caleb. Did you get a load of these people? Three days, and I'm still not tired of them. Of course, if you linger like I do, they'll get you chopping firewood or nailing shingles. But I think there's a future for more mustard around here."

"This place does have its appeal."

"No offense, Levi, but I've got to say . . ." He led me away from Lyla. I noticed that he wasn't carrying the .22 rifle. "Listen, Sharly and I are talking real seriously about staying here. This might be the end of the road for us."

"Yeah?" I tried to view the town as a permanent home for myself, but I couldn't. "I thought you left Idaho to get away from these hard winters. We're at seven thousand feet here, brother. They have some cruel winters without much shelter from that wind."

"It's the people, I guess. Sharly likes it, and I already talked to a preacher who will disciple me in the Word if we stay."

"A preacher?"

"Hey, the Caspertein clan is only half alive if we're not preaching the Word, right?" He slugged my shoulder. "I've got to learn the Bible better. You're not mad, are you?"

"About taking my name or staying in Norwood?"

"Well, the name just kind of caught on, like a traveling circus." He laughed. "No, I'm talking about staying in Norwood. You guys saved our lives and taught us what life is all about. We want to do the same for others."

"No, I'm not mad. I'm glad to hear it. I'll miss you, Forest, but I think it's great. Mom and Mia are coming to the end of their journey soon, too. A couple more weeks, and we'll be in Meeker. Let's talk more tonight. I better go find Mom before she finds out I didn't come to her straight-away!"

Annette and Mia were a tearful mess as we reunited. They'd been worried, not certain whether to send Forest back for me or to wait for my arrival. They doted over Lyla, and I mentioned only that we'd left the riverside settlement together after Annette had sufficiently made known the Caspertein name in the area. She said they hadn't had another conflict since the settlement had tried to steal their burros.

Night closed quickly on Norwood, and after a reunion with Vorca and Caleb, I returned to the husband and wife who'd taken in Annette and Mia. There were other beds available in the town, but I chose to sleep on the floor by the fireplace, and Lyla reluctantly left my side to bunk with Mia. The two weren't the same age, but they had similar personalities. I already dreaded the gossip that would surely come from the laughter upstairs as I spread my bedroll across the carpet.

"Seems like a nice girl," Annette said as she sat on the sofa with a cup of tea. Everyone else had gone to their rooms. "You'd think I'd remember those stunning gray eyes of hers when we went into that settlement, but I don't. She's beautiful, Levi."

"She and some others were kidnapped near there. Lyla had no one. To say she insisted on coming with me is an understatement." I shook my head and lay back on the floor. "The first conversation I had with her, she made it clear she's a Christian. Made me raise an eyebrow."

"Raising an eyebrow and traveling alone for a week are two different things."

"Mom, I'm just her guardian."

"Does she know that? Levi, I've known her for two hours, and I've already seen the way she looks at you. Believe me, I was young once. That Caspertein charm can be hypnotic."

I chuckled.

"I don't think you need to worry about anything. Lyla's too headstrong to be impressed with me." I looked up at Mom. "Is that what Dad did when you two met in Gaza—hypnotized you?"

"Body and soul."

"Mom, please."

"Does she know about you going east to help Jenna?"

"Yeah, I told her."

"So, what're her plans?"

"You'll have to ask her. Like everyone else does, she's just latched onto us so we can protect her for a while. When she regains her confidence, she'll go her own separate way. Look at Alice, and now Forest and Sharly."

"With Lyla, it's more than that, Levi, and I think you know it." She sipped her tea. "Your father had it, and now you do, too."

"Had what?" I felt in my vest for my Bible, but realized Lyla still had it.

"We've crossed half this country, and everywhere we go, you've attracted people. They're not drawn to me or Mia. They come because of you. You have something from God, Levi, something that few ever witness. Maybe they come to you to be safe, at first. You're right, that's Forest and Sharly. But you give them a purpose, and identity. It's so easy for you to share Christ and to set people up with a firm faith because Christ is so real inside you. You become part of people's existence. It's a gift from God, something your new nature from the Holy Spirit produces."

I thought of the Servalites. They now had an identity, a purpose. Kip Brogdon led them, but only because they thought he was me. Others had joined the Caspertein family—Alice, Vorca, Caleb, Gilly . . . Some joined by choice, and some were drawn in by circumstance. Had this been what Lewiston had tried to tell me when he and the others had considered calling their settlement after my name?

"You're saying my influence runs deeper than me just being friendly?"

"You know what I'm talking about, then. Your dad knew he had it. He said it was a blessed burden from God. Hundreds relied on him in San Diego, like a tree that gives shade to animals and seeds to the birds. Once Corban Dowler trained your dad in the things of the Lord, your dad knew he was immortal—until God called him home. He traveled the world. Sometimes I joined him. Everyone he met, he touched them deeply, whether friend or foe. He became a life-giving spring to all. He wasn't a perfect man, but he gave his all for people. And because he gave his all, God gave him that influence to get inside lives. You can't think lightly of it, Levi. You have to guide people carefully, especially since their lives are so wrapped up with yours."

"Like Vorca?"

"Well, Vorca will survive no matter what. That woman—I'm not sure she even knows we're present sometimes!" She laughed a laugh that I'd missed. "She loves that boy, Caleb. A good name, by the way. You know what? He hardly ever cries!"

"Definitely a Caspertein."

"Yeah, right! I'm a Caspertein and I cry constantly!" We laughed together, though muffled as the house was quiet now. "And don't get me started about Mia. This pregnancy—oh, my! Norwood has been a godsend. I don't think I could've spent another night in camp with that girl! What an emotional roller coaster."

We watched the fire for a few moments.

"Mom?"

"Yeah?"

"I think I'm in trouble with Lyla."

"You mean you're falling for her? I know." Annette knelt and kissed me on the head. "At least you admit it. It means you're more likely to do right by her, and not just leave her behind to help Jenna."

"What's doing right by her? What's that mean?"

"God will show you." Then she left to go to her room.

I stared at the ceiling for a long time, wondering what God would show me. Everything about this trip had been planned out—except for this. What was I supposed to do with a wife? How did this fit into my plans? Or God's plans?

Chapter Twenty-six

Norwood should've been a safe haven for us. The town was welcoming, and our bodies were in such need of the rest after scorching days and chilly nights of living in the elements for so many weeks. Since leaving San Diego, we'd traveled over six hundred miles. I should've been elated for a little respite so near the end of our journey.

Instead, I was restless and worried about something. I left the house early the next morning with my rifle, vest, and canteen, and hiked out of town to pray. Whatever was bothering my spirit, God needed to reveal it to me. His light needed to illumine me.

On the north side of town, I sat on a rock surrounded by dandelions, and gazed farther north. I would've been a fool to approach God for answers by claiming I was deserving of answers. No proud soul received from God what that proud soul demanded of Him. Rather, I began my conversation with my Father in worship, by praising Him for His ways, His preservation, and His wisdom in all things.

In reaching out to Him, I examined more closely the sincerity and willingness of Jesus Christ in comparison to myself. Dad had taught me that no wisdom was ever found by looking at folly, so I didn't look at my mistakes alone, but rather also at Christ's light that I might measure my greater need of Him. And what need I had! The past was a mess of hurt and fear, from which my family was elevated only by our hope and trust in God. My life had never been more confusing—Lyla whispering to my heart and Jenna's safety calling out to me. And the future of many seemed to rest on my shoulders, even though I'd thought I was to walk alone to New York. So, what did all the travelers in our band expect from me?

Suddenly, God touched my mind—a memory of something fleeting rose up from my dilemma. A beast of threat and terror was looming, and I gasped in fear when I realized I'd nearly missed the warning altogether! We were in grave danger. Once again, I'd been careless and confident, perhaps in an attempt to push the past away. But my past, Annette's past, and Mia's past—it wouldn't evaporate. Evil incarnate had chased me from Coronado Island. How presumptuous of me to believe I'd defeated the enemy by time and distance!

For another moment, I sat on the rock, thanking God for illuminating my mind and directing me to face what seemed ridiculous to face.

"Yes, Lord," I said, wishing I could refuse His instruction, but knowing I couldn't, not if I was one of His consecrated children. "I will go. Even if it kills me."

I tried not to look north anymore, but my eyes still lingered. So close to Meeker! So close to our Caspertein relatives, and now, after such terrible effort, God was calling me to go another direction!

Slowly, I walked back to town, my stomach growling, but feeling too sick at heart to eat. Never had obeying God seemed so fruitless, but to turn from obeying Him would most certainly lead to disaster. Instead, I needed to trust Him in the face of impossibility.

When I reached the house where Annette and Mia were staying, I passed it by and kept walking. I arrived at a sidewalk garden where a man was weeding around stakes in the ground.

"I'm looking for a man who smokes a pipe," I said. "I met him yesterday. He said something about having a shortwave radio. Sound familiar?"

"Sure, but Old Man Cotter hasn't smoked that pipe in at least ten years, ever since the town ran out of tobacco. He just sucks on that old thing."

He pointed me to a shabby house that had no visible antenna. I walked over to the porch a block from the main thoroughfare, and knocked on the man's door. Though the houses nearest the town center were carefully maintained, Old Man Cotter's house had been neglected by himself, and apparently by the townspeople as well.

When he answered, his hair was askew and he wore no pants. True to what the gardener had told me, Cotter was sucking on the end of a cold pipe. But I wondered if I was wasting my time.

"Mr. Cotter, you told me yesterday that some military is moving up from the south. I need to know about that."

He shifted the pipe in his mouth from side to side.

"You gonna believe Cotter the Coot? Ain't no military out there, not that Norwood's ever seen. Ain't no prospects for anyone to come through Norwood. Waste of time to be comin' this way."

"You said yesterday you had a radio. I don't need to use it. I just need to know what you heard."

"Don't got no radio, youngster. Who would I talk to? No one out there to talk to, except maybe the Pacific States once in a while. Seems they's the only ones who's got a radio nowadays—in the West, anyway."

"So, you do have a radio." I frowned through his senility. "Where's your antenna?"

"What's that now? What do I want with antelope meat?"

"The military . . ." I leaned toward his left ear as he cupped it. "The military. Where are they?"

"The armored unit? Oh, last I heard, they were in Pagosa Springs, talking about intercepting at Meeker."

"Meeker!" I took a step back. As we'd traveled, our target of Meeker hadn't been a secret, but we'd been guarded, I thought, or at least cryptic about our final destination with anyone but those who traveled with us. How would General Brogdon know we were going to Meeker? Like the old man had said, there was no reason a military division or even a scouting party would pass northward through Western Colorado. Resources were few and towns were scarce. There seemed only one reason why General Brogdon would be moving toward Meeker.

"They used the word intercept?" I asked.

"Intercept what?" he yelled back at me.

"How long ago? When did you use the radio?"

"Tuesday."

"Okay, well, what's today?" I hadn't kept track of the calendar days.

"Thursday."

"Thank you." I shook his hand, smiling, and hopped off the porch. "Keep your ear on that radio, old man!"

"What's that? What's that about an air raid?"

I didn't know where Cotter's radio or antenna were located in town or outside the town, but he couldn't know what he knew unless he'd overheard a transmission somewhere. General Brogdon was local, and Norwood was about to be visited!

Back at the house, the smell of breakfast didn't detour me from marching to my pack and drawing out my map.

"Tea, Cuz?" Mia asked. She and Lyla sat in somebody's pajamas at the dining table. Annette was moving around an oven with the host of the house. I smelled eggs. "What're you up to?"

I spread my map across the living room floor where I'd slept, then looked up at their expectant faces. How much should I say? They'd try to stop me. They wouldn't understand that I'd begged God for a light, and He'd shined on my next move. Now, I was beginning to understand why I needed to go.

But this was my family. I'd acted in secrecy before, thinking I was protecting them, and they'd only been hurt.

"Come over here, all of you. Please."

"What's going on?" Annette was the first to sit on the sofa. "What's wrong?"

I waited until Mia and Lyla were settled. After their late night chatting, it was no wonder their eyes looked puffy.

"General Brogdon was in Pagosa Springs two days ago." I placed a finger on the map. "He's on his way to Meeker, I'm pretty sure."

"Meeker!" Mia jumped to her feet. "How could he know where we were going? We haven't told many people about Uncle Rudy!"

"We haven't told anyone who hasn't been traveling with us," I said. "But there were others who could've said something."

"Well, Vorca didn't tell anyone!" Annette stated. "And the kids certainly didn't."

"I didn't say anything," Mia said. "I would never talk. I'm trying to leave anything to do with the Brogdons far behind."

"Forest and Sharly know to keep things quiet," Annette continued. "Gilly hasn't been with us long enough to tell anyone."

"Well, there've been others." I hesitated. "Two others. But neither of them would talk unless they were forced."

"Who?"

"Alice. The general must have her."

"She would never talk, Levi!" Annette looked worried. "Would she? I didn't know her very long, but I thought she was as tough as they come."

"Yes, she is, but everyone has a breaking point. If the general knows our route, or even that we were going to Meeker, it means he has Alice. I've been out praying. I believe God wants me to go meet General Brogdon. If he has Alice, if she's still alive, I'll try to get her back."

"There's no meeting and talking with men like Galt Brogdon." Annette clenched her teeth as she talked. "You can't reason with the devil, Levi!"

"But we can stand against him. This has gone on long enough. Now, he's probably kidnapped one of our own. Alice is like family to me. Besides, she's a sister in Christ."

Lyla cleared her throat.

"You said there were two people who might've talked if coerced. Alice is one. You told me about her. Who's the other?"

I tore my eyes from the map to look into their faces. Were they ready? Could they handle what I had to say?

"Kip Brogdon received Christ a few weeks ago. Periodically, Alice and I have talked to him, even saved his life."

"You dare speak his name in here?" Annette scowled at me, then glanced at Mia. "Levi, you know what that monster did to her!"

"Aunt Annette, it's okay. I'm not a little girl." Mia nodded at me. "He's the one you stayed back to meet before Shiprock, right? He's the one who warned us with the smoke signals, isn't he? He saved our lives."

I told them everything—Kip's dying profession of faith and his miraculous recovery from the virus, his search for a Bible, and his assumption as leader of the party known as the Servalites.

"Your father would be turning in his grave," Annette said, "if he knew Kip Brogdon has taken his name."

"After Dad, it was my name. I've been using it for hundreds of miles. But I wasn't about to take charge of a whole company of followers who needed to be led. Kip was ready, able, and willing."

"Yeah, for his own use!"

Annette was aching for a fight over this, and I could've quarreled with her, but instead, I took a breath and answered calmly.

"I'm going to find a bike and ride south on Highway 141 to Telluride. That's thirty miles away. There's an airport there. If General Brogdon came up from Pagaosa Springs in the last couple days, it would take him about two days to ford a few rivers. I'm guessing he spent the night at the airport. If I don't run into him by Telluride, I'll come back."

"That's it?" Annette waved her hands in the air. "That's your plan? You're running off alone again?"

"Well, I don't have to, if you want to come with me."

"I'll go." Lyla looked at Mia. "Wanna go?"

"No!" Annette said. "None of us are going!"

"I could live the rest of my life without ever seeing the Brogdons again," Mia said, "but you're not going alone, Levi. Half the reason he's after us still is because you stole me back."

I glanced at Annette's face. She looked like she was about to scream, but I nodded sadly at her, and her resolve softened. Or maybe she realized there was no arguing with me about this.

"He might have thirty or forty men with him." I checked the level of water in my canteen. "That's a lot of guns."

"That never stopped you from rescuing others." Annette's voice was resigned as she walked to the door where her bullpup was leaning in the corner of the coat rack. "Why would we expect it to stop you now when you're going after Alice?"

"If we can find another .308 rifle in this town," Lyla said, "I'm a fair shot. Just give me some of those gel-tranqs."

"Mom, try to find another .308 for Lyla. Trade one of the burros if you have to."

"Forest already gave us back his .22," Mia said. "I'll take that."

"Then while you guys are getting ready," I said, "I'll find us some bikes. We need to leave in an hour."

The four of us pedaled quietly out of town in the mid-morning sunlight. Even with all our gear, I set a pace that tested the rusty gears on our mountain bikes. We'd reach Telluride in two hours if we kept our speed up. But once out of town, we realized we could go even faster since our route was mostly downhill.

"How do you know you're not leading your family to their deaths?" Lyla asked as we coasted down steep, cracked pavement. She and I were in the lead, riding side by side, with our rifles on our backs. "Is this the kind of recklessness I can expect from the Casperteins?"

"God has something for us all to witness, but I don't know what. If trouble starts, Mom'll be worried about me, so make sure you worry about Mia." I switched gears to pedal faster. "She's not used to being pregnant."

"What do you want me to do?"

"Keep her out of the fight," I said. "She only has the .22. It won't be effective against an armored convoy, even if we get within range for her to fire."

"I'll keep her back. You can count on me, Levi. Just do what God wants you to do. You saved me. God will help you save Alice, too."

I jumped a root that had emerged through a crack in the pavement.

"How'd you know this was a mission from God?" I asked her.

"Because you seem to be in your right mind, but no one in their right mind would ride a bike out to meet the general of an army like this. So, this is like a warrior of God kind-of-thing." She laughed, her dark hair flying in the wind behind her. "I'm expecting big things from God because of you. I've been with you for almost a week now, and already my faith is stronger because of you, Levi."

"I should feel bigger by that kind of talk, but I just feel smaller."

"That's because you're in the zone."

"The zone?"

"The God Zone." She changed gears and sped ahead. "Are we going this slow for a reason?"

Three hours later, we reached Telluride and its small airport. As suspected, a ten-vehicle convoy was rolling out of the airport perimeter. One of the massive hangers still standing had undoubtedly been their quarters overnight.

Lyla and I were in the middle of the road when we saw the vehicles turn toward us, a quarter-mile away. We hit our brakes, and Annette and Mia stopped with us.

"I was hoping you were wrong, Levi." Annette took her rifle off her back while still straddling her bike. Mia and Lyla did the same, but I left mine on my back. "We have no cover. It's just grass on both sides of the highway. Levi, are you listening?"

"Yeah," I said, but I was really praying, asking God what His plan was. Why was I here? Why had I ridden to face so many men with rifles—and risk my family's safety as well? "Get in the grass and keep your heads down. Use the radios. Mom, you take the north. Mia and Lyla, take the south. If you start shooting, reposition in the grass every few shots, then retreat from the area before you're overrun."

"What about you?" Annette asked. "Levi, this makes no sense. They are literally here for us. Why are you giving yourself to them?"

Mia and Lyla walked their bikes to the side of the road and laid them down.

"I have to end this with Galt Brogdon."

"What's your plan?"

"I didn't make one." I looked from the slowing convoy to her worried face. "This is God's plan. All of it. I don't even know what I should say. I just know I'm supposed to be here."

"That's it?" She scoffed and adjusted the comm over her ear to stay in touch with Mia who wore the other one. "Levi, we need to get out of here! He'll kill you. He'll kill all of us!"

"Mother, go get in the grass."

The convoy stopped eighty yards away, an easy distance for Annette to shoot, but just as easy for the general's troops.

Annette went to lay in the grass. She crawled a few yards, then lay low. On the other side of the road, Mia and Lyla lay prone, side by side, a bolt-action .308 hunting rifle against Lyla's shoulder. She had thirty gel-tranq rounds for her weapon.

The convoy left formation and spread out. Two Humvees blocked the highway's two lanes. Two others drove into the ditch to complete the blockade. The six remaining vehicles reinforced their defenses.

I smiled as men piled out of their Humvees, rifles aimed at me. Someone had recognized me—probably Galt himself.

"All these men just for me, Galt?" I chuckled, remembering that Dad had told me stories of his own exploits for God in distant lands. "It ain't easy being a Caspertein."

Stepping away from my bike, I gave it a shove toward the ditch. The front wheel wobbled as it coasted unmanned, then toppled over. If the vehicles roared up the highway, at least the bike wouldn't be run over.

Not far to the south, the grass had claimed some structures, now burned from what I guessed was a Pan-Day fire. Rolling hills and trees stood in the distance. Not exactly a battlefield setting, but there would be no real battle here. A dozen rifles were already aimed at me, and my rifle was still on my back. If shooting started, it would be a slaughter—the slaughter of me.

I started walking down the middle of the highway. From the convoy, a solitary man stepped from the cover of his vehicle—General Galt Brogdon. More of his men spread out in the grass on both sides of the road. No doubt, they were scoping for my family who they'd certainly seen move into the grassland.

When we were ten yards apart, the general and I both stopped. He wore a sidearm, his holster unclipped. I remembered how he'd so coldly killed Jose Hernandez on the bridge in San Diego. This man had ordered my father's death, and killed hundreds, if not thousands more.

"You've caused me a lot of trouble, Caspertein." His face seemed to be more lined since I'd seen him weeks earlier. "I should've put you down like a sick dog when I put your old man down."

This didn't seem to be the moment for me to be mouthy or clever, so I held my tongue and waited for the right words from God.

"I've lost a lot of men because of you, from Cadiz to here." He spit on the pavement. "The men—I don't care about them. I can always find more men. But you ruined vehicles, too. That cursed phosphorus. I've thought about how I'd make you talk and tell me where your stash is. Your death won't be quick, I promise."

Still, no words came to me, but a commotion was coming from his men. I heard a yell and reshuffling. But the general and I kept our eyes on one another. This was personal.

"Just tell me what you did to my son." He shifted his feet, and I sensed he was truly pleading for the truth, as only a father could. "I don't think you killed him, but you Christians are a contradictory sort when cornered. Kip wouldn't disappear like he did unless someone did something to him."

I opened my mouth, but it still wasn't the time to speak.

"General!" one of his men called over a loud speaker. "We have movement at nine o'clock!"

Brogdon frowned and used his hand to shield the sun from his eyes. I turned as well, expecting to see Lyla or Mia relocating to a better location to the south. Instead, I saw a mass of people, a line of men and women, marching toward us. Some were on horseback, a number had rifles, but as they came nearer through the grass, I noticed most carried only walking sticks and backpacks.

"So, you finally brought backup, Caspertein. It's not like you to ask for help from others. Who did you find to help you out here? It doesn't matter. I'll kill them. I'll kill them all!"

The Pacific States soldiers adjusted their stances to sight their rifles on the newcomers.

"They're not with me," I stated.

Brogdon placed his hand on his sidearm. The people kept coming.

"Who are they? There must be . . . two hundred of them! This town burned. No one has resisted us for over a week. Where did they come from? We're in the middle of nowhere."

As they drew closer, I began to pick out familiar faces. And then, from the front, near the middle, a young, curly-haired man stepped ahead of the others. His faded red jacket was dusty and weathered, but recognizable.

"Hold your fire!" Brogdon ordered his men. "No one shoot!"

Kip Brogdon was all the way to the ditch before the general gasped.

"Son? You're alive?"

"Hey, Dad." Then Kip nodded at me, a light in his eyes. "Levi."

"Morning, Kip," I said. "That's quite an army you brought along."

"Christian soldiers." Kip smiled. The Servalites stood casually opposite the ditch. A few of them waved at me, but for the most part, they looked tired and solemn, likely concerned about the Pacific States soldiers. "These people just keep gathering. They came for direction, but I'm the one learning."

"Kip, who are all these people? Why are you with them?"

"They're just Americans, Dad, ready to start over. And, at least some of them are Christians."

"Christians? *You? You've* gone native on me?"

"Not native, Dad. I just woke up. That's all. We saw your convoy driving north yesterday. We walked all night to get here. Figured you were still chasing the Casperteins after President Criswell ordered you to stop."

"Who do you think you are?" He snarled at his son.

"I'm just an AWOL soldier." Kip said, his posture strong and tall. "But I'm also your son, your only son, the son who's led your most experienced soldiers for years now. I know everyone you have here. I've trained half of them. The rest—we grew up together, swam the bay together, partied together. I'm Kip Brogdon."

"No son of mine would ever be with these weak . . . these Christians!"

"And yet, here I am." Kip was surprisingly confident. "Why didn't you stay on your scouting mission eastward, Dad? You know the Appalachian Federation is pushing west for territory as well. Haven't we caused the Casperteins enough trouble?"

"Look who's talking."

"Oh, I know. Levi and I have talked it out. I'm disgusted about my sinful past, deserving of the worst punishment."

"You've gone insane."

"No, God opened my eyes." He nodded. "So, do you want me to tell your men, or do you want to tell them?"

"Tell them what?"

"That you've breached the president's orders. We both know you've lost power this past year. Rumors are, there's some sort of resistance gathering north of San Diego. But here you are."

"The Casperteins are behind everything, son! I'm telling you!"

"The president doesn't care who you blame. Come on, Dad. We've talked about this for countless nights. You groomed me to think like you, remember? You taught me to hide our weaknesses. Go east, Dad. You're done here."

"You don't give me orders!"

"No?" Kip took one step to stand nose to nose with the old general, whose face had never seemed so unsure. "Who does give you orders? You want to tell your men you're so far off the reservation that they might not be welcomed back home to their own families? Or are you still getting on the wire, making bogus reports about breakdowns as you hunt the Casperteins? Get back on mission, Dad, or this will go very badly for you and all these men."

"Levi has the bullpups stashed somewhere!" Brogdon pointed at me. "With those rifles, we could rule this country, take it over! Even the Appalachian Federation would fall to its knees!"

"It's over, Dad." Kip stepped back.

"It's not over," I said, causing them both to look at me. "He's got Alice, unless he's already killed her."

"Alice? Dad, you have Alice, the one-armed woman? Where is she? Tell me!"

The general's face reddened. I'd never seen one man dismantle another man's arrogance so handily as Kip had his father's. Finally, his head bowed.

"She's in the truck."

"Is she alive?" Kip asked. "That's right, Dad. I know your methods, because I used them for years. Tell me! Is she alive?"

"Yes, okay? She's alive. I'm not an animal."

"Go get her, Levi. We'll wait here."

I didn't hesitate. Moving around father and son, I jogged to the blockade of Humvees. The soldiers' rifles followed my every move. They kept glancing up the road at their commander.

"Alice, the woman!" I called to the men. "I was told to fetch her. Where is she?"

A soldier with bars on his shoulders looked at the general, then at me, and shrugged.

"There." He pointed a thumb at a rear Humvee.

I ran to the vehicle and threw open the back door. Alice lay on the back seat. Her face was battered and swollen, and she clutched her midsection with her arm.

"Alice?" I climbed into the back seat. "Alice? It's me, Levi. Can you move?"

She opened one swollen eye; the other couldn't open at all. I guessed she had bone fractures. Her face would never be the same.

"Levi?"

"Yes, Alice. It's me. Can you move a little?"

"I think so." She sat up with some help. "You came for me? You came back for me!"

"Of course, I did." I pulled her into my arms. "That's what family does for one another."

"Levi, they made me talk. *I talked.* I'm so sorry!"

"I know, but it worked out perfectly." I carried her beyond the vehicles. "You led them right into my hands."

"What's happening now? I didn't hear any gunfire."

"You're gonna get fixed up first. Then, if you're still willing, Mom's been packing your heavy staff halfway across the country. I think that poor burro is ready for someone else to carry it again."

"Oh, I missed you!" She cried, her one arm hooked around my neck.

Chapter Twenty-seven

With Alice in my arms, I walked toward both Brogdon men. Instead of stopping in front of them, I veered off and hopped the ditch. Knowing the Servalites like I did, I was certain Alice would be in good hands. Several men and women received her and carried her behind the line of marchers, then I returned to the road.

"Dad's headed east, Levi," Kip said, his hand on his father's shoulder. "You can get word to me if he causes more problems for you. President Criswell would love to get a call on the radio from me. After all, the man practically raised me while Dad was claiming the West Coast for him. Right, Dad?"

"My own flesh and blood . . ." the general murmured.

"If you're ever back this way, Dad, we might cross paths a second time. Then again, we may be going in the same direction. It's in the Lord's hands."

Kip held out his hand, perhaps a gesture meant for the soldiers who were watching as well. For an instant, I thought the general might draw his sidearm and shoot his own son. But he briskly shook his son's hand, then turned and walked away. Together, Kip and I watched his father return to the lead Humvee. He climbed in, the convoy turned around, and they headed down the highway.

"He might still be a problem for you," Kip said, regret in his voice. "The president's been losing confidence in him for months. Dad's supposed to be sticking to Interstate 40, setting up outposts along the way. But he keeps radioing back to H-Q for more men, more trucks, more resources. He's way off course now, probably telling Criswell some story to justify this alternate route. It wouldn't be so dire, Levi, except we know that the Appalachian Federation is trying to take over the Plains Zone as well. They're headed this way, and every mile they take, the Pacific States loses."

"Honestly, I wasn't sure how God was going to get us out of this one." I felt like falling on my knees and weeping. "You came through, Kip."

"It's what you would've done for me. Where are you headed next?"

"Norwood, about thirty miles northeast."

"You have bikes? Who's with you?"

"Annette, Mia, and a friend."

"Mia's here?" Instead of gazing into the grass to locate her, he turned his back to where she might've been. "All the more reason for us to go our own ways, I guess."

"Yeah, I guess so."

"We have a few two-wheeled carts. Let me see what we can spare. You can pull Alice behind your bike."

"Hey." I held out my hand. "For whatever reasons we're parting ways once more—and we know those reasons—may the Casperteins and the Servalites meet again."

"It'd be my pleasure." He shook my hand. "I sure hope I can live up to that name."

"You already are, Kip." I admired the people who were milling around behind him, now relaxing their brave stance. "You already are."

"Make sure she rests," a female physician among the Servalites instructed Annette as we prepared to leave. "Will you be able to let her rest when you get to where you're going?"

"By nightfall," I said, "she'll be in her own room in a real bed."

"Don't baby me, Levi!" Alice barely submitted as two men set her in a cart attached to the back of my mountain bike. There wasn't much padding in the cart, but Alice wasn't one to complain, even though the cart was small and her legs hung off the back. "I'm only riding in this because there aren't enough bikes for me to ride one, too."

"Of course," I said, not about to tell her how bad she looked.

Since the heat of the day was upon us, we shed our jackets. Annette used the extra clothing to cushion Alice's head and position. Kip had made himself scarce, but Mia seemed to sense he was nearby. She held my bike with her own, glancing often at the groups of people settling into various campsites for the night, even though it was barely afternoon.

"You okay?" I asked Mia as we peddled away from the waving Servalites. To them, I wasn't important, just a close Christian friend to the Serval, their leader.

Annette and Lyla pulled ahead of us a short distance. I was happy to see Lyla fitting in so well with my family.

"I'm okay, Cuz." She changed gears as we sped up. "It's strange that Kip's really a Christian now. I don't know how to think of him."

"And how's that?" I asked. She frowned at my question. "He was once a man who was dead inside, willing to take. Now, he's a different man who's alive inside, ready to give."

"Levi, I carry his baby." She almost whispered, as if I didn't already know that truth. "What's the right thing to do here? I mean, there are enough kids without fathers in this torn-up world."

I touched my brakes and slowed gradually so as not to disturb Alice. Mia stopped as well.

"What are you saying?" I asked.

"What is there for me in Meeker?"

"Family, safety, a home." I swallowed over a lump in my throat. "Mia, if you're worried about a father for the kid, you're a beautiful young woman. Any good man would be tripping over his own feet to love you and be a father to your child."

"Come on." She smiled. "Who are you to speak of safety? You cast caution to the wind constantly, and run into danger for God all the time. You don't know for sure that I'll ever find what you're talking about, and I can't depend on you the rest of my life."

"Well . . ." I sighed and shrugged. "All I've got for you is what we've had planned—to get everyone safely to Meeker."

"I don't think my place is in Meeker, anymore. My place may be here with the Servalites. With Kip."

Her face seemed peaceful. I'd never seen Mia so surrendered to such a selfless idea. Her mood swings, Annette had said, had been in perfect order for a pregnant woman for the first three months, but this was more than a mood swing or hormones. This was a woman speaking from a place of spiritual maturity and humility. How she'd matured through such adversity!

"Hey!" Annette called from far ahead. "You guys coming or what? Did you forget something?"

"I'm having a little trouble," I said to Mia, ignoring Annette for a moment, "understanding exactly what you're saying."

"No, I don't think you are, Levi. You talked me into keeping this baby. You led Kip to the Lord. I think God wants this."

"Mia!" I looked at the sky in bewilderment, maybe expecting God to knock some sense into her. "Twenty years ago, he would've gone to prison for what he did to you!"

"Don't explain to me what he did to me." Her voice was soft, gentler than I'd heard her speak in weeks. "I'm not interested in hiding like a victim. It doesn't have to be like that. But if I go to Meeker, that's how it'll be. To you and Aunt Annette, I'll be the Caspertein who was violated. The kid will be loved, sure, but there'll always be a cloud over him. And whispers. Even if no one says it, it'll be on your minds. It's just the truth, even if we wish it wasn't so."

"And the alternative is—?" I gazed back at the Servalites. They were singing a hymn, the instruments and sounds drifting on the wind—an impromptu worship service. "I don't know why I'm fighting you on this, Mia. What you're saying is so unexpected, that's all. It's not logical, but sometimes that's the way the Holy Spirit works."

The cart rocked as Alice moved. She looked up at Mia.

"Kip saved my life in the desert," she said. "I was out of water. It would've been a miserable death. God can change the heart. You could do worse than Kip Brogdon. He has charisma, and he's not bad looking, either. What he's done doesn't identify him any more than whatever we've done identifies us."

"Hey!" Annette and Lyla rode back to us and stopped. "What's the big idea? We've got some serious miles to cover."

"I'm leaving, Aunt Annette," Mia said, tears now welling. "I'm going with the Servalites."

"What?" She laughed, then became solemn. "Mia, you can't be serious! Levi?"

"It's not Levi's decision," Mia said. "I don't have anything back in Norwood that I can't leave behind."

"But we're going to Meeker." Annette pointed northwest. "You're having the baby this winter in Meeker, at Uncle Rudy's. Titus' brother is waiting for us, I'm sure, to show up one day."

"No, I'm having the baby this winter with the Servalites." She smiled at me. "Besides, someone needs to tell Kip more about Uncle Titus, the real Serval."

"What's happening?" Annette's face showed panic as Mia climbed off her bike and dropped it on the pavement. She embraced Annette with the force of a departing loved one. "No, Mia. No!"

Annette seemed in shock as Mia turned from her to hug Lyla.

"Haven't known you long, Sis, but I know you'll tame him."

"Oh, I will!" Lyla winked at me.

"Tame who?" I blurted. "Hey, I'm standing right here, you know!"

"Alice?" Mia kissed the battered woman's forehead and gave her the .22 rifle to hold in her single arm. "When I think of you, I'll remember God teaches us that we gain more by loss than having everything. I hope that makes sense."

"It does." She set the rifle aside in the cart and squeezed Mia's hand. "You take care, huh? I'm proud of you. I can tell God is moving in you right now. Don't lose that."

Mia embraced me, and I held her tightly, not wanting to let her go. Finally, she paused to gaze at us all once more. For a moment, Annette was stunned and speechless. Then, Mia smiled, picked up her bike, and pedaled away.

"I'll bring her back," Annette said suddenly, and stood up on her pedal to ride after her niece.

But I reached out and squeezed the back wheel brake on her handlebars, so she couldn't budge. Wounded, she jerked the steering bar against my grip, but I held tight.

"Let her go, Mom."

"Mia!" she called. "You can't just leave us! I love you!"

We watched after Mia until she reached the camp of the Servalites. Annette wept quietly, then shook my hand off her brake and turned northwest.

"She'll be okay," Lyla assured me about Annette. "I'll ride with her. Sometimes we're only protecting ourselves when we think we're protecting others."

When Lyla had left to follow Annette, Alice looked up at me.

"That girl's got some wisdom, Levi. Where'd you find her?"

"I think God brought her to me."

"Why don't you sound excited about that?"

"Well, I guess because she doesn't fit into my plans." I chuckled. "But God seems to be teaching me that my plans don't matter much."

I pedaled toward Norwood at a comfortable pace, almost all of it uphill, while Alice shared about her activities for the past weeks. She'd led the refugees of Shiprock south, settling them in towns as they passed through them. Before she'd reached Albuquerque, she'd turned north to catch up to us. General Brogdon had picked her up in Gallup, New Mexico, depriving her of sleep and water until she was too incoherent to know if she was speaking or not, but later she realized she'd given away the Meeker destination.

We reached Norwood after dark—Lyla and Annette an hour ahead of us. I helped Alice into the house as she insisted on walking on her own. Annette had fixed dinner, and Lyla served us. No one was very talkative since we were exhausted and were missing Mia. Her absence felt like the death of a loved one, but I knew she'd responded to God's prompting. We didn't need to imagine the dynamics of the relationship she and Kip would have now. It was too miraculous an event for our simple minds or hearts to contemplate without sinking into a somber mood of concern. Mia was beyond my arm of protection for the first time since she'd been born. My cousin had joined another family now. This brought us all a sense of loneliness.

For two days, we sat in Norwood, allowing Alice to rest and heal from the battering of men's fists. Lyla sat with her, and Annette doted over them both. But I avoided the house as much as possible. I was restless to continue the journey, and Old Man Cotter's mysterious radio kept my mind imagining the worst about Jenna. Twice a day, I talked to Cotter, picking his brain about rumors from the east. Sometimes, he spoke coherently, sharing vague details about a Federation force coming to Meeker, searching for Christians. None of it made sense, so I understood he was confusing what he'd heard about the Pacific States and their rendezvous at Meeker, meaning to catch me. Other times, he would talk about noncompliance institutions across the East Coast where people were imprisoned for pushing against the Federation's new laws. Then Cotter's mind would drift to unrelated facts about butterflies or one-hundred year-old Colorado history.

"You'd better be visiting me to say we're leaving tomorrow," Alice said as I checked on her the night of the second day. Lyla had been reading her a Christian novel, *Fury in the Storm*, while sitting in a rocking chair in the corner with a candle in one hand. "No offense, Lyla, but I can't stay here another day and do nothing. I'm going crazy for fresh air and the ground under my feet."

"How do you feel about riding a bike?" I asked Alice as I sat on the edge of her bed. "I fastened an extension onto the left side of the handlebar that'll cup your stump."

"What about my staff? I sort of like walking with it out in front of everyone."

"There's a gun sling on your bike. The staff sticks out a little like a lance, but it works."

"I guess that'll do." She shook her head. "As long as I don't have to ride in that cart anymore."

"Everyone in Norwood agrees that we can stick to the roadways from here to Meeker, so bikes will get us there in a week, half the time that walking would take."

When I left the room, Lyla followed me out and stopped me in the dark hallway. The only light in the corridor came from the candle she held. Even Annette and the couple who owned the house had gone to bed.

"You and I need to talk about what happens after Meeker."

The candlelight made her gray eyes appear like some sort of enchanted stones. There was no avoiding her this time. She wanted answers.

"I'll be heading out to New York."

"Alone?" she raised her eyebrows, obviously testing me, but I'd learned my lesson.

"No, that simply won't do, would it?" I nodded. "It's my understanding that I'm taking you, right?"

"And why are you taking me?" Her smile was creeping out, but she was trying to keep a serious face.

"Honestly?"

"I hope so."

"Because I'm terrified of you." I grinned at her obvious amusement. "And I'll need a cook on the road."

"That's it?"

"Someone'll need to chop the firewood, too. Skin the animals I hunt. Patch up my wounds."

"You're fixing to get wounded right now." She shoved me playfully. "Well, you just described a wife, didn't you? Except I'll leave the wood chopping to you."

"That sounds like something we can work out."

"So, you think we'd make a good team for the Lord, right?"

"That's usually not the first reason people get married nowadays."

"Well, it should be, right?" She raised her chin. "Mia already told me you'd fallen for me, so love isn't a question."

"Mia said that, did she? We didn't even talk about you."

"But we talked about you. She's known you her whole life. She said she could tell by the look in your eyes when you looked at me, and how you acted when you were in the house with me."

I looked at the floor. Of course, Lyla had been on my mind every hour of my days, and often mentioned in my prayers for direction. What did I really know about being a husband except what I'd seen from my father, who'd treated Annette like a princess for their twenty-plus years of marriage? He was my only Christian reference for romance, but I didn't know how things were supposed to go at the beginning. I'd only known my father and Annette as a couple who'd met in Gaza under trying circumstances.

"You don't think it's too soon to talk about marriage?" I asked.

"When you find the right fruit on the tree that God says is acceptable for eating, are you gonna pick the fruit or let it go to another?"

I muffled my laughter, then sighed, hoping no one else in the house could hear us.

"You have a wild beauty, Lyla Suzanne Grady. And, for God, you'll make a fine addition to the Caspertein family. That thought makes my knees weak and my heart do flip-flops. I'm crazy about you, but you've got to let me drive."

"What do you mean? Drive what?"

"You've got to let me propose."

"Let you propose?" It was her turn to cover her mouth to stifle her laughter. "That's your condition? Is that your way of telling me to let you be the man of the family? You want me to butt out?"

"Why, that's a great idea!"

"Okay, I'll stop bugging you. I'll pretend to be the hapless maiden, awaiting your word." She put her hand on her hip and aimed the candle at me. "Just don't wait too long, Levi Caspertein, because I don't do the hapless maiden bit too well!"

She kissed me on the mouth and marched to her room before I could say anything else. In the dark hallway, I waited for my mind to clear, then walked to Annette's door. I knocked lightly, then opened it a crack. Annette was reading her Bible by candlelight.

"Just saying goodnight," I said. We hadn't talked much since arriving back without Mia. It seemed she blamed me, but I knew that gently reaching out to her often brought about the reconciliation we needed.

"Back on the road tomorrow, huh?" She closed her Bible.

"I sure hope we can find Uncle Rudy." I lingered. "Mom, what does hapless mean?"

"Use it in a sentence."

"I won't be hapless forever."

"It means like unfortunate, down on your luck. That sort of thing."

"Like impoverished, maybe?"

"Yeah, maybe."

"Okay, good night." I started to close the door.

"Levi? She's just saying she wants to know that you value her, that you know she's valuable."

"What?"

"Lyla wants to be your partner, not a damsel in distress."

"So, you heard everything."

"I lost a daughter two days ago. When should I plan to gain another?"

"Probably when we get to Meeker. If I have the nerve."

"Your dad needed a little help, too. If you didn't, I'd be worried you were over-confident about yourself."

"Mom, you didn't lose Mia."

"I know. I just miss her."

"Yeah, me too."

The next morning, Vorca scolded me in her own tongue as I insisted she accept the broad seat of an adult tricycle. Like my mountain bike, her vehicle pulled a little trailer of gear that had once been carried by the two burros. For the bikes, we had traded the pack animals. Vorca's protest ended abruptly when Lyla approached to settle the matter. Actually, I wasn't certain what Lyla was about to do or say to settle Vorca, but Vorca seemed to know, so she complied and climbed onto the tricycle. Lyla returned to her own bike with a nod and a smile at me. She was already helping me lead! The bike joints groaned as short, round Vorca sat on the tricycle seat. Her feet were able to reach the pedals perfectly, and the three gears would help her keep pace with the rest of us. It would take little effort for us all to move at ten miles an hour.

"Lyla," I called as she climbed back onto her bike, "move us out."

Alice had already departed minutes ahead of us, taking point on her customized mountain bike. Instead of a rifle, she carried the heavy staff on her bike. There were more practical weapons, but she seemed to hold sentimental value for the heavy metal beam.

Regardless of Gilly's initial attachment to Annette, he'd already found a home in Norwood with a family who had two young men his age. I'd met the father, and he seemed better equipped to handle a teenage boy than we could.

Our goodbyes to Forest and Sharly had been tearful, but the young family was happy to have found a place in the community.

Lyla led the way for us, Forest's silenced .22 slung on her back. Annette carried her bullpup, and in my trailer, I'd packed Mia's shotgun, in case we needed it for birds. Also on my hip, included with the horse trade, was a .22 pistol with nine shots. Since it was the same caliber as the .22 rifle, I could now shoot gel-tranqs with the handgun as well. At a machinist shop in Norwood, I'd paid an engineer to drill the gun's barrel and screw on a clumsy-looking silencer onto its threaded barrel. He said it wouldn't last forever, but as long as the foils inside didn't break, I could shoot silenced rounds.

By noon, we'd reached Naturita, refilled our canteens from a gracious residence, then continued north on Highway 141. We met a few people headed south across the terrain that rolled and twisted around gullies, hills, and rock formations. They were wary but friendly, each of us moving on after a couple courteous sentences about the path ahead, or food. *Is it safe? Is it paved all the way? Do you have any fruit or meat to trade?*

Since Alice stayed about a mile ahead of us, she met travelers first, and remained in radio contact with Annette. I would've liked to have had the comm in my own ear, but Annette needed the distraction. Alice seemed more talkative as well, which I discovered by how Annette constantly responded to dialogue with the black woman far ahead. Since the two were about the same age, I sensed a growing bond between them.

"You know she loves you," Lyla said at the end of the first day. The sun had set and Alice had radioed back that she'd found a good campsite off the road. "If it weren't for you, she'd not be with us."

"Who? Vorca?"

"No, Alice." She glanced at me. "I guess the same could be said for Vorca, though."

Vorca, laboring ahead of us, heard her name, and rattled off a string of words, which I imagined related to the burros once carrying the load that she was now made to tow. Her rant prompted Caleb to pipe up from a dead sleep on her back, as if he were instructing us to pedal faster and talk less. From Vorca's back, Caleb faced us at the back of the group.

"Don't be jealous," I said.

"Oh, I'm not jealous. I'm just admiring your family. Alice is like your aunt, and Vorca's like your awkward cousin. Annette is your mom, sort of. Caleb is the son you named, but never sired. Everyone is here because of you."

"Isn't that okay? I care about them all as if they were my flesh and blood."

"I'm just trying to figure out my place." She frowned. "It's like everyone belongs but me."

"I thought we had that conversation last night."

"Well, we did. I know. It's just that I was once the glue that held my own family together for years. Now I see someone else is the glue in a much broader sense."

"Everyone here has their own value. I don't have more honor. The Bible tells us to honor those who seem to have less honor, just to show we all have the same honor in the Body of Christ. This is why I've risked my life at different times for each of you. You're all very valuable, and without every one of you, something important would be lacking in my life. I may be chosen to be the glue, but everyone here makes up the ingredients."

"How could someone so powerful not know his own influence?" She laughed quietly, and steered closer to me to talk more privately. "If we were alone right now, I think I'd tackle you just to kiss you again."

"If I'm so powerful," I said, "what makes you think I'd allow myself to be tackled?"

"Because I have my own powers as well!"

With that, she crowded my bike, laughing, as she tried to run me off the edge of the road. The commotion, mixed with the noise of my yelling, woke Caleb again, who scolded us afresh with his gibberish, shaking his little fists. Annette ignored us, as did Vorca, by not even looking back.

Chapter Twenty-eight

Six nights later, I stood outside of camp and gazed north. A million stars winked at me, and I worshipped the Creator who showed Himself through what He had made. Behind me, the fire of our camp flickered between the two dome tents where the women and Caleb slept.

Alice appeared at my side, my ears not picking up her soft steps since I'd been tuned to the sounds of wild animals in the night.

"We reach Meeker tomorrow," she said, holding her staff in her hand. Two nights earlier, she'd stopped sleeping inside the tent with Vorca and Caleb. Like me, she'd folded herself inside a tarp and slept under the stars. "You seem quiet today. Even Lyla noticed."

I glanced back at the tent where Annette and Lyla had ceased talking. Vorca and Caleb—their incoherent speech seemingly understood only by each other—were silent as well.

"You're back to one-hundred percent?" I asked.

"Don't let my face fool you." She scoffed. "They broke some bones, but not my spirit. I'm on top."

"The past two weeks have been some of the best weeks of my life." I smiled at the sky. "God has been good to us, giving us just the trials we've needed to show us His greatest good. It's easier to see His hand long after a stormy season. But I'm realizing how much my faith is lacking as I think about facing another storm."

Far away, where the forest clothed the mountain slopes, a mountain lion screamed a lonely cry.

"Is there something wrong that I should know about?" she asked.

"We haven't met anyone on the road for two days." I shifted the bullpup cradled in my arm. "We can safely assume something is amiss not far to the north. Travelers have been diverted somehow. You know the signs."

"The Pacific States knew we were going to Meeker," she said. "Do you think they went around us and arrived early to ambush you?"

"I'm not sure."

"Did you say anything to the others? Up to a couple days ago, the people we met coming toward us claimed everything in the north was in order."

"I'll tell them in the morning—as I explain your absence." From the corner of my eye, I noticed that she squared her shoulders with the pride of being needed once again. "Take the .22 pistol. You'll have nine shots. It'll be easier for you to shoot than the rifle with its bolt action."

"I'll get my bike."

"Leave the radio. You'll be out of range, anyway."

"What do you expect me to find?"

"I'm not sure, but God knows." I set my hand on her shoulder and said a brief prayer. "Whatever happens tomorrow, I'm glad you're a believer, Alice. But don't let the idea of heaven allow you to risk your life needlessly."

"No, recklessness is your department, as your mom always says."

"I don't mind being reckless, as long as my family is safe, and that includes you."

"I feel the same way," she said.

"See you soon."

We embraced, the touch of her left stump on my side a reminder of our history together.

She left five minutes later, pedaling up the road to the unknown. In my mind, I saw her travel up Highway 13, surrounded by grassland once famous for sheep, and streams once known for their trout. But the world was a much more dangerous place now.

"This isn't the arrival in Meeker I had in mind," Annette said the next morning as she checked her bullpup. Lyla did the same with her bolt action .308 rifle. "There's no indication we're riding into a gunfight, Levi."

"Of course." I pushed my bike with its heavy trailer to a rolling start, then hopped on. "We're just taking precautions."

But in my mind, I calculated Alice's progress up the highway to the quiet rodeo town of Meeker. She was eight hours ahead of us. Without a trailer, she could've flown northward at fifteen or twenty miles per hour. Since we were less than forty miles from Meeker, she could've been there by midnight. The fact that she hadn't returned to announce that all was well meant that all wasn't well.

Annette seemed to sense my concern as she caught up to me and passed me a comm. I tucked the earpiece into my ear and clipped the unit to my belt.

"You already know, don't you?" Annette said.

"Know what?" Lyla asked as we rode three abreast up the highway, with Vorca close behind.

"Levi has a sense for danger before anyone else does." Annette switched gears. "We don't want Vorca and the baby to get into a mess with us. Maybe we should ride ahead."

"Yeah, let's go." I gestured to Vorca. "Go slow, Vorca. We're going ahead."

She didn't respond, only continued to labor on her pedals, with Caleb bundled and sleeping on her back, his cheeks rosy from the morning chill. I hoped that Vorca held onto the memory of me rescuing her, so she would be comforted in the face of any new trial. No matter what happened to her, I would rescue her. She was part of our family, too.

It felt good to test the wheels of the bike and trailer as I pulled up short hills and coasted down rolling slopes.

Annette and Lyla had saddlebags over their wheels, but nothing compared to the weight I carried.

An hour later, we saw a figure miles ahead. We halted on the pavement and each of us applied different scopes to our eyes. I used my binoculars and recognized who it was first.

"It's Alice, thank God!" I sighed with relief, stowed my field glasses, and looked south. Vorca was so far behind, she wasn't even in sight. "Let's wait here."

Ten minutes later, Alice raced up to us and hopped off her bike—a true feat to do without wrecking, having only one hand. She tossed me her empty canteen and I handed her my full one. We had several gallons in the bottom of each trailer.

"It's bad." Alice caught her breath and wiped her mouth. She left her bike on the ground, her heavy staff protruding out of the scabbard. "Some sort of troops have taken over Meeker."

"Troops?" Annette frowned at me. "I thought Galt Brogdon was southeast of us."

"No, it's not the Pacific States military." Alice touched her scarred face for emphasis. "Believe me, I would know. But that's not all. It looked like what civilians are left of the town have escaped to the China Wall cliffs north of town. The townspeople are under siege by this military."

"A siege is a good sign," I said. "At least they aren't killing everyone outright. They want to starve them to submission, maybe."

"But where are the troops from?" Lyla asked.

"I didn't get close enough to find out or ask." Alice turned me around and took the map from my day pack. Flattening it on the highway pavement, we crouched around it. "I left my bike here, then scouted around the edges of town. There were lightly armed patrols on foot around what buildings weren't burned. The main force looked like twenty vehicles, all armored, except for one fuel tanker."

"It could be some rogue army we've never heard of," I said. "Years ago, there was the Liberation Organization run by a Commander Morris who slaughtered whole towns across the Plains Zone. These forces come and go. Others could be trying to rise up, too, to take control of resources that Meeker has."

"I remember the Liberation Organization from fifteen years ago," Lyla said. "Twenty armed vehicles and a fuel truck probably means these guys aren't local."

"Was there any indication, Alice, where they came from?" I asked. "Meeker's not exactly a town noted for lots of resources. There's no strategic purpose to cross a state or two and arrive at Meeker to bother the citizens."

"I don't know." Alice pointed at lines on the map. "There are roads east and west, and one that heads south, where we are. On their vehicles, they have a green and white emblem, and over what I think is an old courthouse in Meeker, there's a green and white flag, but I saw all that in the dark, so I can't be sure what else there may have been to identify them."

"Seed on green." I gulped. "That's what they call it. I've heard it on the radio before. It's their national motto, to plant a seed on green pastures. It's the Appalachian Federation. This isn't a coincidence, not in Meeker."

I stood and walked to the side of the highway, staring east, wishing I could see eighteen hundred miles away. What was happening on the East Coast that had brought the Federation all the way across the Plains Zone?

"Levi, what do you mean?" Annette called. "This has nothing to do with us. You said that the Federation has been pushing west, scouting, just like the Pacific States is pushing east, looking for a way to expand."

"No, this is something more. This is somehow about us. Or Jenna. She knew Dad had set up a safe zone for Christians in Meeker. That was twenty years ago. The Federation couldn't possibly know we were coming here also, to find Rex and Uncle Rudy."

"Why would the Appalachian Federation care about Rudy?" Lyla laid a hand on my forearm. "Levi, what are they doing here?"

"I don't know for sure, but it involves us, because it involves Jenna, somehow. The Federation has come all this way for something, and it's not a power grab like the Pacific States, or they would've stayed on Interstate 70 to secure the major cities and freeways. Meeker is of no consequence strategically."

"None of this makes any sense." Annette folded up the map and tucked it into my pack. "We just cut ties with one crazy dictator and army, and now we're dealing with another? I came to Colorado to be safe. What would a blind girl in New York have to do with the Federation and the Caspertein family out here?"

"Well, if they knew us, they should be worried." I smiled mischievously. "But I wasn't aware they knew about us. The Dowlers and Casperteins were really something twenty years ago. But I doubt anyone remembers all that COIL once represented."

"There are at least one hundred people inside the barricade against the cliffs," Alice said. "It seems like a lot of people for such a small town. Maybe they're refugees?"

"Could it be that Jenna is with them?" Annette asked. "If she knew we were coming to Meeker, or that there are Casperteins in Meeker, the Federation may have chased her and other Christians here!"

"Wait," Lyla crossed her arms. "This is all about Jenna, Levi? *Your* Jenna? Blind girl, Jenna? That's what you're saying?"

"It could be. And if the Federation wants to tangle with the Dowlers and Casperteins, so be it. We're not about to stand by as Christians are persecuted. That's one thing the Dowlers and Casperteins have a long history of— sacrificing to redeem the helpless."

"Well, we have COIL weapons." Annette shrugged. "How do we do this? There's only four of us."

"And about one hundred troops," Alice said. "They have some heavy artillery, too."

"I doubt they've crossed our phosphorus rounds." I frowned as my mind worked. "Let's pull into the trees and set up camp. Vorca should be here soon. We're an hour from Meeker. Let's get some rest. We'll ride out at sundown."

✝

Under a crescent moon, Lyla and I crept across the grassy plain. West of Meeker, the White River wove through dry lands of mesas and canyons. Sagebrush brushed against our knees as we approached the China Wall, the three-hundred-foot-tall cliffs that stood over the town.

A vehicle drove from the town to where the siege was taking place. I grabbed Lyla's arm and together, we dove to the ground until the vehicle moved on. Chances were, the driver couldn't see us since he used his headlights and we were in the dark plain off to his left. But we needed to find cover before they spotted us somehow, or before we were forced to face-off with these soldiers.

On the other side of Meeker, Annette and Alice were moving in the aspens high above the town. If they found the right cover to shoot from, Annette would be shooting nearly straight down at the invaders in their siege around the cliffs. Though Alice would've preferred to stalk the enemy more closely, I insisted she accompany Annette. None of us could chance being alone against such an overwhelming and unknown enemy. Nevertheless, such was our experience with countless aggressors that no one in my party had hesitated in planning an attack on this force, for the sake of the townspeople, which possibly included Uncle Rudy and his household.

"Look." Lyla indicated to my right. "Are those trees? It's about the right distance for us."

From her cue, we walked east to find young juniper trees rising from a shallow gully, rimmed with skull-sized rocks. Through my scope, I checked my line of fire on the siege. I was facing the cliffs almost directly, the siege party forming an oval around the civilians. The soldiers' backs were to us.

"This is a good position," I said. "We're about a quarter-mile out, but I'm concerned about our backsides. There are still troops in town that might be able to get behind and flank us."

"I can move one hundred yards toward the cliffs to cover you."

"No, I don't want to split up." Turning my scope on the town, I tried to estimate the enemy's strength. "Stay here with me for now. If we're about to be overrun, we can retreat together." I touched the comm in my ear. "Mom, we're in place, about twelve o'clock from the cliffs. Over."

Lyla and I shed our small packs and stacked rocks up to make a safer foxhole. I lay on my belly aiming toward the cliffs as Lyla fashioned a gun stand to cover us from the town on our right flank.

"Levi," Annette called on the comm, "I'm in a bad position up here above the siege. It's real steep and the angle is tight. Over."

"Do you have a shot at the attackers? Over."

"Only some of them. They're too close to the cliff base below me. I can probably cover you better than I can sharp-shoot at them. I'll watch for your muzzle flash to ID your position. Over."

"Okay, let's get ready."

Behind me, Lyla had stopped moving. We were ready. It was comforting to know that Annette was in an untouchable position where only eagles flew on the high cliff. She could cover me and Lyla as we concentrated on the enemy, to rescue as many people as we could. But then an alternative attack plan came to my mind.

"Mom, I've changed my mind," I suddenly said. "There must be sixty or seventy soldiers surrounding those civilians. I can whittle their numbers down with the silenced .22 long before we have to make any noise with our battle rifles. Over.

A moment passed. Every minute that passed, we risked discovery.

"Alice says that's what she could do also silently from the west. As soon as you're both discovered, retreat to your current positions. Over."

"Okay, let's do it."

I slung the bullpup onto my back and shouldered the .22 rifle that Forest had used over countless miles. He'd been a better shot, but I didn't have to hit a deer in the neck on this night. A shot anywhere on a man's body would do.

"We can't protect each other if you're not with me," Lyla said. "That was your plan."

"If you don't make a peep, they'll never know you're here. I'll come back as soon as I do some damage."

I squeezed her hand to reassure her, then walked across the empty terrain, cutting crossways toward the enemy, their backs to me. The .22 had a sixth of the range that the bullpup did, but silence was the key now. And if I didn't commence firing soon, Alice would start the party without me on the far side.

Within range, I knelt and peered through the narrow scope of the smaller rifle. If Uncle Rudy and Rex had still been living in Meeker, there was a chance they were among those under siege against the China Wall. With Jenna waiting for me in the east, the pressure on me was immense to effectively attack and win. There would be no moving on without total success here tonight.

The key to a stealth attack had been taught to me by my father when hunting a herd of deer for San Diego residents. The key was to shoot the deer that the other deer couldn't see. The gunshot alone wouldn't spook them necessarily. As long as the other animals didn't see the first animal fall, a hunter could continue to fire at additional targets.

I remembered this lesson now, and found a man at the back of an SUV. He was isolated. The gel-tranq slammed into him between the shoulder blades. It wasn't as forceful as the bullpup's .308 round, but the man was visibly impacted, turning to find the culprit, before he fell unconscious.

But he hadn't been totally isolated after all. Someone had heard him fall. That person called out to the unresponsive man, then went over to him. When he found his fallen friend, I shot him before he could sound an alert. He collapsed onto the other.

Moving down the line of vehicles widely spaced in an oval, I found other men in pairs. For more precise shots, I moved within fifty feet. I shot one in the backside where two men sat on a log. When he jumped to his feet, rubbing his wound, I worked the bolt action and quickly chambered another round, then shot his partner before either man could discern what was happening.

I changed magazines and started on a fresh line of ten men when a gunshot came from the other side of the siege line. Hesitating, I looked back toward the juniper trees, which were barely visible as dark shapes far out on the plain. Lyla could probably see me a little better. She would be able to see that I wasn't running for cover quite yet, as planned.

Instead, I walked briskly up to the siege line where men were running for cover and asking one another in confusion what had happened. Most were shouldering rifles and aiming at the civilians against the rock, which I now could see more directly since the vehicle headlights were pinning them to the cliff rock. But the gunshot had clearly come from the siege line, not from the civilians.

Next to two tranquilized men, I took their rifles and threw them under the nearest vehicle, a dark colored SUV.

With a couple strong jerks, I tore the sleeve off one of the men, and opened the fuel cap of the SUV. I stuffed the sleeve into the fuel tank and used a lighter to light it on fire.

Over the hood of the time bomb, I fired down the siege line at men nearly facing me now. The stage of stealth was over. Men saw me and ducked for cover. Others froze in confusion as other shots were fired from Alice's side of the siege. Whatever trouble Alice had found herself in, Annette hadn't found a reason to expose her elevated position by firing yet.

My chamber clicked on empty. I'd gambled on the fiery sleeve long enough. I turned and ran into the plain, swerving to the north for fifty yards in case anyone saw me fleeing.

The SUV exploded and gave the terrain around me a brief glow before the flames settled. I slid into our juniper cover, scraping my hip, and set the .22 rifle aside. I acknowledged Lyla with a nod, then brought the familiar bullpup up to my cheek, and opened fire on anyone standing around the flames or near the vehicle headlights. Four hundred yards out, they couldn't see me, but they could sure hear me. A few well-trained men might've noticed my muzzle flash even though I used a flash suppressor, but with the SUV fire and several men toting flashlights to check on the wounded, their night eyes were certainly ruined.

Lyla fired her bolt-action .308 more carefully, precision firing, showing that she was indeed able to shoot.

"Mom, are you there?" I asked as I reloaded.

"I'm here."

"Did Alice make it out okay?"

"I don't know. She was real close to them so she could use the handgun, then she was gone."

With a fresh magazine, I put phosphorus rounds into one wheel of every vehicle in view. The rapid-acting acid wouldn't eat only the rubber tire, but the wheel assembly and part of the axle, too, I hoped. Their vehicles would be useless in minutes. Escape would be impossible by truck.

When men began to organize a firing line for a counterattack, Annette opened up above and behind them. A dozen rounds were fired at me and Lyla, but nothing struck too closely.

"Here they come, Levi!" Lyla warned from my elbow.

I checked the town. Three vehicles roared from downtown toward the siege line.

"I don't think those are reinforcements," I said. "Hold your fire, Annette. Hold your fire."

"What's happening?" Lyla asked.

"They radioed for a rescue. Look."

The three vehicles fish-tailed to a stop as thirty conscious men from the siege line piled into the vehicles. The doors were barely closed before they sped away again. With gel-tranqs, I broke a few windows as they rushed back to town. In the darkness, not even their superior force was a match for our surprise attack.

"We won!" Lyla cheered. "We did, didn't we?"

"The battle, maybe, but not the war, yet." I rose to my feet. "You only catch them once by surprise. Come on. Let's see to the spoils. Mom, watch the town. We're checking on the townspeople. Any sign of Alice? Over."

"Still no sign. Those soldiers drove into town and set up a perimeter. I can see they're professionals, even if they were disoriented for a few minutes out here. The town is locked down."

"Levi, what if you find Jenna among those people?" Lyla asked as we marched swiftly toward the China Wall. "What about us?"

"What about us? Jenna's one of my oldest and dearest family friends, like family. Nothing has changed or will change between you and me. I thought that was already settled."

"Hey, a girl's got to be reassured every once in a while, that's all." She moved her rifle to her shoulder and held my hand as we walked. "At least until I've got a ring on my finger."

We passed through the sizzling, smoking siege line and approached the townspeople. As we neared their dark, low wall of belongings, I sensed movement against the rock.

"Who's there?" a booming voice challenged.

Lyla and I stopped twenty yards from them.

"We're just travelers. We chased the Appalachian Federation troops back to town for now, but I don't think we've seen the last of them. There's about thirty or forty laying out here on the siege line still alive."

"Still alive?" The man, much taller and wider than me, stepped over what looked like a dead horse—part of their hasty cover during the siege. "How's that?"

"We shot them with gelatin tranquilizers. They'll wake up in about forty-five more minutes."

"Forty-five more minutes?" The man stepped even closer. I wasn't used to looking up at men, but this character was a giant—one I'd seen many years ago when I'd first found my father. His beard added to his bear-like presence. "That'll be enough time to round up their guns and rope them together."

"I think that's a good plan."

The man placed his hands on his hips and studied me. At least, I felt his eyes in the semi-darkness.

"Seems to me the only fool crazy enough to tranquilize a Federation army unit is my little brother, but you're not Titus Caspertein, though you might have his voice and build."

"Uncle Rudy?" I grinned.

"Is that you, boy? Levi?"

"Yep. We weren't sure we'd find anybody here, but we came, anyway." We shook hands, but then he enveloped me in a hug that included Lyla since she'd been standing close to me. "Mom is with me. And Mia joined up with someone else a week ago."

"And Titus?" He held me at arm's length. "Where's that wily serval, anyway?"

"The Meridia Virus got him about three months ago."

"Oh." Rudy took a moment to process the news. "I'm sorry to hear that. My own wife passed years ago, too."

"But the man who used the virus to murder Dad has received Christ. It's quite a story."

"That's certainly a twist. What about Wynter?"

"She died. Years ago in the Sierras, but there was no shame in her passing. Wes Trimble, too, but that's a story for another time."

"Yes, it seems we have some things to talk about." He turned his giant head. "Rex! Get some men and hobble these unconscious soldiers! Watch out for pretenders among them."

A younger version of Rudy bounded over the barrier and jogged past me. Five other men, now emboldened by their bearded leader, joining him.

"Mom?" I called. "What's the status of the men in town? Over."

"No movement outside their perimeter. I think it'll be quiet for the night. The loss of their vehicles will make them think twice about trying anything else for a while. Over."

Uncle Rudy reached for the bullpup, and I gave it to him.

"An NL-X2? After all these years, Titus finally dusted them off, huh? Last I heard, he was stockpiling them for COIL missions, or possibly for the rebuilding of America, if it ever happened."

"I didn't know anyone else knew about that."

"Know about these? Why, up on the mountain, we've got our own stockpile your father shipped to us before Pan-Day. We haven't had any trouble for years, so there was no reason to make them known. Until now. The country is changing again. A new struggle has begun."

Shoulder to shoulder, we watched the men bind the soldiers.

"Levi, it looks safe for now," Annette said. "I'm coming down. Over."

"Roger that. Uncle Rudy and Rex are here. We made it, Mom. We made it!"

Chapter Twenty-nine

"They started arriving about a month ago, I guess." Uncle Rudy walked me through the siege camp that no one was too quick to leave, for fear the Appalachian Federation troops would counterattack. Many were wounded or sick. Annette and Lyla moved amongst them, comforting where they could. "They'd been sent, they said, by Radiant Shade."

"Radiant Shade." I frowned. "What's Radiant Shade, a code word?"

"They said it's a woman who made a voice recording. The woman on the recording told them to go west to Meeker, Colorado, on Interstate 70." We stood together, our backs against the China Wall. "The thing is, they're all Christians, Levi. All were about to be arrested by the Appalachian Federation, but Radiant Shade warned them to leave. So they left. The strangest thing, though, I haven't even told you."

"What's that?"

"A lot of them arrived in town asking for Caspertein. Of course, we took them in, figuring Titus or Wynter were on their way here. We didn't know Federation troops would be hot on these people's heels, but when soldiers arrived in town, and demanded that we hand over the refugees, we stood our ground. That's when there was a scuffle in town, and I led everyone out here. We were trying to escape into the mountains. Rex knows the mountains real well, but they caught up to us here, so we found ourselves cornered, so to speak, against the cliff. Then you showed up a couple days later. So, now I have more questions than answers."

"Like what?"

"If Titus has been dead, and Wynter passed away, and you and Annette didn't invite or send all these people here, who knows us well enough to trust us with all these Christians on the run from a government that's trying to kill them?"

"Radiant Shade." I scratched my beard. "Shade. It must be a code name. There's really only one other person who knew there were Casperteins in Meeker."

"Who?"

"Jenna Dowler."

"Corban's little blind girl?"

"Well, she's not little anymore, Uncle Rudy. And she's not just a girl if she's organizing an exodus of Christians out of Federation territory."

The sun peeked over the mountains to the east. The bound soldiers had regained consciousness. They now sat cross-legged, hands bound behind them, facing the cliff. Rex and two other men guarded them with Annette and Lyla's rifles, and my .22. I cradled my bullpup in my arms.

"You broke the siege line, Levi, but we're a long way from standing on our own two feet here. About twenty Meeker people were killed in town before we ran here. There's food stores in town that the soldiers have probably found and are living off of, so we need to slaughter a few sheep up on the hillside. There's a lot of mouths to feed here."

"Those other NL-X2 rifles—where are they?"

"Rex has a hunting cabin up on Flat Tops Byway. He buried them there. It's about a day out."

"We have ten able men here, it looks like." I surveyed the Christian refugees, a weary lot who had traveled far. "You think they'd stand with us to push the Federation troops out of town?"

"I think so, now that they know they'd be shooting non-lethal weapons. Those troops were only here to take custody of the Christians who escaped their Federation territory. If Jenna Dowler really is Radiant Shade, the Federation is probably trying to identify her, maybe by torturing these people until they talk and give up her identity.”

“True. It makes me want to get to Jenna all the sooner. The Federation will break someone eventually. Then, Jenna is finished.”

“I’ll send Rex up for a few more rifles. While we wait, we can move these people into the trees to the east, there. It’s got better cover if the Federation comes after them again.”

“We need a ten-person watch day and night,” I said. “Men and women, whoever can keep a sharp eye, until Rex gets back.”

“You sound like Titus.” He shook his head. “I sure wanted to see that kid again. If he were here, he’d probably march right up there into town and tell those boys what’s what.”

“Yeah, he would.” I chuckled. “And maybe that’s exactly what we ought to do.”

“You have an idea? Wouldn’t doubt it. Any son of Titus would have his wits, too. Go ahead. Shoot me your plan.”

Two mornings later, I was on guard duty outside camp when Lyla approached me from behind. My eyes remained on the White River Valley and Meeker below. The troops hadn’t attacked or offered to deal with us. By now, I guessed they thought all their men they’d left behind were dead. Instead, we’d been feeding them and caring for thirty-five of their number. It was a responsibility we couldn’t sustain much longer.

“Haven’t seen much of you the last day and a half.” Lyla passed me a thermos of hot tea. One of the events that had kept me from her was my return to Vorca to bring her and Caleb into our provisional camp. "Today's the day, huh?"

"Hope so. How's everyone?"

"We don't have what we need up here. We might lose one of the refugees from a gunshot wound tonight if we don't get him the right treatment. The worry isn't helping morale, either."

"How're you doing?" I took her hand and dared a look away from the town to study her face. How someone could remain so calm and beautiful through such strife and terror was a gift that made my own heart soar. This brave woman would be my wife one day! "Tell me."

"I'm worried about you today, but I stay busy feeding the prisoners. No one else is too excited to do that."

"You don't mind?"

"Not at all. I pray as I help each one. Our God changes hearts, right?"

"He absolutely does."

"Maybe not now, but someday, these guys will remember the kindness we showed them when they were trying to kill us."

"You're an amazing woman, Lyla Grady."

"How amazing?"

"So amazing that I have to ask you a question."

"What question?" She took the thermos from me and took a sip. "You want me to stop worrying? Well, I won't, not with you planning to risk your life today. Why can't someone else put their life on the line? Who walks alone into a town full of gunmen, anyway?"

"Moses and Aaron walked in alone. They faced off with Pharaoh. Joshua and Caleb entered the Promised Land with enemies all around them. I won't be asking the Federation to let our people go, or asking if we can have this land of milk and honey. Instead, I'll be making the Federation an offer. I'll offer them safe departure out of town, because otherwise, they're in a heap of trouble if they face us in a battle. Our phosphorus rounds will demolish all their vehicles, and each of our rifles is worth two of theirs."

"You have more confidence than I do. So, what's your question?"

"I don't have much to offer you but a nail-biting life, Lyla Grady, but if you ask Mom, she didn't mind Dad giving that to her. If you'd settle for me, will you be my wife?"

I opened my palm, showing her a silver ring with a single diamond."

"Settle for you? Are you kidding? What girl wouldn't snatch up a Caspertein when she has a chance?" Her hand trembled as I placed the ring on it. "Where'd you get such a ring? It's beautiful!"

"It was Alice's. How she recovered it is quite a story, especially since I cut off her arm that had the ring on it."

"I love it, Levi. And I love you. I know God brought us together. I never want to leave your side. But you'd better not make me a widow before we even get married!"

Someone whistled behind us and I remembered my job. But there was no movement from town.

"Riders!" someone shouted. "It's Rex!"

Rex arrived through the woods with a dozen bullpups and enough ammunition to arm a division. The horses belonged to the townspeople and had been grazing on pasture land to the east. Two slaughtered sheep were draped over one of the horses. They would feed us for another day, but we needed to get out of this standoff situation once and for all.

All experienced hunters were assigned a COIL weapon. Uncle Rudy nodded once at me. We were ready. It was time to test my plan against the Federation soldiers.

"You know, Levi," Rex said, "if God would've given me more wits, I'd be going into town today instead of you. Dad says you're like Uncle Titus—mouth and marbles."

"Actually, I think it's lack of wits that made me volunteer for this. No one in their right mind would do it!"

"I'm a pretty fair shot." He set a paw-sized hand on my shoulder. It was hard to believe my younger cousin could be so much bigger than me. "Stay out of my line of fire and I'll watch your back."

After having a bite to eat, Rudy, Rex, and I coached the riflemen on the finer—and more dangerous—points of firing non-lethal weaponry. Specifically, they needed to know about the one-second delay between a target being shot, and a target collapsing unconsciously.

"Two heartbeats." Rudy held up two fingers. It'd been twenty years since Dad had sent the rifles to him, but his memory seemed to be clear. "Two heartbeats is the difference between getting my nephew shot or not. You have to anticipate your target, more than you anticipate a deer, because a deer won't take its last conscious breath to shoot my nephew."

Annette adjusted my vest needlessly, and patted my magazine pockets to ensure they were full.

"Why is it always you?" she asked.

"If you ask Rex," I winked at my cousin who was within earshot, "it's because I'm expendable."

Rex slapped his knee, but stopped his guffaw short when he noticed Lyla's glare.

"This isn't a laughing matter," my fiancee said. "Whoever gets him killed has to deal with me."

She stomped away, and Annette wasn't far behind.

Uncle Rudy stood taller than all of us, surveying the people scattered amongst the trees. Cook fires burned every few yards. Silently, we followed his eyes, understanding why we needed to remember this moment. We weren't putting our lives on the line for pride or honor or vengeance. Today, we risked everything for the Christian refugees who'd come to us. These people had crossed half the continent, trusting a woman's voice on a digital recording, a woman called Radiant Shade. If we died, they would die. We couldn't fail. This was for the people of God. This was for Jenna Dowler. This was for Radiant Shade. This was for Jesus Christ.

COIL wasn't a distant memory. It had reemerged, doing the same work COIL operatives had always done inside countless dangerous countries.

My walk into town alone seemed far, especially in the daylight, knowing I was being watched. My cover-shooters, including Rudy and Rex, didn't skulk from shrub to tree. Instead, they spread out in plain view, staying well out of range of the common soldier's rifle.

At the north end of town, I walked up the center of the street. Dwellings along the outskirts of the town had been dismantled or burned years earlier, offering my cover-shooters a better view of me.

On the courthouse lawn, the sculpture of a soldier stood as a memorial of a different war from a different time. Still, no one appeared on the street. No gunshots. No yells. Even the three vehicles we knew were still operational were hidden from sight. I walked back up the street, then turned around again.

The old Hotel Meeker stood opposite the courthouse. A window curtain moved on the second story. Of course, no other building could hold all of the approximate sixty-five remaining Appalachian Federation soldiers. I tried not to imagine the sixty-five gun barrels that were probably aimed at me.

Suddenly, the front door of the hotel opened. I didn't aim the bullpup, only cradled it in my right arm, aimed at the ground in front of me. A man stepped from the shade of the porch into the sunlight of the street. He was a frowning, bearded black man in a dark green, wrinkled uniform. Approaching me, he held his head up, and stopped just a few paces away from me. Several of his men who followed him from the hotel to the sidewalk, stayed a distance away where they couldn't hear if we spoke quietly. Nor could they shoot me too easily since the officer stood so close in front of me.

His hand twitched over a sidearm, the holster still buckled. The name on his uniform read, "Colonel Tentmaker."

"We wish to leave Meeker." His frown didn't fade, as if he disapproved of his own words. And they were words I hadn't expected to hear from the fearsome nation in the east.

"That makes two of us."

"You killed almost half my men, and our vehicles are useless. We have only three left. It's not enough for you to say we can move out of town safely. You need to promise us more than that. We know you probably have snipers in the woods."

"I'll tell them not to fire. You can march out."

"It's two thousand miles back to New York."

"Who said you have to go back to New York?"

His brow furrowed more, then he turned and looked at his men. About twenty were in sight on the sidewalk. Their uniforms appeared just as wrinkled and their faces just as weary.

"The thought had crossed my mind." He faced me. "But I'm no deserter, and my men have families."

"You have no family?"

"No. Just the Chancellor. He raised me."

"Chancellor?"

"Kendrick Obrador."

"I see. You're his pet."

"Careful."

"He sent you on a two-thousand-mile errand, like a hound dog, to track and kill a bunch of men, women, and children." I sighed and shook my head, my eyes steady, proving to him I wasn't intimidated by his years of experience or my seeming isolation. "How's it working out for you?"

"A month of hell." Admitting his misery seemed to burden this man. "The last two nights—you really know how to break a man, don't you?"

"We do our best," I said, though I didn't understand what he was referring to. We'd barely been surviving ourselves for two days and nights in the woods. "Maybe it's time for retirement, Colonel. Unless you feel you must return to your chancellor."

"He'd come for me if I didn't. He's obsessed with the mystery. I can't return without an answer."

"What's the mystery?"

"We're trying to find someone."

"Let me guess: Radiant Shade?"

"So, you know?"

"I know."

"Some of the citizens from the Federation must know who she is, recognize her voice from the recording, something!"

"They're not Federation citizens any longer. They're Meeker citizens. If you hadn't heard, the Caspertein family is in town. COIL has been reinstated."

"Caspertein?" He studied me closer. "It's a name that wasn't on the recording, but some prisoners back in New Jersey had whispered the name before they died. It's a family name?"

"That, yes, and a movement as well."

"I see. And you, you're a Caspertein?"

"That's right. I'm Levi Caspertein. We're thick up in these parts now. You mess with one of us, and you bring on the whole family."

"You did seem coordinated the other night. I've never heard or seen of weaponry quite like what you people used." He exhaled loudly. "If I went west, what would I find?"

"The Pacific States. They have their own troops, territory, laws, ambitions."

"We've heard they're along the coast, but moving east."

"Everyone's grabbing up land lately." I sensed God's urging, so I went for it. "There may be a way to take you out so your chancellor won't come after you, if you were interested in actual retirement out here."

"Are you conspiring with the enemy? From what I've seen so far, the Casperteins, as you call yourselves, aren't very merciful."

"We're not interested in a war, Colonel." I smiled sadly. "If you want out, I can give you a safe exit, and get all your men out of town without bloodshed."

"An out? There's no out for me." He turned again and glanced at his men. "As soon as they get back to the Federation, they'll report that I abandoned my post. The chancellor will come after me. It would be personal for him. He has an assassin he uses precisely for that kind of personal vendetta."

"Well, we can help your troops here believe you died."

"Me? Die? They'd never believe it. I've lived through a hundred battles."

"They'll believe it. They look like they're tired enough to believe just about anything. Tell me what's been going on through the last two nights that has you so rattled."

"What, the banging? The screaming? We're ready to go insane. One more night of sleep deprivation, and we'll all lose it." He shook his head. "Three men deserted overnight. More will leave tonight, I'm sure. They hate me already for this wretched assignment into the Plains Zone. It's taken a toll."

"And if they're cut loose to leave, enough have families that they'll really return? I don't want bands of soldiers roaming the mountains. We have enough of that already."

"No. They'll return. They'll march back to the east, if they're allowed to leave."

"Okay, follow my lead." I stepped around him, shoving him roughly toward his men, and raised my voice. "Every night you stay in Meeker, Colorado, will be another night of terror! The last two nights have been moderate compared to what the ghosts of Meeker have planned for you tonight. You won't make it out of Meeker alive. The three who left during the night? As good as dead."

I walked down the street a few paces, then turned on them suddenly.

"You followed some Christian refugees into this town. How satisfied you must be. How mighty you are! Radiant Shade sent you to your deaths. You see, we aren't refugees. We are riflemen, hunters, and veterans from one thousand conflicts. This is the West. You're in our territory now. You came, but you'll never leave alive. Blood must be shed to atone for your evil intentions, your wicked actions. You can't escape. We know every canyon within two hundred miles—every river, every mountain, every cave. Do you want to leave Meeker? You say you do. You want to return to your families. But we won't allow it, not after what you've done here. Unless one of you dies."

"Dies?" a soldier on the sidewalk asked. He had a crewcut, now too long in places to stand up on its own. "What're you talking about?"

"Blood must be shed for the forgiveness of your sins. Do you want to leave? Our wrath must be appeased."

"Yeah, we want to leave!"

"Then one of you must die. Public execution. Here. Now. In the street."

"You're crazy!" Crewcut yelled, and pointed at Colonel Tentmaker. "None of us is dying for this lunatic!"

"You'll do as I say, Private!" Tentmaker screamed, his voice breaking. "Now, shut your mouth."

"The town is surrounded. In ten hours, it'll be night again. The banging and the screams will continue. You want to leave? Someone must die."

"That's what you're saying, for real?" Crewcut asked. "You kill one of us, and the rest of us can leave?"

"You can walk right out—or drive what's left of your trucks."

Crewcut conferred with his men. More poured out of the front door to cast their votes. I didn't know exactly what they'd been through, but I had an idea. They'd witnessed what they thought was the deaths of thirty-five of their friends, and something had been haunting the town since, not letting them sleep.

"We have a man!" Crewcut announced. "Colonel Tentmaker!"

"You sure?" I raised my rifle. "Everyone agrees? Because if you stay another night, we'll require another life to be forfeited."

"No, we'll leave now. We're done. He's yours."

Men appeared at the windows of their hotel rooms, some of the soldiers without their uniforms. My demands were too bizarre not to witness.

"Colonel?" I aimed my rifle at his chest. "The men have spoken. It's unanimous. Your life buys them their freedom. By your blood, all will be forgiven."

He blinked twice, fear consuming his eyes. This didn't seem to be what he'd trusted me for, but he had nowhere to go. His men hated him. The town wanted his blood, it seemed. He was defeated.

I fired twice, two rapid shots at his chest. In the daylight, the gel-tranqs performed wonderfully. The impact of two rapid rounds threw Tentmaker backwards. His feet flew up, his arms flailed. He landed on the grass of the courthouse, started to rise, then fell still. Except for our ringing ears from the gunshots, the town was quiet. Fortunately, my cover-shooters hadn't mistaken my display of force as a signal to commence firing.

"There are guns aimed at you right now!" I yelled at the remaining soldiers. "Get out of Meeker and never return. Carry with you what you've seen here today, and warn everyone in the Federation. Returning here would be a mistake. COIL has risen from the ashes!"

A couple men lingered to stare at the colonel, but the rest collected their gear and started walking. Their three remaining vehicles pulled out from behind the hotel, laden with gear and men. As they moved down the street, my cover-shooters began to appear on balconies, rooftops, and porches. I wanted our show of force to burn into the soldiers' memories. We were still outnumbered, but in the defeated minds of the Federation forces, they were indeed surrounded.

Uncle Rudy and Rex walked up to stand on either side of me.

"I heard only a little of that," Rex said. "You may be the biggest bluffer I've ever known."

"Takes after his dad—all that tall talk." Rudy signaled his men. "We should search the hotel for stragglers."

"You know, Uncle Rudy," I said, "Dad did have a lot of tall talk, but none of it was bluff. That's why people respected him, and his enemies feared him with just the right amount of fear."

"You're right, Levi." Rudy chuckled. "My little brother didn't have to bluff."

On the courthouse grass next to the war memorial, I sat down. Colonel Tentmaker would wake up in fifty more minutes, and I needed to be the one to help him adjust. That night, we'd release the thirty-five Federation captives. By the time they caught up with their comrades, they'd be too far away to want to return to even any score they might think they had to settle. Besides, the shame of condemning their own colonel to death would keep their mouths shut.

Behind me, a soft footfall fell on the grass, followed by a thump of metal.

"So, Alice," I said without turning around, "you've been terrorizing the visitors in town?"

"A little sleep deprivation goes a long ways." She sat next to me. "The first few nights I stayed in Eagle Mountain, those empty houses had shutters that used to bang open and closed. It's tough to sleep. I figured I'd try it here. I threw in the screams here for free. I'd hoped by the time they fought or parleyed, they'd be willing to concede."

"Effective."

"Who's this guy exactly?"

"He's had enough of Chancellor Obrador, the leader of the Federation. He needed to die off so his men could report him deceased."

"Effective."

"I thought so."

"You show Lyla the ring?" she asked.

"Yeah." I gazed up at the tree line where I imagined Lyla was watching me though my binoculars. "Yeah, I proposed this morning."

"You know she's gonna be more trouble than me, right?"

"Is that a bad thing?" I chuckled.

"No, I guess not." She rolled her staff back and forth on her palm. "When do we head east?"

"Wedding tomorrow. Leave the next morning. We can cover a lot of ground before the snow falls. It won't be easy."

"You're telling me. I have to travel with newlyweds? Ugh." She rolled her eyes. "You'd better send me to scout far ahead and often just so I can get out of camp from you two."

"I don't think we'll have trouble keeping you busy for the rest of the year. It's a long way to New York."

We sat there until Colonel Tentmaker stirred. The surviving residents of Meeker trickled back into town, bringing the refugees from the east with them.

"Thank you, Levi." Alice jabbed me in the leg with her staff.

"For what?"

"For giving me a family again. Because of you, I know where I'm going when I die. But until that day, I'm not alone."

"You're never alone. I'll always come back for you."

"I know. That's why I don't want to be around anyone else."

"Oh, my chest." Tentmaker struggled to sit up next to me. "What happened?"

"Do you know what it means to be born again?" I asked, and he shook his head. "Well, it all begins when you die to your old self. You become a new person in Jesus Christ."

I winked at Alice, and she winked back.

Chapter Thirty

The day of the wedding was also the first day the Christian refugees from the Appalachian Federation territory could enjoy their new freedom to worship Christ. Walking around town with Rex, we witnessed spontaneous groups of two or more gathering for a brief greeting, prayer, or even a song. Meeker had never abandoned its Bibles, since there were Casperteins in the area, so Bibles were plentiful.

"Do you think heaven'll be like this?" Rex asked as we observed two parties of Christians on either side of the street conversing over open Bibles. "I could get used to this. Normally, Meeker people are all about food and water and animals and bartering. You think all these new Christians will stay?"

"Until God scatters them again," I said. "That's the way He works, since wherever He scatters them, they'll carry His message of grace with them."

We stopped on Main Street and Sixth where the outdoor mural had been riddled with bullets earlier that week. Uncle Rudy was locked in a deep discussion with Colonel Dathan Tentmaker, who happened to have a skill for painting. Rudy was explaining Bible scenes for the new painter to paint, but Tentmaker kept interrupting, asking questions about the meaning of certain Bible events. When we moved on, Rudy was reenacting the scene of David and Goliath.

Rex led me east through the trees until we arrived at a meadow of wildflowers. Between two dark conifer trees, three women fussed with a flowery canopy under which Lyla and I would exchange our vows.

"You know, you might want to put that down for your wedding." Rex gestured to my rifle. "It's my duty as your best man to warn you that the bride will want it set aside for a few minutes."

We found a shaded area of the meadow and watched as guests from town began to arrive. With so many lives beginning, I hadn't figured on more than a dozen or so to attend. However, in minutes, as if summoned by a trumpet call, the meadow filled with everyone from town, residents and Christian newcomers alike.

"You think this is wise?" I asked Rex. "The town is unguarded with everyone out here."

"Well, we already know to send for you if another army takes over the town. We'll just sit back and take a nap as you scare them off again, you and your Amazon lady."

"It's comforting for me to know you're so willing to risk our lives for your safety." I punched my heavier relative on the shoulder.

Uncle Rudy walked Lyla down the path, and Rex stood on my left as my best man. Annette, as the matron of honor, cried quietly from the side, and Alice had been talked into wearing a yellow summer dress. But every time the one-armed scout looked down at her appearance, she seemed to scowl both at the dress and at the color. Though Mother had talked her into wearing the dress, Alice hadn't been convinced that she needed to be disarmed, so she still held her staff in her one hand and stood posted at my mother's side.

Lyla wore a white gown, a remnant from a time when both gowns and weddings were more prominent. Her hair had been laced with flowers from the meadow, and her gray eyes seemed to shimmer as they welled brightly with tears. We exchanged vows before God, through which I couldn't stop grinning like a fool, and then we kissed as husband and wife.

We led the procession back to town, backed by the townspeople, and harassed by children throwing clumps of wildflowers in place of rice. Someone had baked a small cake that tasted like pancakes, with green icing that tasted like lard. We both politely choked down a bite, then danced together—as my family laughed with the children at my clumsy attempt at grace.

Toasts of cider were made by anyone who attended, but it was Rex whose toast caught my ear.

". . . And though I'd never dreamed of being a chaperone on a couple's honeymoon," he said, his glass raised, "I will be accompanying them east. I wish you both God's best. Congratulations!"

As soon as I could break away from Lyla, I took Rex by the elbow.

"What do you mean, you're going with us?"

"I thought you'd be happy."

"What about ranching, and your dad, and the town?"

"Dad has more help than he knows what to do with, and besides, my dad and your mom aren't exactly thinking about anyone else at the moment. Look."

"What?" I asked in surprise. Sure enough, Uncle Rudy and Annette were laughing together on the sidewalk under a banner someone had hung that read, "Meeker's Range Call Celebration." We watched them both for a moment, maybe each of us nostalgic over a past that was truly past. Rudy and Annette? Perhaps they would find love, I guessed, but we wouldn't be there to watch it blossom.

A room in Hotel Meeker had been cleaned and prepared for us, and though we'd slept under the stars together for weeks, Lyla and I slept as man and wife—exhausted from the attention and activity of the past days and weeks.

"I love you, Levi Caspertein," she whispered as we drifted to sleep.

"I love you, Lyla Caspertein."

The next morning, Alice was in the hotel lobby, staff in hand, waiting for us to depart. Annette was there with Rudy. Vorca, who would also remain at Meeker, held Caleb on her hip. Rex was outside, adjusting our packs on two trailers attached to our bikes. Four pairs of cross-country skis were strapped to the top of the packs, and Rex handed Lyla a bullpup, which she slung onto her back.

Our plan was to head north on Highway 13, and eventually reach Interstate 80 to travel east. This way, we would avoid the recently-released Federation troops, most of whom were on foot. We doubted our trip east would be as pleasant as our last week of travel since Norwood, but we were sufficiently armed and spiritually prepared for conflict.

Uncle Rudy prayed for our safety, and charged us with the safety of Jenna Dowler, should we reach her in time. With snow falling in three months, we weren't sure what to expect, but we had anticipated even the snow by packing skis and winter clothing.

Alice departed first to scout the way ahead while we said our final goodbyes.

"Your father would be proud of you," Annette said, embracing me tighter than I thought possible. "I hope you don't break Jenna's heart with the news that you're already married."

"Yes, Mother."

"Take care of that wife of yours. You picked a good one, by the way. She's strong-willed, but seeing her take care of all those families in the woods—she's made of the right stuff."

"So, you're saying she's a lot like you. That ain't gonna make it easy, Mom."

"You're in God's hands now," she said, smiling. "And knowing Him, He'll direct you to touch many others with your life."

"I suspect you're right."

We rode out of Meeker, Colorado, as the summer sun rose. The road ahead was unknown, but what road is ever known? We would trust God, and leave the outcome in His hands. We were Casperteins. We were Christians. We were COIL. And we were going to save Jenna.

Thanks for reading *Dawn of Affliction!* I pray it was a blessing to you. I would love to hear your input so I know if I hit the mark. Thanks for your help! —*David Telbat*

What's Next?

~ Dawn of Oppression ~

Book Two of the *Last Dawn Series*

Twenty-one years after the collapse of America, the land has fallen to new regimes and wicked governments, and the Appalachian Federation on the East Coast is the worst of them all. Christians who refuse to comply with new religious tolerance policies are arrested and executed. Chancellor Obrador expects no one to challenge his harsh treatment of so many undesirables. Except he's made one terrible mistake: *he doesn't know that Corban Dowler is still alive!*

COIL rises from the ashes in this second book of the *Last Dawn Series.* In the shadows of New York City, Corban Dowler uses his tradecraft now as an aged man. Although he thinks he's alone, protecting hundreds of Christians across the region, God provides unlikely allies to work beside him. And one of those allies is at the top of the ruthless government.

Brian Steelman has returned from the West to face his past within the Federation. He has hunted and captured more Christians for the government than anyone else, and the Chancellor will do anything to put his top killer back into action. An underground revolt must be squashed before it spreads further. The culprit is a mysterious woman whose code name is *Radiant Shade.* The Chancellor wants her dead at all costs!

Heartbreak and anguish plague the land, but God's light shines where His people refuse to be silenced. Corban Dowler is one of those lights, beside his blind daughter, Jenna, who bears a secret that could cost them their lives. There is little hope for believers across the country, unless COIL's next generation of agents stands against an enemy this land has never seen before.

In America's Last Days, only the steadfast will survive!

For direct retailer links, visit our *Dawn of Oppression* page at https://books2read.com/b/DawnOfOppression.

About the Author

D.I. (David) Telbat is a Christian author best known for his **clean, Suspenseful Fiction with a Faith Focus**. This includes his bestselling and award-winning *COIL Series*, *Steadfast Series*, *Last Dawn Series*, and other Christian Suspense and End Times novels. He wrote his first book at age 14, and he hasn't stopped since!

David studied writing in school and worked for a time in the newspaper field. Getting into serious trouble with the law as a young man became a turning point in his life. The Lord used that experience to draw David into a personal relationship with Him. Re-focusing his life for Christ, he now seeks to honor God with his life and writing by doing what he loves most—writing and Christian ministry.

Subscribe to receive David Telbat's FREE, bi-weekly **D.I. Telbat Newsletter** with one of his Christian short stories, or an Author Reflection, or his Novel News Update. You'll also receive **exclusive subscriber gifts**, such as his *Three For Free*—three-novels-in-one eBook! You can join the adventure by visiting his site at books2read.com/DITelbat/ and click on the "**Follow this Author**" button.